59372084674392   FIG

WITHDRAWN

WORN, SOILED, OBSOLETE

A DARKLING SEA

TOR®

A
TOM DOHERTY
ASSOCIATES
BOOK

NEW YORK

A
DARKLING
SEA

JAMES L. CAMBIAS

This is a work of fiction. All of the characters, organizations, and events portrayed in this novel are either products of the author's imagination or are used fictitiously.

A DARKLING SEA

Copyright © 2014 by James L. Cambias

A Tor Book
Published by Tom Doherty Associates, LLC
175 Fifth Avenue
New York, NY 10010

www.tor-forge.com

Tor® is a registered trademark of Tom Doherty Associates, LLC.

Library of Congress Cataloging-in-Publication Data

Cambias, James L.
    A darkling sea / James L. Cambias.—First Edition.
      p. cm.
    "A Tom Doherty Associates Book."
    ISBN 978-0-7653-3627-9 (hardcover)
    ISBN 978-1-4668-2756-1 (e-book)
    1. Science fiction.   I. Title.
  PS3603.A4467D37 2014
  813'.6—dc23

                          2013025215

Tor books may be purchased for educational, business, or promotional use. For information on bulk purchases, please contact Macmillan Corporate and Premium Sales Department at 1-800-221-7945, extension 5442, or write specialmarkets@macmillan.com.

First Edition: January 2014

Printed in the United States of America

0 9 8 7 6 5 4 3 2 1

For my father

Out of whose womb came the ice? and the hoary frost of heaven, who hath gendered it? The waters are hid as with a stone, and the face of the deep is frozen.

—JOB 38: 29-30

A
DARKLING
SEA

ONE

BY the end of his second month at Hitode Station, Rob Freeman had already come up with 85 ways to murder Henri Kerlerec. That put him third in the station's rankings—Josef Palashnik was first with 143, followed by Nadia Kyle with 97. In general, the number and sheer viciousness of the suggested methods was in proportion to the amount of time each one spent with Henri.

Josef, as the primary submarine pilot, had to spend hours and hours each week in close quarters with Henri, so his list concentrated on swift and brutal techniques suitable for a small cockpit. Nadia shared lab space with Henri—which in practice meant she did her dissections in the kitchen or on the floor of her bedroom—and her techniques were mostly obscure poisons and subtle death traps.

Rob's specialty was underwater photography and drone operation. All through training he had been led to expect he would be filming the exotic life forms of Ilmatar, exploring the unique environment of the remote icy world, and helping the science team understand the alien biology and ecology. Within a week of arrival he found himself somehow locked into the role of Henri Kerlerec's personal cameraman, gofer, and captive audience. His list of murder methods began with "strangling HK with that stupid ankh necklace" and progressed through cutting the air hose on Henri's drysuit, jamming him into a thermal vent, abandoning him in mid-ocean with no inertial compass, and feeding him to an *Aenocampus*. Some of the others on the station who routinely read the hidden "Death to HK" feed had protested that last one as being too cruel to the *Aenocampus*.

Rob's first exposure to killing Henri came at a party given by Nadia and her husband, Pierre Adler, in their room, just after the expedition support vehicle left orbit for the six-month gimelspace voyage back to Earth. With four guests, there was barely enough room, and to avoid overloading the ventilators they had to leave the door open. For refreshment they had melons from the hydroponic garden filled with some of Palashnik's home-brewed potato vodka. One drank melon-flavored vodka until the hollow interior was empty, then cut vodka-flavored melon slices until one was too drunk to handle the knife.

"I've got a new one," said Nadia after her third melon slice. "Put a piece of paper next to Le Nuke for a few months until it's radioactive, then write him a fan letter and slip it under his door. He'd keep the letter for his collection and die of gradual exposure."

"Too long," said Josef. "Even if he kept it in his pocket it would take years to kill him."

"But you'd have the fun of watching him lose his hair," said Nadia.

"I would rather just lock him in reactor shed and leave him there," said Josef.

"Who are they talking about?" Rob asked.

"Henri Kerlerec," whispered Alicia Neogri, who was squeezed onto the bed next to him and half drunk on melon.

"Irradiate his hair gel," said Pierre. "That way he'd put more on every day and it would be right next to his brain."

"Ha! That part has been dead for years!"

"Replace the argon in his breathing unit with chlorine," said someone Rob couldn't see, and then the room went quiet.

Henri was standing in the doorway. As usual, he was grinning. "Planning to murder somebody? Our esteemed station director, I hope." He glanced behind him to make sure Dr. Sen wasn't in earshot. "I have thought of an infallible technique: I would strike him over the head with a large ham or gigot or something of that kind, and then when the police come, I would serve it to them to destroy the evidence. They would never suspect!"

"Roald Dahl," murmured Nadia. "And it was a *frozen* leg of lamb."

Henri didn't hear her. "You see the beauty of it? The police eat the murder weapon. Perhaps I shall write a detective novel about it when I get back to Earth. Well, good night everyone!" He gave a little wave and went off toward Hab Three.

This particular morning Rob was trying to think of an especially sadistic fate for Henri. Kerlerec had awakened him at 2100—three hours early!—and summoned him to the dive room with a great show of secrecy.

The dive room occupied the bottom of Hab One. It was a big circular room with suits and breathing gear stowed on the walls, benches for getting into one's gear, and a moon pool in the center where the Terran explorers could pass into Ilmatar's dark ocean. It was the coldest room in the entire station, chilled by the subzero seawater so that condensation on the walls froze in elaborate geometrical patterns.

Henri was there, waiting at the base of the access ladder. As soon as Rob climbed down he slammed the hatch shut. "Now we can talk privately together. I have an important job for you."

"What?"

"Tonight at 1900 we are going out on a dive. Tell nobody. Do not write anything in the dive log."

"What? Why tonight? And why did you have to get me up so goddamned early to have this conversation?"

"It must be kept absolutely secret."

"Henri, I'm not doing anything until you tell me exactly what is going on. Enough cloak-and-dagger stuff."

"Come and see." Henri led him to the hatch into Hab Three, opened it a crack to peek through, then gestured for Rob to follow as he led the way to the lab space he shared with Nadia Kyle. It was a little room about twice the size of a sleeping cabin, littered with native artifacts, unlabeled slides, and tanks holding live specimens. Standing in the middle was a large gray plastic container as tall as a man. It had stenciled markings in Cyrillic and a sky blue UNICA shipping label.

Henri touched his thumb to a lock pad and the door swung open to reveal a bulky diving suit. It was entirely black, even the faceplate, and had a sleek, seamless look.

"Nice suit. What's so secret about it?"

"This is not a common sort of diving suit," said Henri. "I arranged specially for it to be sent to me. Nobody else has anything like it. It is a Russian Navy stealth suit, for deactivating underwater smart mines or sonar pods. The surface is completely anechoic. Invisible to any kind of sonar imaging. Even the fins are low-noise."

"How does it work?" Rob's inner geek prompted him to ask.

Henri gave a shrug. "That is for technical people to worry about. All I care is that it does work. It must—it cost me six million euros to get it here."

"Okay, so you've got the coolest diving suit on Ilmatar. Why are you keeping it locked up? I'm sure the bio people would love to be able to get close to native life without being heard."

"Pah. When I am done they can watch all the shrimps and worms they wish to. But first, I am going to use this suit to observe the Ilmatarans up close. Imagine it, Robert! I can swim among their houses, perhaps even go right inside! Stand close enough to touch them! They will never notice I am there!"

"What about the contact rules?"

"Contact? What contact? Didn't you hear—the Ilmatarans will not notice me! I will stand among them, filming at close range, but with this suit I will be invisible to them!"

"Doctor Sen's going to shit a brick when he finds out."

"By the time he finds out it will be done. What can he do to me? Send me home? I will go back to Earth on the next ship in triumph!"

"The space agencies aren't going to like it either."

"Robert, before I left Earth I did some checking. Do you know how many people regularly access space agency sites or subscribe to their news feeds? About fifty million people, worldwide. Do you know how many people watched the video from my last expedition? Ninety-six million! I have twice as many viewers, and that makes me twice as important. The agencies all love me."

Rob suspected Henri's numbers were made up on the spur of the moment, the way most of his numbers were, but it was probably true enough that Henri Kerlerec, the famous scientist-explorer and shameless media whore, got more eyeballs than the rest of the entire interstellar program.

He could feel himself being sucked into the mighty whirlpool of Henri's ego, and tried to struggle against it. "I don't want to get in any trouble."

"You have nothing to worry about. Now, listen: here is what we will do. You come down here quietly at about 1830 and get everything ready. Bring the cameras, and a couple of the quiet impeller units. Also a drone or two. I will get this suit on myself in here, and then at 1900 we go out. With the impellers we can get as far as the Maury 3 vent. There is a little Ilmataran settlement there."

"That's a long way to go by impeller. Maury 3's what, sixty kilometers from here?"

"Three hours out, three hours back, and perhaps two hours at the site. We will get back at about 0300, just after breakfast. They may not even notice we have gone."

"And if they do?"

"Then we just say we have been doing some filming around the habitat outside." Henri began locking up the stealth suit's container. "I tell you, they will never suspect a thing. Leave all the talking to me. Now: not another word! We have too much to do! I am going to sleep this afternoon to be fresh for our dive tonight. You must do the same. And do not speak of this to anyone!"

BROADTAIL is nervous. He cannot pay attention to the speaker, and constantly checks the reel holding his text. He is to speak next, his first address to the Bitterwater Company of Scholars. It is an audition of sorts: Broadtail hopes the members find his work interesting enough to invite him to join them.

Smoothshell 24 Midden finishes her address on high-altitude creatures and takes a few questions from the audience. They aren't easy questions, either, and Broadtail worries about making a fool of himself before all these respected scholars. When she finishes, Longpincer 16 Bitterwater clacks his pincers for quiet.

"Welcome now to Broadtail 38 Sandyslope, who comes to us from a great distance to speak about ancient languages. Broadtail?"

Broadtail nearly drops his reel, but catches it in time and scuttles to the end of the room. It is a wonderful chamber for speaking, with a sloped floor so that everyone can hear directly, and walls of quiet pumice-stone. He finds the end of his reel and begins, running it carefully between his feeding-tendrils as he speaks aloud. His tendrils feel the knots in the string as it passes by them. The patterns of knots indicate numbers, and the numbers match words. He remembers being careful to space his knots and tie them tightly, as this copy is for Longpincer's library here at Bitterwater. The reel is a single unbroken cord, expensive to buy and horribly complicated to work with—very different from the original draft, a tangle of short notes tied together all anyhow.

Once he begins, Broadtail's fear dissipates. His own fascination with his topic asserts itself, and he feels himself speeding up as his excitement grows. When he pauses, he can hear his audience rustling and scrabbling, and he supposes that is a good sign. At least they aren't all going torpid.

The anchor of his speech is the description of the echo-carvings from the ruined city near his home vent of Continuous Abundance. By correlating the images of the echo-carvings with the number markings below them, Broadtail believes he can create a lexicon for the ancient city builders. He reads the Company some of his translations of other markings in the ruins.

Upon finishing, he faces a torrent of questions. Huge old Roundhead 19 Downcurrent has several tough ones—he is generally recognized as the expert on ancient cities and their builders, and he means to make sure some provincial upstart doesn't encroach on his territory.

Roundhead and some others quickly home in on some of the weak parts of Broadtail's argument. A couple of them make reference to the writings of the dead scholar Thickfeelers 19 Swiftcurrent, and Broadtail feels a pang of jealousy because he can't afford to buy copies of such rare works. As the questions continue, Broadtail feels himself getting angry in defense of his work, and struggles to retain his temper. The presentation may be a disaster, but he must remain polite.

At last it is over, and he rolls up his reel and heads for a seat at the rear of the room. He'd like to just keep going, slink outside and swim for home, but it would be rude.

A scholar Broadtail doesn't recognize scuttles to the lectern and begins struggling with a tangled reel. Longpincer sits next to Broadtail and speaks privately by means of shell-taps. "That was very well done. I think you describe some extremely important discoveries."

"You do? I was just thinking of using the reel to mend nets."

"Because of all the questions? Don't worry. That's a good sign. If the hearers ask questions it means they're thinking, and that's the whole purpose of this Company. I don't hear any reason not to make you a member. I'm sure the others agree."

All kinds of emotions flood through Broadtail—relief, excitement, and sheer happiness. He can barely keep from speaking aloud. His shell-taps are rapid. "I'm very grateful. I plan to revise the reel to address some of Roundhead's questions."

"Of course. I imagine some of the others want copies, too. Ah, he's starting."

The scholar at the lectern begins to read a reel about a new system for measuring the heat of springs, but Broadtail is too happy to really pay attention.

▲⊤ 1800 that night, Rob was lying on his bunk trying to come up with some excuse not to go with Henri. Say he was sick, maybe? The trouble was that he was a rotten liar. He tried to make himself feel sick—maybe an upset stomach from ingesting seawater? His body unhelpfully continued to feel okay.

Maybe he just wouldn't go. Stay in bed and lock the door. Henri could hardly complain to Dr. Sen about him not going on an unauthorized dive. But Henri could and undoubtedly would make his life miserable with nagging and blustering until he finally gave in.

And of course the truth was that Rob *did* want to go. What he really wanted was to be the one in the stealth suit, instead of Henri. It would be amazing to get within arm's reach of the Ilmatarans and film them close up, instead of getting a few murky long-distance drone pictures. Probably everyone else at Hitode Station felt the same way. Putting them here, actually on the sea bottom of Ilmatar, yet forbidding them to get close to the natives, was like telling a pack of horny teenagers they could get naked in bed together, but not touch.

He checked his watch. It was 1820. He got up and slung his camera bag over his shoulder. Damn Henri anyway.

Rob made it to the dive room without encountering anyone. The station wasn't like a space vehicle with round-the-clock shifts. Everyone slept from about 1600 to 2400, and only one poor soul had to stay in the control room in case of emergency. Tonight it was Dickie Graves on duty, and Rob suspected that Henri had managed to square him somehow so that the exterior hydrophones wouldn't pick up their little jaunt.

He took one of the drones off the rack and ran a quick check. It was a flexible robot fish about a meter long; more Navy surplus—American, this time. It wasn't especially stealthy, but instead was designed to sound just like a swimming mackerel. Presumably the Ilmatarans would figure it was some native organism and ignore it. His computer linked up with the drone brain by laser. All powered up and ready to go. He told it to hold position and await further instructions, then dropped it into the water. Just to be on the safe side, Rob fired up a second drone and tossed it into the moon pool.

Next the impellers. They were simple enough—a motor, a battery, and a pair of counter-rotating propellers. You held on to a handle on the top and controlled your speed with a thumb switch. They were supposedly quiet, though in Rob's experience they weren't any more stealthy than the ones you could rent at any dive shop back on Earth. Some contractor in Japan had made a bundle on them. Rob found two with full batteries and hooked them on the edge of the pool for easy access.

Now for the hard part: suiting up without any help. Rob took off his frayed and slightly smelly insulated jumpsuit and stripped to the skin. First the diaper—he and Henri were going to be out for eight hours, and getting the inside of his suit wet would invite death from hypothermia. Then a set of thick fleece long-johns, like a child's pajamas. The water outside was well below freezing; only the pressure and salinity kept it liquid. He'd need all the insulation he could get.

Then the drysuit, double-layered and also insulated. In the freezing air of the changing room he was getting red-faced and hot with all this protection on. The hood was next, a snug fleece balaclava with built-in earphones. Then the helmet, a plastic fishbowl more like a space helmet than most diving gear, which zipped onto the suit to make a watertight seal. The back of the helmet was packed with electronics—biomonitors, microphones, sonar unit, and an elaborate heads-up display which could project text and data on the inside of the faceplate. There was also a little self-sealing valve to let him eat with the helmet on, and a freshwater tube, which he sipped before going on to the next stage.

Panting with the exertion, Rob struggled into the heavy APOS backpack, carefully starting it up *before* attaching the hoses to his helmet, and took a few breaths to make sure it was really working. The APOS gear made the whole Ilmatar expedition possible. It made oxygen out of seawater by electrolysis, supplying it at ambient pressure. Little sensors and a pretty sophisticated computer adjusted the supply to the wearer's demand.

The oxygen mixed with a closed-loop argon supply; at the colossal pressures of Ilmatar's ocean bottom, the proper air mix was about 1,000 parts argon to 1 part oxygen. Hitode Station and the subs each had bigger versions, which was how humans could live under six kilometers of water and ice. The tons of argon needed to supply the expedition had been gathered locally, by a robot spaceplane skimming the atmosphere of Ilmatar's giant primary world.

The APOS units made it possible to live and work on the bottom of Ilmatar's ocean. The price, of course, was that it took six days to go up to the surface. The pressure difference between the 300 atmospheres at the bottom of the sea and the half standard at the surface station meant a human wouldn't just get the bends if he went up quickly—he'd literally burst. There were other dangers, too. All the crew at Hitode took a regimen of drugs to ward off the scary side effects of high pressure. Every day spent at Hitode knocked about a week off Rob's estimated life span.

With his APOS running (though for now its little computer was sensible enough to simply feed him air from the room outside), Rob pulled on his three layers of gloves, buckled on his fins, put on his weight belt, switched on his shoulder lamp, and then crouched on the edge of the moon pool to let himself tumble backward into the water. It felt pleasantly cool, rather than lethally cold, and he bled a little extra gas into his suit to keep him afloat until Henri could join him.

He gave the drones instructions to follow at a distance of four meters, and created a little window on his faceplate to let him watch through their eyes. He checked over the camera clamped to his shoulder to make sure it was working. Everything nominal. It was 1920 now. Where was Henri?

Kerlerec lumbered into view ten minutes later. In the bulky stealth suit he looked like a big black toad. The foam cover of his faceplate was hanging down over his chest, and Rob could see that he was red and sweating. Henri waddled to the edge of the pool and fell back into the water with an enormous splash. After a moment he bobbed up next to Rob.

"God, it is hot in this thing. You would not believe how hot it is. For once I am glad to be in the water. Do you have everything?"

"Yep. So how are you going to use the camera in that thing? Won't it spoil the whole stealth effect?"

"I will not use the big camera. That is for you to take pictures of me at long range. I have a couple of little cameras inside my helmet. One points forward to see what I see, the other is for my face. Link up."

They got the laser link established and Rob opened two new windows at the bottom of his faceplate. One showed him as Henri saw him—a pale, stubbly face inside a bubble helmet—and the other showed Henri in extreme close-up. The huge green-lit face beaded with sweat looked a bit like the Great and Powerful Oz after a three-day drunk.

"Now we will get away from the station and try out your sonar on my suit. You will not be able to detect me at all."

Personally Rob doubted it. Some Russian had probably made a few million Swiss francs selling Henri and his sponsors at ScienceMonde a failed prototype or just a fake.

The two of them sank down until they were underneath Hab One, only a couple of meters above the seafloor. The light shining down from the moon pool made a pale cone in the silty water, with solid blackness beyond.

Henri led the way away from the station, swimming with his headlamp and his safety strobe on until they were a few hundred meters out. "This is good," he said. "Start recording."

Rob got the camera locked in on Henri's image. "You're on."

Henri's voice instantly became the calm, friendly but all-knowing voice of Henri Kerlerec, scientific media star. "I am here in the dark ocean of Ilmatar, preparing to test the high-tech stealth diving suit which will enable me to get close to the Ilmatarans without being detected. I am covering up the face-plate with the special stealth coating now. My cameraman will try to locate me by sonar. Because the Ilmatarans live in a completely dark environment, they are entirely blind to visible light, so I will leave my safety strobe and headlamp on."

Rob opened up a window to display sonar images and began recording. First on passive—his computer could build up a vague image of the surroundings just from ambient noise and interference patterns. No sign of Henri, even though Rob could see his bobbing headlamp as he swam back and forth ten meters away.

Not bad, Rob had to admit. Those Russians know a few things about sonar baffling. He tried the active sonar and sent out a couple of pings. The sea bottom and the rocks flickered into clear relief, an eerie false-color landscape where green meant soft and yellow meant hard surfaces. The ocean itself was completely black on active. Henri was a green-black shadow against a black background. Even with the computer synthesizing both the active and passive signals, he was almost impossible to see.

"Wonderful!" said Henri when Rob sent him the images. "I told you: completely invisible! We will edit this part down, of course—just the sonar images with me explaining it in voice-over. Now come along. We have a long trip ahead of us."

* * *

THE Bitterwater Company are waking up. Longpincer's servants scuttle along the halls of his house, listening carefully at the entrance to each guest chamber and informing the ones already awake that a meal is ready in the main hall.

Broadtail savors the elegance of having someone to come wake him when the food is ready. At his own house, all would starve if he waited for his apprentices to prepare the meals. He wonders briefly how they are getting along without him. The three of them are reasonably competent, and can certainly tend his pipes and crops without him. Broadtail does worry about how well they can handle an emergency—what if a pipe breaks or one of his nets is snagged? He imagines returning home to find chaos and ruin.

But it is so very nice here at Longpincer's house. Mansion, really. The Bitterwater vent isn't nearly as large as Continuous Abundance or the other town vents, but Longpincer controls the entire flow. Everything for ten cables in any direction belongs to him. He has a staff of servants and hired workers. Even his apprentices scarcely need to lift a pincer themselves.

Broadtail doesn't want to miss the meal. Longpincer's larder is as opulent as everything else at Bitterwater. As he crawls to the main hall he marvels again at the thick growths on the walls and floor. Some of his own farm pipes don't support this much life. Is it just that Longpincer's large household generates enough waste to support lush indoor growth? Or is he rich enough to pipe some excess vent water through the house itself? Either way it's far more than Broadtail's chilly property and tepid flow rights can achieve.

As he approaches the main hall, Broadtail can taste a tremendous and varied feast laid out. It sounds as if half a dozen of the Company are already there; it says much for Longpincer's kitchen that the only sounds Broadtail can hear are those of eating.

He finds a place between Smoothshell and a quiet individual whose name Broadtail can't recall. He runs his feelers over the food before him and feels more admiration mixed with jealousy for Longpincer. There are cakes of pressed sourleaf, whole towfin eggs, fresh jellyfronds, and some little bottom-crawling creatures Broadtail isn't familiar with, neatly impaled on spines and still wiggling.

Broadtail can't recall having a feast like this since he inherited the Sandyslope property and gave the funeral banquet for old Flatbody. He is just reaching for a third jellyfrond when Longpincer clicks loudly for attention from the end of the hall.

"I suggest a small excursion for the Company," he says. "About ten cables beyond my boundary stones upcurrent is a small vent, too tepid and bitter to be worth piping. I forbid my workers to drag nets there, and I recall finding several interesting creatures feeding at the vent. I propose swimming there to look for specimens."

"May I suggest applying Sharpfrill's technique for temperature measurement to those waters?" says Smoothshell.

"Excellent idea!" cries Longpincer. Sharpfrill mutters something about not having his proper equipment, but the others bring him around. They all finish eating (Broadtail notices several of the Company stowing delicacies in pouches, and grabs the last towfin egg to fill his own) and set out for the edge of Longpincer's property.

Swimming is quicker than walking, so the party of scholars cruise at just above net height. At that level Broadtail can only get a general impression of the land below, but it all seems neat and orderly—a well-planned network of stone pipes radiating out from the main vent, carrying the hot nutrient-rich water to nourish thousands of plants and bacteria colonies. Leaks from the pipes and the waste from the crops and Longpincer's household feed clouds of tiny swimmers, which in turn attract larger creatures from the cold waters around. Broadtail notes with approval the placement of Longpincer's nets in staggered rows along the prevailing current. With a little envy he estimates that Longpincer's nets probably produce as much wealth as his own entire property.

Beyond the boundary stones the scholars instinctively gather into a more compact group. There is less conversation and more careful listening and pinging. Longpincer assures them that he allows no bandits or scavengers around his vent, but even he pings behind them once or twice, just to make sure. But all anyone can hear are a few wild children, who flee quickly at the approach of adults.

HENRI and Rob didn't talk much on the way to the vent community. Both of them were paying close attention to the navigation displays inside their helmets. Getting around on Ilmatar was deceptively easy: take a bearing by inertial compass, point the impeller in the right direction, and off you went. But occasionally Rob found himself thinking about just how hard it would be to navigate without electronic help. The stars were hidden by a kilometer of ice overhead, and Ilmatar had no magnetic field worth speaking of. It was barely possible to tell up from down—if you had your searchlights on and could see the bottom and weren't enveloped in a cloud of silt—but maintaining a constant depth depended entirely on watching the sonar display and the pressure gauge. A human without navigation equipment on Ilmatar would be blind, deaf, and completely lost.

At 0500 they were nearing the site. "Visual only," said Henri. "We must be as quiet as possible. Can you film from a hundred meters away?"

"It'll need enhancement and cleaning up afterward, but yes."

"Good. You take up a position there—" Henri gestured vaguely into the darkness.

"Where?"

"That big clump of rocks at, let me see, bearing one hundred degrees, about fifty meters out."

"Okay."

"Stay there and do not make any noise. I will go on ahead toward the vent. Keep one of the drones with me."

"Right. What are you going to do?"

"I will walk toward the settlement."

Shaking his head, Rob found a relatively comfortable spot among the stones. While he waited for the silt to settle, he noticed that this wasn't a natural outcrop—these were cut stones, the remains of a structure of some kind. Some of the surfaces were even carved into patterns of lines. He made sure to take pictures of everything. The other xeno people back at Hitode would kill him if he didn't.

Henri went marching past in a cloud of silt. The big camera was going to be useless with him churning up the bottom like that, so Rob relied entirely on the drones. One followed Henri about ten meters back, the second was above him looking down. The laser link through the water was a little noisy from suspended particulates, but he didn't need a whole lot of detail. The drone cameras could store everything internally, so Rob was satisfied with just enough sight to steer them. Since he was comfortably seated and could use his hands, he called up a virtual joystick instead of relying on voice commands or the really irritating eye-tracking menu device.

"Look at that!" Henri called suddenly.

"What? Where?"

Henri's forward camera swung up to show eight Ilmatarans swimming along in formation, about ten meters up. They were all adults, wearing belts and harnesses stuffed with gear. A couple carried spears. Ever since the first drone under the ice got pictures of Ilmatarans, they had been described as looking like giant lobsters, but watching them swim overhead, Rob had to disagree. They were more like beluga whales in armor, with their big flukes and blunt heads. Adults ranged from three to four meters long. Each had a dozen limbs folded neatly against the undersides of their shells: six walking legs in back, four manipulators amidships, and the big praying-mantis pincers on the front pair. They also had raspy feeding tendrils and long sensory feelers under the head. The head itself was a smooth featureless dome, flaring out over the neck like a coal-scuttle helmet—the origin of the Ilmatarans' scientific name *Salletocephalus structor.* Henri's passive microphones picked up the clicks and pops of the Ilmatarans' sonar, with an occasional loud ping like a harpsichord note.

The two humans watched as the group soared over Henri's head. "What do you think they're doing?" asked Rob when they had passed.

"I am not sure. Perhaps a hunting party. I will follow them."

Rob wanted to argue, but knew it was pointless. "Don't go too far."

Henri kicked up from the bottom and began to follow the Ilmatarans. It was hard for a human to keep up with them, even when wearing fins. Henri was sweaty and breathing hard after just a couple of minutes, but he struggled along. "They are stopping," he said after ten minutes, sounding relieved.

The Ilmatarans were dropping down to a small vent formation, which Rob's computer identified as Maury 3b. Through the drone cameras Rob watched as Henri crept closer to the Ilmatarans. At first he moved with clumsy stealth, then abandoned all pretense and simply waded in among them. Rob waited for a reaction, but the Ilmatarans seemed intent on their own business.

* * *

⌃ rock is missing. Broadtail remembers a big chunk of old shells welded together by ventwater minerals and mud, just five armspans away across-current. But now it's gone. Is his memory faulty? He pings again. There it is, just where it should be. Odd. He goes back to gathering shells.

"—you hear me? Broadtail!" It is Longpincer. He appears out of nowhere just in front of Broadtail, sounding alarmed.

"I'm here. What's wrong?"

"Nothing," says Longpincer. "My own mistake."

"Wait. Tell me."

"It's very odd. I remember hearing you clattering over the rocks, then silence. As if you were suddenly gone. I recall pinging and sensing nothing."

"I remember a similar experience—a rock seeming to disappear and then appear again."

Smoothshell comes up. "What's the problem?" After they explain, she asks, "Could there be a reflective layer here? Cold water meeting hot does that."

"I don't feel any change in the water temperature," says Longpincer. "The current here is strong enough to keep everything mixed."

"Let's listen," says Broadtail. The three of them stand silently, tails together, heads outward. Broadtail relaxes, letting the sounds and interference patterns of his surroundings create a model in his mind. The vent is there, rumbling and hissing. Someone is scrabbling up the side—probably Sharpfrill with his jars of temperature-sensitive plants. Roundhead and the quiet person are talking together half a cable away, or rather Roundhead is talking and his companion is making occasional polite clicks. Two others are swishing nets through the water upcurrent.

But there is something else. Something is moving nearby. He can't quite hear it, but it blocks other sounds and changes the interference patterns. He reaches over to Smoothshell and taps on her leg. "There is a strange effect in the water in front of me, moving slowly from left to right."

She turns and listens that way while Broadtail taps the same message on Longpincer's shell. "I think I hear what you mean," Smoothshell says. "It's like a big lump of very soft mud, or pumice stone."

"Yes," Broadtail agrees. "Except that it's moving. I'm going to ping it now." He tenses his resonator muscle and pings as hard as he can, loud enough to stun a few small swimmers near his head. All the other Company members about the vent stop what they are doing.

He hears the entire landscape in front of him—quiet mud, sharp echoes from rocks, muffled and chaotic patterns from patches of plants. And right in the center, only a few armspans in front of him, is a hole in the water. It's big, whatever it is: almost the size of a young adult, standing upright like a boundary marker.

HENRI was completely gonzo. He was rattling off narration for his audience completely off the top of his head. Occasionally he would forget to use his media-star voice and give way to an outburst of pure cackling glee. Rob was pretty excited, too, watching through the cameras as Henri got within arm's reach of the Ilmatarans.

"Here we see a group of Ilmatarans gathering food around one of the sea-bottom vents. Some are using handmade nets to catch fish, while these three close to me appear to be scraping algae off the rocks."

"Henri, you're using Earth-life names again. Those aren't fish, or algae either."

"Never mind that now. I will dub in the proper words later if

I must. The audience will understand better if I use words they understand. This is wonderful, don't you think? I can pat them on the backs if I want to!"

"Remember, no contact."

"Yes, yes." Back into his narrator voice. "The exact nature of Ilmataran social organization is still not well understood. We know they live in communities of up to a hundred individuals, sharing the work of food production, craft work, and defense. The harvest these bring back to their community will be divided among all."

"Henri, you can't just make stuff up like that. Some of the audience are going to want links to more info about Ilmataran society. We don't know how they allocate resources."

"Then there is nothing to say that this is untrue. Robert, people do not want to hear that aliens are just like us. They want wise angels and noble savages. Besides, I am certain I am right. The Ilmatarans behave exactly like early human societies. Remember I am an archaeologist by training. I recognize the signs." He shifted back into media mode. "Life is difficult in these icy seas. The Ilmatarans must make use of every available source of food to ward off starvation. I am going to get closer to these individuals so that we can watch them at their work."

"Don't get too close. They might be able to smell you or something."

"I am being careful. How is the picture quality?"

"Well, the water's pretty cloudy. I've got the drone providing an overhead view of you, but the helmet camera's the only thing giving us any detail."

"I will bend down to get a better view, then. How is that?"

"Better. This is great stuff." Rob checked the drone image. "Uh, Henri, why are they all facing toward you?"

* * *

"WE must capture it," says Longpincer. "I don't remember reading about anything like this."

"How do we capture something we can barely make out?" asks Broadtail.

"Surround it," suggests Smoothshell. She calls to the others. "Here, quickly! Form a circle!"

With a lot of clicking questions, the other members of the Bitterwater Company gather around—except for Sharpfrill, who is far too absorbed in placing his little colonies of temperature indicators on the vent.

"Keep pinging steadily," says Longpincer. "As hard as you can. Who has a net?"

"Here!" says Raggedclaw.

"Good. Can you make it out? Get the net on it!"

The thing starts to swim upward clumsily, churning up lots of sediment and making a faint but audible swishing noise with its tails. Under Longpincer's direction the Company form a box around it, like soldiers escorting a convoy. Raggedclaw gets above it with the net. There is a moment of struggling as the thing tries to dodge aside, then the scientists close in around it.

It cuts at the net with a sharp claw, and kicks with its limbs. Broadtail feels the claw grate along his shell. Longpincer and Roundhead move in with ropes, and soon the thing's limbs are pinned. It sinks to the bottom.

"I suggest we take it to my laboratory," says Longpincer. "I am sure we all wish to study this remarkable creature."

It continues to struggle, but the netting and ropes are strong enough to hold it. Whatever it is, it's too heavy to carry swimming, so the group must walk along the bottom with their catch while Longpincer swims ahead to fetch servants to help. They all ping about them constantly, fearful that more of the strange silent creatures are lurking about.

* * *

"ROBERT! In the name of God, help me!" The laser link was full of static and skips, what with all the interference from nets, Ilmatarans, and sediment. The video image of Henri degenerated into a series of still shots illustrating panic, terror, and desperation.

"Don't worry!" he called back, although he had no idea what to do. How could he rescue Henri without revealing himself and blowing all the contact protocols to hell? For that matter, even if he did reveal himself, how could he overcome half a dozen full-grown Ilmatarans?

"Ah, bon Dieu!" Henri started what sounded like praying in French. Rob muted the audio to give himself a chance to think, and because it didn't seem right to listen in.

He tried to list his options. Call for help? Too far from the station, and it would take an hour or more for a sub to arrive. Go charging in to the rescue? Rob really didn't want to do that, and not just because it was against the contact regs. On the other hand, he didn't like to think of himself as a coward, either. Skip that one and come back to it.

Create a distraction? That might work. Worth a shot, anyway.

He sent the two drones in at top speed, and searched through his computer's sound library for something suitable to broadcast. "Ride of the Valkyries?" "O Fortuna?" No time to be clever; he selected the first item in the playlist and started blasting Billie Holiday as loud as the drone speakers could go. Rob left his camera gear with Henri's impeller and used his own to get a little closer to the group of Ilmatarans carrying Henri.

BROADTAIL hears the weird sounds first, and alerts the others. The noise is coming from a pair of swimming creatures he doesn't recognize, approaching fast from the left. The sounds are unlike anything he remembers—a mix of low tones, whistles, rattles, and buzzes. There is an underlying rhythm, and Broadtail is sure this is some kind of animal call, not just noise.

The swimmers swoop past low overhead, then, amazingly, circle around together for another pass, like trained performing animals. "Do those creatures belong to Longpincer?" Broadtail asks the others.

"I don't think so," says Smoothshell. "I don't remember noticing them in his house."

"Does anyone have a net?"

"Don't be greedy," says Roundhead. "This is a valuable specimen. We shouldn't risk it to chase after others."

Broadtail starts to object, but he realizes Roundhead is right. This thing is obviously more important. Still—"I suggest we return here to search for them after sleeping."

"Agreed."

The swimmers continue diving at them and making noise until Longpincer's servants show up to help carry the specimen.

ROB had hoped the Ilmatarans would scatter in terror when he sent in the drones, but they barely even noticed them, even with the speaker volume maxed out. He couldn't tell if they were too dumb to pay attention, or smart enough to focus on one thing at a time.

He gunned the impeller, closing in on the little group. Enough subtlety. He could see the lights on Henri's suit about fifty meters away, bobbing and wiggling as the Ilmatarans carried him. Rob slowed to a stop about ten meters from the Ilmatarans. The two big floodlights on the impeller showed them clearly.

Enough subtlety and sneaking around. He turned on his

suit hydrophone. "Hey!" He had his dive knife in his right hand in case of trouble.

BROADTAIL is relieved to be rid of the strange beast. He is getting tired and hungry, and wants nothing more than to be back at Longpincer's house snacking on threadfin paste and heat-cured eggs.

Then he hears a new noise. A whine, accompanied by the burble of turbulent water. Off to the left about three lengths there is some large swimmer. It gives a loud call. The captive creature struggles harder.

Broadtail pings the new arrival. It is very odd indeed. It has a hard cylindrical body like a riftcruiser, but at the back it branches out into a bunch of jointed limbs covered with soft skin. The thing gives another cry and waves a couple of limbs.

Broadtail moves toward it, trying to figure out what it is. Two creatures, maybe? And what is it doing? Is this a territorial challenge? He keeps his own pincers folded so as not to alarm it.

"Be careful, Broadtail," Longpincer calls.

"Don't worry." He doesn't approach any closer, but evidently he's already too close. The thing cries out one more time, then charges him. Broadtail doesn't want the other Bitterwater scholars to see him flee, so he splays his legs and braces himself, ready to grapple with this unknown monster.

But just before it hits him, the thing veers off and disappears into the silent distance. Listening carefully lest it return, Broadtail backs toward the rest of the group and they resume their journey to Longpincer's house.

Everyone agrees that this expedition is stranger than anything any of them remember. Longpincer seems pleased.

ROB stopped his impeller and let the drones catch up. He couldn't think of anything else to do. The Ilmatarans wouldn't be scared off, and there was no way Rob could attack them. Whatever happened to Henri, Rob did not want to be the first human to harm an alien.

The link with Henri was still open. The video showed him looking quite calm, almost serene.

"Henri?" he said. "I tried everything I could think of. I can't get you out. There are too many of them."

"It is all right, Robert," said Henri, sounding surprisingly cheerful. "I do not think they will harm me. Otherwise why go to all the trouble to capture me alive? Listen: I think they have realized I am an intelligent being like themselves. This is our first contact with the Ilmatarans. I will be humanity's ambassador."

"You think so?" For once Rob found himself hoping Henri was right.

"I am certain of it. Keep the link open. The video will show history being made."

Rob sent in one drone to act as a relay as the Ilmatarans carried Henri into a large rambling building near the Maury 3a vent. As he disappeared inside, Henri managed a grin for the camera.

LONGPINCER approaches the strange creature, laid out on the floor of his study. The others are all gathered around to help and watch. Broadtail has a fresh reel of cord and is making a record of the proceeding. Longpincer begins. "The hide is thick, but flexible, and is a nearly perfect sound absorber. The loudest of pings barely produce any echo at all. There are four limbs. The forward pair appear to be for feeding, while the rear limbs apparently function as both walking legs and what one might call a double tail for swimming. Roundhead, do you know of any such creature recorded elsewhere?"

"I certainly do not recall reading of such a thing. It seems absolutely unique."

"Please note as much, Broadtail. My first incision is along the underside. Cutting the hide releases a great many bubbles. The creature reacts very vigorously—make sure the ropes are secure. The hide peels away very easily; there is no connective tissue at all. I feel what seems to be another layer underneath. The creature's interior is remarkably warm."

"The poor thing," says Raggedclaw. "I do hate causing it pain."

"As do we all, I'm sure," says Longpincer. "I am cutting through the under-layer. It is extremely tough and fibrous. I hear more bubbles. The warmth is extraordinary—like pipe-water a cable or so from the vent."

"How can it survive such heat?" asks Roundhead.

"Can you taste any blood, Longpincer?" adds Sharpfrill.

"No blood that I can taste. Some odd flavors in the water, but I judge that to be from the tissues and space between. I am peeling back the under-layer now. Amazing! Yet another layer beneath it. This one has a very different texture—fleshy rather than fibrous. It is very warm. I can feel a trembling sensation and spasmodic movements."

"Does anyone remember hearing sounds like that before?" says Smoothshell. "It sounds like no creature I know of."

"I recall that other thing making similar sounds," says Broadtail.

"I now cut through this layer. Ah—now we come to viscera. The blood tastes very odd. Come, everyone, and feel how hot this thing is. And feel this! Some kind of rigid structures within the flesh."

"It is not moving," says Roundhead.

"Now let us examine the head. Someone help me pull off

the shell here. Just pull. Good. Thank you, Raggedclaw. What a lot of bubbles! I wonder what this structure is?"

Broadtail takes notes as fast as he can, tying clumsy knots to keep up with Longpincer. He feels elation. This is a fantastically important discovery and he is part of the first company to get their feelers on it. Joining the Bitterwater Company of Scholars is the greatest thing Broadtail can remember happening to him. He imagines great things in his future.

TWO

⊤⊢≡ trip back was awful. Rob couldn't keep from replaying Henri's death in his mind. He got back to the station hours late, exhausted and half out of his mind. As a small mercy, Rob didn't have to tell anyone what had happened—they could watch the video.

There were consequences, of course. But because the next supply vehicle wasn't due for another twenty months, it all happened in slow motion. Rob knew he'd be going back to Earth, and guessed that he'd never make another interstellar trip again.

Nobody blamed him, at least not exactly. At the end of his debriefing, Dr. Sen did look at Rob over his little Gandhi glasses and say, "I do think it was rather irresponsible of you both to go off like that. But I am sure you know that already."

Sen also deleted the "Death to HK" feed from the station's network, but someone must have saved a copy. The next day it was anonymously relayed to Rob's computer with a final method added: "Let a group of Ilmatarans catch him and slice him up."

Rob didn't think it was funny at all.

He stayed in bed for about a week after Henri died. At first he was really just exhausted, and then he was depressed, and for the last couple of days he was afraid of what people would say to him. Nobody had liked Henri, but somehow Rob didn't think they'd want to congratulate him. So he kept to his room, slipping out during night shift to stockpile food and prowl the station.

Dr. Sen and Elena Sarfatti, the medical officer, did insist on visiting him for a few minutes each day. Sen was still writing up a report on the incident and wanted Rob to explain pretty much every single minute of the time between when Henri showed him the stealth suit and his return to the station alone. That was actually more boring than painful, because the worst parts were on video and Sen didn't need to ask about them.

Dr. Sarfatti was worse, really, because she wanted him to talk about how he felt.

"Can't I just have the damned antidepressants?"

"Not until we explore why you feel you need them."

"I need them because I listened to a guy get cut up by aliens!"

It usually took about half an hour of circling around the subject before she'd relent and hand over the pills. Some days it was antidepressants, some days tranquilizers, and once she bullied him into taking a memory enhancer. That was a mistake. For sixteen hours afterward every time he thought about Henri (and there wasn't much else for him to think about, holed up in his room), he got a complete, highly detailed instant replay of the whole incident inside his head.

After a week he finally started working again, motivated chiefly by sheer boredom. He did rearrange his schedule (with Sen's implicit consent) to minimize his contact with others. He took to working during the night shift, sleeping during the day, and staying in his room until everyone else went to bed. They started leaving meals for him in the galley, ready to heat up. It was just like being in grad school.

BROADTAIL is tired when he gets back to Continuous Abundance. The village is much as he remembers it: a tall mound about two cables across with the main vent at the highest point. A stone dome covers the vent, and each property owner's pipe leads off to feed a network of smaller channels. The diameter of the pipe is set by law, and interfering with flow rights is a crime and a sin.

The various properties are marked with boundary stones on the lower slopes of the mound and the flat plain beyond. All of them are covered with branching conduits, with different crops growing in different places depending on what temperature and flow speed they prefer.

His own Sandyslope property is on the broad side of the mound where the cold current from the wilderness brings silt. The flavor of the water is comforting and familiar as he passes the marker stones. On his own property, Broadtail finally relaxes. Like all landowners he is only really comfortable within his own boundaries.

As always, he rises up and gives a loud ping to check on the place. The house echoes back sturdy and—sadly—all too clean. The pipe network flows quietly, with no burbling leaks or churning at a blockage.

Broadtail's pipes are not like the others at Continuous Abundance. He recalls using mathematical models based on the proportions of blood vessels in large animals to adjust the diameter of the branches. His crop yields are bigger than anything anyone remembers Flatbody producing by nearly an eighth part, though that is still less than most of the other tracts at Continuous Abundance.

The house is in the middle of the property, three long halls with vaulted stone roofs for protection. Pipes feed into the house, and downstream the waste-laden water supports a bloom of hardy fronds. Broadtail crosses his boundary, pinging for attention. He reaches the door and sets down his reels and supply bags, then calls again loudly for his apprentices. There is no reply.

Typical. Doubtless they are off idling with other apprentices and tenants, instead of working. Broadtail crawls out of his house again and listens. There is a clamor of many voices coming from the commonhouse in the center of the village, just next to the dome over the vent itself. A meeting? Broadtail doesn't want to go to a meeting now. But he is a landowner. It is not proper to stay home.

The commonhouse is packed, people jammed in shell to shell. Talk and sonar clicks make it almost too noisy to move about. Broadtail squeezes into the back, working his way to his favorite spot over in the corner, where a slab of porous stone cuts down on some of the echoes. If only that lout Thicklegs 34 Sandybottom just in front of him would stop grinding his palps, Broadtail would be able to hear what the speaker is saying.

Ridgeback 58 Hardshelf is on the lectern, gripping it with all eight legs as if he's afraid of the audience trying to drag him out. They might actually try it if he keeps ranting on. Everyone is hungry and bored—the hecklers at the back have started pinging in unison, trying to set up a standing wave and drown him out.

"Openwater is common to all! All precedents agree! Everything above the height of a person's outstretched claws is common water. The catch in tall nets should not belong to the landowner but to the public jars."

"Nets don't put themselves on poles!" someone shouts. "If the tall netcatch goes to the public jars there is no reason for us to waste time building tall nets!"

"Then let the town buy some dragnets and put some children to work towing them!" Ridgeback answers. "Share out the catch among all, landowners and tenants."

That gets a loud response. About half the people in the commonhouse are tenants—netmakers, stonecutters, openwater fishers. The craftworkers love the idea of getting catch for free, so they support Ridgeback loudly. The fishers want the right to drag nets over private lands themselves, so they're a bit more muted. The landowners hate the whole idea, and say so. The apprentices are just making noise for the sake of noise, hoping a fight breaks out.

Broadtail hates the idea more than most. His Sandyslope property is off at the upstream end of town, exposed to the cold currents, and his pipeflow is cold and thin. His channels produce only slow-growing plants like ropevine and springbranch, and those can't back many beads. Almost half his food is netcatch, and he has three expensive new tall nets on his land. He waits for the noise to die down and then jumps in before Ridgeback can continue. "How about letting the landowners pay a rent for the right to put up nets? Maybe an eighth of the catch?"

Some of the landowners like that, but most of them just want to be able to put up whatever they want on their own land and eat whatever they catch. The fishers don't like the rent idea at all, because it sounds too much like the idea of charging a toll on openwater. They fight that notion at almost every meeting.

Ridgeback doesn't like it either. "Give landowners the right to rent common water and it's not common anymore! They can trade the rights back and forth, and buy and sell and sublease them. The waters become the property of the richest landowners instead of everyone. I imagine the waters full of nets, blocking navigation."

That really gets the fishers going. They don't like anything which might snag a dragnet or tangle a line. And none of the tenants like the idea of the landowners being any wealthier than they already are. Broadtail is momentarily deafened by some angry pings directed at him. When he gets his hearing back, Ridgeback is calling for a vote.

It's a close one. The tenants are all for the proposal, of course. Many of them vote for anything Ridgeback proposes, as if by reflex. Even the fishers are grudgingly in favor—Broadtail's warning has only convinced them that the choice is between public dragnets and a tangle of private ones, and this way they at least get a portion.

Then the landowners vote. Each gets one vote as a citizen and then another based on flow rights. Broadtail himself gets only half an extra vote because his flow share is so small, but big owners like Flatfront 6 Ventside have six. As a group, the owners have the bulk of the voting power, and can usually pass anything they wish, but this time they are divided. Big rich owners don't care much about netcatch and like the idea of feeding tenants and apprentices at no expense to themselves. Some of them want to reassure the fishers and craftworkers that they aren't trying to monopolize the waters. The small owners like Broadtail are solidly opposed to Ridgeback's plan, but they just don't have enough votes. In the end, the motion squeaks by.

The next speaker with a motion is Sevenlegs 26 Archrock, who wants to reapportion flow rights based on pressure instead of pipe size. She brings it up whenever a meeting is called, but her explanation is so complicated nobody can even tell if it's a good idea or not. Broadtail's too mad to stay and listen, so he crawls to the doorway, angrily pinging any adults in his way, and shoving apprentices aside.

Outside the quiet is almost shocking, as if he's gone deaf. Some children are curled up in the pathway asleep, and Broadtail kicks them out of the way with unnecessary force.

He's tired and hungry, and he needs some stingers to stay awake long enough to get things in order at home. Widehead 34 Foodhouse sells stingers and doesn't ask any annoying questions. Her shop is just across the public road from the commonhouse, set on a tiny plot with no flow rights at all. The front part of the shop is actually on public land, and only the kitchen and Widehead's own quarters are behind her boundary stones.

Broadtail goes inside and taps at the shell by the door for

service. Widehead comes out promptly and pings the room. "Broadtail? Is the meeting over?"

"The important part is. Ridgeback's foolish plan to abolish tall nets passed. I need some stingers."

Widehead brings him a pair of stingers and Broadtail taps the sharp end of the first one with his feeding tendrils. There's a mild pain, and then a nice tingly numbness as the neurotoxin spreads through his system. It relaxes his muscles but makes him feel much more alert and alive. He taps the second and savors the sensation, then calls for another pair.

After half a dozen stingers Broadtail finds the sound of his own pulse almost deafening. He gropes clumsily in his pouch with one foot and eventually gets out three of his beads for Widehead. He goes homeward, trying to move as quietly as he can, but of course his half-limp legs betray him with every step. Outside it sounds as if the meeting in the commonhouse is breaking up. Broadtail doesn't linger; he's tired and hungry and he wants to get home without talking to anyone.

He almost makes it. Nobody stops him until he's on his own property, going to his own door. He hears a loud ping that makes his shell feel as if it's shattering. It's Ridgeback, standing in the public pathway beyond the marker stones. "Broadtail! Come here!"

"What?"

"I am disappointed. You usually vote with me in meetings."

"You usually have good ideas. This one is terrible. I need my tall nets."

"But you get your share of the public catch! You can devote your time to other things and still get food!"

"I get more from my own nets. Schoolchildren pulling a dragnet don't catch much. They slip away, or eat the catch themselves."

"We can put someone in charge of them."

"Who needs to be paid. All too costly for my taste."

"Broadtail, you are too miserly."

"I am miserly because I have a cold barren plot and can't afford to waste my time and wealth winning the friendship of a lot of tenants and apprentices!"

"They are useful friends. They balance the power of the big landowners."

"And small owners like myself are ground up in between."

"Because you have nobody to protect you. If you were my friend I would help guard your interests. And so would my other friends."

"By banning my nets? Go away. I need to eat and rest."

Ridgeback moves closer to Broadtail and lowers his voice. "I am preparing a motion for the next meeting which makes great changes. If you support it you can gain wealth, perhaps even more flow."

"I do not wish for gain, only to be allowed to use what I have and be left in peace."

"You are foolish, Broadtail. Everyone calls you the most intelligent adult in the village, yet you waste all your time digging up old stones and trying to read carvings. A landowner should concern himself with practical matters like politics."

"Get off my property," Broadtail pings loudly. He's sick of Ridgeback's big promises and schemes, and wants to go inside and run his feelers over a good book before sleeping.

"You should not speak that way to me."

"Go!"

Ridgeback steps forward past the boundary stone and raises a pincer, and in Broadtail's tired and stinger-addled brain an ancient instinct kicks in. *Invader on my territory!* He charges Ridgeback and shoves him hard. Ridgeback folds his pincers and shoves back. For a moment the two of them strain and push, their feet scrabbling for purchase on the path.

Then one of Broadtail's feelers gets caught in Ridgeback's pincer, and a couple of segments at the tip get snipped off. The pain makes him even madder, and he raises one of his pincers and jabs it down behind Ridgeback's head. Ridgeback isn't expecting this, and there's a gap between his headshield and his back carapace. The tip of the claw neatly pierces the soft skin and plunges deep into the flesh beneath.

The two of them stand frozen for a moment. Broadtail's shocked by what he has done. Ridgeback wiggles his feelers wildly, but the rest of his body is absolutely still. Then Broadtail pulls out his claw and Ridgeback collapses.

"Ridgeback!" Broadtail pings him and tries to pick him up, but the wound behind his head is spewing fluids like a vent and he's not moving.

Broadtail steps back and bumps against something. It's one of his marker stones. He listens for a moment to get his bearings and gets another shock. During the fight he must have shoved Ridgeback into the pathway. The corpse is in common territory. Killing on private property is a personal matter, but this is murder.

Broadtail doesn't know what to do. His body does, though. It's been far too long since Broadtail last ate or slept, and the fight used up any reserve he might have had. He staggers past the marker stone onto his land and passes out.

BY an unspoken arrangement, Rob took over as maintenance tech on the drones and sensor gear, communicating with Sergei via notes in grease pencil on the door of the workshop. Since Henri had monopolized Rob's services before dying, everybody was already used to doing their own photography and image processing anyway.

Four days after he returned to work, Rob started finding little people.

The first one was on the bench in the workshop, a little figure made of swabs and tape with one cotton-tipped arm raised in a cheery wave. Rob figured it was something Sergei had put together in an idle moment, and left it on the shelf when he finished work.

The next day he found two more figures. One was a little dough girl sitting atop the microwave in the galley, and the second was a wire dancer poised in the middle of his regular table.

Rob spent half an hour that night exploring the station to see if the little sculptures were maybe just a kind of fad. Maybe everyone was making them, just to pass the time and decorate the station. He didn't find any others, though. In his room during the work shift he lay awake for a couple of hours, reverting mentally to age fourteen and wondering if the little figures were somehow part of a plot by everyone else to make fun of him.

On the third night there were half a dozen of them. One, cut from a strip of scrap plastic, on the sink in the bathroom nearest his room in Hab Two. The second, folded from a sheet of nori, in the galley. The third, molded from caulking compound, on the back of the chair in the workshop. Another origami figure made of foil inside the tool cabinet. And a wire angel posed above the hatch into Hab Two where he'd be sure to see it on the way back to his room.

The sixth figure was sitting on his pillow. It was a girl made of swabs and foil, with her cotton hair colored black and a tiny smile on her little cotton face. She was holding a folded note.

BREAKFAST TOMORROW AT 2200?

Rob wasn't any good at sculpting, but he was a decent freehand artist. He sacrificed a page from his personal journal and drew a little cartoon of himself surrounded by tiny figures. The caption read *Sure*. He stuck it on his door and went to bed.

The station used a twenty-four-hour clock, and for simplicity the day began at the start of the first "day" shift. So 2200 was an hour before even the early risers would be up and about. Rob finished rebuilding the flex linkage on one of the drones at 2130, and spent the next half hour fretting about what to do. Should he go meet the mystery person? Should he shower and change?

At 2145 he decided to go ahead and meet whoever it was. If this was some elaborate plan to give him crap about Henri's death, then whoever was doing it was an asshole and Rob could tell him that face to face.

He wound up sitting in the galley at 2150, wondering if this was all some kind of joke. But at 2200 exactly, Alicia Neogri came in and flipped on the lights.

"Why are you sitting in the dark?" she asked.

"Oh, I—"

"Lying in ambush to see who would come?" She put a little figure made of plastic tubing on the table. "What shall we have for breakfast?"

Figuring out what to cook at Hitode was always difficult. For a team of scientists who had grown up in a world of agricultural oversupply, with even the most obscure ingredients available at any market, being limited to what the hydroponic farm could produce was almost intolerable. Everyone brought along personal supplies, and hoarding and bartering were a way of life.

Rob, being an American, had used most of his ten-kilo personal food allotment for sugar and caffeine. But one of the few vivid food memories he had from childhood was eating scrambled eggs on a camping trip with his cousins, so on a whim he had packed a hundred grams of egg powder.

"I've still got some powdered eggs left. We could have scrambled eggs."

"What about an omelette? I have cheese and there are some fresh mushrooms." When Rob looked uncertain, she laughed. "I will do the cooking."

So Rob grated cheese and sliced mushrooms while Alicia put some synthetic oil in the pan and got it hot.

Cooks on Ilmatar had to follow an entirely different set of rules. The tremendous pressure at the bottom of the ocean affected everything. Water didn't boil until it was hot enough to melt tin, bread didn't rise, and foods like rice and pasta practically cooked themselves at room temperature. Added to that were the limits on what was available. The hydroponic garden produced plenty of greens, tomatoes, potatoes, and soybeans, but no grains. They had shrimp and a few catfish but no meat. Dairy products and eggs existed only in powdered form.

For bulk, the staff could always fall back on the pure glucose and synthetic lipids produced by the food assembler. You could have them separately, or combined in a kind of greasy syrup which sounded utterly nasty until you came in from a day in freezing water and wanted nothing but calories in their purest form. Without the hydroponic farm morale would suffer; without the assembler the crew of Hitode would starve.

Alicia was a good cook, at least on Ilmatar. Rob watched admiringly as she flipped the omelette out onto a plate one-handed. It was by far the best thing he'd eaten since leaving Earth.

"So what's up?" he asked after getting a few mouthfuls into himself. "Why the little statues?"

She looked a little embarrassed. "I thought they might cheer you up," she said. "But I didn't want to disturb you."

Rob tried to make sense of the situation. They weren't friends—at least, he didn't know her any better than anyone else at Hitode. Why was she being nice to him?

"Thanks," he said. "It was really nice of you."

They met again for breakfast the next day, and as they finished their toasted bean cakes, Rob cleared his throat and tried to sound casual. "You know, you don't have to get up early. We could meet at 0100 tomorrow if that's better for you."

"Everyone else will be up."

"I know."

"It's hard to flirt when there's an audience," she pointed out.

"We're flirting?" he asked, startled. She laughed, and he joined in, trying to pass it off as a joke.

They agreed to keep having breakfast together early, but that evening at 1500, when most of the staff were relaxing after dinner, Rob sat with Alicia in the lounge playing cards. There were half a dozen others in the room, and aside from a few furtive glances, nobody reacted to Rob's presence.

Encouraged, he started joining Alicia earlier and earlier in the evening, until they were dining together with the "second seating" in the galley at 1300. Rob realized he looked forward to spending time with her, and rearranged his work schedule to let him see more of her. In the process, he wound up spending more of his time out of his room when others were about, and he found he didn't mind it so much after all. A week passed, and then another; Rob hardly noticed.

He was just starting to wonder if she would sleep with him when the aliens arrived.

THE braking burn was brutal. Tizhos lay strapped to her bed, which for the occasion had extruded itself from what was normally the aft wall of her cabin. The fusion motors roared, and the force mashed Tizhos down into the cushions. She tried to estimate how hard—twice Shalina-normal gravity? Three times as much? How much could the ship stand before it broke apart?

The entire voyage had a distressingly thrown-together feel to it. Just to get out of orbit they'd used half a dozen strap-on boosters, and there were drop tanks attached to the drive section to allow faster transit in Otherspace. The expense of getting all that lofted into orbit on short notice was simply staggering—this one mission seemed likely to cost more than a year of interstellar probes.

Instead of popping out on a long, cleverly plotted minimum-fuel rendezvous orbit, they'd drained the drop tanks for a high-speed pass dangerously close to Ilmatar's sun, and now were using half the ship's internal fuel for this punishing deceleration.

She watched the display projected in the center of the cabin. At the moment the ship was passing low over the cloud tops of the giant planet the humans had named Ukko. It would swing out again, matching orbits with the moon Ilmatar, and do a final burn to start circling the moon. All these extravagant maneuvers would leave the ship with just enough fuel to get back to Shalina on a four-month low-energy trajectory through Otherspace.

The motors shut down, and Tizhos unstrapped herself. She rather liked zero gravity. She called up a window, and watched the red and yellow swirls of Ukko's atmosphere beneath the dark sky. Ilmatar was already visible as a little white crescent, rising steadily above the giant planet's cloud tops.

According to the display, Tizhos had about two hours before she needed to strap in again. The perfect time to work on her little personal project.

She had joined the Space Working Group in order to learn about alien life. But until now, she had never left Shalina. The Ilmatar voyage was a wonderful opportunity to study two different alien species: humans and the natives of Ilmatar. The visit would be short, so Tizhos wanted to be able to gather as much information as she could in the time available. After a little thought, she had come up with a clever plan.

The humans spent a lot of time studying the Ilmatarans, so if Tizhos could spend time with one of the human researchers and examine the raw data, she could effectively study both species at once. It seemed like a very efficient way to do things. So she spent her free time practicing English and Spanish, two of the most common human languages.

She was fluent enough to read some of their scientific documents. They had an oddly conflict-based method of disseminating information. Researchers wrote up their findings in stand-alone documents, and others tried to disprove the statements in the document. Somehow, out of conflict came consensus.

Sometimes the ongoing consensus changed dramatically, and Tizhos thought it was significant that the humans used the same term, "revolution," to describe both a shift in scientific theory and a violent social upheaval. Everything the humans did seemed to be the result of competition or rigid logic. How unlike the compassionate, nurturing consensus of the Sholen, she thought.

Tizhos never spoke of it to anyone, but at times she thought it might be pleasant to be able to disagree with others.

STRONGPINCER and the others crouch hidden beneath an overhanging rock, listening carefully. The rock sits in a barren part of the seafloor, but it is in a good place to wait for travelers. Traders and messengers going from the Deepest Rift communities to the Three Domes hotspot pass nearby, but here it is hundreds of cables to safety in either direction. Robbers can pounce on the unwary and there is no one to help.

The gang has eight members now, all fierce fighters. Strongpincer remembers chasing away a gang of twelve, with only three others to help him. That the larger gang consisted mostly of half-grown children is something Strongpincer tries to forget.

He listens again, hoping to hear prey, and feels a surge of joy. It sounds like a whole train—three or four towfins and probably half a dozen adults. As they come closer he hears the adults clicking away to one another, not caring if the whole ocean knows where they are. This train is too big for a band of children or half-starved outcasts to attack; evidently they don't know this is Strongpincer's territory.

To his left, Shellcrusher starts to move, but Strongpincer halts her and says very quietly, "The last one. Pass it on." The others are silently getting into position for a fast climb and some quick, brutal fighting.

Overhead, the first towfin passes. From the churning of its fins, it sounds like it's hauling something big. Two of the chatty adults are trailing behind the towfin. The next one sounds smaller and lightly loaded—Strongpincer suspects a young towfin ready to be sold. Then another, with what sounds like three or four adults hanging on its line.

Strongpincer tenses. The last one is passing now. It sounds like an old towfin with ragged fins, laboring a bit to keep up with the others. Silently, Strongpincer rises from the seafloor and then begins swimming up toward the towfin using powerful strokes of his tail. When he's half a cable away he starts pinging, to get a better idea of what he's up against. There is one adult riding on the towfin's back, and two nets of jars trailing behind it. The adult hears Strongpincer's pings and calls those ahead for help.

Headcracker and Tailcutter are going for the cargo bundles; even if the merchants get away, Strongpincer and his gang get the loot. Shellcrusher and Weaklegs are in formation with Strongpincer, gaining on the towfin and the panicky adult. Halftail is lagging behind, of course.

Ahead he can hear the other towfins coming about, but they are clumsy and can't turn fast. Where are Onefeeler and Hardshell?

He hears them ping up ahead and imagines them walking on the bottom before rising up to attack. Clever—surely Onefeeler's idea. Sometimes Strongpincer wonders if maybe Onefeeler isn't too clever.

The panicking adult abandons his towfin. Fool. Strongpincer gives a couple of powerful strokes with his tail and catches the wretch. A town-bred adult, that's for sure, with his shell all covered with weed and parasites. Big, though. He probably doesn't remember going hungry. Strongpincer grabs him from behind and tries to get a grip on his pincers, but the coward tries to curl up, folding his legs and pincers against his belly. Strongpincer doesn't have the time to waste prying this one open, so he works a pincer point between a couple of the fellow's back segments and forces it in until he can feel the soft membranes give way.

He looks up and pings. Onefeeler and Hardshell are fighting tail to tail against three angry adults behind the third towfin. Shellcrusher and Weaklegs are going to help. Tailcutter's down on the bottom trying to cut open the cargo nets from the fourth towfin. Greedy fool; he could be helping get more stuff. The young towfin is bolting, dragging its rider helplessly on the towrope, and the two adults on the first 'fin decide to run for it as well, prodding their beast until it breaks into a ponderous sprint.

When they notice Shellcrusher and Weaklegs, the other three adults scatter, trying to catch up with their fleeing buddies. Shellcrusher overtakes one of them and gets her massive pincers around the poor fool's body right where the tail joins. There's a burst of panicked clicking and then a crack, and Shellcrusher lets the leaking body tumble down to the seafloor.

The haul is good. The two cargo nets from the last 'fin hold jars of iceshaver roe and skin bags full of smokeweed pith. The other beast has only a small net full of personal baggage and some food for the merchants. Still, the beasts themselves are certainly valuable.

Only one of the gang is hurt—Hardshell lost a feeler, but they grow back, and it won't affect his fighting ability. Strongpincer imagines recruiting some more fighters, maybe even buying some fierce children from a school. For a big gang, there are so many possibilities. Strongpincer dives down to get some roe before Tailcutter eats the whole jar by himself.

TIZHOS joined Gishora at the lander hatch as soon as the ship had established orbit around Ilmatar. Gishora was leader on this voyage, which meant that he had to do a lot of nuzzling and stroking of Tizhos as part of the normal bonding. Neither of them particularly enjoyed it. Gishora was naturally somewhat shy and solitary, almost as reserved as the humans. He was in charge of this voyage only because of his unmatched knowledge of human social rules and languages.

Consequently, their contact up to now had been perfunctory and brief, enough to satisfy the formalities without really establishing a hormonal leader-follower bond.

The two of them suited up and climbed into the lander after the pilot. There was a delay of some twenty minutes before launch, and Gishora took that opportunity to have a talk with his subordinate.

"Tizhos. I have set up a private channel so we may speak frankly. Tell me if you have finished all your preparations."

"I believe so. I made estimates of how contact could affect the Ilmatarans. My notes may lack precision—I had very little information other than the bulletin from Earth."

"I understand. You can refine them as we learn more below.

Remember that we come here to learn and understand, and to correct what may have gone wrong, not to judge."

"Some on board seem to think otherwise," said Tizhos.

Gishora knew who she meant. "I thought it best to bring Irona on the mission so that the Interventionist faction would not feel themselves excluded. But I think even he would agree that he can do little to help in the gathering of facts. So I have a perfectly valid reason to leave him in orbit where he can do no harm."

"I do admit to curiosity, Gishora: Did you bring him in order to have something to threaten the humans with? If they do not cooperate with you, they will have to face Irona?"

Gishora sounded pained. "Tizhos, we have not come here to make threats or demands! Such behavior resembles what we wish to avoid. We only wish to learn all the facts of what happened and prevent future mistakes."

"If the humans refuse to accept our help, what then?"

"In that case, you and I must do our work anyway. And, yes, I do take comfort from knowing I can call upon Irona if force seems necessary."

For a moment, Gishora seemed dominant indeed, and Tizhos felt the warm sexual rush of agreement with a leader.

The pilot called back from the flight station. "Thrusters fire in one dozen seconds."

"Good," Gishora replied. "We wait prepared."

A moment later they heard the hissing sound of the thrusters behind them, and a feeble gravity pushed them into their seats. Then they floated again. "All done," said the pilot. "We begin braking in three dozen minutes."

Gishora made the hull next to their seats transparent, and the two of them became absorbed in the view as the vast landscape of Ilmatar pivoted beneath them. The surface below was a smooth plain of white ice, criscrossed by lines and mottled with occasional spots and splotches of dark material. In a few places mountains of rock pierced the ice layer to rise barren and gray, casting long shadows. The moon was virtually airless, with no clouds or haze to block their view.

There! Just at the terminator line, at the intersection of two chasms in the ice, Tizhos saw a tiny flashing light. From this height she could not see the Terran base itself, but the landing strobe showed up clearly. If she peered hard, Tizhos could almost make out a faint smudge around the blinking light, where the humans had disturbed the pristine surface. A stain on the world.

THREE

THE trial is quick and holds few surprises. A good crowd gathers in the commonhouse, about equal numbers of Broadtail's friends and Ridgeback's supporters. Half a dozen landowners with their militia bolt-launchers are standing by to keep order. Judge Longfeeler 62 Deeprift opens the proceedings by asking Broadtail to recount his version of events.

"I remember the two of us arguing about the net vote after the meeting. Ridgeback steps onto my property and I order him off. He refuses to leave, and we fight. He nips off the end of my feeler, I stab him with my pincer, and he dies."

There are no witnesses to the event besides a few children, but the judge calls Cleft-tail 5 Fisher, who describes the position of Ridgeback's body. Smallbody 19 Doctor confirms that Ridgeback's fatal injury is exactly the type produced by a downward pincer stab. Finally the judge asks Broadtail to clarify some points.

"Do you remember intending to kill Ridgeback?"

"I recall being very angry and striking out at him without thinking."

"Do you remember being aware you and Ridgeback are on common ground?"

"I do not. The fight starts on my property and I remember being too busy fighting to notice where we are. I also remember Ridgeback fighting back and refusing to leave. Is that a mitigating circumstance?"

"The law is very clear. You may not kill another adult on common ground, even if the fight begins on your property. Your personal law stops at your boundary."

"What about his death being accidental? I do not remember intending to kill him."

"Unfortunately it is too easy to tell lies about intentions. The common law can only govern actions. Do you regret killing Ridgeback?"

"I regret it very much. I do not recall liking him, but I am not glad he is dead."

The judge asks if anyone has any information to add. Nobody speaks up. The commonhouse gets very quiet as the judge pronounces the sentence.

"The law is clear: killing another adult on common ground is murder. No one disputes Ridgeback's adulthood, and Broadtail admits killing Ridgeback on the public road. The penalty for murder is equally clear: expropriation and outlawry. The Sandyslope property now belongs to Ridgeback's second-oldest apprentice, and Broadtail is proclaimed an outlaw within the bounds of this community. Does anyone offer him sanctuary?"

A landowner is the ultimate authority on his own property. If another landowner at Continuous Abundance chooses to take Broadtail as a tenant, he is safe—on his protector's land, that is.

Nobody speaks up. Former landowners are notoriously bad tenants, and many who remember Ridgeback fondly might make things difficult for Broadtail's protector. Broadtail is actually a little relieved. He hates the thought of being trapped on someone else's property, lower than any apprentice or new-caught child.

The judge continues. "Because of the circumstances of the crime, I ask if anyone will safeguard him to the edge of town."

Thicklegs 34 Sandybottom and Longhead 10 Bareslope volunteer. Neither of them belong to Ridgeback's faction, and they're both pretty big and have their weapons. If some tenants or apprentices want to try mobbing the outlaw just for fun, Thicklegs and Longhead can give them a fight.

Expropriation means Broadtail 38 (no more Sandyslope, and for the moment he has no profession-name) can't even set foot on his old property again. Young Smoothpincer 14 owns it all now, even Broadtail's beads and debts. The apprentices go with the property just like the livestock.

The hardest thing for Broadtail to leave behind is his library. He has several dozen books, including a few he has made himself. Smoothpincer can sell them, or use them to tie up bundles, or whatever he likes. He has a reputation as a hard worker, not a reader.

With Thicklegs and Longhead flanking him, Broadtail sets out down the road leading to the edge of town. They are joined by some of his friends—Roughshell 74 Westcave, Spineback 22 Coldvent, and Bigfeet 15 Ropemaker—and followed by some of Ridgeback's old cronies. There are some pings and a few shouts of "Murderer! Split his shell!" but nobody does anything. Broadtail is still trying to get his mind used to the idea of exile. As they pass Sandyslope he suddenly feels afraid and lonely despite the crowd. The urge to hold his property against all comers is very strong. He makes himself keep walking, one step at a time. He keeps his pincers clamped shut and folded against his body.

The crowd around Broadtail thins. Nothing is happening, and the crowd gets bored and loses interest. Ridgeback's friends are satisfied with the verdict and nobody wants to join a hunting posse to chase the outlaw in cold water. The apprentices have work to do. By the time he reaches the edge of town, Broadtail has only his escort and a couple of friends left.

At the boundary stones they pause for good-byes. Roughshell asks, "Where are you going?"

"I'm not sure," says Broadtail. "I don't wish to be a scavenger like Bentpincer 89." He flicks his tail toward the little hovel where the old outlaw manages a half-starved existence just beyond the boundary.

"What about fishing?"

"No. Not here, anyway. Too many of Ridgeback's friends are fishers or netmakers. I don't wish for trouble. For now I will go visit some of my scientific friends and find out if they can help." Broadtail takes momentary comfort in knowing that even if he is a murderer and outlaw, he is still a scientist, the author of a respected work.

"Good luck to you," says Thicklegs. Spineback gives Broadtail a bag of roe balls and strips of swimmer flesh. They all brush feelers in farewell, then Broadtail turns and begins swimming steadily out into cold water. The others stand and listen for a moment, then turn and head back toward the warmth of the vent.

ROB was just heading for the galley to meet Alicia for another private breakfast together when the master alarm sounded. All over the station, lights flicked on. The seldom-used public-address system came alive.

"Attention, please, everyone!" said Dr. Sen's voice from every terminal and comm button in Hitode Station. "I would like everyone to meet in the common area in Habitat Four in ten minutes. The station is not in danger but there is something extremely important I would like to talk to everyone about as soon as it is practical to assemble."

Rob hurried, and since he was already dressed and half-way to the common room, he and Alicia were the first ones to show up.

"What is this all about?" she wanted to know.

Rob pulled out his computer and did a quick check of station systems. "Everything's nominal—we're not about to drown or anything. Supplies look good."

"Look at orbital tracking page," said Josef Palashnik, coming in just behind Rob. He had a bad case of bed hair, but was dressed and functional.

Alicia and Rob nearly knocked heads as they looked at his computer. The gas giant Ukko was a big red disk, surrounded by green circles marking the orbits of the moons. Ilmatar was a smaller gold disk creeping along one of the green paths, but Rob could see that there was now a little red circle around Il-matar, with a red triangle moving along it. He tapped the tri-angle and his computer obligingly opened a new window.

SPACECRAFT: Sholen (Aquilan) interstellar vehicle, UNICA class identification INFLUX.

Rob skimmed the technical description of the alien vehicle—most of which was guesswork, anyway. One thing was certain: the Sholen craft was a big one, a giant doughnut a hundred meters across, with fuel tanks and motors filling the hole in the middle. It had room for up to a hundred people, two landers, and immense fuel reserves. The intel said it *probably* didn't mount any weapons—but of course any spacecraft could carry combat drones as cargo.

Sending a vehicle like that across thirty light-years cost a fortune. What was it doing here? Rob suspected he knew, and began to feel queasy.

The room was filling up. Rob and Alicia had claimed seats at one of the tables, but with all twenty-eight members of the Hitode staff crowding into the room, they soon could see only backs and stomachs. So Rob stood up and helped Alicia stand on her chair.

Dr. Sen climbed onto the big dining table, and stood with his bald head nearly touching the ceiling. "Thank you all for coming here so promptly. First, let me reassure everyone that there is no danger or emergency. We are all perfectly safe."

Behind Rob someone muttered, "I sure as hell hope he didn't get me out of bed just to tell me that."

"Now," continued Dr. Sen, "some of you may already know that there is a spacecraft in orbit." The room erupted in click-ings and mutterings as people pulled out pocket computers to check. "It is a Sholen interstellar vehicle, and a lander is just putting down at the surface station. I have received a message from the Sholen commander. Apparently they have learned about what happened to poor Dr. Kerlerec, and have come to evaluate the situation and make sure that we have not violated any of the treaties governing contact with alien species and that sort of thing."

"How'd they find out so fast?" asked Angelo Ponti. "We haven't even been able to send word to Earth yet."

"Actually I have already sent a message. Dr. Castaverde and I agreed that Dr. Kerlerec's death was important enough to use one of the message drones, so I sent it off just two days after the incident."

There was a moment's silence as twenty-seven people did mental arithmetic. Ilmatar was thirty light-years from Earth, but cutting through gimelspace divided that distance by al-most a million, so call it about 300 million kilometers. The drones were big solid-fuel boosters carrying a tiny transmitter, and could hit a hundred kilometers per second. That meant a trip time of only a month, which meant . . .

"The Sholen have been eavesdropping!" Dickie Graves yelled. "There's no way they could get a message from Earth and send a ship here."

"I don't know if we can necessarily make that assumption," said Dr. Sen. "They could have better boosters than ours, or have transmitters positioned in gimelspace to relay messages. At any rate, that is not the most important issue at this moment. What is important is that two Sholen are coming down to Hitode as we speak. The elevator is on its way up to collect them right now. We have two days to make everything ready for their visit."

"What if we don't let them come down?" Dickie called out. "Tell them to fuck off and send them right back home again!"

"Taking a confrontational attitude like that will accomplish nothing, Dr. Graves. The treaty gives both species inspection rights outside our respective home systems. We are obliged to let them examine the station and interview everyone involved in the Kerlerec incident." At that particular moment, everybody managed to be looking at something other than Rob Freeman. "However, I think we can avoid a great deal of difficulty if the Sholen find nothing which might indicate contact with the Ilmatarans, or create any mistaken impression. We should place all the artifacts from the city sites out on the seafloor, encrypt any recordings of Ilmatarans, and relabel the cadaver sections. I also need a group to make a thorough sweep of the area around the station to make sure none of our equipment or waste has been left outside."

"Why do all this hiding?" asked Alicia. "We haven't done anything wrong. All that research is allowed by the treaty, isn't it?"

"Of course it is, Dr. Neogri. But there is a certain amount of public relations involved here. If the Sholen make a complaint about us and can present things like cadaver samples and artifacts, it will affect public opinion back on Earth. I'm afraid it is not enough to simply be innocent of wrongdoing; we must be sure to avoid anything which could be misinterpreted."

Since everyone was still not looking at him, Rob cleared his throat and raised his hand. "Dr. Sen? The Sholen are going to need someone to show them around, aren't they?"

"Yes, they will certainly need a guide. I had intended to perform that task myself but if you have a suggestion I'm sure we all would like to hear it."

"Since they're going to want to debrief me anyway about what happened to Henri, why not let me be the tour guide?"

"That is a perfectly sensible suggestion and I am happy to let you take over that part of the work. Now, we must all get started as quickly as possible. We only have two days."

THE Terran base on the surface of Ilmatar was built at the bottom of a long crack in the ice that the Terrans called Shackleton Linea. The landing area and beacon were up on the edge of the crevasse, and in order to reach the base proper the two Sholen had to seal up their suits and descend the cliff face in an open platform suspended from a crane that looked alarmingly makeshift to Tizhos. Their suit radios weren't on the same channel as that of their Terran guide, so the entire trip down was spent in silence.

The base itself was nothing but a squat foam-covered cylinder, about the size of a lander, standing on a cleared patch of ice on the floor of the crevasse. Clumped nearby were a power plant, an antenna mast, some machinery for making rocket fuel out of ice, and the gaping hole of the shaft down through the ice to the ocean beneath. Some distance off was the plasma furnace for waste disposal, which had made a huge ugly stain of soot on the ice for kilometers around. The whole place was surrounded by a litter of construction equipment and scrap.

Another suited human met them at the airlock, and made some gestures of greeting before they all went inside. According to the glyphs on the hatch, the airlock was built to hold four humans, so two humans and a pair of Sholen made a very tight fit.

Within the habitat it was cramped, overheated, and foul-smelling. The crew consisted of three male humans and one female, and all were dressed in very dirty suit liners. A male with a hairless head stepped forward and extended his hand in a gesture of greeting.

"Welcome to Shackleton. I'm Claudio Castaverde, director of operations up here. We have a room for the two of you, if you need to rest."

"Very kind of you, but we rested in the lander," said Gishora. He spoke the most common Terran language far more fluently than Tizhos could. "We must go down to the main base as soon as we can."

"The elevator is on its way up now. There's nobody aboard so it will be here in just a few hours. In the meantime, if you'd like something to eat or drink, we were just about to have dinner. Would you like to join us?"

Tizhos felt her mouth grow dry with disgust at the thought of eating in such a foul-smelling place, but Gishora was a hardened diplomat. "Thank you very much. That would give us great pleasure."

They did not actually eat any of the Terran food. Tizhos knew that Sholen could safely eat the starches and sugars, but she also knew the humans had a dangerous habit of flavoring everything with animal proteins that would almost certainly cause an allergic reaction.

So Tizhos and Gishora dined on the food they had brought along. Their rations were simple balls of blended carbohydrates and lipids, but each was flavored with a mixture of aromatics, pheromones, and psychoactives, and the balls were coded to be eaten in sequence. The meal began with subtle vegetable tastes mixed with stimulants, progressed to strong spices and disinhibitors to improve the conversation, and wound up with aphrodisiacs and a mild narcotic with a blend of pickled fruit flavors. Tizhos felt mellow and well-disposed toward everyone afterward.

While they ate, Gishora and the Terrans discussed the scientific research they were conducting. The hairless one, Castaverde, was studying the ionosphere and magnetic fields of Ilmatar, and how they interacted with the more powerful fields of the giant planet it orbited. The female was using a series of laser reflectors to measure the movement of the ice plates. The other two males were in charge of maintaining the base and the elevator. All four of them seemed desperately eager to show the two Sholen around. Tizhos had to suffer through a trip out to view the waste incinerator, and tried to stand patiently as the female human went on endlessly about the accursed thing.

"The shell's just hull plating we scavenged from some of the cargo drop pods. Inside it's all lined with native basalt. Satoshi and I spent two weeks in the crawler dragging a sled full of rock back from the nearest outcrop. There's a pure oxygen feed and a hydrogen plasma torch; anything organic gets completely burned up in minutes. No contamination."

"But it produces much soot," said Tizhos. "One can see it from orbit."

The female made a gesture with her shoulders. "The original plan was just to dump all the waste on a piece of rocky surface somewhere and let it sit there for the next billion years.

But you guys wanted us to burn everything. Burning stuff makes ashes."

"You could take it all away from this world."

"Are you kidding?" her voice was shrill over the radio. "That's what, ten kilos of fuel for each kilo of garbage? We're already mining as much ice as you guys will let us."

Tizhos looked over at the station and saw that the elevator capsule was just emerging from the top of the shaft.

"I have enjoyed speaking with you, but I see the elevator coming up. I need to go now."

Despite their best efforts to make the humans hurry, it was more than an hour before Gishora and Tizhos could board the elevator, and then more delays as their gear was loaded and two of the Terrans checked out all the onboard systems. So when the ice wall began sliding upward past the tiny porthole in the hatch, Tizhos felt a tremendous sense of relief.

The elevator was a little self-contained habitat unit, almost as big as the surface station. It had four human-sized beds, a table, a little waste-disposal unit, and a cabinet stocked with dehydrated Terran foods. The two Sholen had their own food-maker and distilled water to drink, and plenty of time for conversation. The descent took thirty-six hours to give their bodies time to adjust to the pressure.

Tizhos actually enjoyed the elevator descent. She and Gishora had complete freedom to talk about their work—Ilmatar and the Terrans. It was almost like being a student again. Tizhos could simply enjoy the company of another smart, curious Sholen for the better part of three Shalina days. Their sexual play became more than just an official duty.

She briefed him about the planet and its inhabitants. "Of course," she cautioned, "most of what we know about Ilmatar comes from the Terrans. They may well have learned more since my last opportunity to read their findings."

"I must ask you to compare what you have read with what we see here," said Gishora. "Note any differences. If you find anything the Terrans have concealed, let me know at once."

"I believe you said we did not come here to judge."

"True. But we must strive for accuracy and impartiality. Just as I cautioned against too much suspicion, we should also avoid trusting them too much."

"I understand."

"Please proceed," said Gishora.

Tizhos called up an image on her terminal. "The moon Ilmatar orbits the giant planet the humans call Ukko. I believe these names derive from the mythology of a human culture exterminated long ago by a more aggressive one. Ilmatar fits a standard model for giant planet moons far outside the life zone of the central star: a rocky core covered by a thick layer of water ice. Diameter of 6,400 kilometers. Tidal heating has liquified the interior, creating an ocean two kilometers deep, buried under a crust of ice a kilometer thick."

"Hence this long ride down. I understand the physical details. Tell me about the things which live here."

"Life on Ilmatar resembles similar ecosystems on other subglacial ocean moons. We know of three others. On all of them, volcanic vents on the seafloor serve as energy sources, giving off warm water and carbon or sulfur compounds. The native organisms make use of both heat gradients and chemical energy."

"Tell me how such a low-energy system can support intelligent beings."

"The Ilmatarans descend—according to human scientists—from smaller species which live as scavengers and predators around energetic vents. At some point the Ilmatarans became intelligent enough to cultivate chemosynthetic organisms, and eventually developed a sophisticated analog of agriculture, using stone pipes and channels to conserve and distribute energy-rich vent water."

"What sort of communities do they form?"

"Again, the information I have only includes archaeological data and some images taken from a distance. It appears that the Ilmatarans live in small communities, each centered on an active vent. They have some sort of division of labor, as the humans have observed individuals performing distinct tasks consistently."

"How much they sound like Sholen," said Gishora. "Small communities, careful stewardship of their resources, mutual assistance."

"I only wish we could learn more about them," ventured Tizhos.

"We will have the human records to examine," said Gishora. "I feel certain you look forward to that with great anticipation, as I do."

"In all honesty, yes."

"Tizhos—this elevator ride may represent our last chance to speak in complete privacy. Tell me if you pay much attention to the politics of consensus back home."

"Only somewhat. I attend my community and working-group meetings." She did not add that she had long ago stopped paying the slightest attention to anything discussed at those meetings.

"I assume you know that our world has not yet achieved consensus about the Terran problem."

"Yes." Tizhos hesitated for just a moment. "I myself adhere to the Noninterference tendency on that issue."

"As do I," said Gishora. "But I find it highly frustrating that most other members of our tendency support a complete withdrawal from space altogether."

"It frustrates me, as well. I suspect most in the space working groups agree."

"Some, but not most. Irona came on this voyage because he takes a prominent part in the Interventionist tendency regarding the Terrans. He wishes to restrict them to their own world, possibly even compel them to adopt planetary-management policies like our own."

"I know. He spoke to me about it several times during the voyage. I can't understand why you brought him."

"I had no choice. The Interventionists support space travel—after all, one cannot meddle in the affairs of other species across interstellar distances without spacecraft."

"So you needed Irona's support to get consensus for the mission, but at the price of including him."

"Exactly. Which means that our conclusions here must support Irona."

"You know your conclusions before gathering data?"

"I fear we must use bad science to accomplish good politics. Our only hope for more space exploration lies with the Interventionists. I know for a fact that Irona has risked a great deal of his own prestige for this mission. If we return to Shalina and announce no need for any form of intervention, Irona loses much influence and the anti-space tendency can point to the enormous waste of resources our mission represents."

"You sound like an Interventionist yourself," said Tizhos.

"Not at all! I loathe the idea of imposing our consensus on the humans—and I don't feel at all certain we would win a violent conflict with the humans. Their world holds ten of them for every one of us on Shalina."

"But surely our technology gives us the advantage!"

"I have seen estimates of capabilities," said Gishora. "They do not reassure me. We have *knowledge* far beyond anything the humans possess, but we have spent generations reducing our ability to use it effectively. Shalina has a single facility building spaceships; we know of at least eight on Earth. Right now we possess twelve starships, each superior to anything the humans can build—but they have thirty that we know of."

"Then I fear I don't understand what you mean to accomplish," said Tizhos. "You fear intervention but support it at the same time."

"We must produce a report which supports Irona's beliefs, but which won't tip the consensus at home in favor of the Interventionist faction."

"That sounds difficult. Especially with aliens involved."

"Very difficult. But consider what it means for the future: Irona and the Interventionists will owe their prestige to us. That gives us a way to control them."

"Tell me if you would like some food," Tizhos asked.

"Please," said Gishora.

She operated the foodmaker, feeling herself settle into the role of a subordinate. A comfortable feeling—especially if she didn't have to make the kind of terrifying decisions Gishora did.

As they began the meal she asked one final question. "You wish to maintain a balance between factions—but so much depends on the actions of the humans. Tell me how you can predict the behavior of alien creatures."

Gishora popped a food ball into his mouth and stretched lazily. "The Terrans have an obsession with rules and pride themselves on behaving rationally. Predicting their behavior seems like analyzing a computer's output—as long as you know the relevant rules and inputs, determining the result poses no difficulty. Of all the elements, I worry least of all about them. They seem entirely predictable."

* * *

STRONGPINCER learns of the attack when a bolt glances off his headshield, waking him from a sound sleep. He pings and is shocked to hear a throng of armed adults converging on the rocks where his followers are camped. Half the attackers are on the sea bottom, arranged in a crescent around the rocks and moving inward. The rest float above, ready to intercept anyone trying to escape. There must be two dozen in all.

"Wake up!" Strongpincer thwacks Hardshell's headshield and pings the others as loudly as he can. "Militia!"

The militia must be from Three Domes; many of the adults there are merchants and don't like bandits, even if they don't prey on Three Domes convoys. For them to come out in force like this is a surprise, but not impossible. It's just Strongpincer's bad luck that they're out looking for bandits here.

Where is Tailcutter? Strongpincer remembers leaving him on watch. The coward is probably swimming away as fast as he can go. Of course, that isn't a bad idea, but how to get away without being cut off and shot full of bolts?

"Onefeeler!" Strongpincer calls out. "Take Headcracker and Hardshell—try to get free. We hold them here."

He's lying, of course. In battle, sacrifices are sometimes necessary. As soon as Onefeeler's group go half a cable, Strongpincer and the rest scatter, each swimming as hard as he can in a different direction. That makes poor Onefeeler and his companions the biggest target, and Strongpincer can hear them getting swarmed by militia.

The squad hovering up above are launching bolts at the fleeing bandits, and a couple pass near Strongpincer as he zigzags desperately. Halftail gets snared in a net, struggling to free himself until half a dozen bolts send him sinking gently to the bottom.

There's one soldier moving to intercept Strongpincer. He knows that he can't afford to get tied up fighting, so he tries to brush past and keep on going. It doesn't work. The soldier jabs with a spear, and Strongpincer has to do a sudden roll to avoid getting an obsidian point in his head. He's not called Strongpincer for nothing: he gets one pincer onto the shaft of the spear and snaps it.

Now the soldier's grappling with him, trying to hold one of his limbs and slow him down. Strongpincer gives the fellow a powerful blow to the head, deafening him for a moment. He loses his grip on Strongpincer's leg. That's all Strongpincer needs—he dives for the bottom, where the rocks and rubble make confusing echoes. The soldier tries a few pings, but evidently he doesn't want to fight Strongpincer alone, and his comrades are busy chasing down Headcracker and Onefeeler. Strongpincer swims away, slowly at first as he weaves among the rocks, then rising above them and picking up speed. The soldier doesn't follow.

Strongpincer swims until he's ready to pass out, then listens. Nobody's following him. The sounds of fighting are dying down. He lets himself sink to the bottom and finds a sheltered spot to rest. The bottom here is silty, and Strongpincer digs in until only his feelers stick out of the dirt. He wonders if any of the others are safe. There's a big rock slab a few cables away where he remembers agreeing to meet, but nobody's meeting anywhere until the militia leave.

VOLUNTEERING to guide the Sholen around didn't get Rob out of his share of the cleanup work before their arrival. Since he was the imaging and video specialist, Dr. Sen gave him the task of going through all the visual data stored in the station network and removing all the frames that showed living or dead Ilmatarans.

The Sholen weren't as far ahead of humans in computer technology as in other areas, but they weren't behind either, and Rob had to assume whoever they were sending would be familiar with Terran systems. So he couldn't just delete the images, he had to replace them. He dug up some of his early files, from when he'd first arrived on Ilmatar and was still learning the ropes. There were plenty of shots of silt, lens covers, his fingers, and black water to use as filler.

Of course, the researchers didn't want to lose their images, so he had to store everything he cut out on a disk, heavily encrypted and labeled ANIME PORN. For verisimilitude he copied in a few videos from his private collection.

Since he spent the whole day on the station network, he was one of the first to see the new feed go up, entitled: "Ways the Sholen Can Go Fuck Themselves." He watched the list grow as the day went on.

DGRAVES: Immediately.

JPALASHNIK: Far from here.

GWEISS: Sideways.

FOUCHARD: With an *Aenocampus.*

PADLER: Sideways, with an *Aenocampus.*

SERGEI: Senseless.

HISHIKAWA: Is that a comment, or a suggestion for the Sholen?

SERGEI: Suggestion.

APONTI: Responsibly.

SAMIAM: In a house, with a mouse, in a box, with a fox, in a car, in a tree, on a train, in the dark, with a goat, on a boat . . .

RADUZ: In accordance with all interstellar treaty agreements.

APONTI: That rules out Fouchard's idea, then.

ANONYMOUS: Any way they like, if I get to watch!

NKYLE: If you ask nicely, they might let you do that anyway.

ANON: Or let you join in.

PADLER: From what I understand, the problem is likely to be keeping them from doing it right in front of everybody.

APONTI: Unless they're both male, or both female.

GWEISS: That doesn't stop some of us.

PADLER: That wouldn't be a problem for Sholen. Their sex roles are based more on status than on physical gender. And yes, public display is apparently an important element.

GGDG: Six ways to Sunday!

MADAMEX: With whoever started this stupid stream.

DGRAVES: That would be me. If you don't like it, don't play.

ILMATAR: Having consulted several journal articles on Sholen reproduction, I would like to suggest 1: The "Missionary" position; 2: The "Lotus" position; or 3: The "Screaming Wombat" position.

ANONYMOUS: Your Screaming Wombat Kung Fu is no match for the Drunken Monkey!

VSEN: I certainly hope this discussion is closed and completely erased by the time our guests arrive, which by my clock is only 26 hours from now.

ROB took a break from his work and ate dinner; it was weird but kind of pleasant to be eating with everyone else. He glimpsed Alicia, but she was hurrying off to the dive room for another shift outside and could spare him only a smile and a wave.

By the time the evening shift was coming to an end, Rob realized he felt gritty and tired. He had been awake for more than thirty hours without a rest, so he decided to go to bed at 1600 along with everyone else.

Alicia was in his room.

"I was wondering if you were going to sleep at all," she said.

"If there was more coffee, I could probably keep going."

"I am all sore and tired from moving things outside, and I expect you must be stiff from sitting at a table. Would you like to trade massages?"

"Um, sure. Wait. I'm not very good at the subtle social cues thing—"

"I have noticed."

"—so before we start, I want to know: by massage do you mean actually rubbing each other's sore muscles, or do you mean having sex?"

There was a long pause, during which Rob wondered if he had just done the equivalent of shoving his head into a wood chipper. But then she smiled. "Muscle rubbing first, then sex."

Rob's massage technique was based on brute force and what he could remember from being on the swim team in high school, but evidently that was what Alicia needed because her groans and grunts had a contented sound. He worked his way from her calves to her forearms, kneading and rubbing until his own arms ached. Her bare skin was still slightly chilly to the touch from being out in the cold water, but under his hands she turned pink and warm again. Like just about everyone at Hitode, she was in terrific shape, with muscles as hard as wood and less body fat than the average famine victim.

When he couldn't make his fingers work anymore, he tapped her shoulder. "My turn."

She made a disappointed sound, but dutifully perched on the back of his thighs and began working on his stiff neck and shoulders. If they did have sex together, he never noticed it because he promptly fell asleep.

LONGPINCER'S apprentice shows no surprise when Broadtail arrives at the boundaries of Bitterwater and pings to signal the house. Apparently everyone at Bitterwater is accustomed to half-starved outlaw scholars showing up without warning.

The apprentice takes Broadtail to Longpincer straightaway. The master is at work on his pipes, commanding a group of tenants and apprentices who are installing a curious gadget in one of the main channels. It seems like a circulator turbine, but the axle is linked to a bundle of twisted ropevine, which is in turn anchored solidly to a heavy stone.

"Broadtail! I don't remember getting word of your coming. But you are welcome all the same," says Longpincer.

"I am an outlaw, Longpincer," says Broadtail. "I am exiled from Continuous Abundance for killing a landowner on common ground."

Longpincer considers this. "Describe the crime."

"I remember a dispute in the commonhouse over nets. The leader of the other faction tries to recruit me to his side. We argue. I am tired and hungry. He refuses to leave. I believe myself to be on my own land and fight him. I kill him, and then learn we are on neutral ground."

"A sad mistake. I am certainly surprised, but I repeat that you are welcome here. At Bitterwater you are under my protection."

"Thank you," says Broadtail. Longpincer is a stickler for the old forms, and when he calls someone his guest he means it. Broadtail can relax for the first time since the trial. He is no longer an outlaw, he is the guest of a sovereign landowner. Within Longpincer's boundary stones he is safe.

Longpincer pings at Broadtail. "Enough chatting—get to the house and eat something at once. You sound all hollow! I expect us to speak a great deal after this task is done." Longpincer turns his attention to one of the hired workers. "You wild child! Feel that pipe joint! Half the flow is going out through the seam. Put it together properly."

* * *

ROB slept nine hours, ate a huge meal, and worked another shift packing up Henri Kerlerec's belongings so that Una
Karlssen could switch into Henri's old room. That way the two
aliens could have adjacent quarters.

Alicia volunteered to help him pack up Henri's stuff, but Rob
told her he could do it himself. "It's easier for one person in
these tiny cabins," he said. "And I promise I won't slit my wrists
in some outburst of delayed grief."

Nevertheless, it was weird going through Henri's things. All
the items that had seemed so affected and annoying were sad
and kind of pathetic now. The ankh pendant that Henri claimed
he'd found in the harbor of Alexandria. The French navy diver's
shirt he wore when he wanted to look macho. The flight suit
with mission patches for Titan, Europa, and Ilmatar.

Rob tried to be reverent, folding things up and packing them
neatly into the Betacloth bags. He found himself wondering: if
someone had to pack up Robert Freeman's gear, what would
they find? Some faded T-shirts with the names of bands or
brands of beer on them. Some imaging software manuals.
A Caltech class ring. Two crew shirts from feature films he'd
worked on.

Henri had been an egotistical pain in the ass, but people
would at least remember him after he died. If Rob got lost in
Ilmatar's ocean and never went home to Earth, who would notice? Five relatives, maybe a dozen acquaintances, and whoever
was in charge of cutting names into the astronaut memorial at
Kennedy Space Center.

When Henri's room was empty, Rob spent another couple of
hours doing general cleanup, getting rid of the mildew in the
bathroom nearest the aliens' rooms.

The sad truth, as Rob looked about the station with a critical
visitor's eye, was that space explorers were terrible slobs. They

might be fanatics about putting things away properly, but no-body had the time or inclination to do the boring daily chores like scrubbing walls or sweeping corners. The Japanese Space Agency designers had done their best, packing Hitode with self-cleaning toilets and smart plastic walls laced with antifungal chemicals, but ultimately one simply tuned out the stains and smells, lumping them together with the low gravity and constant chill as just another feature of life on Ilmatar.

With only four hours to go, he made the mistake of lying down for just a few minutes of rest, and didn't wake up until ten minutes before the aliens were due to arrive.

He dressed in his one clean set of coveralls and hurried through the connecting tunnel to Hab four, where most of the twenty-eight inhabitants of Hitode Station were packed into the common room. Dr. Sen was waiting by the airlock door, dressed in an immaculate white silk outfit that was certainly the most comfortable and elegant-looking thing on the planet.

Not a very handsome group otherwise, Rob thought as he looked around the room. Most of the crew were all pale and pasty-looking after so long without sunlight, and even the naturally dark-skinned ones had acquired a weird grayish tint. The only ones who looked at all healthy were the Ishikawas, who spent all their time in the farm section under the grow lamps. All of them were squeezed into their astronaut flight suits, many of which were getting quite tight across the shoulders and chests as the crew bulked up with swimming muscles. They had insignia from half-a-dozen space agencies, but all had the United Nations Interstellar Cooperation Agency patch prominently displayed on the right shoulder. One big, happy space-going family.

"I can see the elevator," Una Karlssen called from the docking module. "It's just at the last safety stop now. Three minutes!"

It was odd how excited they all were. The elevator had been making its way down the cable from the surface for thirty-six hours, but everyone was counting down the seconds until it docked. To fill the anxious silence, Dr. Sen cleared his throat and spoke. "Let us all try to make sure this visit goes smoothly. If the Sholen do not find anything to complain about, there is less chance of their trying this kind of surprise inspection again."

"I still think we should file some complaints of our own," said Maria Husquavara. "They've got no right to keep coming in here and interfering with our work."

Sen smiled tolerantly. "I have already prepared a message to UNICA addressing that subject at length, but we can hardly turn them away now."

"Besides, the designers forgot to put a lock on the front door," said Pierre Adler in a stage whisper.

There was another nervous pause, and then Una called out "One minute!"

From outside came the sound of scraping metal as the elevator caught the guide rails and began to slide down to mate snugly with the docking hatch. It landed on the support brackets with a heavy thump, and then the docking latches clanged shut one after another. There was a pause while the pumps forced air into the space between the two hatches. Una swung the inner door open and checked the pressure gauge on the elevator hatch. The difference was minor, so she turned the equalizing valve set in the hatch. When it stopped hissing she opened the door to let the aliens out of the elevator.

There were two of them. The Sholen were bigger than humans, covered with sleek dark-gray skin, and wore no clothes other than belts with storage pouches. In the cramped station they walked on their four rear legs, peering about nearsightedly and flicking out their purple tongues to taste the air. The horizontal posture and curiously mammalian faces made them look like giant hairless otters.

"Welcome to Hitode Station. I am Vikram Sen, the director of the facility."

"I call myself Gishora; I present Tizhos," said the leader, indicating his companion. Gishora was a male, with wicked-looking claws on his forelimbs and brightly colored genitalia. The female, Tizhos, was bigger and had a pouch barely visible on her chest.

Among themselves the Sholen gesture of greeting was an embrace that verged on foreplay; with humans they contented themselves with a hug and a few tongue flicks to pick up the scent. Dr. Sen submitted to the process with tolerant grace, like a man who doesn't really like dogs putting up with having his face licked.

Rob hadn't seen any Sholen in the flesh before, and he found himself studying the way they moved. The body could never be mistaken for a Terran vertebrate's, even if you ignored the extra pair of limbs. When the aliens turned, Rob got a glimpse of their segmented spines, a series of jointed bones like femurs.

Dr. Sen was still playing host. "Why don't I show you to the rooms I have selected for your use? We can make sure that all of your belongings are stowed away properly and then perhaps discuss your plans for how to proceed with this investigation."

"I agree," said Gishora.

"Then please follow me this way," said Dr. Sen. He motioned to Rob, who helped carry the Sholen luggage—mostly food and dive equipment, since they didn't wear clothes. Sen put them in Hab One, right next to his own room.

A small group of Hitode staffers followed along. Rob could see some unhappy looks. Simeon Fouchard was the one who broke the silence as they reached the aliens' quarters.

"We would like to know the purpose of your visit," he said.

"This is a serious interruption of our work and we want to know why you are here."

Gishora turned and looked at Fouchard, then at Sen. "We came because of the incident involving the death of a human. He violated the contact rules."

"I know that! Kerlerec was foolish and died for it. It is sad and a nuisance, but it is done. Why are *you* here? What can you do that we cannot?"

"We must investigate how the violation came to happen, and what effect it had on the inhabitants of this world."

"That is intolerable! Dr. Sen is preparing a full report, and you will get a copy. Do you think we will not tell the truth about the Kerlerec incident?"

"Please, Dr. Fouchard," said Sen. "This is not at all a good time to be having this sort of argument. I am sure our guests are quite tired from their journey and would like some time to rest and unpack their belongings."

"No! I will not be silent! They say they are here to investigate, as if they are the police and we are criminals. I say they have no authority here and no crime has been committed."

"Simeon!" said Dr. Sen, tugging the bigger man's arm. He bent close to Fouchard and spoke quietly, but Rob could hear what he said. "I do not like this situation any more than you do, but getting angry and starting confrontations like this will not make things any better."

"Pah! You are too accommodating, Vikram. Remember what planet you come from." He stomped away, muttering in French.

Sen turned back to the aliens. "I do hope you will pardon Dr. Fouchard's outburst just now. He is understandably upset about what is going on."

"I do not understand what angers him," said Gishora.

"Well, I think it is simply that he objects to being investigated. I am preparing a report on Dr. Kerlerec's death and the events leading up to it, and let me assure you that it will be entirely truthful and accurate. This desire of yours to conduct your own inquiry implies that you don't believe we will tell the truth. Among humans that is an insult."

"I understand," said Gishora. "And I apologize if we give offense. But I fear I must continue with my assignment. I must speak privately with Tizhos now, and then we would like to question the witness of the event."

FOUR

BROADTAIL wakes in a hallway of Longpincer's house. He recalls dragging himself inside and dozing off from the effort. There is a good flavor in the water, and he follows it to the dining room, where Longpincer and the work crew are having a whole young towfin.

"I am pleased that you can join us," says Longpincer. "I remember finding you passed out in the hall and thinking perhaps to have some apprentices carry you to a room."

"I'm sorry," says Broadtail. "It is a long swim here from Continuous Abundance."

"Well, tear off some," says Longpincer. "There's plenty for all. I may work my people like a coldwater schoolmaster, but nobody leaves Bitterwater hungry."

"May I ask the purpose of that curious machine I remember you installing at my arrival? Is it some kind of circulator?"

"The principles are similar, but this device measures flow. I remember discovering the idea in a piece by Longlegs, quoting some ancient writings of the Cold Rift ruins. The flow through the pipe turns in the circulator blades, but the axle is attached to a bundle of ropevine secured to a block. So the turning circulator winds up the ropevine until the force of the flow cannot overcome the resistance of the bundled cords. A rod inserted into the bundle near the block shows how much the bundle is twisted, and thus how strong the flow is."

"Remarkable!"

"I plan to install them in all my pipes, and then adjust the pipe size accordingly. My hope is to reduce leakage and overflow. Already it reveals inefficiencies."

"I remember a landowner back in Continuous Abundance who wishes to apportion flow rights more accurately. This is exactly what she would need!" Then Broadtail remembers that he can't go back to Continuous Abundance and falls silent.

Longpincer tactfully changes the subject. "Do you remember the four-limbed creature? The one full of hot bubbles?"

"Of course. I can't recall finding anything stranger in my life."

"My studies of it reveal many curious features. I suspect the outer hide may actually be an artificial covering. Parts of it come apart into distinct fibers like woven cloth."

"Artificial? But who could make such a thing, and why put it on a weird creature like that?"

"I remember wondering the same things. And now I have an idea: you can go and find their origin."

"Me?"

"It all fits together perfectly. In your—situation—you must avoid towns and settled places, but in the cold waters you are the equal of anyone."

"Where there is no law, it doesn't matter that I am an outlaw?"

"Exactly! There are other reasons, as well. You know as much about these strange creatures as anyone else in the Bitterwater Company. Unlike some of the other scientists, you are strong and fit."

"And I have nothing else to do. I hear you, Longpincer, and

I think it is a splendid idea. If you are willing to supply an expedition, I am willing to lead it."

"Excellent! I propose meeting to make plans after we finish eating and sleep."

⊤⊢⧉ humans assigned them two rooms, putting each Sholen in a separate container in their orderly way. Tizhos and Gishora didn't even have to discuss changing their living arrangements. One chamber became a workroom, where they could gather information and look at records. The other became their bedroom, where the two of them could curl up sociably to rest and bond with each other.

The two Sholen could easily see that the humans wanted them to finish quickly and leave, so Tizhos didn't have a lot of time to study their findings about Ilmatar. She skimmed through all their data to see if there was any evidence of contact.

What Tizhos saw seemed tantalizingly incomplete. There were sound recordings of the Ilmatarans, made using drones, and a few blurry long-range video images. The humans did have a large selection of Ilmataran artifacts recovered from abandoned settlements. But Tizhos could only look over the catalog of items and glance at images. She could only hope to find an opportunity to actually see and touch some of the artifacts herself.

They interviewed the only survivor of the Kerlerec incident a day after arriving at Hitode. The others called him Rob Freeman, and he narrated the whole event, from the time the dead human recruited him to the journey back from the vent.

Tizhos found the story fascinating, and pressed the human for details about the Ilmatarans and what they had done to the dead human. "Tell me what purpose you think they intended to accomplish," she asked him.

"Purpose? They were killing him."

"The method seems overly elaborate. Explain why they

would carry him to a shelter, hold him captive for nearly an hour, and then kill him before a large gathering. Tell me if you recognize a ritual purpose, perhaps."

"Uh, I'm not really much of a xenologist."

"Tell me if you have observed this kind of behavior before."

Gishora let her question him about the Ilmatarans for a time before interrupting. "Tizhos, I fear this adds nothing to what we wish to learn. Save your questions for one more knowledgeable." He switched back to the human language. "Explain again why you and Henri Kerlerec wished to approach the native beings."

The human expelled air loudly before speaking. "Henri wanted to get some cool video of the Ilmatarans to show the folks back home. That's what he does. Used to do."

"We would like you to tell us who would have access to this information on Earth."

"Geez, pretty much everybody. I mean, I guess some obscure tribe in the Amazon without net access might have to wait for print media, but everyone else could see it. That's how Henri made his living, you know. Go to strange places, film strange stuff, go home and talk about it."

"Tell me what persons other than Henri Kerlerec would gain benefit from the data you and he collected," asked Gishora.

The human touched his fingers as he spoke. "Whoever his publishers are back on Earth, and the net services, and the science journals, and everyone interested in Ilmatar, and the guys who make alien action figures, and all the comparative biochemists, and I guess the space agencies and their contractors. And probably a couple of million other people I'm forgetting."

"I want to know if this means there was a large economic interest in Henri Kerlerec's activities."

"Well, I guess indirectly, yeah, there must have been. He always used to brag about it, and I guess he was right."

"Tell me if this affected your decision to accompany him," said Gishora.

The human was silent for a moment. "Maybe a little," he said. "I mean, that's how Henri got the suit and that's how come we both figured we wouldn't get into any big trouble. But it wasn't like he tried to bribe me or anything." The human looked around the room, then back at Gishora. "I went along because I thought it was a cool project. Nobody made me go."

"You said everyone could have access to your findings. Tell me if that includes military planners and government leaders."

"Well, yeah, I guess. They can go to Henri's site or watch his videos like everyone else. And all our data is technically property of UNICA or whoever, so I guess the Pentagon or the PLA could see whatever they want. Henri was French, so he was plugged into the whole Euro bureaucratic-corporate-intellectual network."

It surprised Tizhos when Gishora asked about military planners. The question seemed obviously pointless. She spoke quickly to get in a question before Gishora could continue. "Tell me what you did to prevent contact with the native beings."

"Well, like I said, we had the stealth suit and the camouflaged drones. I just had a regular suit, so I stayed way back with the impellers and watched Henri on video through a laser link. It would have worked, too—he got right up to them without being noticed. I guess he just got cocky and waded right into a group."

Tizhos wanted to ask about the behavior of the Ilmatarans, but Gishora cut her off. "This suit," he asked. "I would like you to tell us more about it."

"I don't know a whole lot. It was Russian navy surplus, I think. Henri said his pals back in Paris got it for him and shipped it out with the last supply payload. I don't know if they bought it right from the Russians or whether it fell off the back of a truck."

"Confirm for me that the word 'navy' means a military organization," said Gishora.

"Yeah. They sail around in ships and stuff. You know, on the ocean."

"I do not understand why you ask these things," Tizhos said to Gishora in their own language.

"Irona would ask them. A military force specialized for ocean warfare gave them this device, and major economic organizations stood to profit. We should not ignore this."

"I lack your certainty. You may see connections where none exist."

"If I fail to ask about such things, Irona's faction will demand to know why not."

"IT sucked. Big time." Rob flopped down on his bed.

Alicia began to massage his shoulders. "You are very tense."

"That's no surprise. I just spent four hours getting grilled by those two, and we're not even finished yet. They want me back tomorrow. When am I supposed to sleep?"

"The Sholen don't sleep, why should you?"

"They don't? Bastards." He tugged off his shirt so that she could get at the stiff muscles better.

"What did they ask you?"

"Jesus. Everything. I told them all about what happened with me and Henri, and then they started in like a couple of six-legged lawyers drinking espresso. One of them—the boss guy—was getting totally paranoid. All kinds of insinuating little questions, like the whole thing was part of some huge conspiracy."

"Perhaps it is just the language barrier. They don't know how to say things politely."

"Maybe. But I swear it sounded like they were trying to pin something on me. Like they had an *agenda*."

"Robert"—she stopped kneading his neck—"I just had a horrible thought. What if you are right?"

"First time for everything."

"No, I mean what if they have a—a mission to discredit the work we are doing here? The Sholen have always opposed our presence on Ilmatar."

"Do a little media hit job on us? I can believe it. Dr. Sen's been afraid of that all along, I think. Hey, you're naked! I hadn't noticed."

"Stop it, not now. This is serious: if they do wish to discredit us, what can we do to stop them?"

"When my dad was doing some work for a timber company, I remember him saying the golden rule for talking to media was always have your own camera going. That way if they try any funny editing you can show the original."

"Did that happen very often?"

"I don't know, but they sure worried about it. Anyway, you put up your raw video on a public site right away. Even if you did something really embarrassing."

"You should be photographing yourself when you meet with them. Did you do anything embarrassing?"

"Not really. That's a good idea, though. In fact, let's pass it on to Dr. Sen—put a camera on them every goddamned minute, except when they're in the bathroom or fucking or something. Which reminds me . . ."

"Not yet. I don't want to forget about it." She used her terminal to send a note to Dr. Sen. Rob made it very difficult, but she managed.

BROADTAIL attacks the task of planning the expedition with enthusiasm that surprises even himself. Part of it

may simply be the pleasure of having Longpincer's vast library
to consult. He skims through accounts of other scientific expeditions, taking special note of the equipment and supplies they
describe. He carefully reads every bestiary and compendium of
animals for mention of anything resembling the creature he is
seeking.

Longpincer's kitchen is also a luxury. Broadtail doesn't even
have to go and ask for meals. They simply appear beside him as
he studies, brought by inconspicuous servants. The steady supply of food means he needs little rest, so Broadtail makes good
progress, filling a whole reel with notes and lists of items to
take along.

The first setback comes when Longpincer runs the reel
through his feelers and stiffens with shock at the expense. "My
dear fellow, I know I have a large establishment, but even I can't
arrange this many towfins. It's more than my entire herd."

"But cutting down the amount of supplies reduces the distance we can cover! Each member of the expedition needs one
jar of food for every twenty dozen cables we travel."

"That's something else—the number of staff. I can understand taking along a scout and someone to tend the towfins. But
six guards? A cook? Two assistants for yourself?"

"Very well," says Broadtail. "How about just one assistant?"

"How about just going alone? I recall Narrowhead 99 Far-
swimmer charting the entire Deep Rifts vent system all by
himself."

"His own account refers to Narrowhead almost starving and
nearly being killed by bandits and hostile landowners."

"I think that is just his attempt to make the narrative more
exciting."

"Perhaps, but I am certain that I cannot manage alone. How
many adults are you willing to send?"

Longpincer considers this. "Three. Yourself, to handle

scientific matters and command the party; a skilled coldwater hunter as your guide; and a menial to tend the beast and prepare food. One towfin for supplies. That would let you travel some six thousand cables. A considerable range."

Broadtail decides he can make do with the reduced expedition. "My plan is to search along the old rift stretching from here toward the cold shallows. I remember those strange creatures approaching from that direction, and it seems reasonable that they might follow the line of old vents along the rift."

"Six thousand cables along the rift takes you very nearly to the cold shallows. An excellent plan. Of course, the ancient rift settlements may have old inscriptions for you to examine."

"I recall thinking of that," says Broadtail blandly.

"Try not to forget the purpose of the trip." Longpincer pushes up from the floor of his study. "Very well, I approve. Now I propose we celebrate with a good meal."

"As you are my sponsor, I cannot oppose you," says Broadtail, and the two of them head for the dining room.

WHEN the humans slept, Tizhos spent hours looking over the video of the incident, going over the images of the native beings in complete fascination. She envied the humans. They could work here, doing all kinds of fascinating research on Ilmatar and its creatures. She considered herself Shalina's foremost expert on Ilmatar, and had never even visited the world before.

Sholen robot explorers had discovered Ilmatar, and tunneled through the ice layer to the subsurface ocean. Sholen probes had returned images of life in Ilmatar's waters before humans ever ventured beyond the atmosphere of their homeworld. But the study of Ilmatar by Sholen ended there.

For probably the ten-thousandth time Tizhos cursed her people. They had ventured forth from a ruined planet, rediscovered how to enter Otherspace and explore the Universe, made contact with Terrans and others—and then decided they preferred to spend all their time blowing glass and planting gardens in little woodland villages. Without the convenient menace of the humans to stoke fears of conquerors from space, Shalina probably wouldn't have any spaceships at all.

In a way, it seemed almost cruel for her to see all this information and know that no more would ever come from Ilmatar. This mission would ensure that. She remembered the outrage from Irona's faction when the account of the humans' unauthorized contact reached Shalina. It seemed impossible that the Consensus would launch such a huge and expensive mission to Ilmatar only to confirm the existing arrangement. Soon all spacefarers would leave Ilmatar forever.

DR. SEN approved Alicia's proposal quickly enough, and that turned out to be a problem for Rob. He was an expert with recording systems, he was spending a lot of time with the aliens, and he didn't have much else to do, so Rob Freeman was the natural choice to watch the watchers and take video of everything they did and said. Which meant that all his free time suddenly vanished.

It was a chore, but Rob actually found it kind of fun. It was just like filming wildlife—forget all the externals, concentrate on getting the video. The best cameras at Hitode were all built for underwater use, but Rob managed to scrounge up a few spare keychain cameras and rig them up with suction mounts so that he could record both the aliens and their interview subjects at the same time.

The social part of it was utterly baffling. Tizhos and Gishora didn't seem to mind a bit that Rob was monitoring them. Sholen weren't big on privacy, and the two of them probably understood the reason for his presence. But Rob's fellow humans seemed almost insulted that Dr. Sen wanted him to record their interviews with the aliens. Even when he explained why, they still griped.

"Do not worry about me," said Simeon when the Sholen came to talk with him about the archaeology program. "I know when to keep my mouth shut."

"This is just a precaution," said Rob. "To make sure there's no disagreement over what somebody said."

"Or a way to assign blame if someone does make a mistake. Have you thought of that?"

Rob couldn't think of an answer, so he shut up and stuck to his recording. Simeon's interview went relatively well; despite his prickly temper, Dr. Fouchard had a good grasp of public relations, and had done plenty of media in the past. With the Sholen he was frank but polite. "I think it is an absurdity that you come here presuming to judge us. But I will answer all your questions honestly. Let us begin."

Watching the aliens grill his colleagues gave Rob some interesting insights about them. Where Fouchard was surprisingly diplomatic, Dr. Sen was a lot more acerbic than he would have expected—although Sen did it so subtly the aliens may not have noticed. When Tizhos asked him, "Tell me what is your opinion of Dr. Kerlerec's death," Sen's response was classic: "Right now I am beginning to understand how he must have felt."

And on one occasion Rob was afraid he might have to intervene to prevent a fight from breaking out. Gishora and Tizhos were talking with Dickie Graves, and it was like watching a couple of belligerent drunks on a street corner. The Sholen, especially Gishora, were asking questions that could almost have been designed to piss him off. Meanwhile Graves himself was making no secret of his dislike for the aliens.

"Explain what you study here," said Gishora.

"I'm trying to learn about the language of the Ilmatarans. Not very easy to do when one can't even speak with them."

"Tell us what you hope to gain."

"Gain? Why, I want to get one of those huge salaries routinely paid to linguists, of course. Some of them even make enough to purchase food, or so I'm told."

"We want to know if your studies could be continued by other means," said Gishora.

"Sure! You could build a probe to not listen to Ilmatarans the same way I do. Better yet, don't build it. Much cheaper."

"Tell us what observations of the native beings you have made," said Tizhos.

"I've planted a net of hydrophones to pick up their communications. It would be easier if I could put the phones near their permanent settlements, but someone objected to that, so instead I put them out away from the vents, along routes they often travel. In the two years I've been here I've managed to accumulate about thirty-six hours of usable data. The other ninety-nine point five percent of my recordings are either silence or animal sounds."

"Tell us how you analyze them."

"With great difficulty. Normally, linguists have the advantage of being able to ask their subjects what things mean. Since that's *not allowed*, I have to proceed by induction, comparing what's said with what's going on. Now as it happens, I have been able to make some significant progress, but I expect it would have taken me about two weeks rather than two years without you lot interfering."

"Explain what you have learned," said Gishora.

"As I said, rather a lot. We know their language is based on what I've named *eidophones*, or sounds mimicking the sonar echoes of particular objects. By comparing eidophones with actual echoes I've built up a little Ilmataran vocabulary, and—"

Tizhos interrupted. "Tell me what value you find in this."

"Is this the old 'why are we doing this' question? I thought we laid that particular specter when we met you people. All right, I'll play: there are lots of things we can learn from the Ilmatarans. It appears they have a very long history; they may have developed social structures and philosophies we haven't considered. The biology people have already learned a great deal which may be applicable in medicine or biotech back home. The place is a gold mine—" Graves stopped.

"Continue describing the benefits you can gain here," said Tizhos.

"Oh, no. I see your game. Your people have been trying to paint us as wicked old colonialists ever since Castaverde first set foot on Ilmatar. If we benefit from being here, it makes us look like so many conquistadors out for loot. But if I say there's nothing here of value to anyone, you can pass that along to UNICA with a word about closing down this useless project. Well, I decline." He turned to face directly into one of Rob's cameras. "Hear that? I refuse to answer any more questions because these two are trying to twist my words and manipulate my responses."

"Richard Graves, I ask you to make yourself calm," said Gishora. "We only seek to learn the truth."

"The truth? The truth is that poor old Henri got fed up with your stupid contact rules and went out to have a good look at the locals, but he cocked it up and got killed. Maybe if you Sholen weren't trying to tell us what we can and can't do here, he'd have been properly prepared and it wouldn't have ended so badly. Have you thought of that?"

"You cannot blame us for the actions of humans."

"Oh? Why not? You're trying to blame the rest of us for what happened to Henri, why not spread it around? Seems to me your hands, or paws, are just as bloody as ours. If you want to be the grand panjandrums of alien contact, then you've got to accept the responsibility for when things go wrong!"

"If Henri Kerlerec had obeyed the rules I do not think he would have died," said Tizhos.

"Oh, so they're for our *protection,* are they? Thank you, Mummy, for telling us we mustn't go down to the park without Nanny."

Gishora interrupted. "I feel that we should stop now and meet with Richard Graves at a future time, when all may be more calm."

As Graves left the room he muttered to Rob, "Self-righteous *pricks.*"

WHEN Gishora and Tizhos finished their interviews, they dined privately in their room. The food was delicious, and Gishora had misted the room with psychoactives to relax them both and put them in the mood for some erotic play. Despite that, both Sholen were quiet and sad during the meal.

"It seems clear to me that nothing happened here except a stupid act by a human who died as a result," said Gishora.

"The humans have said that from the beginning," said Tizhos.

"I see no reason to doubt them. If they had planned this, they could have hidden the whole thing and reported the human's death as an accident."

"We still can choose to go home and report that."

"I fear we cannot." Gishora toyed with a food ball, then put the plate aside and flopped back on the cushions. "Irona and the others of his faction have very strong feelings about the humans and this world. If we report that humans have done no harm here, I doubt they will believe us. Instead they can claim we secretly support the humans' activities—and that we no longer follow the ideals of the Consensus."

Tizhos began stroking his belly in a friendly but not pas-sionate way. "I feel trapped. If we report that an accident hap-pened here, then Irona's faction gains strength and leads us to conflict with the humans. If we report falsely, then we cause that conflict ourselves."

"In such a situation, we should make the best of things," said Gishora. "We must act to preserve our own influence, so that at least we have the chance to guide and limit the conflict."

"You plan to accuse the humans of violating the treaty, then?"

"I do, and it makes me terribly sad. Console me."

"ARE we the only ones?" asks Shellcrusher. The three of them are sitting at the base of a big chunk of basalt a dozen cables from their old hideout.

"Likely," says Strongpincer. "Those militia don't take pris-oners. They take heads."

"So what can we do?" asks Weaklegs. "Are they still looking for us?"

"The militia don't have any towfins with them, and fighting is hungry work. I expect they are going home, not hunting us. So that's all right. But the three of us can't rob convoys by our-selves."

"Back to rustling worms?" Shellcrusher sounds disgusted.

"No," says Strongpincer. He actually likes that idea, but he knows that he has to propose something bold, to keep Shell-crusher and Weaklegs from drifting away. "Listen to this: we strike out through cold water, leaving the militia behind. On the other side there is a line of vents and towns where nobody knows who we are. We can make a new start there, maybe hire on as convoy guards, or find some landowner who's looking for workers."

"You want us to clean pipes and tend nets? I remember leaving home to get away from that!" Shellcrusher floats up, as if she's getting ready to swim off—or maybe she wants room to fight.

"Relax," says Strongpincer quickly. "Leave that to apprentices too weak for anything else. No, I imagine us striking suddenly when the boss trusts us. Think about it: a whole convoy or a whole farm, split among us three. Sound good?"

Weaklegs makes an approving click, but Shellcrusher is still floating just out of pincer reach. "Where do you plan to go? Over to Deepest Rift?"

"No, we need to put more distance between us and anyone who knows us. I think we have to head across the basin."

"That's a long swim."

"There are ruins and some old vents along the way," says Strongpincer. "We can hunt. I think we can make it."

Actually, he isn't certain at all, but Shellcrusher and Weaklegs don't need to hear that. Strongpincer doesn't like the idea of starving to death out in the basin, but he hates the thought of losing his followers even more.

WHEN it came to Alicia's turn to be interviewed, she insisted on taking the Sholen outside the station and showing them her animal traps, to demonstrate how well they were hidden from the Ilmatarans and how minimal their effect on the local environment was. Rob was happy to go along—as he suited up he realized he hadn't been in the water since his unauthorized mission with Henri.

Tizhos went alone with Rob and Alicia. The Sholen had their own suits, and Rob watched with interest as Tizhos got into hers. The Sholen suits were a century beyond anything available on Earth, complex hybrids of living systems, smart nanotech materials, and advanced molecules. They could function in any environment from deep ocean to deep space, and were self-regulating and self-repairing. The only external stores the Sholen needed were small oxygen tanks.

The really cool part was watching the suit tailor itself to its wearer. When Tizhos pulled her suit on it was baggy and bright green in color, but once it was on, the fabric began to tighten and shift, until it fit the Sholen like a coat of paint. The color changed to match her skin—or maybe it just went transparent; Rob wasn't entirely sure. Except for the helmet, she almost looked naked, even down to the colored skin around her genitals. Apparently the Sholen just couldn't relate to each other in a nonsexual way. Rob allowed himself a couple of seconds to imagine Alicia in a skintight transparent suit.

Alicia was already outside, and when Rob and Tizhos joined her, the three of them began to follow the circuit of traps, which extended in a ragged loop a kilometer or so out from Hitode. Despite their months of experience in Ilmatar's ocean, the two humans had to work to keep up with Tizhos as they swam. She kept her limbs folded and swished her tail side to side like a fish. Her suit sprouted what looked like shark fins to help.

The first set of traps were on the rocky ridge to the west of Hitode. Alicia had anchored them where a gentle current funneled through the ridge; the moving water brought a surprising amount of stuff into her nets.

Tizhos spent a long time looking at the little creatures in the nets and listened closely to Alicia's explanation of how the mesh was big enough to let hatchlings and nymphs pass through, so that there would be minimal impact on the local ecosystem. Rob thought the alien was more interested in the rocks.

"These stones look like building stones," said Tizhos, when Alicia finished explaining about the nets. "Is this a settlement site?"

"The whole rift is nothing but a long string of ruins. As the hot spots move, the Ilmatarans abandon their old towns and build new ones. Simeon believes they have been doing it for at least a million years."

There was a silence for a time as the three of them tried to comprehend a million years of history. Rob just couldn't. It felt like when he was ten years old and visiting his uncle outside Chicago.

Uncle Saul lived on Ridgeland Avenue in Berwyn, and young Rob had gone for a little walk around the neighborhood. He'd gone down Ridgeland for block after block, expecting to come at last on some obvious boundary like a river or a highway or the edge of town. But after going the better part of a mile, Rob began to feel the sheer scale of Greater Chicago. The avenue seemed endless in either direction. Each of the cross streets stretched off to the horizon. The houses were close-packed, neat rows of them extending to infinity. Just trying to imagine all those houses, with all those people, all living their lives, had been impossible for young Rob, and he'd gone running back to his uncle's house in sudden inexplicable panic.

Now he had the urge to go swimming back to Hitode and not think of Ilmatar's history again.

Tizhos broke the silence. "Your civilization claims an age of four or five thousand years. My species has fragmentary records perhaps twelve times as old. Compared to these beings we seem like infants."

"If we are the infants, why do you insist on protecting them from us? Shouldn't it be the other way around?" asked Alicia.

"I leave such matters for Gishora and others. Show me your other trap sites."

The next site was the highest point of the ridge. "I picked this location because it gets lots of little transient currents. The main circulation driven by the Maury rift passes to the north of us."

"You so easily give these things your own names," said

Tizhos. "Maury, Shackleton, Dampier. They sound alien to this world. Even the name Ilmatar comes from a human legend."

"How else can you describe something if you don't give it a name? We can hardly use the Ilmataran sounds," said Alicia.

"I understand," said Tizhos. "But I also remember history. On my world—and on yours, too—when conquerers come they change all the names."

Rob suddenly discovered he had no patience left for Tizhos. "Why are you guys so damn suspicious of us? All our exploration has been perfectly peaceful—our spacecraft don't even have weapons! Why all the talk about us trying to act like some kind of invading army? If you haven't noticed there are only thirty of us."

Tizhos touched his arm, probably trying to soothe him. "I do not doubt that you mean no harm and wish only to learn. I sympathize. But history shows cultures always struggle, and the strong destroy the weak. We Sholen nearly destroyed ourselves four times, and when we did not fight each other we ravaged our world until it nearly lost the ability to support life."

"So? That's your problem, not ours!"

"The Consensus has expressed a desire to help other worlds avoid our mistakes. We offer you our wisdom."

"Oh, I get it—if you screw up your own planet enough, that gives you the right to go around telling other people how they should live."

"It pleases me that you understand."

Alicia was touching his other arm. "Robert, let it go."

He looked at her, then back at Tizhos. "Right. Sorry. I probably need to get more sleep or something."

There was a slight awkward silence. Then Alicia spoke up. "Tizhos, could I suggest a small change of plan? There's something else I'd like to show you."

"I do not feel fatigue yet."

"Good. It's about half a kilometer to the west. We'll have the current with us coming back."

As they swam, Rob managed to get up next to Alicia. He turned the hydrophone as low as possible for privacy. "What's all this about?"

"Something I want Tizhos to see. I was planning to show you, but then they dropped in on us and I never got the chance. Maybe we can come back together."

"But what is it?"

"You'll see," was all she would tell him.

The three of them crossed a section of flat silty bottom, then came to a little hummock of jumbled stones. Rob was no archaeologist, but this looked older than most of the other ruins. The stones were all rounded off, and silt filled in all the crevices.

"This side," said Alicia. She led them around to the north side of the hill. "This is an old vent, and the flow is too irregular and cold for the Ilmatarans to use for agriculture. Now, let's all hold hands, and then everyone turn off all your lights. Even the ones inside your helmets."

Rob was in the middle, so he had to use his voice interface to get everything turned off; he didn't want to risk letting go of Alicia in the darkness. When the lamp on Tizhos's chest flicked off, the three of them were in complete blackness. For a moment Rob couldn't even tell if his eyes were open or closed.

Then he saw something out of the corner of his eyes. A faint shine, like moonlight. As his eyes adjusted, the shine got brighter, and he could see that it was the rocks. There were swirls of pale light on the stones around the vent mouth, extending out across the bottom to where they were standing.

He began to notice colors. The vent itself was now glowing faintly green, and there were green streaks where the current was strongest. Around the green was a pale halo of orange, and tendrils of blue and yellow followed the paths of eddy currents across the old stones.

Now he could see more clearly. The swirls were made up of millions of tiny points. It was like looking at a galaxy. He began to lose his sense of scale. Now he could see slow waves of brightening moving across the swirls of color as the water temperature changed. It was the most beautiful thing he had ever seen.

Tizhos was the first to turn her lights back on. The dim safety light on her backpack was like an arc lamp after the darkness. Rob reluctantly cued up his own lights and displays, and saw with some surprise that they had been watching the glow for nearly twenty minutes.

"I certainly did find that phenomenon interesting," said Tizhos. "Although I expect your eyes could see it better than mine. Have you determined the cause?"

"Microorganism colonies. I think the colors relate to chemical concentrations in the water. The luminescence is just a byproduct of phosphorus metabolism. That's not what's important. Tizhos, nothing on Ilmatar has eyes. You and Rob and I are the only things in the entire universe that have seen this."

There was another moment of silence while Rob and Tizhos digested that.

"Wow," was all Rob could say.

"If we weren't here, studying Ilmatar, nothing would ever have witnessed that. If we don't make contact with the Ilmatarans, they'll be like those little colonies, shining in the dark with nobody to see them."

BROADTAIL'S expedition is proceeding well. He has a dozen pouches full of interesting finds: some small creatures he doesn't recognize, a couple of plants new to him, some lovely old stone tools from a ruined settlement, and a piece of shell pierced with regular patterns of holes that he is convinced are old writing. He also has an entire reel of notes, including tentative translations of half a dozen old inscriptions. What he does not have is any trace of the strange creatures he's looking for.

The team is camped at a ruin—yet another extinct vent, with the usual jumble of silted-up houses, scattered pipes, and domestic trash. There is a thick coating of silt over everything, and Broadtail is pleased to note that his theory correlating silt depth with the language of inscriptions and the style of artifacts seems to be holding.

His two helpers are working well. Sharphead is one of Longpincer's employees, a coldwater hunter with lots of terrifying tales of dangerous creatures and bandits. Shortlegs is a small adult, still growing and barely able to read or tie knots. But she can lead a towfin, moor the beast downcurrent from camp, prepare simple meals for the group, and carry Broadtail's spare note reels when he goes exploring.

Shortlegs bangs a stone to call them to eat. She has mixed a fresh egg from the towfin with some shredded jellyfrond and the last of the vent-cured roe. Sharphead is already eating when Broadtail swims up. They don't follow any order of precedence out here.

"Eggs and roe," says Sharphead. "No more meat?"

"Do you recall catching any?" says Shortlegs. "If there is any here I don't taste it."

Since it is Sharphead's job to catch meat for them, he sensibly quiets down and eats.

"This is a small town," says Broadtail. "But I remember you saying there is a larger one a few cables along?"

"Yes," says Sharphead. "A huge city, or ruins anyway. Three or four old vents—one of them makes a little warm water."

"Good hunting there?"

"Oh, yes! I remember catching a spinemouth there—twice your size, at least! I—"

"Excellent!" Broadtail cuts him off before another old hunting story can begin. "I plan to move there after sleeping. I hope to find many old things and take many notes, and you can hunt good food for all of us."

"I THINK we must tell them now," said Gishora when Tizhos returned to their room. After the long swim in the cold ocean, she was hungrier than she had ever been in her life. As fast as the foodmaker could produce balls of high-energy food, she gobbled them down. To speed up the process, she had turned off the textures, aromatics, and psychoactives, and just ate calories like a human.

"They appear likely to become angry," she said between bites.

"I know that. I expect them to become angry no matter when we tell them."

"Then perhaps we should do so at the last possible moment."

"I don't feel certain about the wisdom of that. Tizhos, you know a great deal about human psychology and cultures. Describe their attitudes about deception."

"All their cultures condemn it, to a greater or lesser degree."

"Now explain to me how the humans here may react, based on that."

"I understand now! You feel that waiting may be perceived as deliberately misleading them, and that this may provoke unfavorable reactions. Very well, let us tell them as soon as possible."

"After they have rested and eaten. Tell me if you ever served as a Guardian."

"During my youth I worked as a forester."

"We may face violence. Let me know if you feel ready for that."

"I do," she said, although in truth she did not.

WHEN they got back from their long swim with Tizhos, Rob and Alicia got out of their suits layer by layer and combined their hot water rations for a shower together. By the time they dressed and made their way to the dining room, most of the others had eaten already, so the two of them stir-fried a pan of whatever bits and scraps they could round up, and ate it over a huge mound of mashed potatoes.

"I'd kill for some butter to go with this," said Rob. "Real butter and maybe some cream."

"Don't talk about things like that. Besides, don't you like artificial grease?"

"I just wish it tasted like something. Hey, when the Sholen leave, let's see if we can steal their foodmaker. It can make all kinds of stuff, not just synthetic fat and sugar."

"That would be an interesting way to commit suicide."

"How come? They eat regular food, right? It's not like they're based on chlorine or something."

"Oh, true—their DNA is different, but that all gets broken down anyway in your GI tract. No, I was thinking about toxins and allergies. A lot of the flavorings we put in food are really poisons the plants make to defend themselves. We've evolved to tolerate some of them, but only from Earth plants."

"Well, maybe we could just use it to make bland stuff. No poison flavors."

"There's also the chiral sugars issue, getting the right amino acids, vitamins . . ."

"Spoilsport," he said. "I was just dreaming of having it make me a cheesecake. A real one, without a lot of weird fruit or chocolate. Or a big tender steak. Hey, maybe we could reprogram it! Have it make anything we want!"

"Do you know anything about programming Sholen equipment? Does anyone?"

"From what I've read their systems really aren't much better than ours. A whole different technology path; they like to build very sophisticated single-purpose analog systems instead of just slapping digital processors into everything the way we do. We could slip into their room and take a look at it."

"Wait a minute," she said. "When did this stop being just a joke?"

"When I thought about cheesecake," he said. "I think I could probably kill someone for a cheesecake right now."

"You need a distraction." She put a hand on his thigh and squeezed gently. "Is this working?"

"Not yet. I'm still thinking of cheesecake."

"How about this?"

"I'm wavering. Cheesecake—sex. Sex—cheesecake. Tough call."

"What if I do this?"

"Okay, now I'm officially distracted."

But afterward, lying on her bunk, he couldn't sleep. The idea of getting his hands on the Sholen foodmaker and fooling with it was just too appealing. It wasn't really the food issue; he was just curious. He also had some vague idea about maybe learning how the thing worked and passing some technical tips back to researchers on Earth. Maybe even pick up a patent. Could you patent alien tech? Probably not.

Alicia was sound asleep. When they shared her bunk, she insisted on being between him and the wall. "I would rather be crushed than fall on the floor," she explained. So it was simple enough for Rob to slip out of the bed, grope around for his clothes, and creep out into the hall.

He was halfway to the Sholen's room when he realized he was being an idiot. They didn't sleep! There was no way he could sneak in there; no matter how late it was the aliens would be wide awake. And during the day shifts when the Sholen were out of their room, Rob would be stuck tagging along with them, recording interviews. Alicia was right—it was a dumb idea all along.

Rob stopped off at the bathroom, mostly to have an excuse for getting up. Then he decided he was thirsty and headed for the dining room to see if there was any tomato juice. To his surprise the room was occupied. Dickie Graves, Josef Palashnik, Pierre Adler, and Simeon Fouchard were sitting around one of the tables drinking vodka Bloody Marys.

"Am I interrupting something? Sorry."

"No, have a seat," said Graves. "We were just talking about the Sholen problem. What's your position?"

"My position? Uh—I mean, I wish they'd go away again so things can get back to normal. And I guess I hope they don't make a big deal out of what happened to Henri."

"Naturally. Of course, the only reason they're here at all is that Sen's being an utter doormat," said Dickie. "They've got no right to be here, no right to come meddling in our affairs, and certainly no right to sit in judgment on us."

"They came a long way. It would be rude to send them home again," said Pierre.

"Well, it's rude to drop in unannounced, too."

"Also very expensive," said Josef. "Do the math. For them to arrive so soon after we sent message drone—"

"Means they're eavesdropping!" said Graves.

"Naturally, but that is unimportant. We also eavesdrop on their message traffic, or at least I hope we do. No, it is cost of getting a vehicle that big from Shalina orbit, through gimelspace, and then to Ilmatar insertion. You saw plot of their orbit after emergence—very high-energy trajectory, fantastic waste of propellant. Whole voyage must have been like that. This single mission must have used more fuel and boosters than Sholen space program in six months!"

"I wish we could afford missions like that," said Fouchard. "I hate long voyages in space."

"You miss the point. Scientific expeditions do not travel that way. Even diplomats do not. Only military missions look like that."

Everyone thought about that for a moment.

"I still say Sen should've called their bluff," said Dickie at last. "Tell them good day, terribly sorry, no tours without an appointment."

"We must assume they have enough power to make us comply," said Josef.

"How? Drop bombs on the surface? Bad luck on Castaverde and his team, but we've got four kilometers of water and ice for protection. And supposing the Sholen did go all out and blow us up—what does it get them? The Big Six stop pretending those black-budget interstellar military vehicles don't exist, and it's war."

"Oh, surely not," said Pierre. "The Sholen are a very peaceful species."

"So peaceful they have blown their own civilization to bits every few centuries," said Fouchard. "They are peaceful because the alternative is extinction."

"I think they're all bluff," said Graves. "Look at the way they talk to each other—posturing and puffing out smells. This is the same thing writ large. Dominance displays—it's how they think. If Sen had any balls, he'd stand up to them. They'd leave us alone quick enough."

"They can cause trouble for us back on Earth, though," said Pierre. "A lot of people still think of the Sholen as the wise space brothers. If they say we should leave Ilmatar, you'll have demonstrations in Brussels and Washington demanding our return."

"And are other ways to use force against us," added Josef. "A vehicle that size could carry troops. Sholen could occupy base, or evacuate us by force."

"Force only works if you're willing to pull the trigger," said Dickie. "They won't go that far. All we have to do is refuse. If they want to start a fight, then poof, it's war. And if they're the ones who start it, then even the lunatic fringe back on Earth will turn against them."

"All right, Dickie. You've said it a dozen different ways, but the fact is you're not Dr. Sen, and neither are any of us. He's not going to try to face them down. So why are we here?" asked Pierre.

"I think we ought to be making some contingency plans. Get ready in case the Sholen do make a move," said Graves.

"Doesn't that depend on what they can do to us?" asked Rob. "I mean, if they've got guns and bombs and stuff all we can really do is get ready to die."

"Not necessarily. I've been thinking a lot about this. You can only kill an enemy you can find. We could wage asymmetrical warfare."

FIVE

ROB woke Alicia just before 2400. "I've got breakfast," he said. "You want some tofu chili?"

"I do, but it disgusts me to say it. On Earth I would never eat chili at all. It is nothing but a ragout with too much pepper."

"You want plain tofu instead?"

"I am almost hungry enough to say yes, but because we are in love I will eat your chili."

Their long swim the previous day meant they were still ravenous, so they polished off the pot of chili, generously laced with synthetic oil and hydroponic tomatoes. They were still sitting together as the others began to drift into the common room.

When just about the entire complement of Hitode Station were having breakfast, Tizhos and Gishora came in. Gishora gave a kind of loud bark to get everyone's attention.

"I wish to speak to all of you," he said. "I consider the subject of great importance."

Dr. Sen popped up from the table where he was breakfasting with Simeon Fouchard. "If it actually is of great importance then I think it would be a rather good idea to wait and announce it after all of us have finished eating our breakfasts and can give you our full attention."

"I do not wish to wait any longer. Allow me to speak."

Sen sat down and made a go-ahead gesture. "I certainly can't stop you."

Gishora stood on his two hind legs, raising his head to the ceiling. "My colleague and I have reached a conclusion. It appears to us that Henri Kerlerec died as a result of accident and carelessness. We do not believe anyone at this station intended to violate the contact agreements."

Rob realized he was all tensed up, and gave a sigh as he relaxed. He wasn't the only one, either.

"However," Gishora continued, "we cannot avoid the conclusion that other errors and unauthorized contact attempts may occur in the future, as long as Hitode Station remains an active facility."

Alicia's face was white. "No," she whispered.

"I discussed the matter with my colleagues here and in orbit, and we have reached consensus. We cannot allow you to remain. The risk of further contamination appears too great. We request that everyone here prepare to evacuate the station. Our spaceship can transport all of you to Earth, with fifty kilograms of mass per person for baggage. You may leave other items on the surface for future transport. We plan to return the dismantled station to your space agencies."

Dr. Sen broke the silence before the crowd could erupt in protests. "This is—this is a most unexpected and, I must say, a most *unfortunate* proposal for you to make. I'm afraid it's quite out of the question. I suggest you take the matter up with the UNICA council back on Earth. I'm certain they will consider the whole matter with great seriousness."

"We have made a large number of similar requests in the past," said Gishora. "I cannot believe this will produce a different result. As I said, we have reached consensus: you should leave at once, and then we can discuss a new set of acceptable protocols to prevent any more incidents like the death of Henri Kerlerec."

Sen was on his feet again, standing in front of Gishora. To Rob he looked like a child arguing with a bear. "Before we give you an answer I would like the opportunity to discuss it privately with the rest of the station crew."

"I do not understand what you need to discuss," said Gishora. "Tell me if you understood my words."

"Well, we—" began Sen, but Fouchard cut him off.

"Tell him no, Vikram! He has no right!"

Sen gave Simeon Fouchard a nod. "Dr. Fouchard is essentially correct. You don't have any sort of authority to order us to leave."

"The situation seems too important for any delay," said Gishora. "To protect the inhabitants of Ilmatar you must leave now."

"And what if we don't want to go?" yelled Dickie Graves.

Gishora turned to face him. "Then we must remove you."

For a moment the room was silent. Then half a dozen people started yelling at once. Sen said something quietly into Gishora's ear and ushered the two of them out of the room. The shouting continued. Dr. Sen let the noise go on for a couple of minutes, then used a tray as a gavel to bang for quiet.

"I understand that you are all angered by this unreasonable request they have made of us. But we will not accomplish anything of substance by standing here and making a great deal of noise!"

"We're not leaving!" said Graves, and Fouchard followed up by banging an open palm on the tabletop and shouting, "Never!"

But Una Karlssen stood up with a completely horrified look on her face. "You're all mad!" she said. "I don't agree with the

Sholen either, but this kind of macho posturing isn't going to solve anything. Even if we don't like it we have to do what they ask, and let the diplomats work it out later."

"And what if they're right?" said Antonio Diaz. "Maybe we should leave before something else happens."

That prompted another round of shouting, and Dr. Sen had to use his tray gavel again. "Please!" he said. "Everyone deserves a completely fair hearing. But I do not wish to turn this into a philosophical discussion about the ethics of interstellar travel or the wisdom of the contact rules. We need to concentrate our attention on how we are going to respond to this ultimatum."

"What choices do we have?" said Alicia.

"That is a very good question for us to consider," said Sen. "Once we have determined what we *can* do, it will then be easier to decide what it is that we *should* do."

"Kick their asses back to Shalina!" yelled Graves.

"For the sake of simplicity we will refer to that option as 'Active Resistance' for the time being, if you don't have any objections," said Dr. Sen. "Others?"

"This is madness! I think we have to do what they say," said Una.

"Let us call that option 'cooperation,' if the term is acceptable."

"Collaboration is more like it," said Graves.

"And your suggestion should be labeled 'Suicide,'" Una shouted back.

"Please! We are not going to accomplish much of anything if our discussion keeps breaking down into arguments and wrangling. Are there any other proposals that anyone would like to make?"

"What about passive resistance?" asked Alicia. "It's probably true they can force us to go, but we don't have to help them clear the place out. We can't fight, but we can peacefully refuse to leave."

"*Satyagraha*," said Dr. Sen. "We will refer to this option as 'passive opposition.' Are there others?"

"Run away!" called Pierre Adler. A few people laughed, but he shook his head. "I'm serious. We've got a whole planet to hide on. They can't make us leave if they can't find us."

"That is tactics, not strategy," said Josef.

"I think Lieutenant Palashnik is correct," said Dr. Sen. "Let us decide what we wish to accomplish and then discuss how to go about it."

"What about Castaverde and the surface crew?" asked Pierre. "They deserve to be part of this."

"I think that you are quite correct in pointing that out," said Sen. "Before anyone makes any additional statements let us set up a link with the surface habitat."

But even while Pierre was establishing the link and setting up a screen the debate went on.

"I want everyone to know that nothing is going to make me fight the Sholen," said Una. "You can all go along with Dickie's stupid idea, but I'm not going to be a part of it."

"Can we at least agree that we will all abide by the decision of the entire group?" asked Dr. Sen.

"No!" Antonio broke in. "What if the majority is wrong?"

"What if *you're* wrong?" someone shouted at him.

"This is not getting us anywhere," said Dr. Sen. The wall screen went live, displaying the common room on the surface, and the crew there holding coffee cups. "Dr. Castaverde, what do your people think about this ultimatum the Sholen have given us?"

Rob was getting bored. He leaned over to whisper in Alicia's ear. "I bet we could go away and have sex together and come back without anyone noticing."

"Robert, this is important!"

"I know, but listening to Dickie and Una going back and forth with this did-not, did-too is really boring. Sex is more interesting."

"Wait until we are finished."

An hour of argument later, Rob's patience was used up. He took advantage of a momentary silence after Antonio finished describing the moral hazard of any violent confrontation with the Sholen.

"Excuse me," he said. "I know everyone thinks they have something really important to say, but I'm pretty sure everyone's minds are already made up and nobody's going to change their opinion. So why don't we just go ahead and vote on what to do?"

"Rob moves that we end debate," said Pierre. "All in favor?"

Nearly everyone raised a hand. Dr. Sen diplomatically abstained, and both Dickie and Una sat with arms crossed, glaring at each other.

"Motion carries!" said Pierre Adler. "Thank God."

They voted. Dr. Sen handed out slips of scrap paper and asked everyone to fill in their choices, then collected them and announced the result with Pierre looking over his shoulder.

"Dr. Castaverde? Would you please tell me the votes from the surface facility group? Send it privately to me, please? Thank you." He cleared his throat. "We have a total of six votes for opposing the Sholen with force. Seven abstentions, including my own. Five votes for full cooperation. Fourteen for passive resistance. It would appear to me that the passive resistance plan has won by a clear plurality. We will not cooperate with the Sholen in dismantling this station or closing down the operations here—but we will not engage in any sort of violence. I will inform our Sholen guests of what we have decided, but I want to make it very clear to everyone that I expect you all to abide by this decision we have made."

* * *

Tizhos began to notice an interesting change in the behavior of the humans, though at first she wasn't quite sure what to make of it. She returned to her room after reviewing some of the Terrans' research findings, and discovered a pool of amber liquid on the floor. It had the distinctive odor of human liquid waste, along with various unfamiliar pheromones.

She first assumed it was the result of a failure in one of the station's systems, and contacted Dr. Sen to inform him of the incident. Robert Freeman came out to check, and quickly determined there was nothing wrong. "The sanitary lines are all in the center of the hab cluster," he said. "You're a good six or eight meters away from the nearest plumbing. I don't see how a leaky pipe could put stuff over here without getting anything in the other rooms or the landing outside."

"Tell me how this substance got here, then."

"Well," the young human's face turned pink. "It sure looks like somebody came in here and took a leak on the floor."

"Explain the phrase 'took a leak.'"

"Urinated. Peed. Um, excreted liquid waste. Don't you guys do that?"

"Not in the same way. Our bodies conserve water and expel all wastes in solid form."

"Oh. Well, you know how we've got two systems? This is a mix of water and waste chemicals. Nitrogen compounds, mostly. Don't worry, it's pretty sterile."

Tizhos was puzzled. On Shalina, the significance of the gesture would be obvious—marking someone else's space as a form of challenge. But with humans it might simply be an error. "Tell me if this kind of accident happens frequently."

"Uh, well, sometimes. Maybe someone was confused about which one was the toilet, or maybe they just couldn't hold it."

The next curious incident came later that same day, when

Gishora and Tizhos were doing a follow-up interview with Simeon Fouchard. Tizhos brought along her bag containing personal items and her computer. But when she opened it to begin the session, she found everything inside wet. This time it wasn't liquid waste, but a substance the Terrans identified as stain for microscope specimens. The stuff bonded to cellulose—which meant that the composite materials in the bag fabric and the case of Tizhos's computer were now bright purple.

At mealtime the two Sholen took their accustomed places in the common room, but found that their seats were coated with adhesive. Peeling themselves off the seats required the use of solvents and was quite painful, not to mention undignified. And when they returned to the room they shared, all the cushions they had piled up for sleeping were gone—they eventually turned up floating in the moon pool in Hab One.

Twice they were informed of important messages, only to discover the source was an unattended terminal in one of the laboratories.

As the humans were finishing their active period and preparing for their nightly hibernation, Tizhos decided to mention her suspicions to Gishora.

"I suspect the humans of performing these acts deliberately."

She had expected suspicion, possibly derision or denial, but not Gishora's obvious amusement. "Certainly. That you took so long to realize it surprises me. One or more of the humans has decided to harass us."

Tizhos really was surprised. "I do not understand why. It seems so unlike them."

"Because they do not want us here. They do these things to make us wish to leave."

Tizhos felt a rush of anger. The humans were challenging them! She willed herself to be calm, no easy feat under Gishora's amused stare. For a moment anyway, Tizhos felt the strong half-sexual, half-childlike love of a subordinate for a leader.

"If someone deliberately harasses us, we should complain," she said.

"Explain to me why. I doubt Vikram Sen knows of these things. If he does know, I am sure he wishes to end them. Complaining only weakens us."

"Then we should find the person ourselves!"

"Not an easy task. Tell me if you volunteer for it."

"Yes!" said Tizhos.

STRONGPINCER and his companions move easily along the old rift. Though it is coldwater, a few of the vents give off trickles of lukewarm flow, enough to support some mats and weeds, and a few grazing swimmers. They catch enough to keep going, and when they stop to rest the ruins of settlements provide lots of good places to hide.

Strongpincer is determined no militia will catch him resting. He leaves one adult on guard, even taking a turn himself while Weaklegs and Shellcrusher have their rest.

So it is Strongpincer who hears the sound of a towfin in the distance. It's moving toward him, and as it approaches he picks up the sound of adults swimming along with it.

Another militia band! His first impulse is to creep away quietly and then swim as fast as he can. But he can only hear a few adults, and they're being so chatty it's hard to imagine them as militia. Traders, then? Perhaps.

He pokes the other two awake, then speaks to them softly. "Towfin coming. Three adults. Get your weapons and prepare to rush them." Strongpincer wishes the other two understood numbers, so he could tap instead of speaking. He remembers wishing that many times.

They take up their spears. Strongpincer listens. The towfin

is less than a cable away now. He lets it get closer, holding back Shellcrusher and Weaklegs with a pincer on each one's flukes. At a quarter of a cable he says "Go!" and prods them, then grabs his own spear and surges out of the ruin.

BROADTAIL'S little expedition cruises along above the seafloor, making the easy passage to the next ruined city. Sharphead is in the lead, listening more for any likely food animals than anything else, as bandits are few in these waters. The towfin follows half a cable behind, with Shortlegs steering it and Broadtail trailing behind on a rope, pinging down to study the bottom.

Broadtail hears some interesting echoes from below—worked stone?—and lets go of the rope in order to drop down and get better echoes. From ahead he hears a loud ping. It sounds like Sharphead, but he can't make out what the hunter is saying. Then he hears the towfin give a cry of alarm and realizes they are being attacked.

There are three bandits, and Broadtail hopes that maybe if he can get together with Sharphead and Shortlegs the three of them can hold off the enemy. He swims hard toward the towfin, listening.

Three bandits coming from ahead. Silence from Sharphead. Shortlegs and the towfin making an incredible racket as the youngster tries to turn the beast. Broadtail passes above the towfin and stops, waiting for the bandits to come on. He tastes blood in the current and realizes that Sharphead is probably dead.

One large bandit splits off from the other two and swims toward Broadtail. He backs up, trying to stay near the towfin but it is thrashing about so much he doesn't dare get too close. That may keep the bandits away, too. If he can just hold off this one, he hopes they get discouraged and leave.

The big bandit shows no sign of that, though. She rises toward him like a stabbing spear, her pincers folded, aiming to ram. He turns to present his hard-back shell, and then she hits. It almost feels like something cracks, but he can't stop to check. Her pincers are out now, stabbing for his underside, looking for gaps. He grabs one of her pincers in his own and turns his head toward her. Broadtail gives a loud ping, hoping to deafen or confuse her, and pushes free.

But she's not going to let him go, and comes for him again. She's trying to grab his shell from the side. Can she really be trying to crack him? He briefly recalls hearing stories of such feats, and she may be big enough to do it. He flexes his body and again gets free. For a moment he can listen.

The towfin isn't thrashing any more, it's swimming slowly away. The other two bandits have Shortlegs. One has her pincers trapped while the other is methodically stabbing her.

Then his opponent is on him again, her pincer tips feeling for the edge of his headshield. He locks his head back to close the gap and whacks her with his flukes. Before she can grab him again he swims hard for the bottom, going away from the towfin. He hopes that the bandits prefer to chase the beast loaded with food and supplies rather than hunt down a lone scholar.

She doesn't give up. He ducks around a cluster of old stones—automatically noting to himself that they seem to be part of a building, probably an outlying child-farm or fishing-station of the ruined city. He grabs a stone with his legs and freezes, hoping she'll miss him, but she isn't fooled and dives, pincers open wide.

He doesn't wait for her. Broadtail swims as fast as he can, not really caring which direction, as long as it's away from these killers. The big one follows, and Broadtail is afraid that in a long chase she will catch him. Then he hears a faint call from the other bandits, and his pursuer slows, stops, and finally turns back toward them as they follow the towfin.

Broadtail swims on, trying to put as much distance between himself and them as he can. He imagines they might follow him after looting the towfin. He swims and swims into cold silence.

ROB'S double life was a lot of fun for the first couple of days. During the waking cycles he was mild-mannered Rob Freeman, video tech for a great metropolitan research station. But at night he stalked the mean streets of Hitode Station as the Midnight Avenger, righter of wrongs and foe of alien oppressors.

The four of them had agreed to try at least one prank each per day, and Dickie had brought Angelo Ponti into the conspiracy. It rapidly became apparent to Rob that some of the plotters were much better at suggesting cool pranks than at actually doing them. Simeon in particular was a fount of ideas but claimed to be too busy to execute any.

The four of them who actually did stuff had very different styles. Rob personally leaned toward high-tech pranks: the stain in Tizhos's bag was his doing, and he followed it up by disconnecting the light switch in the aliens' room. Josef's ideas all had an appealingly direct vulgarity, based on body fluids. Angelo, in Rob's opinion, was the one most likely to get caught. He'd been the one who stole the cushions from the aliens' room, which meant that he'd gone through half the station carrying them.

But it was Dickie Graves who really worried Rob. The ideas he suggested when the plotters were brainstorming were all very rough; some of them might have been recycled from the old "killing Henri" game. The glue on the chairs scheme was the mildest thing he proposed, and even then Rob had to insist that Graves use a dilute glue instead of the pure stuff, which would have taken the aliens' skin off.

Dickie's second prank was equally harsh. He got some of the trypsin used to break up proteins and "accidentally" spilled a whole bottle on Tizhos's smart environment suit. The suit's adaptive surface and self-repair mechanisms did their best, but the damage was simply too great. Everything but the backpack and the helmet turned to goo.

About half an hour after Tizhos discovered the damage, Dr. Sen posted a general announcement to the station network.

> **To:** Everyone
> **From:** Station Director
> **Re:** Accidents
> It has recently come to my attention that there has been a very extraordinary series of unfortunate safety lapses in the past two days. Several of these incidents have involved our two Sholen visitors, and it would be extremely unfortunate if they should come to harm or even depart with an unfavorable impression of this project. I would like to urge all station personnel to be extremely cautious and take pains to avoid any incidents of this kind in the future.

IRONA sent them a request for a conversation over the secure link. Tizhos could see that Gishora wished to put it off as long as possible, but after two more messages from space, he asked her to set up a connection.

"I wish you would explain to me what the humans have decided to do. You said they offer no violence, but also refuse to cooperate."

"That accurately describes the situation," said Gishora.

"It sounds like a paradox."

"Not at all. Tell me how many offspring you have, Irona."

"None," Irona replied with a slightly indignant tone. "My community seeks to reduce its population, so we have agreed not to reproduce."

"I have one. When my child Giros does not wish to do something an adult has requested, she does not attack us. She merely disregards us. Sometimes she even makes herself limp if we try to move her bodily. The humans have chosen a similar tactic."

"Then you need help. Even a human gone limp does not sound like more than two adult Sholen can lift."

"Rather than going limp they have simply refused to do anything we request. In particular, the elevator capsule remains down here attached to the station. We cannot command it, so we have no way to evacuate them. I do not see how we can use physical force at all."

"Then it seems the humans have imprisoned you."

"Not at all. Vikram Sen informs me that Tizhos and I may leave at any time. For now I do not consider us to be in any danger. But we cannot bring down anyone to help us remove the humans."

"Tell me how many attacks the humans have made against you," asked Irona.

Gishora's body stiffened, and in the chamber with him Tizhos could smell a wave of aggression. But he kept his voice neutral. "I know of no attacks, Irona. Tell me why you think they have made any."

"Your equipment requests. Material damaged by biological agents. Those sound like attacks to me. Add to that their stated refusal to leave. The human behavior seems increasingly hostile. I suggest you and Tizhos depart at once for your own safety, and leave the matter to myself and the Guardians."

"We have suffered no personal injury—"

"Yet."

"—and the station director has expressed great regret about these incidents. I believe the majority of the humans mean us no harm."

"And I do *not* believe that," said Irona. "Tell me if you have considered the possibility of a deception on their part. They may seem peaceful while actually preparing for violence."

"Of course I have considered that, Irona. Please do not insult my intelligence. Tell me if you have considered the possibility that Tizhos and I understand human behavior better than any other Sholen. I do not believe we face any danger. Tizhos, tell me if you agree."

Tizhos didn't know what to say. She felt loyalty to Gishora, more than she had ever felt to anyone since leaving her parents. But . . . the damaged equipment did worry her, especially the destruction of her suit. Until the replacement arrived she would die if the station suffered any kind of life-support failure. That felt a little too close to a direct attack.

"I—I do not believe the humans intend us direct harm," she said. "If they did, a station like this presents a great many ways to kill us and make it seem accidental." She could smell Gishora's approval, and found it incredibly difficult to go on, but she hunched her upper shoulders and continued. "However, I must point out the risk that the damage to our possessions and our quarters could lead to a real accident. And I do not think that the station director can prevent the other humans from doing what they wish. I believe they have separated into factions, and at least one faction desires open conflict."

"There! Your own subordinate agrees with me, Gishora. You do face danger."

Gishora kept himself perfectly controlled, though Tizhos could smell his irritation. "Let us form a consensus, then. I agree that danger does exist here. Let us also agree, however, that any aggressive moves on our part might well provoke the humans."

"A show of force might intimidate them," said Irona. "As you yourself have said, the humans respect rational behavior. I suggest we make violence an entirely *irrational* option by showing them we can retaliate."

"I perceive a flaw in that plan: we cannot retaliate against violence. Therefore we must continue with a policy of peace."

Irona sounded triumphant. "I have a way to get Guardians to you even if the humans remain in control of the elevator."

"Tell me why I do not know about this, Irona. As the leader of this mission I should have *complete* knowledge of all our capabilities."

"I only recently rediscovered the method. Now that we face the real possibility of violent conflict, I have begun searching all our records about warfare. They contain a great many interesting things. I have used the fabricator on board to manufacture capsules capable of matching the pressure at the sea bottom. I can send down the lander with Guardians in the capsules, and simply drop them down the elevator shaft."

"Gishora, if Irona really can send us a few Guardians, I would feel safer," said Tizhos. "That would remind the humans of possible consequences, as Irona wishes, without provoking them."

Gishora surprised her by agreeing without argument. "Very well. Send down some Guardians as a precaution. Now if you will forgive me, Irona, I feel very hungry and would like a meal."

Tizhos broke the link. Neither spoke for a moment. Then she hung her head very submissively. "I regret disagreeing with you."

"No, no. You did the correct thing. You stated the truth as it appeared to you. I would prefer truthful dissent to loyal lies. No, I feel sad because Irona may speak the truth."

"I fear I do not understand."

"Violence may work. I hate violence, Tizhos, and I hate what the fear of it has done to our people. We cannot control our passions, so to keep from ravaging our world again we must become a civilization of scattered villages, too small to do harm. I thought the humans represented a different way—a civilization of logic and order. But it seems their passions can get out of control just like ours."

"I know of one encouraging thing," she said, trying to make herself feel cheerful. "Irona's project will take quite a bit of time to implement. We can spend that time reviewing all the discoveries made by the humans."

He still sounded a little sad, but his posture improved. "I agree. We still have so much to learn. Let us make use of our opportunity."

BROADTAIL is hungrier than he can ever remember being. He is in cold water, far from any active bottom trench or hotspot. His sonar pings reveal nothing but silt on the seafloor. Otherwise the water is almost silent. The ice above is low here, and sometimes he can hear it creak. From time to time he comes upon floating threads soaking nutrients from the water, and devours them greedily. They are thin and bitter and do little to sustain him. His bag of provisions trails empty from his harness. The small growths and bits of weed on his shell are getting thin, starving to death and dropping off. He swims slowly; a hundred or so steady strokes and then drifting until his strength returns.

He has only a vague idea of where he is. There is a big empty basin that separates the Three Domes hotspot from the line of vents that includes Continuous Abundance and Bitterwater. He thinks he is somewhere in that great emptiness, and he thinks that if he follows the current he can reach some settlement. But he doesn't know how far he must go, and he suspects he is starving to death.

He swims on, his mind drifting as he goes. The hunger and loneliness call up old memories from childhood. He remembers being small and afraid, and trying to flee the adults with their nets and harnesses. He vividly remembers his first full meal, eating and eating the wonderful rich fatvine roots, the adults putting more before him until he actually cannot cram anything more into himself.

The memory of that first meal only reminds him of just how hungry he is. If he can't find something soon he's going to start getting sleepy, and if he falls asleep in this cold emptiness, he'll probably starve to death. He sends out a few pings, hoping to scare up some swimmers or even just some threads, but the only echoes are the sharp irregular sounds of rocks and the endless muffled dullness of silt.

And then he catches another sound. It is faint, a long way off—a tiny tapping noise. Broadtail drifts and listens, getting a fix on how far away it is. Hundreds of cables away, but it's something. At this distance he can't tell if it's civilized adults making something, nomads fighting or cracking open shells, or maybe just a big snapshell calling for a mate. It doesn't matter to Broadtail; he sets his course toward the sound and calls on his very last reserves of strength for the swim. Either he will eat it or it will eat him.

ROB and Alicia finished their weekly shower together and were getting ready for bed. When you had only limited amounts of hot water, bathing became a tricky part of the relationship. Sure, it was nice to get all warm and clean together, and it was natural to segue directly into getting into bed together—but having sex did raise the problem of spending the next seven days all crusty and uncomfortable, or wasting half a dozen antibacterial wipes just hours after having a bath. So by mutual agreement, they observed a moratorium on sex for at least two days after bathing.

"All the same," Rob said, "I don't think I'm ever going to think that the smell of neoprene and urine on your skin is particularly arousing."

"You Americans worry about smells too much."

"Try growing up downwind from a paper mill and then tell me that. Anyway—should I stay here tonight or go to my own cabin?"

"Whichever you prefer. But if you do stay here, try to be more quiet when you go sneaking out in the middle of the night."

There was a pause while Rob looked at Alicia and tried to figure out just how mad at him she was. "Um, sorry. I didn't want to wake you. I was just—"

She held up a hand. "It would be a very bad idea to lie to me right now, Robert."

"You know what I've been doing?"

"It is not hard to guess. You start slipping out at night and someone is playing tricks on the Sholen."

"It's not a big deal, really. Just some harmless pranks."

"What are you trying to do? Convince them that we are a lot of foolish adolescents?"

"Hey, keep it down. Look, we want them to go away and quit bothering us. Dr. Sen's the only one who could do that and he won't. This way at least we can give them an idea of how unhappy we are."

"It is idiotic!"

"Well, maybe it is, but at least we're doing something!"

Alicia made a sound of annoyance. "It would be more useful

to hit yourself with a hammer. And who is this 'we'? Are you a king, now?"

"Never mind. Goodnight." Rob left her cabin feeling angry and embarrassed. Of course playing practical jokes on the aliens was silly. He didn't need her to point that out, thank you very much. As if she was a 100 percent serious every second of her life. She needed to lighten up. That was her problem: she needed to lighten up. Not get all high and mighty and pass judgment on him for doing a few harmless practical jokes. Europeans had no sense of humor.

He went to the common room to get a snack, then headed for his own cabin. But in Hab One something was going on. Half a dozen people were gathered around the door of the aliens' cabin, including Gishora and Tizhos. Beyond them the door of the room was blocked by some kind of orange membrane. After a second Rob recognized it as a float balloon. The archaeologists used them to move heavy items. Someone had inflated a really big float balloon inside the Sholens' room.

Dickie Graves moved up next to Rob and nudged him. When Rob looked at him he winked. Rob grinned. Even Alicia would agree this was a good one. Worthy of Caltech.

Dr. Sen and Sergei were fussing about with some test equipment at the doorway. "Portable spectrometer. They're afraid it's filled with hydrogen," muttered Dickie.

"Is it?" whispered Rob, suddenly alarmed. Not even Dickie would risk filling a balloon with flammable gas in the confined space of the station. Would he?

Dickie shook his head almost imperceptibly, then nodded toward Sen. The station director peered at the spectrometer display, then made a neat ten-centimeter incision in the balloon with a dissecting scalpel. It gave a sigh and began to wrinkle. Sergei started shoving it into the room, forcing out the air.

Dr. Sen turned around and addressed the crowd. "I am reasonably certain that the person responsible for this incident is here watching at this moment, so I would like to make it clear that there must be no more practical jokes of this kind. This may seem to be very amusing, but I am becoming concerned that if pranks of this kind continue they will cause a serious accident."

Did his gaze rest longer on Rob and Dickie than on the others? Rob wasn't sure.

Sergei got the balloon squashed down to a manageable bundle, and the two Sholen went inside to inspect their quarters. The onlookers began to drift away.

Dickie gestured for Rob to follow, then led the way down to the geo lab.

"Pretty good," said Rob when the door was shut.

"The best yet, I'd say, and entirely harmless. Poor Sen looked a pompous ass standing there giving us a dire warning about the dangers of inflating balloons."

"Yeah. Listen, Dickie—do you think this is working? Are we accomplishing anything here?"

"As to that, we're achieving three very important mission objectives. First, we're showing the Sholen what we think of them. Second, we're having great fun doing it. And finally, as a bonus, we're getting Sen thoroughly annoyed. What more can we ask for?"

"Do you think it'll drive the Sholen away?"

Dickie nodded energetically. "Oh, yes—although not for the reason I thought originally. I was expecting them to give up and go home, but now I reckon Sen's going to ask them to leave just to save his own dignity."

Rob went back to his own quarters for the night. He thought about stopping to tell Alicia about the balloon gag, but decided against it. Let her find out from everyone else, and wonder if

he'd done it himself. He got into bed and dozed off thinking of
ways to top Dickie's prank.

⌐▲⊏▼⌐⊏⊐ getting the balloon removed from their quarters, Gishora and Tizhos invited Vikram Sen inside. "We wish
to discuss with you the lack of progress in evacuating the station," said Gishora.

"I believe I have already explained several times to you that
we have all agreed we are not leaving," said the human.

"Yes, but you must understand that tendencies within the
Consensus on our home world advocate much stricter controls
on human activity beyond your home star system. Possibly even
within your own system. Many aboard our ship belong to those
factions. They constantly urge action. I cannot put them off forever."

Vikram Sen shook his head from side to side. "I am very
sorry to hear that. Perhaps you should go away and resolve
your internal differences in privacy."

"I fear we cannot," said Gishora. "Tell me if you remain determined to resist."

"We cannot prevent your people from doing what you want
to do, but we will not help you in any way—unless you choose
to leave. I am sure everyone would help you most energetically
with that. No, Gishora, if you really wish to make us leave you
must carry us bodily to the elevator."

"Please explain to me why you choose this course of action,"
said Gishora. "You cannot prevent us from removing you. Already a lander full of Guardians sits on the surface. I lack understanding of what you hope to accomplish."

The human expelled air from his nostrils audibly. "We are
protesting the use of force to compel our obedience. By refusing to cooperate we are demonstrating that physical force can

only control our bodies. It cannot control our thoughts. You can physically remove me from this station, but you cannot make me agree with you. Do you see?"

"I see only a faction resisting consensus. You place your individual goals above the greater good."

"If we are going to defer to the opinion of the majority, let me remind you that the Earth has a population of more than eight billion, while there are less than one billion Sholen on your homeworld. It would seem that your people are the willful minority," said Dr. Sen mildly.

Gishora hesitated, his body posture communicating a certain unease. Tizhos jumped into the opening. "We have greater wisdom," she said. "Sometimes a small group can show the larger community the proper course of action."

Vikram Sen widened his mouth. "That is what we are attempting to do here. Now if you will excuse me, I would like to get some sleep."

THAT same night, Rob suited up and swam out to the sub with Dickie and Josef to discuss matters in private. The sub was officially known as the Ilmatar Aquatic Rover, and had been built by a team of Russian and American engineers and hauled to Ilmatar in one piece.

Josef had taken advantage of his position as chief pilot and de facto captain of the sub to name it the *Mishka*, which was now proudly inscribed over the control station in big Cyrillic letters.

The *Mishka* was not a graceful ship—the main hull was a fat round-ended cylinder twenty meters long, with tiny viewports at the front, a hatch on the underside, and two impeller pods on each side. It could only putter along at five knots—but its nuclear-thermal generator was rated for a decade of use, and the sub could make its own oxygen out of seawater for life support. With enough food aboard, it could sail clear around Ilmatar.

The *Mishka* had another feature, which wasn't mentioned in any of the press releases. The designers at Sevmash and Electric Boat had made her as stealthy as any front-line attack sub in Earth's oceans. Her ungainly hull was shaped to avoid any flat surfaces, and was coated in rubbery anechoic material that was supposed to make it invisible to the Ilmatarans. Rob suspected it would work as well as Henri's stealth suit.

He climbed in through the bottom hatch and took one of the seats behind the control station. Josef deliberately kept the internal temperature just above freezing so that passengers could stay suited up without boiling themselves.

"I think maybe we should quit for a while," said Rob. "I get the feeling Dr. Sen knows what's going on."

"He is very wise man," said Josef.

"Sen?" Dickie snorted. "He's like a pappadum. All hollow inside. He isn't capable of anything but bluster. I reckon this means the Sholen are worried and have been complaining to him. That's a good sign for us. We need to increase the pressure now."

"You think so?" asked Rob.

"Absolutely. A few more little 'safety lapses' and they'll suddenly discover an excuse to return to their ship."

"Or strike back," said Josef.

"Let them! That puts them in the wrong."

"Dickie," said Rob, "I want you to tone it down, okay? We don't want to really hurt the Sholen."

"We don't? All right, we don't, then. Don't worry. I've got plenty of ideas that won't harm one downy epithelial derivative on their heads. But no letting up now! Keep turning the crank!"

"What's that?" asked Rob. The sonar imaging display over Josef's shoulder came on, displaying six large targets about two hundred meters up, descending slowly in a neat hexagonal array.

Josef turned and squinted at the screen, then gave them an active ping. "Metal objects. I hear little motor noises, too—like thrusters."

"What the bloody hell are they? Bombs?" For once Dickie Graves looked genuinely worried.

"Not bombs," said Josef. "Pods. I have seen something similar to drop underwater commandos from planes. Pressurize pod in advance and drop from high altitude. The pod opens in deep water and troops can go to work without wasting time equalizing. Ours have sonar-damping exterior."

A hundred meters up the six objects showed clearly on video as streamlined cylinders with fins, very much like old-fashioned bombs. "Are you sure those aren't going to blow us to bits?" Rob asked.

"We find out."

Just then the six pods came apart in a flurry of bubbles. When the video and sonar images cleared up, Rob could see abandoned casing sections dropping rather more rapidly to the sea bottom, and six Sholen in smartsuits making for the station with powerful tail strokes.

"What the hell is going on?" asked Dickie.

"I think the Sholen just decided to turn the crank," said Rob.

SIX

BROADTAIL wakes to find himself being towed. There's a rope around him just behind his headshield, and someone is pulling him along through cold water. He listens. Whoever's pulling him is alone, and is having a hard time of it.

He pings. The person towing him is a large adult with no left pincer, a male by the taste of the water. He has a number of bundles and packages slung on his body, which explains why he's struggling along so slowly. They're about half a cable above a silty bottom.

"You're awake!" The large male stops swimming and turns back toward Broadtail. "I remember thinking you a corpse. My name is Oneclaw 12 Schoolmaster."

"I am called Broadtail."

"No more than that? No good number? Or is your full name a secret? Do I rescue someone best left behind? A bandit? A fugitive?"

"An exile. I am Broadtail 38."

"That is a good number, 38. It signifies 'Warm Water,' of course, but it is also 2 times 19, or 'Child' times 'Place.' A good number for a teacher, though not as good as 82. But 38 is also 4 plus 34, 'Food' plus 'Harvesting'; and it is 'Property' plus 'The World' signifying greatness and rulership; all in all a very good number. I congratulate your teachers."

"Where am I? I do not remember."

"I am not surprised. I do recall finding you, drifting and asleep in cold water. I remember being amazed to hear any life at all in you. Have some food." Oneclaw gives Broadtail a bag full of pressed fronds. "As to where you are, you are about a hundred cables from my camp, and at least a thousand cables from anyplace worth visiting."

While he eats, trying not to gobble the tough fronds too fast, Broadtail asks, "You are a schoolteacher?"

"Yes. I catch the hardy young of the cold expanses, break them, train them, and give them new lives in the vent towns. A hard life, but a noble one. Besides, my number suits me for it: 12 is 2 times 6, and I carve children like stones. It is also 2 plus 10, and I bind children with cords."

Broadtail considers his options. He is far from any civilization, he has lost all the notes for Longpincer, and aside from the food he is devouring he is on the edge of starvation. He cannot bear to go back to Bitterwater alone and with nothing in his net. "Do you need another teacher?"

"I always need some extra pincers." He waves his own single limb. "But you must be strong and swift to catch the young and subdue them. Can you do that?"

"I can."

"And you must have knowledge to impart. Do you know anything worth teaching?"

"I am literate. I know geometry, quadratics, and logarithms. I know the dictionary, and I study ancient remains and writings. I know all the practical arts of the vent farmer. I am a member of the Bitterwater Company of Scholars."

The schoolmaster isn't impressed by his affiliation. "How far do you know the dictionary?"

"Up to 4,000 or so, and a scattering of others."

"Ah. Up among the plant names. Beyond that, there is a vast expanse of obscure tools, followed by some less-common stones, and then a series of recondite but intriguing concepts. If you study ancient writings I take it you are a scholar?"

"Of a sort, yes. I am the author of a book about old inscriptions."

"Do you have it?"

"No. It is back in my old home, if it survives at all."

"I see. Still, it is good to encounter an educated adult. A person in my profession does not meet many. Children who can barely speak and farmers who hoard talk like beads. I have a book of my own, if you are interested in looking at it—a new form of dictionary, in fact. I rearrange the words according to a more logical scheme, beginning with important ideas like existence and continuity rather than commonplace things like stone and food and death."

Broadtail can feel his strength returning as his stomach fills. "I think I can swim now," he says.

"Good. I have a lot of things to carry. I am returning from selling off a batch of apprentices, and I have a load of supplies. I have no helper now—I remember my last assistant leaving because of an argument about how to instruct the youngsters. I hope you are not the sort who thinks education should only cover practical matters. My pupils get the broadest possible training. I cannot teach them everything, of course, but I can at least give them a taste of things like mathematics, geology, navigation, history, and physics."

"I am hired, then?"

"You are. You get food and shelter in my camp—we can take

it in turns to go hunting—and a third of the profits from the sale of the pupils you help train. You also get trained yourself, by a master in the art of schoolteaching. But I warn you, this is not a job for the weak or the fearful. A school of hungry youngsters can rip an adult apart if he isn't careful. We swim far, often on small rations. Sometimes you must fight the bigger children to keep the others obedient. And the waters here are dangerous— tricky currents, hungry hunters, and other things."

That brings an echo of memory. "I remember a noise, a tapping or hammering sound."

Oneclaw's answer is hushed. "There are strange things in the waters here. A whole abandoned city lies not far from my camp. Sometimes there are strange sounds and flavors in the water. I have a theory about them, but I wish to wait until we reach the camp to tell you."

They swim on, resting every few cables, until the camp is in echo range. Broadtail is a little disappointed at how small and shabby the place seems. Oneclaw has a crude little shelter built of uncut stone and gobs of silt, and there is a very rickety pen of netting and poles to hold the pupils. A couple of ragged catchnets on tall poles flutter empty in the current.

"Home again!" says Oneclaw. "I am greater than any venttown landowner; my domains extend for hundreds of cables in every direction. Nobody ever challenges my boundary stones."

The memory of Ridgeback keeps Broadtail from going along with the joke. "How many students do you normally keep?"

"I can manage three or four myself, but with help, possibly as many as ten. It depends on how many we catch, of course. There is a warm current about fifty cables from here where wild children school. I plan going out with you to net as many as we can. Start with twenty or so, since half of them usually die or get eaten by the others."

* * *

BY the time Rob and the others reached the station and shed their suits, the Sholen coup was complete. Dr. Sen was speaking over the PA system. "In the interest of safety I must ask everyone to cooperate with the Sholen soldiers. Follow all their instructions. They have weapons and we do not. I am as distressed by this as everyone else, but we are in a fragile shelter at the bottom of an alien sea. Fighting would be suicide for all of us."

"Cowardly bastard," said Dickie Graves. "We can take them down right now if we move fast. We've got tools, knives—"

"No, Dickie," said Josef. "Dr. Sen is correct. It would be madness."

Graves looked almost ready to cry, but he nodded. "All right, then. For now."

Rob went upstairs to look for Alicia. He found the six Sholen soldiers in the common room with Gishora, Tizhos, and Dr. Sen.

The troops were still suited up, and their outfits looked different from the other two—thicker and bulkier, with armor plates on vital spots and rigid fishbowl helmets instead of flexible hoods. The six of them didn't leave much space in the common room for any humans.

They were definitely armed: all six had funny-looking snub-nosed rifles with three barrels big enough to shoot golf balls slung on their backs, and shovel-handled pistols in chest holsters. Two of them watched Rob as he stopped, hesitated, then hurried out through the doorway into Hab Two.

Alicia was in her room. "Are you all right?" both of them asked simultaneously when he came through the door. He held her for a long moment, then she helped him get out of his damp suit liner and into a slightly less damp coverall.

"All comfortable now?" she asked. "Because now I wish to scream at you."

"I don't think they sent in the soldiers just because of a couple of practical jokes."

"How do you know? You keep expecting the Sholen to be reasonable! They are alien intelligences, Robert—they do not think as we do."

"It seemed like a good idea," he said, instantly aware of how lame it sounded.

"It was childish, and it accomplished nothing—except to anger the Sholen."

He glared at her. "Well, I guess you'd better start packing, then. They're going to stuff you into the elevator along with the rest of us. You'll have to go back to the Marianas Trench now. Have fun."

She swore at him in Italian and German as he turned to go. A bundle of his spare clothes hit him in the back of the head.

STRONGPINCER finishes the last of the tow-fin meat. He pings the camp. The place is a mess, with shell fragments, empty containers, skins, and heaps of loot from the convoy all scattered about. Most of the containers are empty, but Strongpincer remembers happily all the delicacies inside them.

His new shell is hard and spiky, and he's bigger and more fearsome than ever. The other two are still soft, sheltering among the rocks and eating whatever he brings them.

It is a good time to make plans. The food is running out, but they still have one healthy tame towfin and a load of equipment. Selling everything at one of the vent towns would bring a heap of beads, and the chance to live on public-house food and sleep in a shelter.

But Strongpincer can imagine the beads used up, and his

little band wandering cold water again. He wants more. Strong-pincer wants to be a householder, with his own ventwater, a shell all overgrown with parasites, and food just for the picking. A towfin and a convoy's worth of loot aren't enough to buy even a small house.

But they are enough to outfit a larger band. All he needs are more people. Other adults are troublesome, though. He remembers disputes over who is leader. Even with his new bulk he imagines conflict. No, no more adults.

Children are another matter. Get half a dozen youngsters just before their first adult molt, give them food and teach them a few simple words, and Strongpincer has a force that can tackle a medium-sized farm or fishing station.

He knows where to look for children: out in cold water they live in little schools. Strongpincer imagines leading Shellcrusher and Weaklegs into the cold to round up new followers. He plans how to train the youngsters, and as he drifts off to sleep he thinks happily of conquest.

T W O days after the Guardians arrived, the first humans left the station. Gishora chose three to ride the elevator: Maria Husquavara, Anand Gupta, and Pedro Souza. He put Tizhos in charge of removing them.

The first two went peacefully to the elevator, carrying their own gear. But Souza objected, and sat in his room.

"Are you going to shoot me, then?" he demanded, gesturing at the Guardians' holstered handguns.

Tizhos tried to reason with him. "I see no need for violence. I feel sure you understand that you cannot remain here. We all wish to avoid conflict. Therefore you should come along now."

He began singing loudly, ignoring her. Tizhos began to feel frustrated. She made a logical argument, and humans respected logic. For him to refuse made no sense.

"Your behavior seems irrational. It accomplishes nothing. It only produces conflict, which we all wish to avoid."

"Do we? I'm not going without a fight. *We shall oooverCOME— some—day!*"

It felt like a failure when Tizhos turned to the Guardians. "Carry him to the elevator. Treat him gently."

Rinora, the biggest Guardian, went into the human's room and grabbed him with arms and midlimbs. Souza continued singing loudly as the Sholen carried him from the room to the elevator. Nearly half the station complement crowded into the common room, with Guardians holding them back from the elevator docking hatch. As Rinora carried Souza through the room, some of the other humans began singing along with him.

The tension grew almost palpable. Tizhos caught the scents of aggression and fear from the Guardians, and it didn't take an alien psychology expert to see the humans' anger. The crowd in the common room pressed against the outstretched midlimbs of the Guardians, but the Sholen held their places and deposited Souza in the elevator. Tizhos herself fastened the hatches and then typed the command to start the elevator on its long slow climb. She had removed the internal controls to prevent the occupants interfering.

"What if the humans open the hatch?" Gishora had asked.

"Then they drown," she said. "We cannot prevent them from behaving stupidly."

BROADTAIL sleeps and eats a great deal, then helps Oneclaw put the camp in order. In practice this means Broadtail does the work and the old teacher makes a series of mostly irrelevant suggestions. Broadtail suspects he knows why Oneclaw's other helpers are gone. However, the work is satisfying; Broadtail realizes he misses having property to tend.

First he repairs the catch-nets, and rearranges them so that the upstream ones aren't blocking the others. The waters around here are mostly lifeless, but something might be attracted by the tastes of food and waste in the camp. The fibers of One-claw's nets are full of knots and little side-strands tied on, and Broadtail is a little shocked to realize the nets are made of old books.

"Don't worry," Oneclaw reassures him when he mentions it. "I don't use my books for net-mending or braiding into rope until they are frayed beyond repair. Often I have my students make new copies before I get rid of the old reels. A school goes through cord almost as fast as it uses food."

The shelter is in reasonably good shape, though Broadtail does wish it were bigger. He can't pull it down and build a bigger one without more help than Oneclaw can provide. But he can clean out some of the accumulated silt and the incredible clutter of Oneclaw's possessions. The two of them have a fairly fierce argument about getting rid of things, and at last Broadtail consents to simply move all the pieces of broken jars, frayed and tangled books, bits of shell and bone, and other trash to a cache outside the shelter, rather than dumping them in the midden at the edge of the camp.

Oneclaw sorts through all the rubbish, separating the stuff Broadtail may remove from the things he absolutely cannot part with. Among the treasures Broadtail catches a curious echo, and moves closer to feel the object.

"What is this?" He feels it carefully with his feeding tendrils. Part of it seems to be an ordinary siphon, but the outflow goes into a stone with several holes bored in it.

"A noisemaker," says Oneclaw.

"A what?"

Oneclaw takes the device in his good pincer, holds the siphon plunger in his feeding tendrils and pumps it vigorously. The water rushing through the bored stone makes a hideous high-pitched sound and for a moment Broadtail cannot hear anything else. The room is obscured in confusing echoes.

"Where does this come from?"

"It is my own creation. There is a passage in Swiftswimmer 11 Stonymound's *On Currents and Vents* about a device found among the ruined square shelters in the Long Rift, which makes sounds of different pitch depending on how much flow there is in a pipe. I remember reading the passage and trying to make my own. This is the result."

"I am impressed!" Broadtail feels like an apprentice for a moment, amazed by the knowledge of an adult. But he is also a little bit disappointed—he remembers the faint hope that such a strange object might be the work of the mysterious four-limbed creatures.

"I remember you saying something about a ruin near here. Do you remember exploring it?"

"Only once. You wish to go poking about an old city? Remember you are a schoolteacher now! We have work to do, and cannot indulge in scholarship."

"Don't worry. I intend doing all my work. But, yes, I also hope to visit the ruin. I'm interested in strange things."

THE day after the first load of prisoners went up in the elevator, Rob was in the workshop, cleaning up. Not packing—despite the presence of the soldiers, the staff of Hitode Station still adamantly refused to cooperate. But there was always mildew and crud to fight, so Rob took up a sponge and some ammonia and scrubbed the walls as though they weren't going to abandon the station in a month.

Dr. Sen tapped quietly on the door, then came in and shut it behind him. "Robert, if I remember correctly you cast your vote for the policy of passive resistance at the meeting."

"Uh, yeah. I did."

"I confess I am a little bit curious about why you selected that particular option rather than one of the other two possibilities."

"Well, they didn't make much sense. I mean, maybe it would have been cool to grab Tizhos and Gishora and stuff them into the elevator, but what would happen then? They'd come back with more goons and weapons, and we'd be the ones getting roughed up. Kind of like what happened anyway. They're the giant flaming turtle here, and we're just little Japanese guys with electric tanks."

"I think I understand what you mean. And what are your objections to simply doing what the Sholen have asked us to do?"

"Oh, I guess I don't like being bullied. And it all feels like there's some kind of big symbolic thing going on here, like we're not really the issue. I get the idea this is all for the benefit of people on Earth and Shalina."

"That is a very perceptive thing for you to say. And now I wish to ask you another question, if you don't mind: do you know that I am aware of your little project with Dr. Graves?"

Oh, shit, Rob thought. "Uh, no. Look, I'm sorry about that. I guess it was kind of childish, but—"

"It was extremely childish, to be accurate. In any other circumstances, I would almost certainly send you directly back to Earth on the next support vehicle. However, given what has happened here in the past few days, I am going to overlook your actions. The fact that you appear to be willing to take some considerable risks in order to defy the Sholen makes you very suitable for another little clandestine project you may wish to put in motion."

Rob put down the sponge and wiped his hands. "What kind of project?"

"The *satyagraha* project cannot succeed if all of us remain here within the station. I have come to realize that Pierre had a valuable insight when he suggested that we all run away and hide. Consequently, I am pointing out—not suggesting or ordering, mind you—that you could be one of six or eight people to leave the station."

"I don't understand. Run and hide where?"

"You could deploy the two Coquille modules. Each of them will support a crew of three or four for a considerable length of time. If you were to conceal them several kilometers away, it would be nearly impossible for the Sholen to locate them— especially if they do not have access to the submarine. Again, I am just pointing this out. I am certainly not ordering you to do anything."

"I get it—they can't haul us all away if a bunch of us are hiding out in the ocean somewhere. Cool. But what if they just say screw it, dismantle Hitode, and leave?"

"Then those who have gone out to the Coquilles will die of starvation," said Sen quietly. "I hope I did not give you the impression that I think this plan would be completely free of risk. It is very difficult to predict what other humans will do, and considerably more difficult to anticipate the behavior of aliens."

"So why do it?"

"It would buy us some time. The message drone has reached the Solar System by now and transmitted its signal. I do not know what sort of ultimatum the Sholen have delivered to the UN, but either UNICA or one of the national space agencies— or one of the space military forces—will almost certainly launch a mission to assist or recover us. At the very least, they can send a message drone with specific instructions."

"It sounds like you're breaking orders in order to wait for orders."

"Perhaps it is a paradox, but that is something to discuss at another time. Now, as I said, I cannot order you to do this. I am only suggesting it, do you understand? You may call it dishonesty if you wish, but I prefer to think that I am encouraging my people to use their own initiative. I do need to know, though: are you willing to crew one of the Coquilles?"

"Yeah, I guess."

Sen sighed. "Robert, this is a very important moment. Not merely in our lives, but possibly in history. Would it be too much to ask for you to say something a bit less bathetic? If I am to write my memoirs someday I would like to have good material to work with."

Rob smiled at that. "Okay. Um—'If the Sholen want me to leave Ilmatar they're going to have to drag me.' How's that?"

"It is good action-film dialogue, which I suppose is really the best one can hope for," said Sen. He looked at Rob over his little Gandhi glasses. "I hope you are sincere. As I said, there is a great deal of risk."

"Well, yeah," said Rob. "I'm in."

"That is good. Oh, I expect you will be interested to know that Dr. Neogri has said she would like to participate as well. I believe the two of you are good friends?"

"Why didn't you tell me that before?"

"I did not want your decision to be affected by your hormones. While war for love is inspiring in legends and epic poems, we must be governed by cynical pragmatism. Now please excuse me as there are others I must speak with."

ONECLAW takes Broadtail out on a long patrol to where a current flows through the abyss. The water of the current is just barely warmer than the cold sea around it, but that is enough to support a faint bloom of tiny organisms and a layer of slime on the rocks of the bottom. Those in turn feed a population of small crawling animals and little swimmers, and those are food for some larger hunters and a pack of wild children.

The two teachers sit half-buried in the mud of the bottom, listening to the children and communicating by quiet shell-taps. There are nineteen young ones in all, but most are too small, little creatures no bigger than Oneclaw's good pincer and incapable of language. The six large ones are about the right size for schooling.

The children are trying to hunt, but are doing it very badly. They can spread out to trap and drive prey well enough, but they cannot agree on which is to be the catcher. As soon as there are some swimmers clumped together, all the children rush forward and the hunt dissolves into separate chases and fights among the hunters. Broadtail hears some swimmers thrashing as the children's pincers snatch them, but he also hears plenty of them getting away. And in the middle of one brawl between a large older child and a little one, he hears a call of distress cut off by the sound of a pincer being snapped off.

"Listen. The waters are getting quiet," taps out Oneclaw. "I expect they are sleeping. Are the nets ready?"

The nets are ready. Broadtail has them slung on his back, all neatly folded, with weights to make them spread out when thrown. The two teachers move forward very slowly, staying on the bottom and trying not to make any noisy movements.

The children are on the bottom, sleeping off their tiring hunt. Some of the older ones have concealed themselves, burrowing into the silt to blur the echoes off their smooth shells. The younger ones just curl into balls and sleep anywhere. Broadtail touches one little one fast asleep atop the shell of an older child. He gently shoves the little one off, then drops the net over the big one while Oneclaw grabs the trailing ropes.

The youngster comes awake frightened, and tries to flee. The net wraps around it, and its terrified struggles only get it more tangled up. When it tries to swim, it gets only a few arm lengths before the rope goes taut. Oneclaw has the other end, and is braced against some rocks. The child darts this way and that, but the old teacher keeps his grip, letting the panicked youngster wear itself out before hauling it in and trussing it tightly.

The struggle awakens the rest, and Broadtail picks out one healthy-looking one—a female by the shape of her palps—and gives chase. She is frightened and has a nice smooth shell, but he is bigger and has more reserves. She darts away but soon tires, tries a sudden burst of speed, then some violent maneuvers—but Broadtail isn't going to get drawn into that. He hangs back, keeping her in hearing but not bothering to match her increasingly jerky moves. When she drops exhausted to the bottom, he moves up, pinging so she can't creep away silently. She crawls a bit, but he can see she's on the verge of collapse. When the net goes over her, she doesn't even struggle. Broadtail tows his new student back to where Onepincer is waiting.

They capture a total of five, including one big stupid child who sleeps through the whole thing until Oneclaw starts winding a rope around its tail. One of them is malformed: what should be the big final joint of its left pincer is just a tiny nub, making the whole limb nearly useless.

"Hold that one while I pith it," says Oneclaw, working his one good pincer under the back of the child's headshield.

"Why not let it go?"

"I imagine it living an unhappy life," says Oneclaw. "There are few places in the world for one with such a deformity."

With a sudden thrust he drives his single pincer into the child's brain.

Some of the little ones gather around the corpse and begin to feed while the two schoolmasters confer about names.

"I leave that to you," says Oneclaw. "Names are but temporary identities, as easily discarded as a shell. The number is the meat and soul. You bestow their names, but I number them."

"As you wish. The female there: I suggest calling her Smooth-shell."

"No shell stays smooth once one leaves the cold water. I imagine her as encrusted as any pipe-farmer."

"Perhaps. But as you say, the name is only the surface."

"A piercing jab! Very well. A number to go with that name. I propose 13. A difficult number for some, as it is prime and thus has no interesting factors, but 13 is appropriate for a fast one like her. And it is auspicious, since it combines Food and Property. Choose another."

"The big sleepy one. I name him Broadbody."

"Fitting. Broadbody 27, as it seems he likes to sleep in silt. It is 3 cubed, so I expect to make him swim and swim and swim. Also, 27 is 21 plus 6, as befits one with a body as heavy as stone. And it holds out the good thought of Warm Property in 18 plus 9. What about the little male?"

"Smallbody is the obvious choice."

"Such a small fellow needs a good number to compensate. I propose 54: Wealth. It is 3 times 18, which means much warmth, and it combines Solidity and Abundance. There is hardly a better number, excepting always 94."

"I name the last one Sharpclaw, because I remember getting a painful jab from her."

"She needs a number to keep her from fighting too much. I suggest 39. Boundary stones prevent conflict."

Broadtail doesn't say much as they head back to the school compound. Herding the children keeps him and Oneclaw busy, and he doesn't want to offend his new employer. But, privately, he is scornful of the old schoolmaster's reverence for numbers.

To be sure, Oneclaw isn't the only adult to become fascinated by the ordering of words in the dictionary. Some writers go so far as to use mathematics to guide their choice of words, or encode hidden meanings in books through spacing and numerical intervals. Others grope for secret messages in ancient texts, or assign prophetic meaning to numbers found in nature.

Broadtail is a skeptic. He knows that dictionaries are composed by adults, and that different communities use different systems of numbering words. He recalls studying ancient sites and trying to tease out the meaning of archaic writings and carvings. Speech is universal—even wild children speak—but writing is a made thing, and varies as much as ways of making nets or laying pipe.

About halfway back to Oneclaw's school, he catches an odd flavor in the water and drops back from the group to taste it better. A very odd flavor indeed—something like rock oil and something like some of the mats that grow on rocks, but much more complex than either taste. What's especially maddening is that he is sure he remembers tasting it before, but not when or where.

That reminds him of something, and he swims hard to catch up with Oneclaw.

"Everything all right?" asks Oneclaw.

"Fine. I remember you mentioning odd sounds and flavors in the water around here. There's a funny taste just back there. Do you know what it is?"

"Ah, yes. The ruins upcurrent are home to many strange

phenomena. I hear noises, sometimes sense things moving about. I have a theory about the cause."

"I recall you saying something about that."

"Yes. You are an educated adult, so I assume you know all about the shape of the world. In the center, rock giving off heat. Outside that, the oceans we know. And surrounding all is the infinite ice, cold and lighter than water. But is the rock beneath our legs really solid? We know there are vents and rifts, some quite deep. There must be channels for water to return to the vents. I believe that within the rock below us there are vast tunnels and chambers filled with hot, rich ventwater."

"It is certainly plausible. I remember reading books of speculation along those lines."

"As do I. But I do not recall encountering anywhere the idea that those caverns may be *inhabited*!"

"Inhabited? But how? Most vents are too hot to approach. Adults die in agony in a channel full of ventwater."

"I don't mean adults. At least, not adults precisely like ourselves. You know about animals, yes?"

"Yes, a great many kinds."

"And they are different in different places—some suited to coldwater, some suited to the rocks around a vent, and so forth. Now imagine creatures—maybe even creatures like ourselves—who come from the boiling world underground."

Broadtail ponders this. "They would be very hot themselves," he says. And then it hits him like a bolt. "Oneclaw! I remember finding a strange creature near the Bitterwater vent—large and utterly unlike anything I remember touching before. And I remember the great *heat* of its body!"

He can hear Oneclaw's hearts race with excitement. "Is this true? You really recall such a creature? You need not lie to humor me, Broadtail."

"No, I remember it perfectly. The scholars of the Bitterwater

Company all know about it." Broadtail feels a surge of hope. He imagines returning to Longpincer in triumph, with valuable data about the odd creatures. "Promise me that once these children are sold, we spend time seeking these strange noises and flavors. It is of tremendous importance."

"Of course. I am making a note of it."

SEVEN

TWO days after Dr. Sen recruited him, Rob was ready to leave Hitode Station. He couldn't pack a bag or do anything obvious, but he did gather up a few essentials and tuck them into a waterproof pouch to bring along—his computer and one of the little people Alicia had made for him.

The last thing he collected before leaving was the drones. They were just too useful to leave behind. The teams going into hiding could use them to communicate, to keep an eye on the Sholen, and doubtless some things Rob hadn't thought of. And for the same reason, it was a good idea to keep them away from the Sholen. Without drones they'd be limited to the area they could search themselves in suits. Swimming Sholen were a lot easier to spot and hide from than the drones.

He avoided the common room. There were always a couple of the Sholen soldiers there, and he didn't like the way they sniffed the air whenever a human came in. Could they tell if he was nervous by the way he smelled? Dogs could do that, he remembered reading somewhere.

So Rob made his way through the labs and work areas on the lower level. Everything was a mess down there now. The human staff weren't helping with the evacuation—but the scientists all hated the idea of leaving their precious specimens behind. They had worked out a bit of benign hypocrisy: all the important specimens were carefully packed up and labeled for shipment—so that if and when the Sholen finally did remove the whole base from Ilmatar, there would be at least a remote chance that someday the specimens could get to Earth.

To Rob's surprise, the female Sholen envoy, Tizhos, was in the workshop when he got there. She had one of the fish-shaped drones on the worktable, and was poking at its innards with some of the micro-scale tools.

"What's up?" Rob asked her. He did still think of it as *his* workshop, and even though he was about to leave the station he didn't like the idea of some alien messing the place up.

She looked up and her posture shifted—Rob couldn't tell if it was the cramped room or some Sholen social thing. "I wish to understand the operation of these devices. They seem very cleverly made."

"Yeah. We use them a lot. They're pretty much off-the-shelf stuff. Plenty more just like them in Earth's oceans, Europa, anyplace there's liquid water." He was careful not to mention that the primary users on Earth were navies. "Don't you guys use them?"

"I believe past cultures on my world employed such devices. At present we prefer to employ tailored organisms, with technological implants as needed."

"I think that some . . . organizations back on Earth tried that. People just think the idea of cyborg sharks is a little scary."

Tizhos put down the tools she'd been using and moved aside. "Tell me if my presence interferes with your work."

"Oh, no problem. I was just . . ." Rob thought frantically. "I was just going to make sure the drones are safe for shipment. I mean, we're not going to be using them here any more, right?"

"That seems a sensible precaution."

Rob took a seat at the worktable and started to safe the first drone. He took out the power cells, primary and backup, and made sure that all the pressure seals were open.

As he worked, he could feel Tizhos hovering, watching him. She finally spoke up. "I have a question. Please explain why you open up those valves inside the device."

"Oh, that's just to make sure there's no pressure seals. Remember we're at the bottom of an ocean here. Take a sealed system up the elevator and then to a spacecraft in orbit, and something's going to pop."

"I understand. Very prudent."

"Thanks. The power cells get packed up separately, so there's no risk of anything getting turned on accidentally, maybe generating heat and starting a fire."

There were a total of sixteen drones, but half of them were unusable due to damage, corrosion, or incurable software problems. Rob had put those aside to scavenge for parts. He finished safing the eight active ones and packed them up, four to a case. He was extremely aware of Tizhos's gaze as he stuffed the power cells into the cases next to the drones. It seemed painfully obvious that they weren't made to fit, but if he left the cells behind he wouldn't be able to use the drones himself.

"Well, if you'll excuse me I'll just put these away." He hefted the two cases and was very glad of Ilmatar's low gravity. At ten kilos each, carrying eight drones at once was quite a load.

Tizhos stepped out into the hall, but didn't move out of his way when he got to the door. Did she *know*? He was pretty sure that he couldn't overcome a female Sholen unarmed, even without two cases of drones trying to pull his arms out of their sockets.

"Excuse me?" he said.

"Tell me why you need to move the drones. Tell me where you intend to take them."

"Ah—this is a workshop, not a storage room. Can't leave them in here to clutter things up."

She considered that for a moment, and it wasn't just exertion that made Rob's arms tremble. Finally the Sholen stepped out of his way. "Forgive me for interfering in your work," she said. "I wish to know about things."

He grunted and edged his way along the narrow passage toward the moon pool. He could feel her watching him but didn't dare look back.

Alicia was already there, looking annoyed. "What took you so long?"

"Tizhos wanted to watch me pack up the drones."

"Josef has been waiting in the sub for an hour already."

The two of them suited up and rolled into Ilmatar's icy ocean. The drone cases were considerably lighter out in the water. The other three conspirators were already outside: Dickie Graves, Simeon Fouchard, and Isabel Rondon, all puttering about as if they were doing something useful. As soon as Rob and Alicia left the station the five of them swam over to where the Coquille modules were stacked.

The modules had never been used—when the Sholen got word of them they had filed a strong protest, and UNICA had decided not to press the issue then. They were still in their shipping configuration, folded into giant hockey pucks four meters across. The smooth white plastic of the shipping shroud was coated with a centimeter of silt on the downcurrent side. As Josef moved the sub into position overhead, the downblast from the steering thrusters filled the water with a cloud of particles.

Rob swam up out of the soup, then over to the sub. He found the hoist and pulled the cable free, then let himself sink down onto the stacked Coquilles. He could see nothing but silty water, brightly illuminated by four divers' shoulder lamps. Holding the hook in one hand, he felt for the lifting point in the center of the Coquille shroud.

There! He hooked on the cable, then switched his hydrophone to broadcast. "Okay, we're hooked on."

They backed off to about ten meters while Josef turned on the hoist and took up the tension in the line. The Coquilles were mostly composites and plastic, so in the dense water of Ilmatar they were pretty close to neutral buoyancy. The sub bobbed a bit, then it and the Coquille began to rise until the folded shelter was hanging a good ten meters above the seafloor.

"You three: take hold!" Josef broadcast over the hydrophone. Rob and Alicia let themselves settle to the bottom as the other three grabbed the landing skids, and the sub moved off ponderously.

"So what do we do now?" Rob asked Alicia. "I understand why we can't go help set up—this way only Josef knows where both Coqs are—but it does leave you and me with nothing to do for a couple of hours at least."

"Robert, I hope you are not trying to interest me in any sexual adventures. This water is too cold."

"Relax. I don't think about that *all* the time."

"You may think about it as much as you like, but I am not sure we will have many opportunities."

"We can try to be quiet when Josef's around."

"We will be too busy. I want to use our time in the Coquille to get some field work done. We are not going on vacation."

"Great," he said. "A romantic getaway in an alien ocean and you just want to do field work."

A splash caught his attention. Someone was leaving Hitode Station through the moon pool. Rob turned off his suit and helmet lights and motioned for Alicia to do the same. He cranked up the gain on his hydrophone.

The breathing gear sounded Sholen, but there was only one

individual. The Sholen troops always worked in pairs. Was it Tizhos or Gishora?

Alicia and Rob swam quietly after the lone Sholen, staying well back and relying on sight and passive sonar. Their quarry moved away from the station heading upcurrent, stopped to examine some of the catch-nets in the rocks, then veered off toward the warm water exhaust from the power plant.

"It is Gishora," Alicia said over their secure link. "Tizhos is bigger."

"What's he doing?"

"I think he is looking for specimens."

"You mean he's doing science? I don't get it."

"Why not? He has some free time; he gathers some data. It seems perfectly reasonable to me."

Rob was glad they weren't using a video link, so he could roll his eyes in complete privacy. "Well, let's hope he finishes up before Josef comes back for the second Coquille."

"I think that if his work is sufficiently interesting, he will not notice anything."

STRONGPINCER leads his band through the cold water, staying low near the bottom. There are large predators out here, some of them big enough or stupid enough to tackle a group of adults. It's also easier to navigate when he can taste the silt in the water and occasionally ping to hear the landscape.

He remembers there is a current whorl somewhere out here where young ones gather. His earliest memories are of being in a school with others, fighting over scraps left by bigger children, hiding from adults with nets. He remembers his first kill: he is very hungry and finds a trapworm egg case. A larger child tries to take it. Strongpincer attacks, ignoring the other's jabs, dropping the eggs, going for his enemy's underside. He grabs the base of the other's pincers and cracks the joint in his strong grip, he hacks at gills and feeding tendrils, he gets a sharp pincer into the other's tender mouthparts, and finally pierces the thin shell between body and tail.

When it is over, Strongpincer finds himself missing a couple of legs and a feeler, but his opponent is dead. He feasts on the remains, then calls some others to share, and from then on Strongpincer is a power in the school.

That school is where he's trying to go right now. He does not imagine finding his own schoolmasters there, but he figures it must be a good spot to look for children. If the old school is empty, he imagines his band camping while they catch some new recruits for the gang. And if there are schoolmasters there—Strongpincer is bigger and stronger than he remembers being when he left the place. He wouldn't mind the chance to teach a schoolmaster some things.

A sound wakes Strongpincer from his memory. It is a faint, steady hum. It is difficult to tell which direction the sound is coming from. Strongpincer pings the others to quiet down, then swims in a wide circle, listening carefully. The sound seems to be strongest off to the left, which is very strange indeed. As far as Strongpincer knows, there's nothing that way but an expanse of empty sea bottom.

So what is the hum? It isn't any kind of animal—it's too steady. He listens but it never changes pitch or volume. A vent, perhaps? Possibly a pipe farm? Water through pipes can make all kinds of noises. A vent out here would be isolated, vulnerable. Easy pickings? Or abandoned, free for the taking?

He turns toward the sound, but soon realizes his bearing is changing as he homes in. The noise is *moving*. It is also getting fainter even though he and the others are swimming hard.

Strongpincer pauses for thought. A moving sound means some kind of creature, and if it can swim faster than a strong adult like himself, it must be quite large. He is content to hunt smaller prey. The three bandits give up the chase and turn back toward the current. There are swimmers to catch there, and rocks coated with edible growths. And he imagines that when they find a school of youngsters they can eat any they don't recruit.

THE ride out from Hitode with the second Coquille was slow and unsteady. The Coquille tended to swing astern as the sub moved, which angled its flat shape downward, turning the whole thing into a giant sea anchor trying to drag the sub into the sea bottom. Josef had to pitch the sub's nose up at about forty-five degrees and redline the motors to compensate for the drag. Changing directions meant coming to a halt, turning the sub with the thrusters, and starting off again.

The three of them had picked the ruins at the extinct Maury 19 vent as the best hiding place. Nobody back at Hitode knew where they were going, so there was no way the Sholen could learn their location without going out and searching. The Maury 19 site had lots of jumbled rock, including ancient Ilmataran cut building stones, which would hide the Coquille's sonar signature.

Setting up the Coquille was even more difficult than moving it. As designed, it was supposed to simply hang from the submarine while a couple of divers released the catches at the side of the shipping shroud and then began inflating it with an APOS unit. The flexible-walled shelter would unfold, and presto! An underwater house!

It didn't work that way. When Rob and Alicia released the catches and began inflation, the Coquille stayed sullenly inside the shipping shroud while precious argon bubbled uselessly into the ocean because the little pump in the APOS unit couldn't generate enough pressure to blow up the big Kevlar-and-foam shelter unit.

So Alicia monitored the inflation level while Rob moved around the outside of the shelter, manually cranking the four support struts into their extended position. Since extending any one strut too far would jam the others, this meant Rob had to give each strut a couple of cranks with the extremely inadequate folding crank tool, swim to the next and repeat the process, over and over and over until the Coquille reached its full four-meter height. He could feel blisters developing on his hands, and every muscle in his upper body ached by the time the job was done.

Alicia spent the time fiddling with the inflation pump. Too much pressure and the gas backed up and bubbled away. Too little and the sides of the Coquille began to buckle inward. She lost several liters of argon before finding an inflation rate that matched Rob's pace cranking open the struts.

After an hour of exhausting work the Coquille was inflated. Rob took a breather and let Alicia extend the support legs. Then Josef, who had spent the whole time aboard the sub keeping it in exactly the right position with the side thrusters, lowered the structure to the seafloor.

More work with the folding crank tool followed as Rob and Alicia got the legs adjusted to keep the shelter level. Then they could swim underneath to the access hatch and climb up into their new home.

Rob went first, out of some atavistic impulse to make sure it was all right before letting Alicia inside. He cracked the hatch and then opened it, looking around to make sure nothing had shifted and was about to fall on his head. The light control was just inside, and after working in the ocean darkness by shoulder lamps, the LEDs were blinding.

The interior of the Coquille was all new and clean—shockingly so after his months living in Hitode's high-tech squalor. All the

equipment was still packed in a layer on the floor, neatly covered with shrink-wrap.

Rob cleared the hatch and winced a little as he slopped seawater onto the nice clean interior. Like getting the first scratch
on a new toy. Alicia surged up next to him, squinting in the
brightness.

"Atmosphere test," he said, then switched off his APOS and
cracked his helmet.

The smell nearly knocked him out. It was a powerful new-
car smell of fresh plastic, a hint of ozone, and something unfamiliar that, after a moment, Rob realized was simply fresh,
clean air. He'd been breathing his own and everyone else's
funk for so long the absence of any stench was shocking.

The two of them got to work unpacking. They peeled up the
shrink-wrap layer and began stowing all the items where they
belonged. Everything had a helpful little label telling where it
should go. It was like a tremendous birthday present. There was a
compact life-support unit with its own radiothermal generator,
four hammocks to go in the upper section of the shelter, a little
aluminum worktable, a stove, a dehumidifier/potable water
extractor, a freezer for food and specimens, a medical kit—
everything a small team would need for extended field operations.

The interior was a single space. They stacked the equipment
against the walls and unfolded a table in the center. The hatch
in the floor was off center, so that a fourth person could sit at
the table as long as nobody needed to go in or out. The hammocks hung overhead, just above an average astronaut's
head—which meant that Josef had to stoop.

The Coquilles had been designed to serve as temporary
bases for exploration beyond the immediate surroundings of
Hitode. The mission planners had imagined that archaeologists
might set one up at a particularly good site for intensive digging,

or biologists establish themselves at a rich vent to study the native life. Thanks to Sholen (and some Terran) concerns about "colonization" the Coqs had never been used.

"What do you think?" Josef poked his head into the hatch and called out, making them jump in surprise.

"It's great! Sen couldn't pay me to leave!" said Rob. "It's going to be a little cramped with three of us, but not too bad. I don't snore."

"And I'm certainly going to spend as much time as possible outside, observing and collecting," said Alicia. "This site is a good example of a relatively rich current-fed ecosystem."

"You do that," said Rob. "I can keep the hab running, Josef's got the sub to tend, and we've got a month's worth of food. When we get tired of each other we can go check out the other Coquille. It's like a little vacation."

GISHORA only noticed the missing humans at the evening meal. He counted those present, and the count came up six short.

"Tizhos!" he called over their private link. "Gather the Guardians and search the habitat. Six of the humans have gone missing."

While Gishora made sure nobody entered or left the common room, Tizhos and the four Guardians made a systematic sweep through the habitat modules. They could not account for six of the humans. A search of the dive room revealed that their suits were gone as well, and when Tizhos led two Guardians outside, they found no trace of the submarine.

She reported back to Gishora in person. "I believe they have left the station."

Gishora motioned Vikram Sen over. "Doctor Sen, I would like you to tell us where the missing people have gone."

"I am very sorry but unfortunately I have no idea where they are," said Sen. "Nobody at the station knows."

"I want you to tell me what purpose they intend to accomplish."

"As to that, you must understand that I did not order them to leave, so this is entirely speculation on my part. But it may well be that they have left Hitode because they don't want to be dragged to the elevator, hauled up to the surface, and forced aboard your space vehicle. But, as I say, that is just speculation."

"It seems a foolish act," said Gishora. "They can remain outside in their suits for a dozen hours, possibly as long as two dozen, but no longer. They will accomplish nothing."

Tizhos had been consulting her personal computer, and rubbed against Gishora to get his attention. "I see a problem," she said in their own language.

"Tell me."

"The humans brought along two temporary shelters, to aid in exploration. I did not see either of them outside when I searched. According to the mission plan, each one can support three humans for several weeks."

Gishora turned back to Vikram Sen and spoke in English. "Tell me if they have taken the temporary shelters."

"What a clever idea!" said Sen. "With the submarine they could take the Coquilles a considerable distance. You are going to have a very difficult time finding them."

"Tell me if you have a way to communicate with them. You must ask them to return."

"Sadly, no. They are undoubtedly beyond hydrophone range. Perhaps if you stop removing people from the station they will return."

Gishora was silent for a moment, then spoke to the whole

room. "I must state that this action represents a very uncooperative attitude," he said, then beckoned Tizhos to follow him back to their room.

At first he walked slowly, but halfway there he seemed to brighten up, and his pace became almost jaunty.

They gave Irona the bad news over a secure link to the ship in orbit. Tizhos thought the whole idea of encrypting their conversation seemed rather silly—after all, the humans could listen to what they were saying by simply putting an ear to the door of their room. But serious matters demanded the formality of pointless security.

"It saddens me to report that some of the humans have fled the station," said Gishora.

"I don't think I understand," said Irona. "Explain how they can survive."

"Consult the original exploration plan: the humans brought along two small portable shelters."

"Yes, I remember now. We used diplomatic pressure to prevent them from expanding across the planet with these so-called 'temporary' bases."

"They have now deployed them, and six humans now hide somewhere on the ocean floor. Vikram Sen claims they do this to protest our actions here," said Gishora. "He says they acted without his permission."

"It surprises me that you believe such a statement," said Irona. "You often describe humans as rule-bound and hierarchical. It seems more reasonable that they have a plan. They challenge us to take action."

"I prefer to wait them out," said Gishora. "They cannot have an indefinite supply of food."

"We can assume nothing. Our own supplies cannot last forever, and those of us in orbit will eventually get too much radiation exposure. The humans may wish to keep our ship here until Terran military forces can arrive. You may not have considered that."

From his sudden change in posture Tizhos could see that, indeed, Gishora had not thought of that. The notion seemed ridiculous—did the Terrans even *have* military forces that could reach Ilmatar and fight a Sholen ship? But the idea appeared to disturb Gishora a great deal. "I wish to avoid conflict if we can," he said.

"Then I believe we must capture these hiding humans as quickly as possible," said Irona. "Get all of them aboard and then leave this world. If you remember, I said at the very beginning that the success of this mission depends on rapid action."

"Above all we must avoid violence," said Gishora. "The humans may return on their own."

"I doubt that," said Irona, and Tizhos could almost smell the scent of scorn through the video link. "We must retain the initiative and send out searchers."

"If you think we can do that without provoking greater conflict, I agree," said Gishora.

"I do. Tell me if you need more Guardians. I can send more down with the elevator, now that we control it."

"No," said Gishora quickly. "This station can barely accommodate the six already here. Wait until more of the humans leave. Tizhos and I will try to find where the humans hide. It may take a little while," said Gishora, and broke the link.

"Tell me if you really believe we have enough Guardians," said Tizhos as soon as she was sure Irona couldn't hear.

"I do. Vikram Sen has said the humans will not cooperate, but will not fight us, either. The six Guardians already here seem sufficient. And we still have no idea where the missing humans have hidden themselves, so they may yet return."

"Oh, but I do know their location!" said Tizhos. "One of the shelters, at least. Remember that I have explored the station computer network. Their submarine automatically joins that network whenever it comes within laser link range. The station system keeps a copy of the submarine's log, including position and time records. Look here!" She happily manipulated her terminal, connecting to the Hitode system and calling up the submarine logs. "After taking away the first shelter the submarine returned and the log automatically updated. You can see the complete profile of its voyage."

Gishora looked disappointed. "Explain why we still have access to the station's network at all," he asked after a moment.

"Oh, we don't. Vikram Sen locked us out shortly after you asked the humans to leave Ilmatar. But as part of our investigation I got copies of the dead Henri Kerlerec's files, including his codes and passwords. They still work. Sen has not deleted him yet."

"Well done, Tizhos," said Gishora, though he still did not sound pleased. "But I feel we can wait a few days before sending these results up to Irona. I don't want to rush if I can avoid it."

Tizhos's sense of triumph faded and she cringed. "I have bad news, then. I have made it my habit to send up copies of all my notes and logs every few hours. Irona already has this information, if he chooses to look."

Gishora cuffed her, but not hard. No more than a token gesture. "I fear that means we can't delay too long in telling him about your discovery. Someone may compare times and dates later on. Tomorrow, then—but not too early." He slumped on his cushions and looked beaten. "I hoped to use this delay to spend more time studying Ilmatar. Instead we must continue to act like warriors. I hate it."

Tizhos moved to lie beside him, and they cuddled and stroked each other, and after a time both could at least pretend to feel better.

EIGHT

AT Coquille 2, Rob, Alicia, and Josef settled into a comfortable exile. Rob had been worried that the three of them crammed into the tiny habitat would soon be at one another's throats, but in fact the biggest problem for him was loneliness.

Alicia was in a frenzy of data gathering. If and when the Sholen finally dragged her up to orbit she'd have terabytes of new information about Ilmatar and its native life. She concentrated on collection rather than analysis, which meant she spent about ten hours a day suited up, making video recordings of organisms she ran across, gathering specimens to freeze, and collecting hydrophone recordings. She went over the whole vent complex with a camera, documenting everything. Most evenings she climbed back into the habitat so tired she could barely make it into her hammock.

Josef, on the other hand, was keeping tabs on the Sholen. He didn't dare take the sub too close to Hitode, but he did spend hours sitting in it, powered down on the sea bottom with a laser link to a drone at the extreme limit of range, listening on the hydrophone for any sound of activity at the station.

Rob looked after the habitat. Since it was brand new, that should have meant he had nothing to do except watch cartoons.

But Theory, where everything works as intended, turned out to be a long way from Ilmatar. Rob had to fix systems that had been improperly installed back on Earth—or improperly designed in the first place.

The dehumidifier posed the biggest problem, especially given that it was also their main source of drinking water. It started out producing just a tiny trickle, and then quit entirely on the second day. Rob took the whole device apart and rebuilt it, and in the process discovered that the compressor wasn't compressing. That eventually turned out to be the fault of a loose shaft on the turbine pump, which Rob secured with a generous glob of epoxy.

When the thing finally began to produce a steady trickle of water and a nice flow of warm air, Rob felt justifiably proud of himself. Human survival on Ilmatar depended on Rob Freeman.

"We have water again," he told Josef when the lieutenant climbed up through the hatch and unfastened his helmet.

"Good," Josef grunted. "Only one bottle left aboard *Mishka.* Sholen are more active today. Sounded like they are training."

"Training for what?"

"Good question."

Alicia came through the hatch half an hour later.

"We've got water," said Rob, handing her a cup of instant tea.

"Ah, warm. I think I have located a nest of some large pelagic swimmer. There are half a dozen eggs, about a liter each. I am going to set up a camera to watch them develop. We may get to see them hatch!"

"Great. Did I mention we aren't going to die of thirst because I fixed the water extractor?"

"Oh, yes," she said. "When will there be enough to wash?"

"Sweetie, I do miracles every day but that's just crazy talk. You can take a shower when the Sholen capture you, or when a relief ship gets here from Earth. Until then, you get two anti-septic wipes per day. Use them wisely."

She shrugged. "A little dirt will not kill us. What do we have to eat?"

"Nothing but emergency food bars. If this was a proper expedition we could have brought along supplies from Hitode. There's a little kitchen and a fridge. But since taking a big bag of food out of Hitode would have attracted some attention . . . we get food bars. Take your choice: chicken flavor, beef flavor, or vegetarian flavor."

"Make soup," said Josef. "Stretch the bars that way, too."

"That's not a bad idea," said Rob. "I'll make us a pot of beef flavor food bar soup, with water from the extractor. Which I fixed today."

"Thank you for fixing the water extractor, Robert," said Alicia, almost managing to keep the sarcasm out of her voice. "I don't know what we would do without you."

"Damn right you don't," he said, and began cutting up a food bar with his utility knife.

TIZHOS felt uncomfortable leading a squad of Guardians, but Gishora had convinced her that he had to remain at the station. She did her best to establish the right sort of rapport with the fighters, but she only had a short time and could not overcome the tremendous differences in outlook and background that separated her from the Guardians.

She did achieve a basic level of sexual attraction, since the unit included three males and only one other female. That required her to flirt outrageously and pretend to find them attractive. Of course, they did have the appeal of youth and health, but she couldn't really discover any common interests to share with them. All their real affection still went to Irona.

So when Tizhos set out from Hitode Station leading four

Guardians to capture three humans, she hoped she could accomplish the job without any fighting. She didn't bring along any obvious weapons of her own. Her Guardians had nothing but tools—and about twice as much mass as any human.

The humans at Hitode still refused to repair the impellers, and the fugitive humans had the submarine, so Tizhos and her team had to swim all the way out to the temporary shelter. After the grueling five-kilometer swim even the healthy young Guardians needed a long rest and some food, so they paused about two hundred meters from the rubble field that concealed the habitat.

Long before Tizhos wanted to continue, the timer clicked softly. "We must end our rest now," she said to the Guardians. "Use your stimulants."

All of them, herself included, swallowed a wafer laced with high-energy compounds and neurotransmitters. In a moment Tizhos felt clearheaded, energetic, and a trifle aggressive.

"Come on!" she called out, and began swimming.

She passed the edge of the rubble field and switched her sonar unit to active mode. The high-pitched pings created an image of the ruined Ilmataran city around her, and about half a kilometer away she could make out a large blank area where something absorbed the sound waves instead of reflecting them. The shelter.

Her unit detected one large moving target near the void. The sound of the breathing apparatus identified it as a human. When the Sholen approached within about two hundred meters the human reacted, hurrying to the shelter entrance and saying something indistinct by hydrophone.

They'd been spotted. No point in trying to be stealthy, then. Tizhos activated her own hydrophone, at maximum volume so the humans could hear. She spoke in English. "We have arrived in order to take you back to Hitode Station. Cooperate in a peaceful way."

She heard no reply until her party reached a hundred meters from the shelter. Then a hydrophone, tinny and shrill, broadcast: "We refuse to leave! Go away!"

Tizhos noticed the Guardian nearest her unsheathe his tool. Interesting: she had not known anyone on the expedition but herself and Gishora understood any human languages. "No need for that," she said. "Put it away."

He hesitated. "Their statements sound aggressive. They may have weapons."

"Remember what we discussed. If they resist, you may use force, but only use weapons if they do."

Thanks to the stimulants, Tizhos felt not at all tired when the squad reached the shelter. The tiny entry hatch was located underneath, so only one Sholen at a time could enter: a very bad situation, tactically.

She selected the biggest Guardian. "Nirozha, you first, then Shisora. I will follow. Gizhot, I want you and Rigosha to remain outside and receive the prisoners as we send them out. Tell me if you all feel ready."

The Guardians gave aggressive hoots, like dancers ready for a competition.

"Then go inside now."

The humans had tried to lash the hatch shut, but Nirozha braced himself in the entry tube and used his midlimbs to shove it open far enough to cut the cord with his knife. The hatch popped open and he surged inside. Shisora followed swiftly in case of trouble.

Tizhos struggled up the tube, her life-support pack scraping the side as her belly pressed against the ladder. She wondered briefly how a bulky Guardian like Nirozha had managed to fit.

Then she pushed through the hatch into the shelter. The humans had turned off the lights so she could see only the jerky beams from the Guardians' shoulder lamps.

She aimed her light up. Three humans dangled in hammocks in the upper section. Nirozha had also seen them and began climbing the flimsy ladder up to them. They made no aggressive moves, which pleased Tizhos.

A sudden screaming made her jump. All three humans began shrieking as Nirozha approached. He tried to pull one of the human males out of his hammock, but the human started struggling and kicking. Tizhos recognized him as Richard Graves. For some reason he did not use his arms.

"Wait here. I will go up to assist Nirozha," she told Shisora. The ladder felt as if it could barely support her weight. In the upper section she could hardly find room to move with three humans and Nirozha crowded in. The Guardian and Richard Graves still struggled. Nirozha grabbed his legs with all four arms and pulled, but he still did not come out. His shouting increased in volume. Tizhos found it hard to think.

She could see something around Richard Graves's wrists attaching him to the ring supporting the hammock. Tizhos wondered why the humans had restrained themselves.

"Please quiet yourselves!" she called out, but the humans continued shouting. She could not make out anything they said, but their tones sounded angry.

Nirozha used his knife to cut the restraint holding Richard Graves to his hammock. The human struggled free of Nirozha's grip and danced around the upper part of the shelter, swinging from handholds and jumping over the other two humans. Finally the Guardian got his midlimbs around the human and half-passed, half-tossed him to Tizhos.

She had to use three of her arms to hold Richard Graves, and could barely get down the ladder to the lower level, especially with him struggling and kicking his legs. Shisora and Tizhos held him down and tried to get him into a drysuit, but he continued kicking and struggling, still shouting.

They got him suited and tossed him into the water for Gizhot and Rigosha to deal with.

Next Nirozha captured the human female. Despite her smaller size she proved even more difficult for him to handle than the male. Twice he got her in his grip only to have her wriggle free. She struck and kicked him repeatedly, and finally Nirozha backhanded her with his left midlimb, knocking her down to the lower level where Shisora could pounce on her.

Getting her into a suit felt worse than trying to wash an uncooperative infant. Infants didn't kick as hard and scream insults. Infants didn't grab at your own suit hoses, or throw equipment across the shelter, then break free when you had to let go to retrieve it.

And then, when they had her legs into the suit for the third time and were trying to capture her arms, she punched Shisora in the ribs once too often.

He hit her back, a powerful blow with his midlimb. And then he hit her again. He held her down with his upper arms and began hitting her with his midlimbs, over and over again. Her screams changed in pitch, getting higher and louder.

Tizhos still held the female's legs down. I should stop this, she thought. Before she gets badly hurt. But it felt so satisfying to watch the human being pounded. Tizhos's suit reeked of anger and frustration, and watching Shisora work the human over felt almost as good as doing it herself.

The screams stopped, and suddenly Tizhos snapped back to reality. "Shisora, stop. I order you to stop!"

He got in one more blow, then sat back on his four rear limbs, breathing heavily. The human didn't move. Circulatory fluid leaked from her mouth and nostrils, and Tizhos could see sections of skin changing color.

The female human's suit included a medical monitor, and when they turned it on the readouts showed lots of blinking red alert signals. Gizhot had the most medical training, and Tizhos knew enough first aid and human physiology to assist, but neither had ever tried to aid an injured human before. The little medical kit in the shelter contained a manual and some emergency drugs, but they didn't do much. Eventually her heart stopped and she stopped breathing.

The remaining male offered no resistance. The one outside slipped away during the confusion. Tizhos led her little team back toward Hitode, towing the dead human's body herself. Nobody spoke much.

BROADTAIL is teaching the youngsters how to speak properly. Each student is kept in a pen, and Broadtail moves along the row with a bag of clinger meat. They strain against the netting of the pens, snatching at him, but he keeps behind the row of little stones marking the limit of their reach.

He stops before each pen and conducts a little lesson. The student doesn't get any meat until it can say "Give me food." Half of them fail. Broadtail recalls Oneclaw's advice.

"Most of them fail at new lessons, but I expect improvement. Hunger is a good teacher."

The female at the end of the row, Smoothshell, can only snatch feebly. Broadtail doesn't remember her eating anything in the pens. She fails all her lessons. Is she too stupid to learn? In that case she is nothing but food for the others.

But she sounds clever enough. Her pings are rare but sharp. Broadtail recalls her almost getting herself untied from one of Oneclaw's clumsy knots. Perhaps she is simply stubborn. He decides to try something he dimly remembers from his own youth.

"Food," he says, and loudly eats a bit. Then he places a chunk of clinger flesh where she can reach it. "Food," he repeats as she grabs the bit. "Food."

"I give you food," he says, putting out another bit. He listens as she gobbles it. He waits.

She strains against the netting, clacking her pincers, but she can't reach the bag.

"Speak to me," he says. "Speak or starve. Choose now. I think you understand me."

He waits. She stops struggling, tries one last surprise lunge, which brings her extended pincer almost close enough to touch him, then is still. He waits some more.

"Food," she says quietly.

"Good. What do you want?"

Another long pause, then she says "Give me food."

Broadtail shoves half a dozen clingers toward her. "Very good. I give you food. I give Smoothshell food."

"Holdhard," she says a little more loudly. It is not a name he recognizes.

"Where is Holdhard?"

"I am Holdhard."

"You are Smoothshell."

"I am Holdhard."

This is a curious development. Normally children her age don't have personal names. They can barely comprehend themselves as individuals.

"Very well, Holdhard. I give Holdhard food." He gives her the last two bits of clinger. "Broadtail gives Holdhard food."

He waits a little longer, then turns to go. As he leaves he just catches her saying "Broadtail gives Holdhard food" very quietly.

ROB and Josef found Dickie Graves about half a kilometer from Coquille 1. Actually he found them—they were making a very stealthy approach to the Coq with Rob listening on all the external microphones for any hint of Sholen presence when a rescue strobe started flashing nearby. The sudden light made

Josef cry out in surprise, but his hands on the thruster controls were perfectly steady, and he swung the sub around for a sudden getaway before Rob heard Dickie's voice and told him to wait.

Dickie had been in the water in his suit for two days, so during the voyage back to Coq 2 he gobbled down a couple of emergency food bars while telling his story.

"The Sholies have gone utterly feral," he said between bites. "They killed Isabel. Four or five of them came to drag us back to Hitode. We tried passive resistance—the old activist public theater script. Tied ourselves in with cable ties. Look what that bastard did to my wrists! Chanted at them. 'We will not be moved! We will not be moved!'"

"What *happened*, Dickie?"

"I don't know all of it. They stuffed me into a suit and tossed me down the hatch, then went for Isabel. I could hear a lot of fighting inside, and then screams. Then they called for a medic and one of the Sholies guarding me went inside. Then one of them sticks his head out and tells the guard 'The female died.' I know enough of their language to understand that, but I pretended I didn't and waited until they started dragging Fouchard out. He was still alive. Then I swam away as quick as I could and hid in the ruins."

"Could it have been an accident?"

"Don't be a fool, Freeman. They murdered her. Bloody butchers. I got out because I'm a witness. I hope Fouchard's all right."

"What is the condition of Coquille 1?" asked Josef. "Usable?"

"No. Bastards took the power unit. I went in once or twice to spare my APOS and get some food, but I was afraid they might come back."

Rob watched Dickie eat for a few minutes. "Dickie, this is important. What were you guys doing? Was it any kind of provocation—or something the Sholen might mistake for provocation?"

"Why am I suddenly on trial when they're the ones who killed Isabel? No, we didn't do anything. We resisted, of course—I kicked my legs like a four-year-old and tried my best to wear them out. It was all pretty standard protester antics, though. No direct violence."

"They don't follow the same rules we do," said Rob. "They've got that whole unanimous-vote government thing going. I guess active dissent is like some kind of a crime."

"Back home we call that fascism, remember? The mask is off now."

STRONGPINCER pulls his claw out of the youngster's body and waits for the legs to stop twitching.

"Any older ones hiding in the rocks?" he calls to Weaklegs.

"Nothing but hatchlings."

Strongpincer begins cutting open the underside to get at the organ meat in the thorax. His plan is a failure. There are no older juveniles ready for training. Nothing but little ones, good only for food.

"Some dead ones here," Shellcrusher pings. "Pretty big."

Strongpincer breaks off the pincers to eat as he swims over. There are two dead ones, both torn and nibbled by scavengers, but each has a neat hole just behind the headshield, just the size of an adult's pincer. He feels the bodies all over. One has defective pincers, the other's head is small and misshapen. Failures.

He remembers his own time in a school: adults culling the weak and deformed, leaving the bodies for the survivors. He remembers his own gladness at realizing he is strong.

"There are schoolmasters nearby," he says. "Taste the waters carefully and find out which way they went."

Strongpincer hopes to salvage his plan. Schoolmasters can dominate the young, but they are often weak and cowardly when dealing with adults. He plans making a show of violence to overawe them. Isolated in coldwater among half-taught young, schoolmasters are often more than half wild themselves. Despite their blather about learning, they respect strength and cruelty. Strongpincer is strong and knows how to be cruel.

BACK at Coquille 2, Dickie told his story again, at greater length and without as much chewing and swallowing. When he was done, Alicia was the first to speak.

"What do we do now?"

"We've got to fight them," said Graves. "They've obviously taken the gloves off and the longer we wait the more harm they can do."

"Can I talk to you alone for a second?" Rob asked Alicia.

"Where?"

"Just over here." The two of them huddled by the rack of suits on the opposite side of the Coquille from the worktable. "I think you should turn yourself in," he said.

"What?"

"Go back to Hitode and give yourself up. I don't want you getting hurt."

"You are very noble, Robert, but I will not do that."

"This is serious, Alicia."

"I am serious, too."

He looked into her eyes and came to a decision. "Okay, then. If you're staying, then so am I."

The two of them returned to the table, where Josef and Dickie pretended they hadn't heard every whisper of their conversation.

"Okay," said Rob. "We need to figure out how we're going to defeat the Sholen."

* * *

BROADTAIL is untangling some of Oneclaw's books. The old teacher has some interesting works. Aside from standards like the *Comprehensive List of Words* by Roundbody 1 Midden or the *Collection of Useful Arts* by the Coldvent Company of Scholars, there's a copy of *The Anatomy of Communication* by Flathead 67 Lowbasin, and the favorite of eccentrics everywhere, *The Source of Flow* by Longhead 52 Deepsand.

He's running a copy of *Sound-Pulses Directed Downward* by Widehead 66 Coldruins through his feelers when Oneclaw comes to the entrance, pinging loudly.

"Quickly! A band of adults with a towfin are coming! Take up a weapon—they may be raiders."

Broadtail grabs a bolt-launcher and hurries outside. There are two adults approaching the shelter, and he can hear another and a towfin about a cable away.

"Who are you?" calls Oneclaw as they approach.

"We are a horde of desperate killers," says the leader. "Give us what we want or we attack."

Broadtail pings them. He recognizes the speaker—it is the leader of the bandits he remembers plundering his expedition. Anger floods through him. Why can't they leave him alone?

"Go away!" he shouts.

"Why so fierce?" Oneclaw taps quietly on Broadtail's shell.

He answers aloud. "These are bandits. But not a desperate horde—cowardly ambushers and robbers."

"I remember you," says the leader. "And I remember attacking you in cold water. A fair fight, with no marker stones near. No law."

"You are inside my boundaries," says Oneclaw. "It is my law here, and I say peace. Agree, leave, or fight."

"We are three, all strong and fit. You are two, with one missing a claw."

"Then come and fight!" cried Broadtail. He quotes the epic *The Conquest of The City of Three Vents.* " 'Nothing is certain but your death.' "

For a moment nobody says anything.

"We ask your protection, then," says the leader to Oneclaw. "My name is Strongpincer. My band and I wish to rest here."

"Don't trust them!" Broadtail taps out on Oneclaw's shell.

"Of course not," is the silent reply. "But I do not want fighting if I can avoid it." Aloud, he says "I have a little fodder and some food, but little else to give you. You may rest and tether your beast by the boundary stones. I do not take you under my protection and you must leave when I ask."

"Agreed."

The newcomers set up camp just inside Oneclaw's boundary, not far from the pens holding the students. By all law and custom they should lay aside their weapons, but Broadtail doubts Strongpincer cares much for law and custom.

TIZHOS found Gishora in the dive room, getting into a suit. "Tell me if you intend to go out again."

"Yes," Gishora answered. "I have little to do within the station. You perform your tasks extremely well." With the suit covering Gishora and the strong smell of the Ilmataran water, the words of praise had little effect.

"You know of the potential for danger outside. I urge you to take along Guardians."

"The Guardians know little of proper scientific technique. I find it difficult to gather specimens with them around. Each time I go out I must teach them again not to make noise or stir up the silt."

"They did not come here to do science."

"Exactly." Gishora was entirely suited but for his hood. "I feel no fear outside alone. The humans remain in hiding."

Tizhos lowered her voice. "Irona contacted me privately. He expressed concern about how slowly the evacuation proceeds."

"No doubt time seems to pass more slowly aboard the ship in orbit. Here I can barely find time for all the things I wish to do."

"He said his Guardians complain that you spend more time doing science than hunting for the humans."

"*His* Guardians? I did not know Sholen have become things one can own, or that our mission has become Irona's personal property, rather than a working group assembled for a task."

"The Guardians, then. Instead of critiquing my speech you should worry that they complain about you to Irona."

"When I hear something which causes me worry, I will worry about it. The fact that some of the Guardians complain does not bother me."

"I feel that you should pay more attention to Irona's concerns. I think most of the others aboard the ship agree with him about the humans."

Gishora stationed himself on the edge of the pool. "I know— but the faster we send up the humans, the less time remains to study this world. We have lost, Tizhos. Irona's faction wish to end exploration here, for both Sholen and humans. Now that both sides have used violence, I see no way to salvage the situation."

Tizhos cringed a little at that.

Gishora didn't sound angry, though, and continued speaking. "Therefore I must gather as much information as I can while we remain here. We may never get the chance again. You might consider doing the same." With that he sealed up his hood, then rolled into the water and disappeared.

BROADTAIL and Oneclaw take turns staying awake and on guard while the bandits are camped by the school. They don't get much teaching done, although Broadtail does keep up the language lessons while feeding the students.

He's trying to get Holdhard to say "Give me that food," when he hears Strongpincer approaching. He turns, keeping his spear ready.

"A good class of young ones," says Strongpincer. "Any of them ready to sell? I could use a few apprentices."

"They're still just learning proper speech. We still have much to teach them."

"How much do they sell for? I've never bought one."

"I remember buying one for a thousand beads at Continuous Abundance."

"Do you remember doing something else before teaching?"

"I do. I recall being a landowner, and being exiled for murder." He hopes that makes him sound more formidable.

"I must be wary around such a dangerous adult, then," says Strongpincer, then turns and starts to swim away. As he does, something tied to his harness rattles oddly, and Broadtail gives a little ping to find out what it is. It's some kind of box, carved of stone.

"What is that?"

"What? This thing?" Strongpincer taps it with a leg.

"Yes. Where do you remember finding it?"

"In some ruins. Hiding out from militia. Why do you ask?"

"I'm interested in objects like that. May I feel it?"

Strongpincer hesitates, then hands it to Broadtail. The lid of the box fits very closely, and inside is an object unlike anything Broadtail can remember. He sets down his spear and takes a reel of cord from his harness to make some notes.

"Please tell me everything you can about its origin," he asks.

"What's it worth to you?"

"You can have all my wealth," says Broadtail. "Which is nothing. I am alive only because of Oneclaw's charity."

"Then give it back."

For a moment Broadtail wants to fight Strongpincer for it, but then he realizes he has put down his spear. He passes the box back. "Do you have anything else like it?"

"What do I gain by letting you handle my things? You admit you have nothing."

"You are a guest here. I am certain Oneclaw is also interested in strange things."

Strongpincer turns to go. "We camp by the boundary, and one of you always stands guard. That is not how one treats a guest. I owe you nothing."

"What do you want for it, then?"

Strongpincer stops and turns back to Broadtail. "I need some apprentices. Trade me four of the young ones here for the box."

"They are not mine to trade."

"Tell Oneclaw, then. Or—"

"What?"

"You sound like a good fighter. As he sleeps, gather the young ones and come with me."

"I owe Oneclaw my life. I remember almost dying but for him."

"And now you are no better than an apprentice here. You have nothing that is not his. I can show you where I recall finding the box. Others may be there. Leave the schoolmaster."

Broadtail is tempted. He doesn't even like Oneclaw very much. But . . . "No. It is wrong to even suggest it."

"Calm yourself. Think about it. Consider my offer carefully—and consider what you can expect by staying here. I must go." He turns again and strolls off. The students clamor for food as he passes.

DICKIE Graves let the current push him toward Hitode, kicking occasionally to keep himself oriented and maintain depth. He took shallow breaths, trying to stay irregular. There was a plastic bag over the hydrogen vent on his backpack, and from time to time he emptied it. Presumably the Sholen would be listening for the regular bubble-bubble-bubble of an unmodified APOS.

According to the inertial compass he was less than a kilometer from Hitode. Which meant he'd be coming up on the outer line of hydrophones soon.

The raid was his own idea: a trip by impeller to the jumbled rocks at Maury Epsilon, then an easy two-klick swim, sabotage one of the hydrophones and swim away before the Sholen could react. Over time he could make the station deaf, or force the Sholen to send out patrols—which could be ambushed.

It was all just like Von Lettow in Africa: keep the enemy uncertain and force him to guard all possible targets. Classic guerrilla strategy. The Sholen might have advanced nanotech and stuff like that, but their society had forgotten how to make war. They were making themselves into sheep while humans were still wolves. Dickie Graves thought he was a particularly fearsome wolf.

According to the inertial compass he was just a hundred meters from hydrophone six. He let himself drop to the sea bottom and began to crawl, moving from rock to rock. This was familiar territory; he'd helped set up the hydrophone net. Number six was just ahead, perched atop a boulder to keep it from getting covered with silt. He'd come at it from the side and cut the data cable, then grab the phone and swim like hell.

He had covered sixty meters creeping along the bottom when he heard someone swimming. His helmet sonar pinpointed the source: a single individual coming out from Hitode. For a moment Dickie was afraid he'd been heard, but then the swimmer veered off to the west, heading for one of the nets. Dickie toggled up the sound volume and listened. It didn't sound like a human swimming. It sounded like a Sholen.

Dickie hunkered down behind a rock, waiting, barely breathing. He pressed the deadman button to shut off his APOS for extra quiet—the oxygen inside the suit would last him a few minutes if he didn't exert himself.

The Sholen meandered along, stopping from time to time to pick up rocks or bottom-dwelling life. Finally the alien reached the nets and began taking out the various swimmers and flotsam caught there.

Dickie considered his strategy. If he took out the hydrophone first, the Sholen might hear and come to investigate. But if he tried to neutralize the Sholen, it would certainly make enough noise to alert the aliens inside Hitode Station. The urge to strike back at one of them was strong, but in the end Graves restrained himself. Concentrate on the job you came to do, he told himself.

He let go of the deadman button and took on some oxygen, then pressed it again and pushed off against the rock, launching himself at the hydrophone. Halfway there he had to let go of the button and start swimming. The phone was certain to hear him.

The hydrophone was just where he'd installed it, a bright orange casing taped to a boulder, with a long optical cable trailing off through the silt. He slashed the cable and pulled the hydrophone off the rock. No sense in wasting it; properly set up it could be an early warning system for the new camp.

He swam hard, trying to get away from Hitode before someone came to investigate. His own external pickup detected a sonar ping. The Sholen was swimming toward him. Damn.

GISHORA heard the noise of something swimming rapidly and checked the helmet display. He could see no icons indicating other divers around Hitode. So either the noise came from one of the renegade humans, or an Ilmataran organism. Either way, he ought to investigate.

It swam toward a clump of rocks. He gave it an active sonar ping, to get a better image of whatever it was. Four limbs, about half the length of a Sholen, bulbous head and backpack. A human, then. Gishora felt a little bit disappointed at that.

"I want you to stop swimming away," he called out. "I see no way for you to escape."

The human ducked behind the rocks and Gishora swam faster to catch whoever it was. In the human's wake the water contained a great deal of silt. All Gishora could see was the cloudy cone of light from his helmet lamp. It made him feel disoriented and a little frightened. He had to keep checking his faceplate displays to be sure to stay level.

The rock outcropping was a welcome bit of firm reality in the dark chaos of the silty water. Gishora touched it, holding on as though some powerful current might sweep him away.

Something struck his head hard, knocking him down. The displays went crazy, and he could hardly make sense of the text and symbols flashing across his vision. He tried to get up, but felt something land on top of him, clinging to his back.

Gishora gave a cry of surprise, then tried to reach behind him to dislodge the human. He felt cold water against the back of his head, pouring into the suit, separating the clinging inner membrane from his skin. It was so cold it burned. He couldn't see anything. The water was full of silt and bubbles.

Then he felt a sharp pain in his abdomen, and more cold water. Amid the flashing lights in his hood he saw the MEDICAL ALERT icon and the OXYGEN SYSTEM FAILURE symbol. Behind them, half-obscured by the swirling silt, he glimpsed a face. It was the human Richard Graves, baring his teeth inside his helmet and raising his utility knife for another stab.

The blade jabbed into Gishora's upper right shoulder. He

tried to grab the human, but the cold and the pain made it hard to move, and his suit was filling with water.

Gishora couldn't see Graves anymore, but he felt the blade slice into the muscles of his back, and again into his side behind his midlimbs. He couldn't hold his breath any longer, and coughed and choked as the burning cold water entered his lungs.

BROADTAIL hurries back to the shelter and wakes Oneclaw. "Those bandits want to take the students!"

"Are you certain?"

"Yes. I recall Strongpincer suggesting I kill you and join his band with the students."

"I assume you choose not to?"

"Yes, of course."

"I ask because it is not illogical for you to be in league with the bandits. I remember worrying about that when rescuing you."

"I am no bandit!" says Broadtail indignantly. "I am a scientist!"

"You might be a bandit scientist. But never mind that now. I trust you. We have more important problems. How can we stand against a whole gang of them? Perhaps we should flee."

"In cold water they can snatch us one at a time. Fortifying ourselves within the shelter is the only way. Two of us with spears can hold the entrance."

"A good plan, worthy of Shortleg 88. But we cannot fit all the students inside."

Broadtail looks around and makes a quick inventory of their supplies. "I imagine bringing in the two best and leaving the rest."

"Which ones?"

"The two females. Holdhard is small but clever. Sharpclaw is strong. I imagine both fetching a good price as apprentices."

"I agree."

The two of them go out to fetch the two students. Broadtail can hear one of the bandits—probably the big one—moving with them about half a cable away. But nothing happens and they return to the shelter with Holdhard and Sharpclaw. One-claw takes them inside and secures them while Broadtail begins fortifying the doorway and plugging gaps in the walls of the shelter.

He hears someone approach, and takes up his spear. It's Strongpincer.

"Do you accept my offer?"

"Rob Oneclaw and join your band? No. I refuse."

"Then I plan to take what I want."

"And we plan to fight you."

Strongpincer moves a couple of steps toward Broadtail, who swings up his spear, keeping the point between the two of them. Broadtail handles his spear well, like a landowner who hunts and drills with a town militia. Strongpincer backs away. Broadtail waits until the bandit is half a cable away, then goes inside.

He gives food to the students, to keep them quiet while he and Oneclaw prepare. The old teacher has all his weapons piled in the middle of the shelter. It isn't a very good arsenal. There are four hunting spears, but one of them has only the sharpened end of the shaft instead of a proper obsidian head. He has a couple of hammers, a single bolt-launcher for close-in work, and the noisemaker.

"Do you imagine this working?" Broadtail asks Oneclaw, holding up the noisemaker.

"I cannot remember ever actually using it in combat. It does give us the advantage of surprise—I doubt coldwater bandits ever read Swiftswimmer."

"Then I suggest using it only in the direst emergency."

"Agreed. Do you hear them coming? That is the worst part of any fight like this: waiting for the enemy to actually do something."

STRONGPINCER knows about attacking a fortified shelter, and what he knows is that surprise is the best tactic. Drop down out of the water onto a farm without being heard, cut off the landowner and apprentices from the shelter, and the battle is all but won.

But when the defenders are barricaded inside, everything changes. Even if there are gaps in the shelter—and Oneclaw's shelter is old stonework—anyone attacking an opening risks a spearpoint in the head.

But even that is better than the alternative of trying to wait out the defenders. Doing that requires enough food and patience to outlast them, and Strongpincer has neither.

There are the students in the pens, and a few bits of gear left around the school worth taking, but Strongpincer knows all the really good stuff is inside the shelter. He suspects the two students inside are the best of the lot, as well.

Strongpincer decides to attack. His band has three good fighters against a couple of schoolmasters and two students, and one of the masters is deformed. He knows that getting Shellcrusher inside the shelter is all he needs to win.

He lets Shellcrusher and Weaklegs rest a while before attacking. The schoolmasters won't come out, and he wants to give them the chance to be bored and sleepy themselves.

When he judges they have slept enough, he wakes his team and the attack begins. The three of them surround the shelter and come at it from different sides, probing for weaknesses.

Shellcrusher has the door. It is barricaded with all manner of junk, but that makes it hard to defend as she gets her powerful pincers into seams and starts to pry the door apart.

Weaklegs and Strongpincer attack small gaps in the stone-work. They have spears, and Strongpincer instructs Weaklegs to probe the hole and draw the attention of those within. He himself is less aggressive, keeping to one side where a bolt-launcher cannot hit him, jabbing with his spear at the opening and making a lot of noise.

He gets a response: a spear thrusts out from the opening, probing the open water. Strongpincer tries to grab it but whoever is at the other end is quick enough to pull it back out of reach.

After a bit more poking with his spear, Strongpincer risks trying to pull away some of the stones around the opening. He drags down some smaller chunks and gets no reaction. Perhaps those inside are occupied trying to keep Shellcrusher from breaking in the door.

He grabs a larger stone and braces his legs against the wall as he pulls. It shifts a little, but then he feels a sharp pain as something jabs his left pincer joint. He jerks back and feels his wounded claw. It is a small puncture, the kind that heals up, but it makes him wary. He jabs at the hole with his spear again to drive back whoever stabbed him.

From inside he hears excited pinging, then a loud crunching noise as Shellcrusher finally tears the door apart. Strongpincer abandons the little opening and swims around to back up Shellcrusher at the entrance.

Just then comes the most awful noise Strongpincer remembers ever hearing. It is a throbbing high-pitched tone that drowns everything else out and leaves him deafened when it stops.

BROADTAIL gropes about, trying to find Oneclaw. He is completely deaf. Someone bumps him and he barely restrains the urge to stab. It tastes like Holdhard, so he places a pincer on her back to calm her. He remembers facing the bandit with Oneclaw to his left, so he moves to the side, feeling with his free claw.

He finds Oneclaw and taps his shell. "No more sound. I cannot hear. We must get out now." The device makes them as helpless as their attackers; it is useless for defense but he imagines them using it to cover their escape.

Through his feet and tendrils he feels something moving up ahead. Are the bandits coming in? "Make the noise again and then push out of the shelter," he taps to Oneclaw. He feels around for his spear and picks it up, bracing himself for the awful sound.

Being deaf means the noise isn't as loud, but it still feels like a pincer jabbed straight into his head. Holdhard flinches but Broadtail holds her steady, then charges, pulling her along. He hopes Oneclaw is following.

The bandit is just outside the doorway, off guard from the new blast of noise. Broadtail jabs with his spear to drive her back, then swims straight up. Holdhard gets the idea and soon is swimming as fast as he is. They go up until he cannot taste the sea bottom anymore, and Broadtail feels mild fear. He has no way to sense his surroundings—there is nothing to touch, nothing to taste, and he still cannot hear. Only his pincer resting on Holdhard's back gives him any contact with reality. For once it is almost pleasant having another person so close.

He slows and then stops, then concentrates, trying to orient himself. He levels off as best he can by feel, then swims in a random direction. He lets go of Holdhard, but his tendrils can still feel her swimming along with him. He is a little surprised that she isn't going off on her own, but he doesn't mind having an ally.

A sound! Broadtail can make it out very faintly. His head still feels like it's buried in mud. The sound comes again, louder, and this time he recognizes it. It's Oneclaw's voice, calling out for help. The old scholar is cut off in mid-cry, and after that Broadtail hears nothing more. He picks a direction at random and swims away. Holdhard follows.

IRONA reached Hitode Station nine hours after Gishora died. He came with two more Guardians, using the last of the rapid-deployment pods as the elevator was still going up with a load of humans. Tizhos gave him a report on the situation as he peeled off his suit and dabbed himself with scent.

"The humans appear to feel very unhappy and contrite about Gishora's death," she told him. "Several have spoken to me privately, assuring me that they have no doubts of the incident's accidental nature."

"Tell me if you have examined the body."

"Yes. It appears that some individual stabbed Gishora repeatedly with a blade similar in size and design to a human-made utility knife."

"That does not sound like an accident."

"No," said Tizhos. "Someone killed him."

"Tell me if any human currently in the station might have done it."

"I consider that very unlikely. I watched Gishora depart shortly before his death, and I feel reasonably certain that all the humans remained in the station. He refused to take a Guardian along."

Irona growled a little at that. "It surprises me you even considered one of the Guardians as a suspect."

"I failed to make my meaning obvious. I meant only that Gishora ventured outside alone, with nobody present who might have seen his attacker."

"I accept your apology," said Irona, caressing the underside of Tizhos's neck. "So it seems the rebellious humans killed Gishora."

"Yes," said Tizhos sadly. Irona's sexual overture was proper for a leader, especially at a time of transition, but Tizhos felt absolutely no attraction. She did her best to respond, if only to avoid conflict.

"Tell me if you expect more violence."

"I do not know. The rebellious humans may attempt more raids, or they may feel as shocked by this as the others. Certainly the humans here at Hitode seem very unlikely to commit any violent acts."

"If I remember, you and Gishora said the same before he died. We must assume all of them can and will resort to violence. From now on they must remain in their cabins except when eating. No more science, no more maintenance."

"Tell me if you think the station can remain habitable without anyone to maintain it."

"Of course it cannot. Which gives the humans a very good reason to leave." He nuzzles her, then gives her flank a brisk pat. "Go inform the humans of the new rules. Make it clear to them that I will not tolerate disobedience. Tell them their little holiday with Gishora just ended."

BROADTAIL is tired and hungry, and is far from Oneclaw's school compound. He judges it safe to descend to the bottom. He senses another swimmer behind him and nearly turns to fight before remembering it is only Holdhard.

"Are you hungry?"

"Holdhard wants food."

"You don't have to use your whole name. We two are alone."

"I want food."

"Much better. You sound like a landowner. We search for food on the bottom and share what we find." He began a gradual dive, aiming for a section of bottom that sounded like angular stone. Perhaps old ruins—a good place to forage.

"Share?" She sounds suspicious.

"I give you part of what I find, and you give me part of what you find. Share."

"Why?"

"Because we are both hungry."

She is quiet as they drop a couple of cables, then asks, "Why share?"

Broadtail feels his pincers ready for a stab before he carefully folds them. "Which of us is bigger?"

"You are."

"If we fight over food, who wins?"

"You do," she says very softly.

"Exactly. If we don't share, we fight. I don't want to fight. Sharing means we both get food and nobody gets hurt. We can rest and take turns listening for danger."

More silence, and then: "Why don't you want to fight? You're bigger."

He waits until they set down on the rocks. No swimmers or bottom-crawlers, but some of the stones have a good thick growth mat. He shows Holdhard how to scrape the growth, and savors the weak flavor for a bit before answering her. "Holdhard, when we fight we can't do other things. We can't build, or hunt, or even search for mats like this. When we share, we get more than when we fight. You and I can scour these rocks because we are not fighting. Do you remember visiting a vent settlement? Perhaps as a hatchling?"

"I remember—there are many little ones like me and we are eating wonderful food, but an adult drives us away."

"Vent farms have all kinds of wonderful food, because the landowner and the apprentices work together and protect the farm against bandits. They build pipes and shelters, and are stronger than all but the biggest bandit gangs. They are rich because they can work instead of fighting. Do you understand?"

"Working makes food?"

"Exactly! Fighting only steals food, but working makes more."

"You work? You make food?"

"I remember being a landowner and making much food. And I remember fighting, and losing all my wealth. Now I suggest eating and resting before talking."

They eat until several stones are quite clean, then find separate niches for resting. As he feels himself drifting into unconsciousness, Broadtail briefly worries about Holdhard. Why is she still with him? Does she intend attacking him by surprise in order to steal his things and devour his corpse?

No, he decides. She is too clever for that. In effect, she is his apprentice. It is odd to have an apprentice with no land or flow rights. He has nothing for her to inherit, except what he knows. Very well, then, Holdhard can be his science apprentice. A curious idea, but it puts an end to his fretting and he sinks into sleep.

Broadtail wakes. Someone is tapping his shell. It is Holdhard. He tries to make sense of what she is tapping, then remembers she doesn't know the dictionary. "What is it?"

"Food!" she says. "Come catch it!"

He follows her downcurrent to a spot where the two of them can hide amid rocks and mud. They listen, and he hears it: a large creature swimming. It must be nearly his own size. It sounds familiar.

Then Broadtail remembers, and his pincers stiffen as if he's going into battle. This is one of the odd creatures! The sound it makes while swimming is unmistakable.

"Holdhard," he says quietly. "That is not food. But we must follow it as quietly as we can."

"It is not good to eat?"

"No. I remember tasting one—the flesh is awful. We do not eat them. However, I do want to learn about it. Come along."

The two of them follow the four-limbed animal as it swims awkwardly downcurrent. It slows as it reaches a large object. The object is as big as a large house, but sounds like soft mud. It is difficult for Broadtail to get a good impression of its shape or what it is made of.

He can barely contain his excitement. So much to learn! He speaks quietly to Holdhard. "Do you wish to be my apprentice?"

"Yes," she answers without hesitating.

"Good. Then we begin the task at once. We stay here and listen and take notes. We learn everything about these creatures."

"What do we eat?"

"Eat? We have rocks to scour. This is more important than food. This is science!"

NINE

BROADTAIL listens to the creatures constantly, stopping to eat or rest only when his feelers are so tired he can no longer tie knots in his line to make notes. He cannot remember ever being so happy and excited. Not even his memories of becoming the master of the Sandyslope property can compare with this feeling.

Holdhard comes and goes. She listens with him for a time, then goes off to eat or rest. He shows her how he takes notes, and she is fascinated by how he knots the cord to represent words. But she lacks his patience and prefers not to go hungry. When she finds extra food she leaves him some.

The creatures' behavior is complex. They have a shelter and seem to be using tools. They do not hunt, or gather food, but now and then go inside their structure and return with what sounds like solid material in what must be a stomach. To Broadtail this suggests that they have a food cache, which in turn implies a high degree of planning and forethought.

The creatures communicate. Of that Broadtail is certain. They call to one another often, although Broadtail finds it odd that the calls are only when there is some obstacle between the communicating pair. At close quarters they are silent. The calls are long and complex, with little or no repetition. They are not sending each other echo-patterns; it is more like long strings of simple tones.

Like a reel of knots, he thinks. They are writing with sound. He makes a note, but his feeding tendrils feel thick and clumsy and he falls asleep still holding the cord.

He wakes with a tremendous hunger. He eats a couple of floaters Holdhard leaves for him. The flesh is pulpy and unsatisfying, but better than nothing. He listens. No activity. Perhaps the creatures are resting. He goes over his last notes; he remembers being too tired to think clearly.

"Sound writing," is what his last note says. He remembers his thoughts now.

And suddenly, as if his mind has molted and is kicking aside the old shell, he understands. The creatures are intelligent beings. Like adults! They build and plan and speak. They use tools, which they either make themselves or get from others. Which implies an entire society!

Broadtail is thinking so fast his tendrils can barely keep up. His notes are little more than place-markers for his ideas. Where do these things come from? Are there any records of them? What do they eat? How does their anatomy compare with any—

He stops, and his excitement turns to fear. He remembers the captive specimen struggling and making noises during Longpincer's dissection. Longpincer would not do that to an adult, or even a juvenile.

It is not murder, he thinks. He distinctly remembers capturing the creature near an unclaimed vent. A fair fight. And he remembers the dissection taking place in Longpincer's house, on Longpincer's property. All legal. That is reassuring. But dissecting a stranger is still a terrible blunder. They may hold grudges, or demand recompense. Broadtail hopes to persuade Longpincer to apologize to them.

He hears a sound from the shelter and listens. One of the creatures is emerging. A second follows. Sounds of hammering and digging.

What is proper behavior? Broadtail imagines several courses. He can pack up his reels and make for Longpincer's house. Inform Longpincer and the other scholars—and incidentally establish his own claim to this new discovery.

Or he can go hunt for food, to keep himself from getting hungry as he continues his monitoring. After all, his notes are very rough. A complete monograph requires much more information about the creatures. Holdhard can help.

Or . . . he can approach them. Speak to them. Do they understand the speech of adults? He imagines them vindictive, dissecting him in revenge for the specimen at Longpincer's, or to protect their property.

He remains undecided. His mind is like a stone held up by the flow of water from a pipe. When he does decide, it is a simple practical matter that determines his course: he has only one empty reel left. He expects it will take a netful of reels—a whole convoy's cargo of reels!—to record all he wishes to know about the creatures. Getting more means telling Longpincer, and Broadtail discovers that he simply doesn't want to share the creatures with anyone.

He must approach them. It is the most sensible course.

He rolls up his reel and stows it, then climbs out of the little den he has made among the rocks. Holdhard is sheltered nearby. "Remain here," he says quietly. "Stay hidden. If you hear fighting, take my reel and flee."

Broadtail swims toward the creatures' shelter. He goes slowly and makes no attempt to be quiet. Half a cable away he starts pinging, both to announce himself and to learn as much about the camp as he can in case he must flee a hostile response.

ROB had almost finished getting the heat-exchanger set up when he heard a set of loud, regular sonar clicks. It sounded like a large animal. He flicked on the spotlight and had a look.

Fifty meters away was an Ilmataran, swimming slowly toward him. It was a good-sized adult, festooned with tools and bags of stuff. Its pincers were folded back along its sides. Rob didn't know if that was a good sign or not.

He controlled his impulse to panic, to flee back to the Coquille—and his second impulse to pull out his utility knife. It didn't look hostile, and it was alone.

Rob wished someone could tell him how to act. Henri would know what to do. It might be completely wrong, but at least he wouldn't be standing there like a squirrel in the middle of a driveway watching a car bearing down on it.

Should he call Alicia? If things got ugly he didn't want her out here. See what the alien wanted, first of all.

Rob took a deep breath, stood up, and turned on his speaker. "Hey!"

The Ilmataran halted in the water about ten meters away.

Well, at least it wasn't tearing him apart. Yet. Rob took a step toward it. "Hey there, guy," he said, in the same voice he used to talk to his roommate's cat back on Earth.

The Ilmataran hovered there a while, then moved forward. Rob and the alien were about six meters apart now. He was closer to an Ilmataran than anyone but Henri had ever been. No stealth suit this time, either. He, Robert Freeman, was making contact with a new intelligent species.

What the hell was he supposed to do? Shake hands? Pat its head? All his training had been about *avoiding* contact, not how to do it. He turned on his helmet camera so that if he did screw up royally, at least posterity could see what not to do.

The alien made a complex sound, like a green twig snapping. Was it talking to him? According to Dickie Graves they communicated by sending each other sonar images.

Could he maybe use his sonar display to decipher the alien speech? The thought was so exciting that for a moment Rob forgot how nervous he was. It would be pretty damned awesome if Rob Freeman was the one who figured out how to communicate with a whole alien civilization.

He told his sonar software to bypass the signal processor and feed the sound straight into the imaging system. That took a few minutes, during which the alien made some more sounds.

"Okay," said Rob when he was done. "Try talking to me now." He knew it couldn't understand him, but maybe his response would encourage the alien.

It said something else, a long sound pattern like a distant volley of gunfire. Rob looked at his sonar display. Gibberish. A screen full of static. Evidently the Ilmatarans didn't buy their sonar from the same supplier.

Oh, well. It had been a great scientific advance for about five minutes.

They spent half an hour there, standing a couple of meters apart, trying to talk to each other. Rob couldn't get his sonar software to make sense of the alien's sound images, and it was absurd to think it could understand English, no matter how loudly and slowly he spoke.

"I give up," Rob said at last. "I know you want to talk to me, and I want to talk to you, but we just can't. I'm sorry."

Maybe the Ilmataran had reached the same conclusion, for it was silent for a good five minutes. Then it spoke again, but this time it sounded very different. It wasn't making sonar echo-patterns, it was just making simple clicks. It sounded like a telegraph—click-click-click-click, pause, click-click-click-click-click-click-click, pause, more clicks.

Morse code? Numbers?

Rob took a screwdriver from his tool belt and began tapping it gently against the wrench. Start simple: one tap, pause, one tap, pause, two taps. One plus one equals two. Then he tried two taps, two taps, four taps. Was he getting through?

The alien surged forward until its head was almost touching Rob's knee. He had to force himself not to flee, and one hand went to the utility knife on his thigh.

It clicked loudly once, then waited. For what? It clicked again. Rob tried tapping his tools together once.

It raised its head then, grabbing for his arm with one of its big praying-mantis pincers, and for a moment Rob thought sure he was going to wind up like Henri. But it put his hand to its head and clicked once.

Rob tapped the wrench once, then patted the Ilmataran's head. "Okay, so does one click mean you, or your head, or touch me, or what?"

He tried an experiment. He took its pincer and very gently moved it to touch his own chest, then tapped once. But the creature didn't respond.

BROADTAIL ponders. What is he to call this creature? There is certainly no number for it in any lexicon. He shall have to give it a name. Something simple. He taps out sixteen: two short scratches, four taps.

This results in silence. Does it not understand? Or is it offended? Broadtail certainly means no insult. The name Builder is appropriate: the creature builds things. Until he knows more about it, that seems the most accurate thing to call it.

Standing this close to the thing, Broadtail learns much about it. He hears a single heart pumping loudly within it. Sometimes it seems to beat more loudly than other times; possibly part of its digestive process? But the creature's stomach is nearly empty. There is a constant series of clicks and buzzes coming from the back hump, and the creature releases bubbles into the water in a regular cycle that seems to be connected to the noise somehow. He has so many questions! It is extremely frustrating to be limited to simple words.

They are interrupted by a second creature that emerges from the structure. It is similar in size and body plan to Builder, though when Broadtail pings it he can discern some minor variation in its internal organs. Without more of them to study, Broadtail can't tell which differences are significant and which are simply individual variation. It approaches noisily, then halts about four body-lengths away and calls out to the other one. They exchange calls and the second creature approaches slowly. Its heart is also beating very loudly. The two exchange more calls, then the creature he calls Builder guides Broadtail's pincer to touch the second being's body.

Broadtail names it Builder 2.

WHEN they finally went back inside the shelter, Rob and Alicia were both exhausted. They'd been up for about twenty hours, and neither had eaten since lunch. They tore into some food bars and each had a bowl of the food-bar soup.

Rob peeled off his damp suit liner and got into the slightly less clammy one he kept for sleeping, then the two of them cuddled up inside one sleeping bag in his hammock.

Neither one could sleep at first. They were both too excited. Alicia had to keep unzipping the bag to get her computer and make notes. "This is magnificent!" she kept saying.

"When that guy came up to me I didn't know what to expect," Rob told her.

"You handled it very well, Robert. We have established peaceful contact with the species."

"Well, with one of them. We don't know if he speaks for anyone else."

"Do you think it came here looking for us, or was it an accident?"

"That's a good question. He—"

"Why do you assume it is male?"

"I don't know. There's no real difference between the sexes anyway. I guess now that we've been introduced I feel kind of weird calling it 'it.' Do you want me to start saying 'her' instead?"

"No, but I will tease you without mercy if it does turn out to be female."

"I'll risk it. So what do we do tomorrow? More trying to learn the language?"

"Yes. I want to find some of Dr. Graves's notes and try to develop a way to do real-time translations."

The silences between statements were getting longer as they warmed up and began to relax. "I guess you want to handle that?" Rob asked her.

"I will need you as well. I am no communication expert, and you have spent more time speaking with the Ilmataran than anyone."

Rob was about to ask if she thought the Ilmataran could really afford to rent an apartment in Houston without credit cards, but then he realized he was dreaming and let himself fall completely asleep.

BROADTAIL is trying yet again to communicate with the Builder creatures. It is maddeningly difficult—much more so than teaching children. Children can at least speak.

This is like teaching the dictionary to someone born deaf. He remembers reading about a case like that at the Big Spring community. Yet the Builders can hear, he is certain of that. They just don't hear speech.

When he places an object in their hands and taps out its number, the creatures can remember perfectly. But whenever Broadtail attempts to teach them something more complex, they just cannot grasp the meaning. The misunderstandings are almost comical. He remembers using his pincers to demonstrate "upcurrent" and "downcurrent," only to have the Builders reply with the number for "pincer." He can't even say "yes" or "no" to them!

"What is that sound?" Holdhard asks suddenly.

Broadtail can hear it also: a sound like water rushing through a pipe, and a chorus of loud hums, and the echo of something big moving through the water. It's about ten cables away, closing in swiftly.

It's so big and noisy Broadtail doesn't need to ping it to get a clear idea of its form. It is shaped like an adult, but vastly larger—nearly the size of the shelter. Like the shelter, it sounds as if it is covered in soft mud. It moves toward them at a steady speed. Holdhard fidgets but does not leave. Broadtail remains where he is, waiting to learn how the Builders react to this new threat.

The two upright creatures do not hide. They have turned to face the thing and are waving their upper limbs. Broadtail cannot tell if that is a threat or a sign of panic. The thing slows and drops toward the sea bottom.

"I think that large creature is tame," he says to Holdhard. "Much like a towfin or a scourer. Listen: it is slowing as it approaches. A hunter would speed up. If I am wrong, take my notes to Longpincer at the Bitterwater vent."

The hums get deeper before stopping, and the thing comes to a halt just next to the shelter. Two more of the creatures emerge from beneath the thing. One is about the same size as Builder 1, the second is larger and carries more tools. The four Builders float together, then turn and move toward Broadtail. The huge beast remains absolutely still and quiet behind them.

The beast disturbs Broadtail. How can it eat? The water around the ruins is too cold to support such a large animal. Nor is there a stockpile of food for it.

Then he wonders: is it a beast at all? Now that it is not moving it is completely inert. He can hear no motion, not even the fidgeting of a tethered beast. It resembles a shelter more than any living thing. Within its shell he can hear nothing.

But it is a shelter that can move. How? The upright creatures do not push it as they swim; it would take a vast number of adults to shove something that big.

Another mystery. These creatures spawn mysteries. (The thought leads Broadtail to a brief speculation about how the creatures do reproduce; he resolves to ask them at the earliest opportunity.)

The four of them stop just outside pincer reach and wait. Broadtail says "Greetings!" in the hope that maybe one of the new arrivals can understand him.

"YOU'VE been *talking* with them?" said Dickie.

"Sort of. We can't understand their calls or anything, but I think this one's trying to teach us some kind of simple number code," said Rob. "At least, he hands us stuff and then taps his pincers together. The number of taps is the same for the same item."

"That's *great!*" said Dickie. He sounded different. For the first time since—well, since the Sholen had arrived—Dickie Graves didn't sound angry. "Send me all your notes. I had some tentative correlations from remote observation but this is just wonderful."

"All we really have is names for things like rocks."

"That's a good beginning. Let me just get at my notes—" Graves started muttering voice commands to his computer. "Did you make recordings?"

"Of course," said Alicia. "I am sending them to you now."

"Super. I'll need to dig up my analysis software to see if I can identify specific eidophones. Once I can do that, I can start making correlations and try to tease out a grammar. This is so exciting! Oh—" he paused and sounded almost surprised at himself. "I killed a Sholen. I think it was Gishora."

THE creature Broadtail calls Builder 3 makes very rapid progress learning language. The two of them work together, stopping for Broadtail to eat and sleep. When Broadtail returns to work he is startled by the creature's progress. It seems to be learning even when Broadtail isn't teaching.

The biggest problem is that the creature learns words like a hungry child eating roe, but has no grasp of how to put them together. It taps out words all jumbled together, so that instead of making a statement like "Builder gives Broadtail the stone" it bangs out "Stone Builder large tail grasp into" or "Grasping stone Builder tail wide."

Still, they definitely are making progress. Unlike the other Builders, number 3 can actually understand speech and even utters a few echoes, though horribly distorted. As quickly as he thinks the creature can understand, Broadtail starts asking it questions. Some of the answers make sense; others only mystify Broadtail even more.

He rests with Holdhard, tired out from a lot of teaching. She shares some swimmers, caught in one of the nets of the Builders. "What do you speak to them about?" she asks.

"Many things. Where do they come from? What are their tools and shelters made of? What do they eat?"

"Do they answer you?"

"Yes, but—I don't know if we understand each other correctly. I remember asking where they come from, and hearing the reply 'ice above.' I don't know if that means they are from some shallow place where the ice is only a few cables above the bottom, or something else."

"I remember you saying Builder 3 gets the words all jumbled up. Could he mean above the ice?"

"There is nothing above the ice, Holdhard. It extends upward without end, growing colder and less dense with each cable of distance."

"How do you know?"

Broadtail realizes that he doesn't know. It is something he remembers reading in many books, and accepts because there is no better theory. But what if there is something above the ice? He feels his pincers stiffen as though some huge predator is swimming near. Despite his fatigue, he pushes off from the bottom.

"Where are you going?" Holdhard asks.

"I must find out if you are correct!" he calls back.

ROB spent nearly eight hours seething inside the shelter before he could get Graves to leave the Ilmatarans alone and talk to his fellow humans. "So how the hell did you kill a Sholen?"

"Back at Hitode. I was sabotaging the hydrophone net, trying to set things up for future infiltration. A single Sholen came along and tried to stop me. We fought, I won. Stabbed it with my utility knife."

"Jesus, Dickie, what are you trying to do? You can't just go around killing people!"

"I didn't kill any *people.* I killed one of the *Sholen.* You know, the ones who killed Isabel." The anger was back in his voice.

"Yeah, yeah. We're enemies. I know. But still. Are you sure it was Gishora?" asked Rob.

"Yes. My computer was recording ambient sound at the time, and I've compared the noises he made with some old samples of Gishora speaking. When I baselined the phonemes it was a perfect match."

"I'm going to assume what you just said isn't complete bullshit," said Rob. "Okay, so you shanked Gishora. So what? Just randomly killing people—or Sholen—doesn't accomplish anything."

"Oh, but it does!" said Graves. "The Sholen put great store in personal loyalty. Leaders and followers develop an intense bond with a strong sexual component."

"Yeah, we know all about that. The whole bonobo thing."

"Exactly. With the leader gone, the followers are going to be emotionally devastated and competing for the leadership role. Imagine a human family after a parent dies."

"Um, Dickie, if someone stabbed my dad I guess my sisters and I might be a little disorganized, but I'm pretty sure we'd also be kind of *pissed off.* What if the other Sholen try some kind of reprisals? What if they kill someone back at Hitode?"

"They would not do that!" said Alicia. "The Sholen are—"

"What?" asked Dickie, turning on her. "Nonviolent? Remember how nonviolently they beat Isabel to death."

Rob felt queasy. Sholen were bigger than humans, and had claws and teeth. He could picture angry aliens rampaging through Hitode, people trying to flee, blood running in the drains under the floor grid. "Jesus, Dickie. Do you *want* them to kill more people?"

"If that's what it takes to make the others understand, yes! Everyone here—you, and Sen, and all the others—think this is

all some kind of a *game*. We follow the rules and the Sholen follow the rules and nobody gets hurt. Well, it *isn't* a game, and
I'm sure the Sholen don't think it is, either. They brought weapons, which means they're prepared to use them. To kill us. We
have to be ready to do the same."

Everyone except Josef Palashnik looked uncomfortable, but
nobody said anything for a moment. Finally Rob spoke. "I've
got to ask this," he said. "Does anyone think we should surrender now? Give ourselves up to the Sholen and try to defuse
the situation?"

The other three all shook their heads. "We cannot abandon
the Coquille now," said Alicia. "We've made such a break-
through with the Ilmatarans!"

"Okay," said Rob. "We're staying, at least for now. But I think
it would be really dumb for us to do any more attacks against
Hitode or the Sholen—*especially* solo missions. If we are going
to do anything, we have to agree on it and plan it out *in advance*. Does that sound good to everybody?"

"I'll try to come up with a list of objectives in the next couple
of days," said Graves.

"I figured you'd want to spend time with the Ilmatarans,"
said Rob, not without a little malicious pleasure.

Dickie's face was a study in conflict. Finally he nodded. "All
right. Good idea. We'll lie low for a while."

BROADTAIL is hungry. The rocks for a cable
around are scoured clean, and even with the Builders' help he
and Holdhard cannot catch enough swimmers, unless they do
nothing but hunting, which is the last thing Broadtail wants.

He reaches a decision, and finds Holdhard digging for larvae in the soft bottom. "I must go to Longpincer."

"Your friend?"

"I hope so. I remember him lending me servants and a towfin, and all are dead or lost now. But this discovery of ours is important and must be shared."

"How can you share the Builders?" she asks. "You do not own them."

He remembers being surprised several times by her mix of cleverness and ignorance. "Share the knowledge about them. This is the most important discovery I can think of. I imagine dying by accident or violence, and all I know about the Builders lost. I must go to Longpincer." That is the easy part to say. He pauses before the hard part, then surges ahead. "And I invite you to accompany me as my apprentice."

She considers the offer. Broadtail knows he is a poor choice for a mentor—no property, no wealth at all but his notes and what is in his mind. Does she understand the value of that?

"Is it far?" she answers at last.

"Yes—we swim across-current to the rift, then follow it to the Bitterwater vent. The first part is hardest, with nothing but coldwater hunting as we go. At the rift there are swimmers and rocks to scour."

"Here. I have six larvae. We need food for the trip."

In the morning the Ilmataran was gone. Alicia and Dickie swam out from the Coquille in opposite spirals, but they found no sign of it within half a kilometer. While the two of them were out searching, Rob took the opportunity to have a talk with Josef in the privacy of the submarine.

"I think the Sholen are going to come looking for us," he said. "It's a big ocean, but the longer we stay out here the better the odds get that they'll find us. You're the Navy guy—what can we expect when they show up?"

Josef stared off above Rob's head. "Depends on weapons," he said. "Simplest is knives, maybe spears. Good underwater, easy to make, and Sholen are stronger than humans. We fight

by keeping hidden, setting ambushes, and running away before Sholen stab us."

"Right. Anything else?"

"Possibly firearms. Many Special Forces on Earth have
guns modified to work underwater. Very short range, though:
only five or ten meters. Also maybe handheld micro-torpedo
launchers."

"Is that those funny guns they have? With the big barrels?"

"Most likely. Microtorps are like little drones with grenade-
size warheads. Usually self-guided, not very smart. Can be
dodged, but explosions are dangerous several meters away."

"Jesus! How can we fight against any of that? We don't have
guns or anything."

"As I said: keep hidden, set ambushes, run away."

"If we assume they've been bringing down more troops by
elevator, then there could be at least nine Sholen soldiers at
Hitode. It would be dumb to send out all of them, so assume
they keep back a third as a garrison. That leaves six who can
come looking for us. Even if they don't have guns or torpedoes
I don't like those odds at all. Sholen are big."

"You are both right, you and Graves."

"What do you mean?"

"You say we cannot fight against guns and microtorps. True.
He says we must fight. Also true."

"You sound like the guy in *Robot Monster*. 'Must! Cannot!'
So tell me, Great One, what are we supposed to do?" Rob demanded.

"Not sure. First task is survival. For now do nothing foolish.
But at some point that changes."

LONGPINCER and about half of the Bitterwater
Company are gathered in the dining room. Broadtail enters,
with Holdhard helping him carry reels of notes. Longpincer

makes a sound of dismay as he realizes all that line is from his own store-holes.

"So, Broadtail," he says, "tell us this amazing discovery of yours. We are all eager to hear you."

Broadtail seems almost larger than usual. When he speaks there is none of his customary hesitation and overpoliteness. He crawls briskly to the end of the room and begins to speak, occasionally pausing to get a new reel from the pile beside him.

"I announce a discovery," he says. "A very important discovery. There exist creatures capable of adult speech, the use of tools, and the construction of buildings and waterways. But they are not adults, or children, or any creature known in the world. They come from *outside the world*. A group of them are camped no more than a hundred cables from here, in the ruins of the City of Shares. These reels record my impressions of them, and some conversations with them."

"Are you inventing stories?" asks Sharpfrill. "How can something come from 'outside the world'?"

"I recall similar confusion myself. Think of swimming up to the very top of the world, where the ice is. Now think of chipping off some ice. This is something which is done, correct?"

"Correct," Smoothshell puts in. "In the highlands they use nets filled with ice to lift weights."

"Now imagine chipping, and chipping, tunneling up and up into the ice. Where does it end?"

"Many reels speculate on that," says Sharpfrill. "They say the ice extends infinitely far, or that the ice supports impenetrable rock."

"More to the point," says Roundhead, "the archives of the Two Rifts Kingdom recount a project to do just what you describe. In the reel the workers tunnel nearly six cables into the ice before abandoning the task as pointless."

"According to the beings I speak of, the ice extends twenty

cables. And beyond it is—nothing. Emptiness, like the interior of a bubble. And that emptiness does extend a great distance. I am not sure how far. Possibly infinite."

"Then where do these beings come from?"

"Within the vast emptiness are other worlds. They pass through the emptiness in things like moving houses."

"Broadtail," says Longpincer. "This is all quite incredible. Have you any proof?"

"Here!" Broadtail takes an object from his belt and passes it to Longpincer. "A tool made by the strangers. Can you even identify its substance?"

"I remember something tasting like this," says Longpincer tentatively.

"You do! Remember the specimen at the vent? Remember our dissection in this very room? These are the same type of creature. But they can speak! And they make tools! They are adults." He passes out more objects. "More samples of their work. Can any animal do this?"

"Broadtail, this claim is most extraordinary," says Sharpfrill. "You are surely aware that it requires more proof than a few strange artifacts."

"Of course. My studies are by no means complete, and I plan to make another trip to the site. I invite all to come with me."

"I suppose you must go ahead and prepare?" asks Sharpfrill.

"Not at all. Let us all go at once if you wish."

"There is no need to rush off unrested and unfed," says Longpincer. "Let us listen to the rest of Broadtail's findings—reserving our comments and questions for another time—and let him show us the site after sleep and a meal."

Broadtail awakens and for a moment is unsure of where he is. Then the flavor of the water reminds him: Longpincer's house. Someone is standing nearby.

"Broadtail," says Longpincer. "Come outside with me. We must speak privately."

Broadtail follows his host out of the house via a small passage, not the grand entrance-chamber he remembers using. Once outside they swim to one of Longpincer's boundary-stones. Neither speaks until they stop.

"Broadtail, your account of the strange creatures worries me."

"In what way?"

"I have two worries. The first is for you. Are you absolutely certain these creatures are as you describe? They really exist? Intelligent beings capable of speech and the use of tools? You are sure this is not a mistake or a hoax?"

"I am sure. It cannot be a hoax. There are the artifacts, and the creatures themselves—you remember dissecting one. It requires a hoaxer much wealthier than yourself, with experts in all the sciences. The Bitterwater Company cannot create such a hoax. Is there a greater company of scholars with more resources?"

"Perhaps the Long Rift confederation of scholarly companies."

"And can you think of a reason for them to travel thousands of cables just to trick one landless adult?"

"I cannot," Longpincer admits. "Well, if you are certain of what you remember finding, then I have no more fear for you. But that leads to my second worry. If—as you maintain—these things are real, and come from someplace beyond the world, why are they here? *What do they want?*"

"I do not know," admitted Broadtail. "I propose that we ask them."

"I recall thinking about this before coming to you," says Longpincer. "Do you remember them fishing, or quarrying?

They are at the Sharers ruins. Is the vent active again? Do they claim the land for themselves?"

"The city vent does not flow," says Broadtail. "And I do not know if the strangers even need ventwater. You recall the great heat of the specimen at the dissection? Their house gives off warm water. I believe they somehow generate their own heat."

"Well, they must want *something*," says Longpincer. "Otherwise why come here?"

"I do not know. I cannot remember discussing it." Broadtail feels slightly embarrassed for not thinking of it.

"I suggest you do so at your next meeting with them. Bitterwater is the nearest vent to the Sharers ruins. If these creatures claim territory, I must know of it."

"I understand." Broadtail does sympathize with Longpincer's concern. Even villages fear invasion, and Longpincer's property is smaller than most villages. He is vulnerable.

"There is one other thing to discuss," says Longpincer. "I am reluctant even to speak of it, but—what is your attitude toward these beings?"

"I am curious about them, of course."

"Are you their friend?"

"Longpincer, I remember you taking me in and supporting my studies despite my being landless and outlaw. I am your guest and your ally. I do not imagine that changing."

"I am glad. Your announcement is so strange it makes me wonder about, well, everything."

"I remember thinking the same way."

"I suppose we should rest now, before we eat and travel." Longpincer leads the way back into the house.

THE company dines in Longpincer's house before setting out. The food, as always, is delicious and abundant. Bags of roe, a rockscraper with the shell removed, and stimulating venomous threads from cold water. Broadtail explains a few more things as they all eat.

"I recall saying the creatures speak. Actually it would be more accurate to say they tap. They know a few dozen words from the dictionary, and can tap out the numbers for them. But they do not seem to understand actual speech. One of them can make out a little, but not reliably."

"They tap to each other?"

"No, not that I remember hearing. Rather they communicate among themselves with simple howls and grunts, which I believe represent words to them, much the way numbers do in the dictionary."

Sharpfrill is skeptical. "But to organize words by numbers in order to tie reels—or tap shells—one must have the words in the first place! How can creatures incapable of speech understand that it even exists?"

"I cannot explain it. I only report my own experiences. Come hear for yourself." But Broadtail wonders: is he tricking himself? Are the creatures no more than imitative animals, repeating his movements and shell-taps? Their narrative could be nothing more than Broadtail's own brain finding patterns in random noise.

He recalls reading of such things, like Blunthead 40 Hotvent's famous attempt to decipher ancient carvings by including cracks and growths to produce the desired meaning. Now Blunthead is remembered only for his foolishness rather than his genuine accomplishments.

For just a moment Broadtail is tempted to call it all off; find some excuse to cancel the trip and salvage his reputation. But that passes. He is *sure* the creatures are intelligent, and if he is wrong, who better than the Bitterwater Company to test his conclusions?

"I am aware of how fantastic my statements are," he tells the group. "Therefore I beg all of you to be as rigorous as you can in testing what I say and examining all the evidence I present. I prefer to be proved wrong than to live in error."

There are murmurs of approval from the others. Broadtail decides that it is better to be thought an honest fool than a liar or a crazy adult.

TEN

ROB was in his hammock catching up on sleep when his computer started beeping urgently. The hydrophone was picking up a large group of moving sound sources approaching the Coquille.

"Alicia?"

"Down here," she said from the little worktable. Always trying to fit in a little work, even though she was wearing down to a stick figure. "I see it, too. It doesn't look like Sholen. Do you think it is our Ilmataran friend?"

"I hope so. Looks like he's brought along at least a dozen others. This could be trouble. I'll suit up and—"

"And what? Let me sit in here and listen to everything by drone? Don't be absurd."

The two of them suited up. The slimy, clammy feel of the thick neoprene made Rob shudder. It had been—how long?—since the suits had been properly cleaned, or even completely dry. It was like putting on a secondhand condom.

They emerged from beneath the shelter to find eleven Ilmatarans scuttling about the camp, poking the anechoic coating on the Coquille, tasting the outflow from the portable generator, feeling Alicia's catch nets and chattering among themselves in a concert of creaks, clicks, and crackling sounds.

An individual approached them. It looked like the one they'd spoken with before, but Rob wasn't sure. He stood still as it came close enough to touch him, then clicked out 38. That was the identifier the other had used. Rob looked through the little lexicon Dickie had put together and tapped once—"Ilmataran," or at least that's what he thought he was saying.

The alien turned and spoke to its companions. A couple of them came clattering forward and began running their feelers and feeding tendrils over Rob and Alicia's suits. They chattered among themselves a bit, then the first one addressed Rob again: "49-91-16," which worked out to "Ilmataran extend-pincers touch (human?)."

"I think it is asking if they can touch us," said Alicia.

"It's a little late to ask permission. Do you have any problem with letting them run their feelers over you?"

"Only if it will not make you jealous."

"Okay, I guess." Rob tapped one of his hanging tools with his screwdriver. A moment later all the Ilmatarans surged forward. Rob stepped back nervously, wondering if maybe he'd agreed to get dissected or something worse this time.

About half of the group began touching him all over, chattering together all the time. They felt the material of his suit, probed the neck joint where the helmet attached, and gently moved his arms and legs to see how the joints worked. One became interested in his backpack, and Rob could feel it gently tugging on his air hoses and feeling the bubbles emerging from the hydrogen vent. Alicia had her own little circle of admirers.

"I think we should ask them what to call body parts," said Alicia. "It would be wonderful to learn what they know about their own physiology."

So for an hour Alicia and Rob sat within a clump of Ilmatarans, touching body parts and recording the tap-codes for each. They spent a couple of hours with the Ilmatarans before the natives began nodding off. It was kind of comical. Rob would be demonstrating his fingers or the sampling tongs to one of them, and suddenly the Ilmataran would go silent and curl up into an armored ball for about half an hour.

The first one who'd found them hung on the longest, but when he finally needed a nap, Rob and Alicia were alone for a while.

"Maybe we should go inside," he suggested.

"Not yet. I don't know how long they will sleep like this. I should hate to waste time getting undressed and suited up again."

"So, what do you think? Are we communicating?"

"A little bit. I think Graves is right—their eidophones are imitations of sonar echoes. Unfortunately, what they consider important elements of an echo are not what our sonar devices use for imaging. The computer can *recognize* some of their words but not interpret them."

"So for now we're stuck with tapping."

"Yes. The first one—the one with the wide flukes—he is a good teacher."

"You can tell them apart?"

"You cannot?"

"Not really. There's the one with all the crap growing on him, and the really big one. The rest all kind of blur together."

"The one with the encrustations also seems to be a high-status individual. I don't know if you noticed, but the others initiate conversations with him almost twice as often as they do with each other."

"How the *hell* did you have time to notice that?"

"I dug up some chimp-behavior software and modified it to track interactions. I think I can create a social model with some more observations."

"Jesus. You never stop collecting data, do you?"

"What else is there to do? I cannot make love to you every hour of the day, and eventually we must surrender and let the Sholen take us away. This may be the only chance ever for anyone to study the Ilmatarans directly."

The two of them were quiet for a time, watching the sleeping Ilmatarans.

"You really think we're going to have to give up?"

"Robert, we have ninety-two food bars left. Unless you wish to starve to death, that means we cannot stay longer than six weeks."

"I'm pretty sure I can get the food machine running again."

"That will provide calories, but we will need protein and vitamins. The APOS units will not work forever, either. We will eventually run out of argon. And we forgot to bring extra pressure drugs, so once our little medical pack is empty we will have to worry about neuropathy. And—"

"Okay! I know, I know. If you know we're going to have to give up, why are we out here?"

"I already told you. We can gather data. For six weeks."

WHEN Broadtail wakes again most of the others are already busy. Three of the company are over with the creatures, showing off tools and examining some of their items. Longpincer and two others are gathered a little apart, conversing quietly. When Longpincer hears Broadtail moving about he calls him over.

"Speak with us, Broadtail!"

"Gladly! What are you discussing?"

"These creatures of yours."

"Do you think they are truly intelligent, now that you can touch and hear them?"

"Even if they are not, they are certainly strange enough to be an important discovery. I congratulate you."

The praise stimulates Broadtail like a bag of stingers.

"There is a question we are all ignoring," says Sharpfrill. "There is a flaw in your account of these creatures. If they truly come from beyond the ice, how do they pass through the ice into the ocean?"

"You doubt their story?" asks Broadtail.

"I merely suggest that we do not assume everything they say is correct. Even if there is no deliberate deception, they may not understand us perfectly, or may claim knowledge they do not really have," says Sharpfrill.

"That is possible," admits Broadtail.

AFTER two days of interacting with the Ilmatarans, the four of them ate food bars and made plans inside the Coquille.

"Six weeks," said Rob. "Maybe as much as ten. Then the food runs out and we have to give up."

"Impossible!" said Dickie. "We're making breakthroughs every day with the Ilmatarans. We simply *cannot* let the Sholen pack us off back to Earth now."

"Well, if the alternative is starving to death, what choice do we have?"

"Fight them. Drive the Sholen off Ilmatar."

Rob was too boggled to say anything.

"Tactical plans," said Josef. "How do you propose to retake Hitode?"

"I've got it all figured. We trick them. You take the submarine around to the north and make a very noisy approach, maybe even signaling by hydrophone. The Sholen send out a party to investigate. Then the three of us approach from the south, and as soon as they're outside the station, we slip in through the moon pool."

"That's it?" Rob asked. "What if there are guards inside?"

"What if there are? I think I've demonstrated that a human can kill a Sholen in a fight."

"You got lucky."

"Luck is an illusion. I was willing to use deadly force when Gishora wasn't."

"And what about when they killed Isabel?"

"They had the advantage of numbers, and we all were hand-cuffed and unarmed. I don't think the Sholen will stand up as well against enemies who are ready and able to fight back. Remember, it's been ages since they've had a war among themselves. They don't know how to do it anymore."

"That's not enough," said Rob. "We don't have any weapons but our knives. Unless they—"

"Pistol," said Josef. He got up and went for his equipment case. Inside it, locked in a scratched, dented box with a flaking Russian Navy insignia on the cover, was an odd-looking double-barreled pistol, like a black plastic derringer.

"Four-point-five-millimeter caseless four-shot *Spetsnaz* underwater pistol," said Josef. "Each barrel holds two rounds, ignition is electrical. No reloading on this planet."

"Why do you have a gun?" asked Alicia. Rob was too busy admiring the mechanism.

"Usual reasons," Josef said with a shrug.

"Why didn't you tell anyone about this before?" Dickie demanded.

"Told Dr. Sen when I arrived. He said keep hidden."

"And you listened to him?" asked Graves.

"Sen is mission commander."

"You could have used it! When the Sholen first arrived—"

"Four shots. Six Sholen. Also did not want to draw first blood."

"This changes everything," said Dickie. "That thing evens the odds." Graves was as excited about the gun as Rob was, that much anyone could see.

"Dickie," said Rob, "I'm not trying to start a fight here, but—I think you're starting to enjoy this too much."

Graves just laughed. "And you're not?"

"Of course not! I'm—"

"You're getting the chance to play the hero, Freeman. No more fetching and carrying for the scientists, no more scrubbing the mildew, and you've got a woman in your sleeping bag every night." Rob started to interrupt but Dickie drowned him out. "Look at your damned coverall!" He thumped Rob's chest. "The UNICA symbol's as close to the *Star Trek* logo as they could get without paying a royalty! We're all here because of all those old space adventure stories. But it wasn't like that, was it? Just a lot of hard work and rules and bad food. Now, though—now you're having a real outer-space adventure and you're enjoying it just as much as I am."

"It is not the adventure he means, Dickie, it is the killing," said Alicia. "You are proud of stabbing Gishora."

"Absolutely. He was a sanctimonious shit and I'm not a bit sorry he's dead. We're in a war now—you can't go apologizing every time you win a fight."

"Correct," said Josef. "But only fools and madmen fight for thrills."

"This has nothing to do with thrills. I'm talking about maybe winning this instead of just sitting here waiting for them to find us."

"Okay," said Rob, trying to drag things back on topic. "We'll hit them again. But I want to make sure we have a goal—a *realistic* goal—and a plan. Something more concrete than just 'go shoot a couple of Sholen.' That's just murder for the sake of murder. No way are we doing that."

"Do something to degrade their ability to fight," said Josef.

"Exactly!" said Dickie. "I've been doing a bit of reading— T. E. Lawrence on guerrilla warfare. His Arabs used to strike at the Turkish railways and telegraph lines. Infrastructure attacks, we'd call it."

"But we cannot attack Hitode itself," said Alicia. "All of us depend on it to stay alive."

"If we just creep about sabotaging hydrophones it won't accomplish much," said Dickie.

"They have guns," said Josef. "Microtorp launchers for underwater. Also some kind of pistol."

"All right, then," said Dickie, "turn it around. They can't go blowing things up inside Hitode, either. So that's the logical place for us to attack."

"You want to get inside?"

"That's right. Storm the moon pool and get in. Maybe grab their suits, or sabotage them. That would be a pretty serious blow right there. No way to search for us if they can't leave Hitode."

Rob thought it was a terrible idea, but he didn't have anything better to suggest. He did ask, "Can we do it? There are only three of us."

"I've been thinking," said Dickie. "What about the Ilmatarans?"

"What about them?"

"Would they be willing to help us?"

"Richard, you cannot involve them in our quarrel," said Alicia.

"No, think about it! Native allies! There's heaps of examples from history—French and British recruiting Indian tribes in America, T. E. Lawrence and the Arabs—"

"Will you cut it out about freaking Lawrence of Arabia? This isn't Syria in 1915!" asked Rob angrily.

"Why shouldn't we involve them?" Graves demanded. "You've already gone ahead and made contact. We've tossed out all the rules. High time, too."

"We have not tossed out all the rules," said Alicia. "We chose to stop obeying the contact restrictions, but that does not mean we can go completely wild."

"The Sholen think so," said Graves.

"Do they?" asked Rob. "Dickie, they could be unleashing a dozen different kinds of shit on us if they really thought we were out of control. Remember what happened to Lawrence's Arab buddies a century or so later, when they started getting all jihad on everyone."

"That was different," said Graves, but he sounded uncertain.

"So is this whole situation, which is why trying to be Lawrence of fucking Arabia in an ocean full of aliens is completely stupid. We aren't going to involve the Ilmatarans, period."

"We aren't?" asked Graves. "How can you stop me, Freeman? I've got all the language data, and I actually know something about alien communication. I don't need your permission."

Rob fumed silently for a moment, then brightened. "Okay, Mr. Language Genius, let's hear it. Explain what you want to do in Ilmataran number code. You don't have to tap it out, just give me the numbers."

"Let me see," muttered Graves, looking at his own handheld. "One three nine thirty-five."

"'Ilmataran swimming place not-moving' is how my computer translates it. I wouldn't know what that meant if you said it in English."

"I think immobility includes the concept of death."

"It is still nonsense," said Alicia. "In both senses of the word. Would you follow an alien into battle if they were speaking words without meaning?"

Graves was silent for a moment. "All right," he said at last. "You've made your point, both of you. Bugger. We'll have to do this alone."

TWENTY-EIGHT hours later, Rob and Dickie Graves swam toward Hitode Station from the south, pushing off from rock to rock in order to avoid making recognizable swimming noises. They kept a secure laser link open, and were using bags to capture the hydrogen bubbles from their APOS packs.

Somewhere far to the north, Josef and Alicia were creeping closer to the station in the sub, getting ready to make a lot of noise before running for the ruins. If everything went according to plan, the Sholen would go haring off in pursuit of the sub and give Rob and Dickie the chance to sneak into Hitode. Rob had synched up timers for everyone, and his was now counting down to the big moment.

From where he and Dickie were hunkered down in the silt, Hitode was visible only as a vague glow beyond a rocky rise ahead. This side had always been a blind spot (or maybe a deaf spot) for the hydrophones, so unless the Sholen had planted more microphones Rob and Dickie could get to the top of the rise before anyone picked up the sound of them swimming.

The counter reached zero. Nothing happened—the little microphones on their sonar units weren't sensitive enough to pick up submarine engine noises more than a kilometer away. Hitode's hydrophone net was.

Allow the Sholen a couple of minutes to notice the sound, five minutes to suit up, and another ten minutes to get clear of the station. Then we move, thought Rob. He looked over at Dickie, who had Josef's underwater pistol clipped to his belt. Rob hoped they could manage the whole little coup by bluff, because Dickie seemed way too eager to pull that trigger.

* * *

TIZHOS heard the sound of hurrying Sholen and followed the noise to the dive room, where four Guardians stood still as their suits assembled themselves around their bodies. Irona was already there, holding a large metal box in his middle arms.

"Tell me why they don their suits in such a hurry," said Tizhos to Irona.

"The microphones outside detected the Terran submarine," said Irona. "We prepare to pursue it."

"The submarine? You know it for certain? Do the sound patterns match?"

"Perfectly. Now please stay out of the way, Tizhos, while the Guardians prepare."

Tizhos took out her own computer and connected to the station network. After a bit of fiddling she was able to listen to the sound pickups from outside. There was the submarine's signature, no question about it. What was it doing? She watched the projection of the sound source's movements and felt puzzled.

She pushed her way back to Irona, who was pulling on his own life-support device. "Irona, tell me what purpose the humans attempt to achieve."

"I assume you mean with the submarine. I have no idea. They appear to move back and forth just at the edge of detection. Now I must—"

"Irona, I believe the humans attempt to fool us."

He opened his helmet again. "Explain."

"Nothing else can account for the motions of the submarine. It looks like someone trying to attract our attention. Note also that the sound comes from just the extreme range of the hydrophones. The humans built those hydrophones; presumably they know very well how far they can hear. This seems like a trick to me."

With visible reluctance, Irona agreed. "Tell me your idea of the purpose of this activity."

"I can think of two possibilities. Either they wish to test how well we can make use of the hydrophones, by seeing how we react to this; or they wish to lure the Guardians away from the station. Either way I suggest remaining here as the best course of action. Deny them information and refuse to take the bait they offer."

Irona considered, then gave off a burst of dominance pheromones. "No, Tizhos. I have a better plan." He turned to the Guardians, now all suited up. "The humans may plan a trick. All of you go out, and swim beneath the station supports to the north. Four of you remain hidden under the station; the other two swim noisily to the north no more than two hundred meters. Now: come take your weapons."

Irona opened the metal box. Inside it Tizhos could see eight stubby, wide-mouthed guns. "Tell me what you have there," she said.

"A weapon from the last war," said Irona. "I requested three dozen made from old plans before we left Shalina. Once soldiers fought underwater using weapons like this. They contain four small autonomous vehicles, each of which carries an explosive charge. Direct hits, or even near misses, can kill."

Each of the Guardians took a weapon from the box. They sat on the edge of the dive pool and checked out the weapons with obvious familiarity. The very fact that they seemed to know so much about them made Tizhos even more nervous. How long had Irona been preparing for a conflict?

"Irona, I question the wisdom of this. A human has died because of us. Handing out weapons only makes things worse."

"You are mistaken. The humans resist because they still believe in the possibility of defeating us. Once they see we have them outmatched, they must give in. Now: we cannot wait any longer. Go!" he ordered.

The Guardians rolled into the pool one after another and sank out of sight.

"Here," said Irona, handing Tizhos one of the weapons. "Put on your suit and come outside. I may need your help."

ROB and Dickie moved along the sea bottom toward Hitode, no longer swimming but crawling. So far, so good. There had been a bunch of chaotic echoes around the dive pool, then the sound of several swimmers moving off to the north. Now it was quiet around the station.

They inched forward, stirring up little clouds of silt whenever they moved. Dickie was so focused on not being heard rather than staying unseen that Rob had to remind him the Sholen had eyes and cameras as well as hydrophones.

When the two of them were less than twenty meters from the station, there was no point in trying to stay concealed because all the external lights were on, turning the area around the station into a glaring white bubble in the darkness. The two men pushed off from the bottom and began kicking toward the dive entrance, trying to cover the distance before whatever person or software was watching the cameras could react.

Suddenly Rob's sonar picked up a source outside the station. He squinted into the glare of the lights and thought he saw movement underneath the bulk of Hitode.

"Dickie—" was all he could say before a much louder voice nearly deafened him.

"STOP AND SURRENDER!" Six Sholen-sized silhouettes emerged from their hiding place under the station.

"Crap," said Graves. "Play along and get ready," he said to Rob through the laser link.

"What?"

"Hello! We give up!" said Dickie over his own speaker. "We surrender!" He dropped to his knees on the sea bottom. Rob could see one hand near the pistol.

"Dickie, what are you doing?" Rob whispered over the link.

Graves casually touched the pistol. Evidently none of the Sholen recognized it as a weapon. He gripped it and put a finger on the trigger but didn't raise his hand yet. The Sholen were only twenty meters away now. Rob could see they were carrying things in their upper arms. Weapons?

"Get your knife out, Freeman." Graves raised the gun.

"No!" said Rob. Then the sound of the gun hammered his ears. One of the Sholen jerked and Rob could see a little fountain of bubbles and a cloud of blood. Graves fired again but apparently missed his next target. The Sholen had stopped and were all aiming the boxy devices they held in their upper arms.

Rob flung himself backward, kicking as hard as he could, trying to get away from Dickie. The gun went off again but Rob couldn't see if anyone was hit. Then he heard several brief whooshing noises and looked back in time to see Dickie Graves silhouetted against the flash of an explosion. He was surrounded by a perfect halo of bubbles and pieces of him appeared to be coming off.

The blast hit Rob in the next instant. It was beyond just noise. The shockwave pulsed through his body, a tremendous feeling of pressure that for a second left him unable to breathe. Two more followed the first like heartbeats. Rob blacked out.

When he could think again, Rob was on the sea bottom, facedown in the mud. His helmet's faceplate was half covered by a little pool of blood dripping from his nose. His whole body felt bruised, but none of his bones were broken. Despite a great desire to just stay there on the cold mud until he died, Rob got onto his hands and knees and then started kicking. He swam away from the light, struggling along as best he could.

He couldn't hear anything but a skull-splitting ringing noise, and wondered if more of those little torpedoes were homing in on him. But the lights of Hitode got dimmer behind him as he swam and nothing happened. Either the Sholen were as deaf and dazed as he was, or they didn't want to shoot an unarmed man.

The blood on his faceplate distorted the heads-up display, but he managed to find the rendezvous point where the sub was supposed to meet him. No point in trying to be stealthy—he switched to his external speaker and yelled for help until Alicia came out and dragged him into the sub.

FOUR hours later Tizhos picked through the fragments on the dissecting table. The human tissue and entrails reeked of iron and methane. Tizhos wasn't really interested in that. She'd seen a dead human before—shortly after contact the two civilizations had swapped nearly a dozen cadavers.

The suit was what Tizhos was searching for, in particular the computer. Normally the main memory was located in the chest plate just below the helmet mount, but the first of the little torpedoes had struck the human right in the chest, churning the computer components together with his lungs and ribs. That would reduce normal computers to so much scrap, but the humans on Ilmatar used ruggedized equipment. Their devices were a mass of chips embedded in heat-conducting ballistic resin. One could use them to hammer nails without damaging the electronics.

There! Tizhos cut away the ruined heart muscle. Behind it the computer nestled against the spine on a bed of crushed bone. It looked cracked, but she might be able to salvage some of the memory.

This human, Richard Graves, was a language expert. The files he'd left behind in Hitode's system held a wealth of information on Ilmataran communication. Tizhos hoped to find an even better trove in the human's personal computer. He had been out away from Hitode for more than a week; he might have new discoveries about the world and its inhabitants.

Oh, and of course Irona also wanted her to recover as much data as possible. Not the science material, though. He was only interested in trivia like navigation coordinates and inertial-compass readings. Tizhos would give him that, just to keep him happy.

When she had all the information she needed, Tizhos went to her room to make herself attractive. She daubed color onto her genitalia and scented herself heavily. Normally Tizhos preferred to be honest in her attraction and subtle in her displays. This time she had to be blatant.

She found Irona in the little operations center off the common room, trying once again to squeeze some signal out of the hydrophone data. Tizhos took up a posture of sexual dominance and embraced him from behind.

"I know the location of the remaining shelter," she told him.

"Excellent," said Irona. "I will prepare the Guardians at once." He sounded like an eager subordinate.

"Not yet," she told him. "I want you to do something first."

Irona looked at her then, and she could feel the sexual tension disappear. "You wish to make a *trade*?"

"A *concession* to help achieve consensus," she told him.

"Tell me what you want."

"Only this: speak to them first. I have repaired one of the drones. Send it ahead of the capture expedition. Ask them to surrender."

"It seems unwise to give them warning before our arrival."

Tizhos held him closer and stroked the back of his neck. She could feel him tense up as he resisted bonding with her. "They have no place to go. I fear that coming upon them suddenly might cause them to lash out in panic. Again, I only ask that you speak first."

Irona relaxed a little, and allowed himself a perfunctory nuzzle against Tizhos. "I agree. Send along the drone."

BROADTAIL is worried. He remembers the Builders going off in their moving shelter. He doesn't know where they are, or the reason for the move. He worries that perhaps they are afraid of the Bitterwater Company. Perhaps they think this is Longpincer's property and they are trespassing.

During their absence he and the other scholars take the opportunity to examine the camp of the Builders without any interference. Broadtail even attempts to enter their shelter. There is a narrow passage at the bottom, and he must fold all his limbs in order to fit inside. The walls are perfectly smooth, except for a series of bars evidently for pulling one's body along.

The top of the passage is covered; the lid is made of the same odd-tasting stone as the walls. There is a circular object attached to the lid. The whole thing is very warm to the touch; the heat is invigorating. Broadtail pulls and pushes without result, but when he twists the round object in the center of the lid it turns, and then he can lift the lid quite easily.

Within the shelter is emptiness. Like a huge bubble. Broadtail pokes one pincer into the titanic bubble, then his head. It is like being deaf. He quickly pulls back down into the water again. He tastes something odd, and runs his feelers over his pincer tip. The thin coating of slime and parasites growing on his shell is sloughing off. The surface of his shell itself is like something long-dead and scoured by scavengers. Whatever is inside that bubble is a poison deadlier than anything Broadtail recalls hearing about.

He lets himself drop down the passage into safer, cooler

water. "Longpincer," he calls out. "Tell everyone to stay out of this shelter. It is filled with some kind of poison."

"A trap?" is Longpincer's first question.

"I'm not sure. The inside is filled with a bubble, and whatever substance fills the bubble is some kind of strong poison. Feel my shell—the surface of my head is completely bare of slime. Like something in a hot vent."

"Ah! The dead Builder!" Longpincer sounds pleased. "Yes, I remember my pincers and tools feeling odd after dissecting it! These creatures must excrete some kind of toxin for protection!"

Sharpfrill joins them. "I remember reading several accounts of vents which emit toxic flow," he says. "Combine that with the heat of these Builder creatures and it seems more and more clear that they come from beneath the ground."

"That is not what I remember Builder 1 saying," says Broadtail.

"Misunderstandings are almost inevitable," Sharpfrill points out. "Or—I do not wish to make accusations, but the idea must be spoken—the Builders deliberately deceive you."

"We can ask them ourselves! Listen!"

All of them can now hear the buzzing, rushing noise of the moving shelter as it approaches.

The Bitterwater Company moves away from the shelter to make room for the moving structure. It comes to rest in the usual spot and three Builders emerge. The Bitterwater scholars surge forward, clicking out questions, but the Builders don't seem to be interested in communicating. They go into their shelter without stopping.

Broadtail wonders where Builder 3 is. He loiters about the moving shelter, hoping it will emerge. Builder 3 is by far the easiest to speak with. It even knows some real speech. He waits, and he waits. No Builder 3. Eventually Broadtail gets tired and goes off to rest. The missing Builder never appears.

When he wakes, Broadtail finds Builder 2 is outside, communicating with Sharpfrill and Longpincer. He swims over to the little group and waits for the alien creature to finish explaining something to Sharpfrill about what is beyond the ice.

He wants to ask if something is wrong, but he doubts the Builder would understand, so he tries a simpler question. "Where is Builder 3?"

"Shelter inside," Builder 2 answers.

"No," says Broadtail. "Two Builders are in the shelter, you are here. Where is Builder 3?"

Builder 2 pauses, then taps slowly. "Is Builder 3 this place here is not."

"Where is Builder 3," Broadtail repeats, then tries "What place is Builder 3?"

"Builder 3 immobile remains. Is Builder 3 cold still." The creature is making odd noises inside its head as it taps. "Cold immobile stone Builder 3."

"Dead," Broadtail taps out, then drops to the sea bottom and lies there without moving, to demonstrate. "Dead," he clicks in numbers. Then he jumps up and swims about. "Alive," he clicks.

Builder 2 moves its head and taps out "Yes. Dead. Builder 3."

"But how is the poor creature dead?" Longpincer asks Broadtail. "An accident?"

"Let me try to ask." It takes Broadtail a long time to formulate the question, and he tries several different ways.

"Stay," says Builder 2, and swims over to the shelter. Builder 1 emerges and the two return together. They communicate with each other somehow—Broadtail suspects there is more to it than just the gestures and faint murmurs he can perceive.

Finally Builder 2 taps out a message. "Grasping I one word thing."

What follows is a long and bewildering series of statements. Only Broadtail can stay and listen to the whole thing. Longpincer and Sharpfrill go off to eat and rest, which is a pity because Broadtail wishes he had someone to help him understand what the Builder is trying to say.

Builder 1 describes a creature, similar to Builders but larger and with more limbs. "An adult?" Broadtail asks, but Builder 1 says no, and makes it clear that these things have only six limbs, multibranched like a Builder's.

It speaks of a large shelter containing many other Builders, several dozen cables away. Builder 3 becomes dead there, apparently because of the six-limbed things. Exactly how or why this happens, Builder 2 cannot make clear.

When Builder 2 finishes, Broadtail swims off in search of Longpincer.

"Ah, Broadtail! Excellent. We are just packing up to return to Bitterwater. Just enough food remains to get us there."

"I think I must stay longer," says Broadtail. "There is something I do not understand."

"I plan to return with more food and some servants," says Longpincer. "But now there is little to eat."

"I suggest you and the others return to Bitterwater then. I plan to follow alone."

"As you wish," says Longpincer. "Though I warn you of great hunger if you stay. All the rocks for a cable in every direction are scoured clean."

"I am well-fed thanks to your generosity. I don't plan on starving. But I must speak with the Builders at length. May I keep another couple of reels for notes?"

"These Builders are a boon to the makers of cord, at least," says Longpincer. "Yes, keep as many as you need."

Broadtail finds a spot among some stones to rest. When he wakes the others are gone. A bundle of new reels and a package of cured fronds rests by his head. He stows it all in his harness and swims off in search of the Builders.

IRONA'S hunting expedition had to wait two days, so that three more Guardians could come down on the elevator. That way Irona could leave Tizhos and one Guardian behind to control the humans in Hitode.

On the appointed day Irona led half a dozen Guardians out in the direction of the last shelter. They all carried weapons. The drone swam ahead, linked by laser to a handheld computer carried by Irona. Tizhos watched the Guardians roll into the moon pool two at a time, with a feeling of dread.

Before the ripples of the last pair had died out, Tizhos went to see Vikram Sen. The Guardian accompanied her, on Irona's orders. He had told her she needed protection while in charge of the station. She suspected the Guardian also had orders to tell Irona everything she did. Certainly he did not have the posture and scent of a subordinate. If she had the time, she could establish the proper sexual bond with him, but she had too many things to get done.

Vikram Sen sat in his little cabin, reading. He said nothing when Tizhos came in. None of the humans spoke to her any more unless she asked them questions, and they often gave her false answers when she did.

"I would like you to record a message asking the Coquille group to surrender peacefully," she said. "I fear violence may occur otherwise. I can call Irona back here if you agree."

He pressed his lips together tightly for a moment before speaking. "May I suggest that your coming in here accompanied by an armed guard makes your statement about fearing violence seem rather absurd? And that perhaps you should have thought about the possibility of violence occurring when you arrived here with a warship full of soldiers and began removing us by force?"

"I did not make those decisions. And now I fear that events have gone out of anyone's control. Two Sholen and two humans have died. I grieve for them, and wish to prevent additional deaths. I hope you wish that also."

"No," said Vikram Sen. "I am not going to help you. You Sholen came here prepared to use violence to accomplish your aims, and now you are unhappy because of the fiasco you yourselves have created. I will not absolve you."

Tizhos left him without saying more. She felt more miserable than ever. She wanted to simply join Irona's consensus, put aside all her doubts and savor the feeling of acceptance into the group.

But she could not make herself do it. She knew too many facts that contradicted the consensus. Others might be good at ignoring such things, but Tizhos always had a stubborn streak when it came to facts. She had entered science because it dealt with facts, and any consensus among scientists must respect external reality.

For lack of anything better to do, she took the Guardian back to her quarters and had sex with him.

ROB was out with Alicia when their Ilmataran contact came up suddenly. It had a disconcerting habit of picking up conversations hours or days later as if no time at all had gone by. "Speech [containing?] not [human] six arms," it said to them.

"It wants to talk about the Sholen," said Alicia.

"You're getting good at this," Rob told her. "Like Jane Goodall or something."

"We have all of Dr. Graves's notes. He was really a remarkable linguist."

Rob didn't argue. "Ask him what he wants to know."

She did her best, and the Ilmataran replied "[Ilmataran] touch feeler not [human] six arms."

"Oh! He wants to see one of the Sholen," said Alicia. "Or touch one. Possibly taste."

"Well that's pretty much off the table," said Rob.

"Not . . . necessarily," said Alicia.

"They've got *guns*, remember? They shot Dickie!"

"But this Ilmataran is not a human. The Sholen are quite likely to ignore him."

"Are you sure?" he demanded.

That silenced her for a moment, but then the Ilmataran scratched out a new message. "[Ilmataran] head grasping six arm not [human]."

"I didn't get that one."

Alicia skimmed through Graves's notes. "Aha! Head grasping is a metaphor. We'll call it understanding or knowledge. It wants to know about the Sholen. We must help it, Robert. It is only fair, after it has taught us so much."

"So the contact rules are completely out the window now? I do see one problem: how are you going to get a Sholen for him to taste? Can't just invite one of them over."

"He can visit Hitode."

"How? I mean, I'm sure he could swim that far, but how do you tell him where to go? They don't use grid squares, and we don't know how they even give directions."

"Why not just take him there? He can hold onto the equipment racks on the sub. We can approach to just outside hydrophone range and send the Ilmataran in alone. In fact . . ." her tone changed. "He could give us a lot of useful information. The Sholen will never suspect a thing."

In the end, Rob had to agree. He could possibly out-argue Alicia, but not Alicia and her Ilmataran buddy with the wide flukes. Eventually they decided that Alicia would accompany Josef and the Ilmataran while Rob stayed behind to look after the Coquille.

"And watch out for him, he's a smooth talker," he told Alicia as she opened the sub's bottom hatch. "If you go running off with some Ilmataran pickup artist I'm not going to catch you on the rebound."

" 'He' is a scientist and a gentleman," she said. "Unlike some people I might name. Good-bye, Robert."

"Be careful."

BROADTAIL tries to restrain his fear as he rides on the back of the moving shelter. It swims at great speed, never pausing for rest, as if it is driven by the flow of a vent. The thing comes to a stop and Builder 2 emerges. The two of them swim forward together, keeping close to the bottom and moving in sprints from stone to stone as if hunting. Eventually the Builder tells him "Swim there at long shelter," and jabs one limb ahead. "I lie still lie here."

So Broadtail goes forward alone, unsure of what waits before him. He begins to hear odd noises and then tastes odd flavors in the water. The temperature is higher than it ought to be. He stops and listens. Ahead is another odd silent space, which he recognizes as a Builder shelter. This one is a dozen times bigger than the one he remembers back at the ruins. Nearby is a hard object that hums and gives off a vigorous hot flow.

And now he hears things moving about. They are emerging from the shelter and swimming in his direction. He risks a ping. Seven of them, larger than Builders. They have tails, and swim with sideways strokes of their whole bodies—much more smoothly than the Builders.

Are they hunting him? He remembers Builder 2 saying that

these creatures only fight Builders—but he doesn't want to learn if that is correct. He scuttles along the bottom and hides to avoid pursuit, then swims back to Builder 2. They return to the moving shelter as quickly as possible. Broadtail and Builder 2 take turns pulling each other. Broadtail can swim faster, even towing a passenger, but Builder 2 has incredible stamina and takes over when Broadtail tires.

They reach the moving shelter, but Broadtail hears something in the distance. It sounds like the six-limbed creatures swimming, but with a steady hum overlaid on the sound. Almost like the things that push the moving shelter along. He wonders if he should tell the Builders. Then he wonders how. Finally he scrambles down to the belly of the shelter and bangs on the door. "The six-legged things are coming," he taps.

"JOSEF, I think we are in trouble," said Alicia. "Broadtail says things with six legs are approaching. I think he means Sholen."

Josef muttered something in Russian. "Must have gotten impellers working. Time for evasive maneuvers."

Alicia expected something fast and exciting, but in point of fact Josef's maneuvers consisted of just a few turns and some long periods of sitting motionless, drifting with the current.

"Warm current here," he said at one point. "Comes from rift. Edges have sharp change in salinity and density. Good for fooling sonar."

They drifted with the current for a few moments, then dropped back down into colder water and settled among some rocks.

"Stay silent and listen," he said, and flipped on the hydrophone. There was no sign of the Sholen.

"Do you think we lost them?"

"Maybe." His impassive face suddenly looked worried. "Oh. Sholen will hunt for us a while, fail, and then go back to following our original course."

"That will take them to the Coquille!" said Alicia. "They will find Robert! They could hurt him. We have to go, now!"

"No. Send a message."

"How—" She caught his meaning then and practically leaped to the hatch. A little tapping brought an answering click. With Graves's lexicon on her pad, she composed a message in number-taps. It was excruciatingly slow, like a nightmare in which horrible pursuers were chasing her and she had to accomplish some long delicate task before they caught her.

She finished tapping it out, then repeated the whole thing for good measure. The Ilmataran replied with a long series of taps.

"Oh, go *on* and stop chattering!" she said. Maybe Broadtail realized the urgency of the message, or maybe her tone of anxiety somehow carried through water and the communication barrier, because the Ilmataran swam off at top speed before she could finish translating his message.

WHILE Alicia and Josef took Broadtail off to show him Hitode Station, Rob stayed behind to look after the Coquille. He was taking a well-deserved nap in his hammock when somebody started banging on the hatch down below. It wasn't latched—why couldn't Josef just open the damned thing? In the next second Rob's mind followed a horrifying course of reasoning that convinced him that Alicia must be injured, Josef was carrying her, probably someone's APOS was broken and they were buddy-breathing . . .

He jumped down to the main floor and opened the hatch. A single Ilmataran pincer broke the surface of the water, then quickly withdrew.

Rob banged on the edge of the hatchway with his screwdriver, warning the Ilmataran to stay outside. He got into his drysuit and rushed through the checkout procedure, then dropped into the water to talk face to face—or face to blank faceless head, in this case. The broad-tailed Ilmataran was there alone. No sign of the sub or Alicia and Josef.

"Many swim to you," Broadtail tapped on Rob's faceplate.

"Many [humans]?"

"Six legs."

"Crap," Rob muttered inside his helmet. How did they know? Maybe they'd tracked him somehow? Maybe a drone had come across them by chance. It hardly mattered.

The sub. Was it nearby? "Shelter swims to me?"

"Shelter swims eight [units]."

"[You] swim to swimming shelter. I swim—" Rob tried to think of a rendezvous point he could communicate to the Ilmataran. "Twenty [units] downcurrent."

"I grasp sounds."

With the Ilmataran going off to carry his message, Rob climbed back up into the Coquille and started grabbing everything he could carry. First-aid kit, spare argon, all the food (they were down to just sixty bars). Tools. Tape! He slid six rolls onto his forearms like bracelets. All his other loot he bundled into a plastic sheet and stuffed down the hatch.

His computer started flashing a warning onto his faceplate. The hydrophone outside was picking up motor sounds. A drone. The Sholen were scouting out the site before moving in.

Rob gave the Coquille's computer some final commands and then dropped out after his bundle. His hydrophone could hear the drone now. He oriented himself to follow the current, then turned off all his external sound pickups and closed his eyes. After his last encounter he'd devoted an afternoon to creating countermeasures for the drones, and now he was going to find out how well they worked.

The Coquille's external floods began flicking on and off, dazzling brightness to pitch darkness at a rate exactly timed to mess with the drone camera's compensation interval. The shelter's speakers also began blaring a random playlist of swimming noise samples and sonar pings, with fake Doppler shifts and intensity curves to mess with the drone's sonar and hydrophones.

It wouldn't work forever, but it might keep the drone from tracking him, and moving downcurrent would keep the Sholen from finding him with chemical sniffers.

Teach *them* to mess with the one guy who knew more about drones than anyone for thirty light-years in any direction.

ELEVEN

AN hour after fleeing the shelter Rob crouched behind a rock on the seafloor, trying not to go insane from sensory deprivation. The sound of his APOS and the feel of sweat running down the small of his back were the only things to remind him the material world existed at all.

His hydrophone was cranked up to maximum sensitivity, and he strained his ears to catch any sound that might be Sholen or the drone approaching. Somewhere down in the reptile part of his brain Rob's fight-or-flight reflex revved into overdrive. They could be all around him, they could be just about to creep over the rock!

When he tried to be more rational, it wasn't much help. Instead of worrying about monsters hiding in the dark, he had the very real fear that the sub wasn't going to come for him. Alicia and Josef had been caught, or couldn't understand Broadtail's message, or had gone to the wrong rendezvous point. He was all alone in the dark with no food, and would have to find his way back to Hitode through the alien ocean alone—or die cold and suffocating under miles of water and ice.

Suddenly Rob felt the water around him move, and heard a very faint scrabbling. His thoughts turned from fear of capture or starvation to dread of something big and spiky about to tear him apart.

He couldn't stand it anymore. He flicked on his lamp. Even dimmed all the way down it was still like a searchlight after the absolute blackness of the ocean. The familiar ghostly gray and brown sea-bottom landscape reappeared.

Something tapped his helmet and Rob screamed aloud, making his own ears ring inside the helmet. He scrambled away from the rock and turned, grabbing for his utility knife as he did so.

There was a huge spiky alien monster perched atop the rock, but it was a familiar one and Rob gave a loud sigh of relief. With his knife blade he tapped out the number that Graves had identified as a greeting.

Broadtail crawled off the rock and raised one deadly pincer. With the barbed tip he tapped out his own greeting on Rob's helmet.

Rob wanted to ask how the Ilmataran had found him, but they still hadn't figured out "how" yet. So he tried to get as close as he could. "[Interrogative] Broadtail swim toward [Rob]."

"[Unknown], yes."

That wasn't much help. Rob tried to come up with a question he knew how to ask. Finally he tried "[Interrogative] Broadtail [Rob] here," hoping the Ilmataran might fill in the missing verb himself.

"Broadtail [unknown] [Rob] two cables."

"[Interrogative]," Rob replied and then repeated the unknown number.

Broadtail took a long time to reply; evidently he was just as frustrated as Rob. Finally he tapped out the number again, then ran his feelers over Rob's helmet, then swam some distance away and swished them loudly in the water before returning and repeating the number.

"You tasted me," said Rob aloud to himself. "You tasted me from a couple of hundred yards away. That's awesome!" He added the number to their growing lexicon and replied to Broadtail. "[Human] not taste."

Broadtail replied with another unknown number, which Rob tentatively put down as an expression of sympathy. Just then the Ilmataran stiffened. "Silent," he tapped, and then crawled to the top of the big rock and stood still.

Rob switched off his lamp and listened to the hydrophone. After about a minute he picked up an approaching hum. He couldn't tell if it was the sub or the Sholen, but just knowing that a friend was nearby made the suspense a lot easier to bear.

HIS joy at getting picked up was a little tempered by the fact that there wasn't actually room inside the sub for three people. Josef and Alicia stayed strapped into the sub's two seats, while Rob crouched atop the access hatch in back.

"They removed the power unit and oxygen tanks from the Coquille," said Josef. "I suspect they may have left alarms as well."

"Well, that's it," said Rob. "I guess we give up now."

"Not necessarily," Josef pointed out. "Is possible to die."

"Josef, how long can the submarine keep us alive?" asked Alicia.

"You're not seriously thinking of camping out in here until the Sholen leave, are you?"

Josef ignored Rob, and ticked off his fingers as he spoke. "Oxygen: as long as we have power, two years. Argon: perhaps two months before reserve is gone. Drinking water: like oxygen. Food: we starve to death a month after emergency bars run out."

"How much food do we have?" she asked. "I have six bars in my bag."

"I have two," said Josef.

"I've got two in my pockets and I grabbed two boxes. Plus there are two boxes hidden in the ruins," said Rob.

"Hoarding, Robert?" asked Alicia a little sharply.

"Not exactly," he said. "I figured you'd want to hold out until we were completely out of food and getting hungry, so I stashed some extra to make sure we could actually survive long enough to get back to Hitode and surrender."

"Practical," said Josef after a moment.

"Very well," said Alicia. "We have fifty-eight bars. If we each have just two a day that stretches our time to ten days. Let us leave the last day for surrendering if we must. What can we accomplish in nine days?"

"Don't you *ever* just give up?" asked Rob.

"No."

"Other than senseless, suicidal attacks against Hitode, I can think of nothing," said Josef.

"Robert?"

"I know what you're going to say. Do science, right? We've got nine days, so you're going to collect more data."

"It is the only logical course of action," she said.

"No, the logical course of action is to make sure we can survive. There's no way we can live in our suits for ten days straight. Even if we could all fit in here, which we can't"—Rob thumped the four-foot ceiling above the access hatch for emphasis—"we'll be half dead from fatigue and stress long before the food runs out. And I don't know if we really can live on two bars a day. We've been doing that and we're all getting pretty skinny."

"You wish to surrender, then. To save yourself a week of discomfort."

"No, goddamnit. I think we should see if the Ilmatarans can help us."

"That is . . . an interesting idea," said Alicia after a moment's silence. "Do you think they *will* help us?"

"I don't know," said Rob. "We can find out. You know— gather some data."

⊤⊨⧫⊻ waited another couple of hours before circling around to the Ilmataran settlement, to give the Sholen plenty of time to leave. With no sub, the Sholen didn't have a lot of "loiter time" on their missions—it was all swim out, do the job, get back to Hitode.

Wary of drones, the three of them left the sub a few hundred meters away and swam upcurrent to the settlement where Henri had been dissected.

Broadtail met them only a few dozen meters from the sub. He swam toward Rob like a torpedo and clasped him firmly in his pincers. "Ilmataran many food ping humans."

"Right," said Rob. He tapped out "Humans reaching for Il-mataran."

"Ilmataran grasps limb. Humans swim."

He led the three of them toward the settlement. Rob had glimpsed it before when the Ilmatarans had brought Henri here a prisoner, but he'd never really had a chance to look at the place.

The heart of the whole operation was the vent. It was capped by a low dome of fitted stone, representing God only knew how much Ilmataran labor. Neat covered channels of carefully cut stone radiated out from the dome, branching and rebranching like some kind of neolithic demonstration of fractal geometry. In a few places, where it was evidently important to keep up the pressure or span a chasm, they used pipes made of hollowed stone segments.

One of the oddities of Ilmatar that had puzzled the first human explorers was the absence of any large mineral deposits at the sea-bottom vents. Only at the oldest and smallest vents could drones photograph "chimneys" reminiscent of the ones on Earth and Europa. Solving the mystery took so long because the answer, paradoxically, was right in front of everyone: the Ilmatarans themselves. Very few of Ilmatar's sea-bottom vents got the chance to build up ramparts of mineral deposits because any active vent was quickly occupied by Ilmatarans and channeled into a productive network of pipes and tunnels. Just like so much of Earth, the Ilmataran landscape was the product of intelligent brains and hands.

Atop the channels were tiny vent holes, each with its own plug of shell or bone. Around each hole were dozens of chemosynthesizing organisms, rooted on movable stones. The Ilmatarans planted their crops where the water temperature was right. Nearest the vent itself were the most impressive growths—like giant ostrich feathers two or three meters high, some of them splitting into twin plumes halfway up. Rob could also see what looked like long threads waving in the flow, flat stones supporting shaggy microorganism colonies, some things with broad spiky fans like palmetto leaves, fleshy cylinders that completely surrounded the outflow from a hole, masses of stuff like black macaroni, and long flat strands almost exactly like fronds of kelp.

But the chemosynthetic "plants" were just part of the amazing food factory powered by the vent. Above the crops, the water was cloudy where free-floating microorganisms fed on the warm chemical-rich water. Small swimmers darted in and out of the cloud, and larger swimmers pursued them. The Ilmatarans had nets set up to catch some of these. Traps made of bone and fiber were staked at intervals around the property to catch bottom-crawlers. Rob could also see beds of sessile organisms kind of like half-buried ammonites, and some larger swimmers tethered to stakes.

Downcurrent from the main vent complex were the buildings. They were not quite as neatly built as the vent cap dome. The walls were sloping piles of smaller stones, roofed by heavy slabs like prehistoric tombs. There were no windows. Each building was fed by a ventwater channel, so the walls supported a lush growth of weeds and microbial mats.

At the upcurrent edge of the working area was the garbage midden, with its own screen of nets to catch scavengers. Ilmatarans liked their garbage, and placed it where the tasty organic molecules would wash off it and enrich the farm. The garbage pile was huge, far bigger than the farm itself. Over time it had been shaped and tweaked to control the flow of current, bringing just enough to circulate the water, but not enough to wash away valuable nutrients from the vent.

The trash pile sprawled over a couple of square kilometers, heaped up at least ten meters above the seafloor. Rob felt his hair prickle a bit as he got another glimpse of the scale of Ilmataran history. How long would it take a single little village to build up a trash pile that size? Centuries? Millennia?

The place was quite busy. Half a dozen Ilmatarans were harvesting some of the crops growing on the pipe system, a couple of others were tending the drift nets and traps. By one of the main buildings a couple of young adults were mending nets, and another pair were twisting fibers into rope.

The sea bottom was crawling with scavengers. Half of them looked like juvenile Ilmatarans. As Rob passed the line of traps at the edge of the property, he saw that a majority of the animals in the traps were juveniles. It was with some relief that he saw an adult throwing them away when emptying the trap.

Broadtail stopped at the main house. "Humans moving toward Ilmataran structure," he tapped out, and led them inside. The door was a very heavy affair made of rigid bone segments lashed with tough plant fiber. The outside surface was armored with overlapping plates of shell. It occurred to Rob that this wasn't just a house, it was a fortress. Who did the Ilmatarans have to fight?

Inside Rob felt a pang of claustrophobia. The corridor was narrow and twisted randomly, and every surface was thick with weed and bacterial mats, making it very hard to see. His sonar gadget was nearly useless in the close quarters. All he could do was follow Broadtail and keep reminding himself that this wasn't going to end the way Henri's visit had.

Eventually they reached a large room, which Rob recognized. The video feed from Henri's suit had shown it quite clearly as he'd been dissected. Rob trusted Broadtail, but he felt for the utility knife on his thigh just in case.

TIZHOS met with Irona when he returned with the Guardians. His account of the raid—one could hardly call it a battle—made her more depressed than ever. "We sabotaged the temporary shelter, but they left aboard the submarine. It cannot support them for long. They must give up or die now," he said.

"I worry about what may happen if they do die," she said, not caring how she sounded.

"Other humans may wish to avoid death themselves. They may urge cooperation."

"I fear we have destroyed any chance to achieve a consensus with the humans. During your mission against the last shelter I spoke with Vikram Sen. Even he now acts angry and uncooperative, when before he seemed willing to work with us."

"It could cause problems if he works against us," said Irona. "We must win his loyalty. Humans follow a hierarchy—if the leader supports us, the others will go along."

"Tell me how you expect to win his loyalty."

"I intend to establish a personal bond."

BROADTAIL remembers feeling this anxious when presenting his work to the Bitterwater Company for the first time. Now, however, he is not worried about himself. Whatever happens, his status as discoverer of the Builders is secure. He can imagine scholars reading his work long after his death. Though he does not speak of it to others, Broadtail imagines Longpincer and the rest of the Company being known chiefly as "colleagues of the great Broadtail." If the same thought occurs to them, nobody mentions it.

Holdhard is beside him, holding his note reels. They are his property, her inheritance as his apprentice. He wonders idly if she imagines him being known as "the teacher of the great Holdhard."

Right now Broadtail is worried because he wishes this meeting to go well. The Builders need help and only the Bitterwater Company can provide it. Without that help, the steady flow of new learning from the Builders will cease. Broadtail does not wish for that to happen.

He listens. The chatter in the room quiets. He forces himself to feel confident and strong, and speaks. "Greetings. I'm sure you all can hear that three of the Builders are here at this meeting. Let me explain why. The Builders are here because of a horrible crime. They have enemies—other beings from beyond the ice but unlike them. These other beings I describe as Squatters."

"*Other* beings?" The room fills with commotion.

"Yes. According to the Builders, these Squatters originate within a different sphere beyond the ice. They are in conflict for some reason—I do not completely understand how or why."

"I think we need to know," says Longpincer.

"I agree," says Broadtail. "But please allow me to finish. The Builders claim they are the makers of a large shelter, off in cold water along the dead vent line downcurrent of Bitterwater. They describe the Squatters arriving and forcing them to leave. Upon their taking refuge in a smaller shelter—I'm sure you all remember our visit to them—the Builders are again attacked and their shelter destroyed."

The room is quiet. All the Bitterwater scholars are householders. Even Broadtail still thinks of himself as one despite the loss of his property. Monsters coming out of the cold to seize one's house is the essence of dread for all of them.

"Is this claim accurate?" asks Sharpfrill at last. "I do not wish to doubt anyone's honesty, but perhaps you do not understand everything they tell you. Is it possible they have some kind of, oh, I don't know, maybe an inheritance dispute with these other beings? Or something of that kind?"

"Let us ask them again," said Broadtail. Loudly, so that all the Company could hear, he tapped out a message to Builder 1. "Squatters construct shelter, yes?"

Some discussion among them in faint swishing noises and barks. Then Builder 1 replies. "No. Shelter build action Builders shelter. Two place shelter Builder two shelter. Squatters large grasp shelter. Squatters two shelter separate."

"His words are sharp and strong," says Broadtail. "The shelters are the work of his people. These others force them to leave. As I recall saying, a horrible crime."

"What do these Squatters want?" demanded Longpincer. "Where do they plan to strike next?"

"I am unsure. Let me ask." Broadtail taps another message to Builder 1. "Squatters grasping object?"

More discussion. Builder 1 eventually replies, "Squatters grasp Builders."

"I believe the Squatters only wish to remove the Builders," Broadtail explains to the Company.

"Let them," says Sharpfrill. "It is not our quarrel." The room echoes with murmurs of agreement.

"The Builders are here now," says Broadtail quietly. "They are Longpincer's guests. As are we all."

That creates a long uncomfortable silence. Everyone waits for Longpincer to say something. He takes a little while to respond, and Broadtail realizes he is enjoying the attention. Lately Broadtail is making a bigger noise. It could be awkward: though this is Longpincer's home, it is Broadtail who brings the Builders here into the house. Longpincer could disavow them. And who could blame him? They are not adults. Longpincer would be within his rights to kill and eat them.

Longpincer elevates himself on his legs so that his words are not distorted. "They are my guests," he says clearly. "Within my boundaries they are under my protection. Their enemies are mine." He quotes the way it is written in old laws. Saying it that way, Longpincer is reminding his other guests of their duty. By accepting his hospitality they make themselves his allies in battle. In any vent town the vote of the community replaces ancient codes, but Bitterwater is alone, surrounded by cold water. Longpincer must take such things seriously.

Broadtail translates for the Builders. "Builders may stay here. We adults fight any Squatters who try to take you." He feels tremendous relief. With Longpincer's consent the Builders can remain at Bitterwater. Broadtail can study them all the time and learn everything there is to know.

"HUMANS stand [unknown]. Ilmatarans stabbing motions [unknown] reaching out toward humans," said Rob. "I think that means they're offering to protect us."

"From the Sholen? Are you certain?" said Alicia.

"No, but that's what it sounds like. I think our broad-tailed friend talked the others into it."

"But we have not asked them to do this—Robert, tell them it is not their fight."

Rob tried. "Ilmataran folds pincers."

"Ilmatarans make stabbing motions," Broadtail replied. "Humans and Ilmatarans make stabbing motions."

"Alicia, I think they've made up their minds."

"Should we leave, then?"

"Sound like you hope we persuade you not to," said Josef. "Stay."

"Robert?"

"You're the one who wants to gather more data, right? At least with them helping us maybe we can figure out how to survive longer. And we'll be right in the middle of an Ilmataran community! So I take it we're staying? I'll tell him."

He tapped out the message, then made himself as comfortable as he could in the low room while the Ilmatarans argued things out. With so many of them pinging and clicking together it sounded like some kind of bizarre concerto for harpsichord and castanets.

Broadtail was translating bits and pieces of the discussion into number code for Rob's benefit, so that he understood at least vaguely what was happening. They were trying to decide where the humans could stay and how to protect them. Some of the Ilmatarans wanted to move them elsewhere. And then, quite suddenly, they all apparently came to an agreement because the pinging quieted down.

Broadtail tapped a new message to Rob. "Humans many food, yes?"

"No," Rob replied. "Humans twenty food."

This prompted one of the Ilmatarans to go to the doorway and make some loud noises. After a bit, a parade of others came in carrying bundles and jars of stuff that they set out on the floor in the center of the room.

"Eat," Broadtail signaled.

"Oh, crud," said Rob. "Alicia, how can we tell them we can't eat their food?"

"Show them," she said, and took out one of the emergency bars.

Rob spent some time going through his Ilmataran lexicon, and then tapped out "Human eat zero food." He held up the food bar and unwrapped it. "Human eat object."

This caused something of a commotion. Rob finally had to slip a bit of the food bar through the little self-sealing adaptive plastic port in the helmet faceplate. It was supposed to allow one to eat while outside the station—but in practice it always leaked. Icy water trickled down Rob's neck, soaking his suit liner, but he got the morsel into his mouth. Its brief immersion in Ilmatar's ocean gave it a flavor of over-salted egg, which wasn't much worse than the way the bars normally tasted. The Ilmatarans crowded around, listening and feeling him as he chewed and swallowed.

Broadtail was brave enough to take a bit of the bar in his feeding tendrils. Watching him eat was almost as fascinating for Rob as his own performance had been for the Ilmatarans. The inner side of each tendril was ridged like a file, and Broadtail basically abraded his food, pulling the tendrils into his mouth to swallow what they scraped off.

"He's eating it! Should I stop him?"

Alicia was busy calling up files on her helmet faceplate. "Yes! Tell him to stop! The sugars ought to be all right, but the fats and proteins may taste unpleasant or cause an allergic reaction."

"Too late," said Rob as Broadtail paused and expelled a cloud of food particles from his mouth.

"Not food," said Broadtail after a moment.

"Builder food not Ilmataran food," Rob tapped out.

That prompted a lot more discussion among the Ilmatarans, during which some of them apparently decided there was no sense letting all the stuff on the floor go to waste. They began stuffing themselves and passing things around. Since their sound organs were entirely separate from the feeding mouthparts, the Ilmatarans could chatter as much as they liked while eating.

"Take samples," said Josef.

"Oh! Yes. Both of you help," said Alicia, passing out some little sample baggies from her suit pocket.

"More data?" asked Rob as he scraped a little of what looked like caviar into a bag.

"Yes, and not just for research. There may be a few things here which we can eat."

THINLEGS approaches Broadtail and Longpincer. "My dear colleagues. I find I must return to my own home. Longpincer, may I borrow the service of an apprentice to load my animal?"

"Of course you may," says Longpincer. "But why must you leave now? So much is happening!"

Thinlegs reaches over with his pincers and taps on Longpincer's shell, loud enough for Broadtail to hear. "That is why I must leave," he spells out. "It is too much. I recall joining the Company as a diversion from the cares of managing my property. The discoveries and opinions of the members are interesting, and some of their ideas are profitable. As I say, it is a pleasant diversion. The Company are better conversationalists than my neighbors and apprentices, and you keep a good larder, Longpincer. But all that is happening now—it is simply too much! Beings from beyond the ice! Creatures capable of thinking and speaking like adults! Two varieties at war with each other! I fear that if I remain I must take a side in this fight and risk my life or my property."

"I am sorry to hear it," says Longpincer. "But I intend to welcome you again."

"I am grateful. But I must go."

Broadtail waits until Thinlegs is too far to hear them, then taps on Longpincer's shell. "How many others are leaving?"

"I recall speaking with two—Narrowbody and Smoothshell."

"I regret this is happening, Longpincer," says Broadtail after a moment's hesitation, "if the presence of the Builders creates difficulties, I can take them elsewhere. Perhaps hide them in a different set of ruins, or take them off to the shallows."

"No. I am their host and I recall saying as much before the Company. This is the best place to keep them."

"I must ask—can you afford this? Have you enough surplus for the Company and the Builders?"

"You need not worry. Even if my own jars are empty, I have beads to spend. Besides," Longpincer's tone shifts to amusement, "I remember you demonstrating these Builders cannot eat my food. Surely that is the best sort of guest to have?"

THE sub could sleep two people in only moderate discomfort, but adding a third meant that someone had to stretch out on top of the underside hatch. The unlucky sleeper always woke up cold, stiff, and with a pattern of little triangles pressed into his skin by the floor grid. When they were awake, Rob and Josef spent as much time outside as possible. Alicia used the cramped space as a lab.

On their second day at the Ilmataran settlement, Rob found Alicia hard at work inside the sub. He was quiet as she prepared another sample and slid the little test strip into the analyzer.

"How's it going?"

She straightened up and stretched. "In two days I have

tested sixty-five Ilmataran foodstuffs. Seven have nutritional value for us, two contain no identifiable toxins or allergens, and one even seems to be palatable."

"You mean the orange stuff you showed me this morning? For some values of palatable, I guess."

"What is the old American saying? Pretend it is chicken?"

"More like rotten eggs."

"That is just the sulfur. Everything here is rich in sulfur. It is the foundation of the ecology."

"And that means half the things we've tested are full of sulfuric acid and carbon sulfide."

"The orange bacterial mats have only trace amounts. And we can get rid of the hydrogen sulfide you don't like by cooking it. That would also break down the complex carbohydrates."

"Mmm. Fried sulfur-reducing bacterial mats. When we get back to Earth we can start a chain of Ilmataran restaurants."

"The usable carbohydrate content is about point one kilocalorie per gram. That is a bit less than lettuce. It will help keep us alive, Robert."

"I know. Sorry. How many more samples today?"

"I am hoping to process another twenty. Our friend Broadtail has been a great help. His people have a very sophisticated classification system based on anatomy and physiology. It is essentially Linnean without the modern genetic component."

"How does that help?"

"It means that I can eliminate entire phyla rather quickly. For instance, we were able to determine that all the animals have tremendous concentrations of metals from the water in their tissues. Which is a shame, because I would like to find a source of protein we can use."

"How about eggs?"

"They are too acidic. To be honest, the best things for us here are the products of decay. All of their energetic molecules are bad for us. But the sugars and starches they use for structural materials are all right."

"We're garbage eaters from space."

"Essentially. I am gaining new respect for oxygen respiration. Speaking of which, how is your work?"

"Longpincer—he's the guy who apparently runs this whole settlement—has given us a little outbuilding. Josef and I just spent the whole morning caulking it with silicone and reactor tape. Josef's test-filling it with one of the spare APOS packs. If it's really airtight, we can dismount the sub's backup unit and fill the whole building with oxygen and argon."

"How big is the building?"

"It'll be snug. We had to leave the bottom part flooded, so the air space is about seven cubic meters. We can put a couple of hammocks in there and any equipment we want to keep dry."

"What about heat?"

"Well—it's chilly. It's washed by outflow from the vent, but by the time it gets down the pipes it's only about ten degrees C. Still, that's better than the ambient seawater."

"Ten is not so bad. I have gone camping in Normandy in worse weather."

"That's the spirit." He was silent for a moment. "Is this really going to work?"

"I do not know. Food is the bottleneck. With enough calories we can survive despite the cold. The 'orange stuff' is useful, but it isn't concentrated enough. We will need to eat kilograms of it."

ROB rejoined Josef outside to inspect the little outbuilding for leaks now that it was full of oxygen. The Ilmataran masonry work was really extraordinary, especially when you considered they had no metal tools to work the stone with. Underwater it was hard to swing a hammer, so most of their stone cutting had to be done by patient grinding instead of chipping and wedging.

The building was beehive-shaped, with the stones fitted together by abrading them into place. It reminded Rob of pictures he'd seen of Inca stonework in Peru. The seams were very tight, and Rob and Josef had used up four tubes of silicone sealant and a roll of reactor tape on the inside of the building. Now they hovered inches above the domed roof looking for suspicious bubbles.

After plugging another tube's worth of leaks, both of them were satisfied that the building was airtight. Josef maneuvered the sub over to their new home and the two of them spent half an hour getting the backup APOS system and spare argon tank moved inside. Since it was designed to run underwater anyway, Rob just put it on the floor below water level and taped the in and out hoses to the wall.

They waited for the machine to cycle the atmosphere in the building and get it to the right gas mix. Then Rob used more reactor tape to anchor the hammocks and a heater.

"Electrical work is exciting," Josef commented, floating chest-deep in seawater while holding a cable from the sub's powerplant.

"Tell me about it," said Rob, wrapping another layer of reactor tape around a connection.

"I notice you are very fond of your tape."

"Greatest stuff in the world. Superman's duct tape."

"When I was midshipman we would sometimes use it to tape people into bunks. One poor fellow got a strip attached to his face and lost eyebrows for a month."

"Ouch. When I was in college all we ever did was go crawling through the steam tunnels. What time is it?"

"1622."

"Damn. Another hour till dinner. I'm dying in here."

"Will survive. Dinner will be emergency bars and orange stuff."

"Makes surrender almost appealing, doesn't it? Give up and get a decent meal. I hope Alicia can find a way to make the orange stuff taste better."

"She is remarkable."

"I know. I sure wouldn't be here if she wasn't." Rob worked in silence for a moment. "What about you? I know you've got your guy back home so it's not your hormones keeping you out here. You could be heading back to Earth and Misha—"

"Mishka."

"Right. Why are you here?"

"Orders."

Rob nearly dropped his flashlight. "No kidding?"

"Am still on active Navy duty, simply on loan to space agency."

"Well, yeah, but the Russian Navy didn't order you to hide out in the ocean of Ilmatar waging war on a bunch of aliens."

Josef didn't answer.

"They *did*?"

"Was given contingency plans," said Josef at last.

"So you've got some kind of secret orders to fight the Sholen?"

"Yes. So did Dr. Sen and others—Fouchard, and Mario."

"What about Dickie Graves?"

"Not to my knowledge. Like you, motivated by hormones, I think."

"Alicia?"

"No. Just stubborn."

"And it looks like you don't know about my undercover identity as Batman, so I guess we're even. What are these double-secret orders of yours?"

"Not very secret anymore. Resist any Sholen incursions at Terrestrial bases, using all appropriate means at my disposal."

"What does that mean?"

"It means I am to fight them, but try not to get killed, and not commit any serious atrocities."

"Just minor ones."

Josef shrugged, making himself bob up and down. "We are very far from Earth and our enemies are aliens."

"You're scaring me, Josef. So you knew something like this was going to happen?"

"Of course. You did not?"

"Well—right after I got picked to come here we had this big briefing about the Sholen and their whole hands-off-the-universe thing. I just figured it was all talk. You know, like governments back home talking about preserving the Moon or whatever when what they really mean is they want a cut of the helium mining."

"When someone threatens you, is best to take them seriously. My government—and yours, and most other UNICA members—have been making plans in case of Sholen attack for some time now. That is one reason we have such a large presence here: Ilmatar lies between Earth and Shalina."

"Kind of drawing a line in the vacuum?"

"Likely. But also there was desire to see if humans and Sholen could cooperate in studying this world. Ilmatar is ideal place for that—neither humans nor Sholen can live here un-aided, and existence of Ilmatarans makes it high priority for research."

"So we've got plenty of incentive to work together here, and nobody's going to start homesteading or playing Cortez."

"Exactly. If we cannot cooperate on Ilmatar, then we cannot cooperate at all."

"I guess we answered that question."

"Yes. Now question becomes whether we allow the Sholen to deny us entire universe."

"You think they really want that? Bottle us up inside the Solar System?"

"The logic of their ideology demands it—or even harsher limits. If they chase us off Ilmatar and other bodies with native life, nothing stops us building colonies on lifeless worlds, possibly terraforming some. Soon those worlds have their own interstellar vehicles, more and more as time passes. We have more people, too—which means in time we catch up to Sholen technology. Then pass them. Right now they are; that will not last. I have seen projections: human population off Earth is growing at about five percent per year. In a century, that's a million people. Another century and humans off Earth outnumber Sholen. They must act now or never."

"Damn. And Henri and I set it all off." Rob slid into the water and put his weight on the hammock to test the tape. "Maybe we should give up before this turns into a real Earth vs. the Flying Saucers situation."

"Robert, you are too harsh with yourself. What did you and Kerlerec do, exactly? You were found by Ilmatarans."

"Because we fucked up. If Henri hadn't—"

"Yes, he made foolish mistake. Robert, we cannot expect to avoid mistakes always. If one mistake destroys any chance to cooperate here, then Sholen are being unreasonable."

Rob was fastening his helmet, and when he replied to Josef it was via the laser link. "I don't know; this all sounds so abstract. So what if it's justified? People have died! Isabel, Dickie, at least two Sholen."

"If you wish to be practical, we can be practical: Sholen have killed humans and we must show them consequences to that behavior. If you wish to be idealistic, we can be idealistic: we are right and they are wrong."

"You make it sound so simple."

"I am simple man," said Josef.

TWELVE

BROADTAIL enjoys helping Builder 1 with its projects. Being at close quarters with the stranger gives him the chance to listen to it carefully. He remembers hearing Builder 1 using tools and marveling at how capable the stranger is with its little many-branched pincers.

The strangers are quite strong, too. Builder 1 can lift pipe segments and stones that would normally take a couple of apprentices with levers and pulleys to shift. Broadtail remembers Builder 1 explaining that it and the others come from a place where everything is heavier than here. Broadtail still doesn't quite understand how that can be, but at least it explains why they are so strong.

All his conversations with Builders are like that. Some simple question or observation brings forth an answer that only opens up a vast store of new questions. Broadtail goes through reels of cord at a tremendous rate, mostly just noting things he plans to ask about in more detail.

When he hears things about the Squatters, he feels the same anger he remembers from his argument with Ridgeback. The Builders are *his* project, and learning from them is like discovering an entire vent complex ready for harvest—with a whole line of vents beyond it, all equally rich.

The Squatters plan to take away this harvest of discoveries? Broadtail is ready to fight them for it. He is ready to fight anyone who tries to steal the Builders from him.

FILLING the building used most of the sub's argon reserve, and there wasn't quite enough to fill all the way down to the door. Instead Rob and Josef rigged up a floor above the water level by simply piling up stones and then laying some stiff mats provided by Longpincer on top of them. The resulting floor was dangerously springy, but they could stand with their heads grazing the roof.

They moved the hammocks and other gear into their new quarters, which Rob dubbed the Dome, and then peeled off their suits for the first time in days.

"Wait," said Rob to Alicia as she got ready to climb into her hammock. "I've got something for you." He took a sealed plastic bag from the net filled with equipment hanging above the waterline. "Here, put it on."

She looked at him quizzically and opened the bag. "It is—a suit liner?"

"A *dry* suit liner," said Rob triumphantly.

"It is wonderful!" she said, pressing her face to the clean dry cloth and inhaling. "I hate to put it on and spoil it."

"It won't fit anybody else."

She unzipped her own damp liner, wrinkling her nose at the mold patches. "I am very tired of being wet," she said.

She stripped off her damp liner, wiped clean with four antibacterial wipes, and then very slowly Alicia got dressed. It was a sensual—but entirely nonsexual—reverse-striptease, and the expression on her face as she felt the clean fabric slide onto her limbs was like a painting of a saint touched by the Holy Spirit.

"Thank you, my love," she said at last.

"Where did you find it?" asked Josef.

"I cleaned it, actually. I used a mix of clean water from the dehumidifier and some Ilmatar seawater. To get it dry I put it in the sub cabin heat exchanger, and finally aired it out over the oxygen feed in here."

"Robert, it must have taken you hours!" she said.

"Well, most of the time I was doing other stuff while I waited for it to dry out."

"You are mad," she said. "Wonderfully."

"WHAT do you think?" Alicia asked Rob as she handed him a bowl of cloudy yellow liquid.

He sniffed suspiciously. "Smells kind of like mushrooms," he said.

"Taste it."

"You're sure it's safe?"

"I have tasted it and I am not dead."

"Yet." He lifted the bowl to his mouth and took a tiny sip. "Kind of sour. Very salty." He sipped some more. "Not too bad. What is it—more microbe soup?"

"Yes. A fermenting organism which breaks down the complex sugars in animal exoskeletons. It grows all through the garbage midden."

"Yummy. What's the calorie content like?"

"Very encouraging. I can filter it down to about one kilocalorie per three milliliters."

"That's great—drink a couple of liters and you can skip a food bar. Is there anything to worry about?"

"The sodium content is enormous, but that is true of everything here, and it has no usable protein. No vitamins, either, of course, but we have the supplements for that."

"Any toxins?"

"Nothing directly harmful. There is always the risk of an allergy, though I think if we cook it enough to break down any complex molecules we should be safe."

"How *did* you cook this, anyway?"

"I taped the metal sample container to the wall, and put one of the immersion heaters into it. I am afraid boiling is the only way we can cook for now, except for the microwave oven on the sub."

"That's pretty smart. Oh, by the way, I was wondering about something. We've been using the toilet on the sub, but it's reaching its limit and we can't dump it into the system at Hitode anymore. So either we discharge it off in the ocean somewhere, or we quit using it—and that means we're going to be dumping our stuff in the ocean directly like we did at the Coquille. Is that safe? For the Ilmatarans, I mean. I don't want to start some kind of space-cholera epidemic."

"For ourselves it is entirely safe as long as you don't dump it nearby. As for its effect on the Ilmatarans—hmm. The wastes themselves are harmless, and I'm sure the native organisms can break it all down in time. I am more concerned about our intestinal bacteria."

"I remember there was some fuss about that before the first mission launched."

"Yes, nobody wanted to unleash a plague on Ilmatar. Let me find the reference." She tapped at her computer screen. "Here is the study: 'Risk is slight . . . Terrestrial bacteria fail to thrive in Ilmataran conditions . . . *not* immediately fatal, though . . . sample showed roughly fifty percent mortality after twenty-four hours . . . no cell division observed . . . ' I think we are safe, Robert. Our bacteria evolved to live inside a human body. It is very different out there."

"Well, that's good news. So how much of this stuff do you think we can collect?"

"It seemed to be fairly abundant. I think we can each have one meal of local food per day. That extends our stay by—"

"Two days. Maybe three. I'm also starting to worry about life support. We're using the spare from the sub already, and we only have one spare suit. If any of them fail, we've got no back-ups. Another failure means somebody dies."

"Surely the food problem will become critical first."

"Well, probably. But the thing about air is, when you need it, you need it right now. You can put off eating for an hour or two even if you're really hungry. You can't put off breathing."

She sighed. "You have a point, I suppose. But what can we do? Can you manufacture another APOS unit? Can we call Earth and have them ship us one?"

"I was thinking about salvage. Josef thinks they left monitors at Coq 2, but what about the other one? As far as I know it's still there. Dickie didn't mention them destroying it when they caught him. We can't use it, and it might attract too much attention if we try to move it, but what about scavenging some parts?"

"Can you do it? I mean, do you have the tools and things?"

"I think so. Everything's pretty modular. Swim in, pull the APOS packs and the nuke, swim out. I could do it in half an hour."

"They will be listening for the sub. We will have to use the impeller. It is quieter."

"We? I was gonna do it by myself. We don't know that the place isn't guarded."

"Robert, do not be ridiculous. Even with an impeller you cannot manage two APOS packs and a power unit. And if something goes wrong you will be alone."

Rob opened his mouth to answer, then closed it. He could see the argument unfolding before him, leading inevitably to Alicia getting her way. So he decided to save himself the effort.

"Tell you what: you can come with me if you get in my sleeping bag right now. If you want—"

She cut him off. "You are trying to make some awful pun about Coquilles and penises, aren't you? I will sleep with you if you promise not to speak it aloud."

TIZHOS did her best, curling up next to the human with plenty of skin-on-skin contact. All his muscles felt tightly clenched, which didn't seem right for a human in a relaxed state. She picked up a food ball and tried to feed it to him.

He jerked his head back, then shook it from side to side. "No, thank you," he said.

Irona had instructed her to scent the air in their room with perfumes and pheromones to establish the mood. The two Sholen would certainly have an easier time bonding with the human if they themselves felt relaxed and affectionate. Tizhos had also created a platter of treats they could all share, and turned up the heat.

"I ask you to try the food," said Irona. "You have no cause to worry—Tizhos has programmed our foodmaker to observe human dietary and culinary constraints."

Tizhos tried to feed him again, and again Vikram Sen pulled back. Finally he took the ball from her hand with his own and nibbled it. "Your foodmaker is an impressive feat of technology, but as I told Tizhos earlier I am afraid I have nothing more to say to either of you right now."

"You misunderstand our purpose. We do not wish to interrogate you. We merely want to renew our friendship with you."

Tizhos handed Vikram Sen another food ball. He took it with his hand, had a bite, and put it down with the other.

Irona moved onto the cushions next to the human on the

other side. He put his midlimb around Vikram Sen's shoulders and Tizhos could feel the little human flinch.

"This does not seem to be going well," she murmured to Irona. "He shows no sign of a favorable response."

"We should try harder," Irona said back to her, then switched to the human language. "Vikram Sen, please tell me why you exhibit such a lack of comfort. We wish only to make you content."

"As I have said on a number of occasions, the only possible way you could make me happy would be to remove your soldiers and yourselves from this station and return the people you have taken. We cannot be friends until that happens."

Tizhos handed the human an ethanol beverage and began lightly stroking his hair. If anything, his body seemed even more tense, but she persisted. References indicated that humans used such activities as a bonding ritual, in their strange, emotionless fashion. Vikram Sen sipped the drink and put it with the unfinished food balls.

"Let me feed you," said Irona, holding a cube of delicately flavored gelatin before the human's face.

"No, thank you," said Vikram Sen, turning his head away.

Tizhos caught a shift in Irona's scent. Was he becoming aroused? A good leader could establish a sexual bond with subordinates—but surely not with an *alien*? Apparently the scented air and psychoactives in the food could overcome that barrier. She felt a pang of worry. Irona's hormones might get the better of his self-control. She could feel herself responding to the scents, and she knew that as leader Irona would experience a much stronger effect.

Irona rolled over, supporting himself above the human on four limbs. "Let me feed you," he repeated, then placed the cube delicately between his own teeth.

282 * JAMES L. CAMBIAS

The human struggled but Irona lowered his head. He pressed the gelatin against the human's tightly closed lips, but Vikram Sen just turned his head aside and closed his eyes tightly. The food fell to the cushions and rolled onto the floor.

Irona kept his body pressed against Vikram Sen's, moving from side to side in sensuous waves that turned the human's struggles into a kind of caress. Tizhos felt almost dizzy from the powerful blend of pheromones in the air. Vikram Sen seemed more like a potential rival than an alien they wished to impress. With one small rational part of her mind she knew she should try to stop things before they got out of hand.

"Don't resist your feelings," said Irona. "We can love each other." He began nuzzling the side of the human's face.

But Vikram Sen's responses did not match what the two Sholen had hoped for. Water flowed from his tightly closed eyes, he struggled and hit Irona ineffectually with his arms, and tried to raise his knee against the weight of the larger Sholen.

The skin glands on Irona's underside sprinkled droplets of strong-smelling marker pheromone on the struggling human. Vikram Sen inhaled a couple of times, then shoved Irona's head away and tumbled to the floor. He regurgitated the contents of his stomach, then got to his feet. His body trembled.

"Stay," said Irona. "We have all evening."

The human got the door open and shut it behind him. Tizhos could hear him shouting something in the hallway. It did not sound like words in any human language she understood.

"Tell me if you think we have succeeded in winning his loyalty," said Irona. Without thinking the two of them began moving into a mating position.

"No," said Tizhos after a long silence. "I do not think so."

AS they approached Coq 1 Rob was cautious to the point of clinical paranoia. The two of them cut off their impellers two hundred meters from the shelter, and began moving along the bottom in short sprints from cover to cover. As much as possible, they pushed off from the ancient walls instead of kicking, because Rob was worried that the Sholen might use some of the captured acoustic analysis software to identify the sound of a swimming human.

When they were a hundred meters away they went completely dark, and paused for up to a minute between movements. It took them half an hour to approach to where they could see the Coquille clearly.

It was dark and silent. On passive sonar it was a hole in the ocean. The only noise was a very faint sussuration from the nuclear power unit as water convected through its cooling fins. Even damped down it was still about five degrees warmer than the ocean.

Rob tapped Alicia's helmet and made a "stop" gesture with one hand, then pointed at himself and then at the shelter. She signed "okay."

He braced himself against the broken stone pipe they were crouched next to and pushed off as hard as he could. He felt himself shooting through the water, slowing until he had to start kicking to cover the last couple of meters.

Rob's extended fingers touched the side of the Coquille, and he felt his way to the lower edge, then pulled himself under it until he came to the entry hatch. It opened easily enough, and Rob switched on his helmet lamp. The sudden light was startlingly bright after minutes in total dark. The motes of silt floating before his face made him jerk his head back in surprise.

He risked a look around before climbing up the little ladder inside the hatch. The Coquille had acquired a coating of gray fuzz, growing in intricate six-branched patterns like moldy snowflakes.

Just before his head broke the surface in the hatchway, Rob

paused. What if Isabel's body was still inside? He felt a sudden queasiness. The image of Isabel Rondon, all bloated and purple like a deer on the side of the highway, flashed into his head and he couldn't dismiss it. He realized he was breathing heavily.

I have to climb this ladder, he told himself. Very deliberately he moved his right hand up to the next rung and took hold. He forced himself to let go with his left and reach up to the top rung. His head moved from water to air, and he looked around the lower level of the Coquille.

There were no corpses. He took a deep breath, then let it out in a powerful sigh as his arm muscles unclenched.

The place was a mess, though. The lab space had been trashed by the fighting when the Sholen came. The walls and floor were covered with patches of mold—real, blue-green Terrestrial mold. Rob's queasiness returned when he realized it was growing where Isabel's blood had spattered. Suddenly Rob had absolutely no desire to open his helmet.

He climbed back down into the cool water and turned on the laser link to signal Alicia. No response. His system couldn't find her. Was she out of line-of-sight? He let himself drop to the sea bottom and tried again. Still nothing.

Sonar wasn't picking up anything but ocean sounds. Suddenly there was an explosion of noise and activity among the ruins. He heard Alicia shout "Robert! Sholen! Get away!" over the hydrophone. His sonar imaged four indistinct figures struggling together among the sharp stones.

Rob clenched his teeth to avoid calling out a reply. They had her. That much was certain or she would not have given herself away by shouting. She was always very rational under stress. He moved as quickly as he dared, pulling himself along the underside of the Coquille to get it between him and the aliens. Then he pushed off toward an old broken dome.

Why weren't they shooting? He got behind a wall and

paused to listen. There was no deadly little swish of the micro-torps. Not even the sound of Sholen swimming after him.

Either they were being ethical and didn't want to kill anyone else, or they were being clever. "Put a tracer on me so I'll lead you back to the rebel base, eh?" he said to himself. "Your advanced alien science is no match for our spunky Earthling pop culture."

But what about Alicia? He had to leave her. She would say the same thing. If he got himself captured trying to rescue her she would be brutally sarcastic. He still couldn't rid himself of the feeling that he was making up justifications for cowardice.

But no—taking on a bunch of armed Sholen with nothing but his utility knife would be courage of the "strap a bomb to your belt and blow up a bus" variety. Rob had vague, lapsed secular Jewish ideas about an afterlife, and martyrdom wasn't how he planned to arrive there.

Rob took a roundabout way home to foil any trackers. He passed through the ruins, pausing in the shelter of a large stand-ing stone to listen with the hydrophone at maximum. There were the usual noises of Ilmataran sea creatures, and a faint gurgle from the current washing through the ruins. He was safe.

From there he set his course across the open water of the basin toward the camp at Longpincer's house. It was a long trip, but the impeller's fuel cells had enough juice. Barely.

He had covered about a kilometer when he glimpsed some-thing moving ahead. Passive sonar barely registered it, and he didn't want to risk an active ping for fear it might hear and come to investigate. So he turned on his lights and had a look.

It was a *Cylindrodaptes*—one of the largest creatures in Il-matar's ocean. Its body was simply a giant tube, open at both ends, with little steering fins around the mouth and another set at the tail. According to Rob's computer, this particular *Cyl-indrodaptes* was sixty meters long and nearly eight meters across, cruising past at a leisurely two knots.

Rob switched off his impeller and watched as it approached. The *Cylindrodaptes* was swimming low over the sea bottom, so Rob had a splendid view of its dorsal side as it passed. It was like watching the *Hindenburg* fly beneath him. The thing's hide was pale gray, with faint ridges running its entire length. At the top of the mouth he could see a tiny bulge, about the size of a human head, which held the *Cylindrodaptes*'s sonar organs and brain.

Cursing himself for an idiot he switched on his camera and started to record it. This wasn't the first footage of a *Cylindrodaptes*—Henri had managed that shortly after arriving on Ilmatar. But Henri's images were all of the front end and the mouth, intended to make the beast look as scary as possible for the viewers back home. Alicia would want him to gather better data.

He turned up the gain on his hydrophone again, wondering if he could hear the *Cylindrodaptes* swimming. It made a very faint swooshing as it moved but was otherwise running silent.

Then Rob became aware of another sound: a rhythmic swish-swish-swish, exactly like the sound of a mackerel swimming. Only there were no mackerel in Ilmatar's ocean. It was a drone.

He checked his sonar display. The drone was coming up from astern at ten knots. How had it tracked him? Some kind of chemical sniffer? No time to worry about that now. Rob gunned his impeller, trying to outrun the drone, cruising low and fast.

Even at full throttle the drone could keep pace with him, and Rob knew that running the impeller flat-out wouldn't leave him with enough juice to get back to camp.

How to fool sensors? Merge, then separate. But what could he merge with? Rocks?

Rob steered back toward the *Cylindrodaptes*, hoping to get it between him and the drone. The robot mackerel was about twenty meters behind him as he reached the great creature rippling its way through the water. He cruised over its back, close enough to trail his fingers along its skin, then dropped down on the other side and switched off the impeller, matching speeds with the *Cylindrodaptes* by kicking slowly and quietly.

He heard the swish-swish-swish of the drone pass by, and for a second he felt hope, but then the drone swung around and came back, moving more slowly this time. Right now he was silhouetted against the *Cylindrodaptes*, and Rob hoped the drone's brain couldn't distinguish them. But then it gave off an active ping and sprinted toward him at close to twenty knots.

Rob twisted the impeller handle viciously, steering under the *Cylindrodaptes* to shelter on the other side. The drone shot past, but then turned again. It could keep this up longer than Rob could. His one advantage was that they were too far from Hitode for a laser link. The drone was autonomous, which meant there was at least a chance of his outsmarting it.

He dove again, ducking under the *Cylindrodaptes* and then forward along the length of the huge creature. The drone passed by and circled, homing in on the noise of his impeller. He reached the beasts's front end as the drone began another sprint.

Then Rob simply cut his engine and waited.

The mouth of the *Cylindrodaptes* gaped around him, too wide for him to even touch the sides with his outstretched arms. Lining the interior of the creature's huge body were thousands of filmy fins, beating together in wonderful spiral ripples down its length. The fins drove the beast forward and filtered nutrients from the water as it swam.

As the mouth moved past Rob could hear the drone swish by, searching for him on the far side of the *Cylindrodaptes*. A moment later, it passed again, circling back.

Rob kept station in the center of the *Cylindrodaptes*'s huge body cavity, about three meters back from the mouth. He could keep up with the creature by swimming, and the longer he waited the longer the drone would have to lose him.

After half an hour it still hadn't found him, so Rob decided it was safe to emerge. He did risk a few seconds of light to get images of the interior, and was amused to notice a couple of fish-shaped organisms tagging along among the *Cylindrodaptes*'s fins. Waving farewell to his fellow parasites, Rob stopped kicking and let the beast's interior flow push him out its back end. When no drone attacked him, he dropped to the sea bottom and let the *Cylindrodaptes* cruise away. Then he switched on the impeller and set a course for Longpincer's once again.

TIZHOS began searching the memory of the captive human's computer and quickly realized what a treasure it represented. The woman had so much data stored she hadn't had time to encrypt it all. Tizhos found hours of video and audio, and pages and pages of notes. Where to begin? The section on animals and plants included spectrographic analysis and even—Tizhos gave an audible bark of delight—fragmentary translations of native Ilmataran studies on them.

This led Tizhos to the language section. She found it very impressive how much the humans had accomplished, even allowing for the fact that the Ilmatarans did much of the work of translation. Very clever of them to use the written form as the basis for communication, rather than trying to analyze and duplicate the sounds.

She did feel frustration along with her excitement. Each discovery raised dozens of questions, and of course the humans had not had the time to investigate any of them. Tizhos found herself wishing she could join them out there, surrounded by fascinating new things.

But she could not. She prepared a rough summary of the data to give Irona, then went to eat in the common room. The Sholen foodmakers now stood next to the humans' cooking equipment, and she constructed a meal that would relax her.

The new captive, Alicia Neogri, sat with some of the other humans. Tizhos observed them surreptitiously. The four humans shared a large fruit from the garden and ate cooked roots. Their social behavior exhibited some interesting features. The majority of humans in the station had displayed happiness that the new captive had returned unharmed. A handful, however, seemed disappointed at her capture.

Interestingly, her dinner companions all came from that second group. This seemed to contradict normal human reactions to those who broke their rules of behavior. Did this second group represent some kind of variant consensus?

That could create difficulties. At present most of the humans seemed to accept the Sholen occupation, even if they did not necessarily agree with it. They did not cause any problems. But if Alicia Neogri had high status among them, they might want to emulate her behavior by causing disruptions.

Tizhos did not want any disruptions. The station seemed too small, too isolated down here beneath kilometers of icy black water. Conflict could too easily damage something and kill everyone, Sholen and humans alike. During her time in Hitode, Tizhos more and more felt the weight of all that darkness around the station.

With reluctance, she got up from her place in the common room and went to the operations office, which Irona had turned into his private command center. "Irona, I have some interesting new information."

"Go ahead, then."

"Two discoveries of note. First, I have reviewed the files in the computer of the new captive. They contain a great deal of value and I would like to send a copy up to the ship at once."

"As you wish." She could smell Irona becoming impatient.

"Among the files I discovered a large amount of material about communication with the native Ilmatarans. I believe the humans can speak with them. Their vocabulary already includes several hundred concepts."

A sharp scent of anger. "That strikes me as horrible news. Tizhos, tell me if you think the humans have contaminated the Ilmatarans with alien ideas and information."

"I consider it likely. Past statements by several of the humans indicate they approve strongly of sharing information with other species." Irona's angry scent is mixed with a faint whiff of despair at that news. Tizhos wants to comfort him. "Of course, we have no proof that they have done so."

"Ask the female about it. And if they have indeed transmitted alien science to the Ilmatarans, we must find a way to control or reverse the contamination."

THIRTEEN

"I DON'T know what we can do," said Rob, using number-taps. "They've got the station, they've got the surface, and even if help is coming it'll take months. I'm afraid we're going to have to give up."

Broadtail was silent for a while. Rob couldn't tell if he was thinking about what he'd said or if he'd just fallen asleep the way the Ilmatarans did.

"I hold small echoes [of] stabbing," said the alien. "Many cords I echo sound [of] stabbing twice adults-with-raised-pincers grasping carved stones."

Rob mulled that over. At times he wondered if he and the alien were having completely different conversations. He looked through the lexicon. "You think we should try to attack the Sholen? Stab them?"

"I sound [of] stabbing twice. Sever many adults-with-raised-pincers outside a wall of ice."

"Cut them off! I get it! Yeah! Good idea. But how?"

"Many large adults tie cords. Sever the cord tied to food."

"There isn't a—you mean the elevator?"

"You and I are a pair."

"That's a great idea, Broadtail. I'll tell the others. If we can figure out how to do it, will you help us?"

"I and many adults swim beside you pincers extended."

"⌐⌐⌐⌐⌐," said Rob. "They can't have an infinite supply of those drop capsules; even if they're fabbing up new ones they'll run out of feedstock eventually. So their only way of bringing in more stuff is the elevator. Cut that off and all of a sudden we're on nearly equal terms. Broadtail suggested it."

There was a pause while Josef thought about it. "How will we get back up without it? I want to stay on Ilmatar, but not my entire life."

Rob waved his hand as if brushing an insect aside. "Trivial. We reconnect the cable later. Forget the cable. If the Sholen haven't packed up the surface base we can fab a new one out of local matter. The important thing is to steal the elevator capsule itself. Without it the Sholen can't go up and down at all—and we can use it as another shelter. Heck, it *is* another shelter: same structure, same life support and power. The only difference is that the elevator has a hard-dock adapter instead of legs, and the buoyancy control system."

"Very well," said Josef. "If we do want to steal it—how? When? Elevator weighs tons."

"We have a sub. If it can carry one of the Coqs it can carry the elevator."

Josef looked thoughtful. "Is feasible, yes. As you say, load is comparable to a Coquille and elevator is neutrally buoyant. But taking cable is impossible."

"So we cut it as high up as possible and make sure it doesn't fall on Hitode. If the Sholen want to go out in suits and impellers to try to reconnect it, bully for them."

"You forget about decompression. We need elevator to decompress going up. How can we capture it if we explode?"

"Use the sub. That's my answer for everything. Take it up a kilometer next time the elevator comes down, so we can be in position when it's on its way back up again. You and I can live aboard for a few days. Plus Broadtail says his people will help. Next time it goes up, we board the elevator, take control, cut the cable, and skedaddle."

"Elevator is probably guarded. Sholen are not stupid, you know."

"I know they're not stupid, which is why I don't think they'd do that. A guard going up has to come back down again, which means the whole capacity of the elevator is reduced by twenty-five percent. It'd be simpler to just send up humans and send down more Sholen techs and soldiers. If they want to keep the passengers going up from messing with the elevator, they can just disconnect the internal controls and send them up without suits."

"Hope the Sholen think the same. Robert, I have question for you. Do you want to find Alicia?"

"Well—kind of. It would make sense for them to get her out of Hitode as fast as possible. But this isn't hormones talking. Snatching the elevator makes sense no matter what."

"Good. Just making sure you know your own motives."

AND so Broadtail finds himself with Holdhard and half a dozen of Longpincer's servants, clinging to the back of the swimming shelter like so many juvenile mudcrawlers on their mother. Just ahead of him Builder 1 is speaking to the human inside through a slender cord. Broadtail isn't sure how they do it, but it seems to work. The alien turns and taps Broadtail's head gently with one digit. His tapping is still slow and full of false starts.

"Rises house approaches. Builds fights. Grasp."

The shelter starts to move through the empty water. Ahead

Broadtail hears the faint echoes of something solid. As they get closer he can make out the echo of the great cable stretching from ground to sky. A few lengths below them an object the size of a small house is clinging to the cable.

Builder 1 pushes off from the back of the ship and swims toward the object. Broadtail wishes he had some cord to take notes on how the aliens swim. Broadtail pings and takes up his spear. He leads Longpincer's servants down and takes up station beneath the climbing house, where the door is. Their job is to prevent the other creatures from beyond the ice from interfering with Builder's work. "If anything comes out, count the limbs," he reminds the others. "Four limbs good, six limbs bad."

The swimming shelter maneuvers above the climbing house. Builder 1 connects a thick cable from the bottom of the swimming shelter to the top of the house, then moves around to the siphon devices on the sides of the climbing house that drive it upward.

They are making a tremendous amount of noise, which worries Broadtail. If there are enemies about, they are surely aware of what is happening. Broadtail doesn't remember fighting these Squatters, but Builder 1 and the other Builders seem very afraid of them. He wonders if he can overcome one in a fight. They are as big as an adult, and their thick limbs could be very strong.

He catches a faint, sharp sound like the noise of Builder tools and risks a ping. The door on the bottom of the climbing house is open and a large creature is emerging. It is one of the Squatters! Broadtail summons as much anger as he can on behalf of the Builders. It is *their* climbing house and the Squatters are uninvited intruders. "Attack!" he calls to the others, and swims toward it.

The creature has a hard object in one of its smaller limbs. Broadtail remembers Builder telling him about the swimming-bolt launchers, so he jabs at the limb with his spear, knocking it to one side just as something shoots out of it, faster than bubbles from a hot vent. The thing goes right past Broadtail and strikes Longpincer's servant Crestback.

There is a sudden very loud noise and Crestback breaks apart into little pieces of shell and meat.

Half-deaf, Broadtail surges forward at the Squatter. It grabs his spear, shoving the head to one side and trying to push him back. Broadtail lets go of the spear and swims forward, pincers extended. It's pointing the launcher at him. He grabs that limb with both pincers and clamps down. It's soft, with a hard center, just like the limbs of the Builder he remembers dissecting.

The Squatter hits him with its other limbs, and he can hear it take another hard tool from its harness. It sounds sharp. He squeezes the limb he's holding until something cracks and hot blood flows into the water. The blood tastes very different from that of the Builders.

He lets go of that limb just as the creature jabs him with the sharp tool. The point grates along his shell without piercing. Broadtail grapples with the Squatter again, clutching with legs and his left pincer, while feeling for the back of its head with the tip of his right. The thing is struggling hard now. It's very strong. Its sharp tool pokes his shell again, making a small hole. He feels the hard covering on the thing's head and gets the tip of his pincer under the back edge. The thing twists and struggles, trying to grab his pincer with one limb but Broadtail gets all his limbs around it.

The outer covering is much tougher than what the Builders wear, but Broadtail is well-fed and angry and finally feels his pincer tip punch through. The water around him grows warm and he feels bubbles. The thing gives a last desperate twist of its body, snapping off one of Broadtail's smaller limbs, but he's got his big claw into it and drives it deeper into the hot flesh until he feels it grate on hard things. There's a spot where two hard things inside the flesh join together. He forces the tip between them and the Squatter stops moving.

ROB opened the hatch cautiously, ready to drop back into the water if he saw a Sholen. He pushed it open a few centimeters and looked through the crack. A human hand grabbed the edge and pulled it all the way open, and a moment later Alicia was tearing off Rob's helmet and half dragging him into the elevator.

"You are a madman! I love you!" she said between kisses. "How did you know I was here?"

"I didn't, I just hoped you were. Are you okay? Did they hurt you?"

"I am well. The Sholen did not harm me. They have moved about half the people from Hitode up to the surface, and they have been bringing down soldiers."

"Is that Robert Freeman?" said Pierre. Rob finally managed to take his gaze away from Alicia's face to survey the room. Pierre and Nadia were standing behind Alicia, both wearing the look of patronizing amusement that married people tend to give young couples.

"How did you get past the guard?" asked Pierre.

"We brought some allies. Ilmatarans," said Rob. "While I was cutting the cable and hooking up the towline, Broadtail—that's the one Alicia and I made contact with first—he grabbed the Sholen as he was coming out of the hatch."

"Is he all right?" asked Alicia.

"Broadtail's fine. The Sholen's dead and one of the 'tarans

got shot." Rob's mouth twisted. "I bet Broadtail's going to take the body back for dissection."

The elevator habitat began bobbing and pitching quite a bit as the sub got under way. Rob shut the hatch to keep water from sloshing in.

IRONA took the news calmly. He came to see Tizhos in the laboratory and smelled almost serene.

"The humans have cast aside all rules and are behaving like wild creatures. They have stolen the elevator capsule and cut the cable."

Tizhos felt a surge of irrational fear. *Trapped!* But it was followed almost immediately by the realization, *more time to work!*

Irona continued. "I have a new project for you, Tizhos. I want you to give it your full attention. Ignore everything else."

"Tell me the nature of this project." She tried not to sound annoyed.

"I want you to make a complete study of all the human files on Ilmataran language. Create a translation protocol that we can use. I expect you want to do it anyway."

"That sounds as though you want to speak to the Ilmatarans."

"I do indeed desire that."

"Tell me why."

"Shirozha reported Ilmatarans helping in the attack on the elevator. The humans have made an alliance with some of them, or conscripted them. It hardly matters which. Since they have cut the elevator cable we must fight them with only the resources we have here."

"I know all that."

"With a supply line to the surface we could afford to wait

them out. No longer. We must end this now. To accomplish that we need allies of our own. Natives who can speak with other natives and find where the humans lurk."

"I cannot believe you wish to make contact with the Ilmatarans! That goes against the entire purpose of this mission!"

Irona's scent turned dominating. "When we left Shalina the Consensus ordered us to prevent future contamination of this world by the humans. That remains the purpose of this mission."

"But you suggest causing contamination of our own!"

"I see no alternative. We must choose between limited, controlled contact—which we can end as soon as we accomplish our mission—and *unlimited, uncontrolled* contamination by the humans. Indoctrinating them into human ideologies, distorting the natural evolution of their society, teaching them harmful practices."

Tizhos thought it over. Irona had a point. And more important—she would get the chance to study Ilmatarans! In person and close up! No matter what purpose Irona hoped to accomplish, Tizhos would see more of the Ilmatarans than any Sholen before or to come.

"I will do all I can," she said.

THEY towed the elevator back to the Ilmataran settlement, taking a roundabout course and stopping several times to see if the Sholen were following. Rob had hoped it would take them a while to figure out what had happened, but according to Alicia the Sholen guard had reported the attack before going out to get killed.

Pierre questioned the wisdom of camping at the Ilmataran settlement. "Wouldn't it be better to pick a hidden spot? Make it harder for the Sholen to find us—and keep from involving the Ilmatarans in all this?"

"The 'tarans are already involved. They chose to be. Broadtail and the others who helped with the elevator raid all volunteered. Anyway, it doesn't make sense to disperse. We need their help to survive, even with the elevator's life support and supplies."

A fleet of Ilmatarans rose from Longpincer's vent farm to greet them as the submarine towed the elevator capsule to the settlement. Broadtail had them tie ropes to the capsule's support skids, and then humans and Ilmatarans began the complicated process of lowering it to the seafloor.

Because the hatch was on the bottom of the elevator capsule they couldn't just drop it anywhere. Unless it was properly level water would flood in every time they went in or out.

Josef operated the sub, staying in touch with Rob via laser link. The elevator's comm system was down, so Alicia had to hang on just outside the hatch, sticking her head inside to relay messages by shouting. Nadia worked the capsule's buoyancy controls by hand, with only a depth gauge and Alicia's eyeballs for guidance.

Outside, four teams of Ilmatarans held the ropes and stood braced on the sea bottom, straining to keep the capsule centered above its intended resting place. Broadtail and Rob communicated by clicks, but there was an awful lag.

Rob's biggest worry was Alicia. Though the elevator's skids allowed two meters of clearance below the access hatch, they were still pretty flimsy. He was terrified that one of the skids would give if they dropped the capsule too quickly, and Alicia would wind up crushed. When it was finally resting on the bottom, he realized he was holding his breath.

BOSSING a team of Longpincer's apprentices and tenants as they help the Builders gives Broadtail an odd mix of feelings—as if he is hungry and full at once. It is good to be in charge, organizing teams and telling them when to haul as if he is a landowner.

But the work also reminds him of his old home, and the memories make him sad. Whenever he remembers Sandyslope he is startled by how much he still desires the place. If he concentrates he can remember the way the water tasted, the feel of the stones, and the chill of the currents.

With a patch of clear ground he could trace the entire Sandyslope pipe system, with all the valves, leaks, and uneven flow spots precisely marked. He can even remember what grows where, and the flavor of the different crops. His jellyfronds always get a sour edge from the sulfur in the stones, but that also makes his spine-beds taller and fatter than any others in Continuous Abundance.

Not his spine-beds. Smoothpincer's spine-beds. Broadtail wonders if they are even there anymore. He remembers Longfeeler suggesting putting in some fiber plants there, as even good-quality spines don't fetch as many beads as rope does.

Longpincer's apprentices haul on the rope to keep the floating shelter in the right position as the Builders lower it. Broadtail goes over to inspect it before they tie off. Work is better than remembering his lost property.

As he runs his eating-tendrils along the rope, making sure there is no slackness, Broadtail wonders if Builder 1 and the other strangers have any feelings as deep and unbreakable as the bond between an adult and his home. Certainly the strangers move about with little sign of grief for their lost shelter. Do they have homes in whatever faraway place they come from? Perhaps they do—in which case all their shelters in the ocean are like a traveler's quarters.

Broadtail intends to ask Builder 1 about this, although he is not certain the stranger knows enough words to understand the question.

* * *

TIZHOS waited alone in the cold ocean more than a kilometer from the station. She had only her helmet spotlight to keep the darkness at bay. She tapped the control in her hand and the big portable hydrophone unit began blaring its message into the water.

The humans had more sensitive hearing than any Sholen, and even they had been unable to duplicate the spoken language of the Ilmatarans. Tizhos hadn't even bothered. Instead she had concentrated on creating a Sholen-to-Ilmataran lexicon based on the native beings' written number code, using the Sholen-to-English dictionary and the captured notes.

The method was horribly inelegant and cumbersome, and it required literate Ilmatarans to understand it. Tizhos had no way to know if all the inhabitants of the region even used the same number code to write with. If they didn't, she might be broadcasting gibberish, or horrible insults.

And if they weren't literate at all, she was simply advertising her position to any hostile native or predator within hearing range. With the hydrophone cranked up to maximum volume that meant nearly five kilometers.

Tizhos had her all-purpose tool in her lower left hand, set to knife mode, but she didn't think it would do her much good if something like an *Aenocampus* or a band of Ilmatarans with spears decided to attack her.

STRONGPINCER hears a sound. It's a rhythmic tapping or clicking. He can't quite figure out what is making it. It doesn't quite sound like someone hitting something, or clicking pincers. He moves clear of the rocks where he is resting with his little band and listens.

Numbers. It's sounding out numbers. That means an adult, probably a towndweller. The noise is a long way off, which means it's very loud. Why is someone making numbers so loudly?

He remembers raiding the schoolmaster's place, and listening to the old teacher telling the young ones about making words by tying knots in strings.

"Smallbody!" he calls. "Come up here!"

Smallbody scrambles up to the top of the rock.

"What does that noise say?"

Smallbody is silent, straining to hear. "It says 'Adults ocean approach food adults multiple food.'"

"What does that mean?"

"I'm not sure."

"'Multiple food,' you say? That sounds fine with me. Wake the others. Let's go."

TIZHOS was about to give up and go back to the station when her sonar unit started clicking. She called up the visual display and saw a group of large creatures approaching swiftly. They were drawn up in a crescent formation, and held the alignment as they came. Ilmatarans.

Her suit stank of fear, and the hand gripping her all-purpose tool ached from tension. But she resisted the urge to flee. Instead she touched the control unit and turned down the volume on the hydrophone. No sense in deafening her guests.

THIS is utterly strange, Strongpincer thinks. No adults within hearing, or if there are, they are hiding. Just a large animal and some made objects sitting on the sea bottom making noise.

Strongpincer halts his band when they're about three body-lengths from the thing. The repeating message stops, there is a brief silence, then a different pattern of clicks.

Smallbody translates. "'Me and multiple adults are a group.'"

"I remember you going to a school," Strongpincer says to Smallbody. "Do you know what that thing is?"

"No. I don't even remember anyone telling me about anything like that. But it's making numbers."

Strongpincer doesn't like being puzzled. "Kill it, save the meat, take the stuff." He starts forward, choosing where he will stab it.

The numbers are replaced by a horrible noise, like the schoolmaster's noisemaker but even louder. It is like being bashed in the head with a huge stone. Strongpincer clutches the sea bottom with his legs and flattens himself into the silt, not daring to move.

The noise stops. When Strongpincer can hear again, he pings. The others are all hunkered down as well. The thing is still standing before them. It touches some of its objects and the number clicking begins again.

"Smallbody," Strongpincer pings. "What is it saying?"

"'Adults fold pincers.'"

"Tell it we agree. Then ask it what it wants."

A long exchange of clicks and pings between Smallbody and the thing. Finally Smallbody says, "It's hard to understand it, but I think it wants to hire us."

"Hire us?"

"Yes, it says it has tools and rope and things for us if we do what it asks."

"What does it want us to do?"

After some clicking, Smallbody answers, "It wants us to go to villages and talk to other adults."

Strongpincer feels himself grow calmer. "We can do that. Now let's talk about the price."

* * *

TIZHOS led the Ilmatarans back to the station. It was not her idea. She was getting tired and cold, and her suit stank despite the pheromone filters. When she finally packed up her things to go, the Ilmatarans tagged along. At Hitode they camped around the nuclear power unit's heat exchanger, snatching up some of the small swimmers that lived in the warm outflow, and scraping microorganisms off the rocks nearby.

She pulled off her suit and dried off, then went to talk with Irona. She would have preferred to eat and rest first, but she knew he would come and bother her if she didn't report in.

"As you requested, I avoided speaking of any scientific matters. They do not know where we come from. Interestingly, these Ilmatarans did not display much curiosity about that, either. They seemed more interested in getting as much food and as many tools as they could in exchange for helping."

Irona gave an approving gesture, but added, "Try to keep the number of tools small. Give them food or consumables. Leave as little trace of our presence as possible."

Tizhos tried to keep from taking an irritated posture. "I have identified some problems with doing that. They do not seem to enjoy what our foodmaker produces. Giving them food would require someone to catch native organisms."

"What about all these things the humans have stockpiled? They have hundreds of native creatures in jars or frozen."

"You would let the Ilmatarans *eat* those samples?"

"I doubt we can afford the propellant to take them all back to Shalina. We will incinerate as much as possible."

For once Tizhos is glad that she reeks of Ilmataran seawater, because it's all she can do to keep from flooding the room with hostile scents. She even feels a slight urge to bite Irona. But she controls her feelings and says only, "The humans treated those samples with preservatives. I do not believe the Ilmatarans can eat them anymore."

"Ah, well. You really cannot think of anything consumable we can give the natives?"

"No. But I doubt giving them tools would cause any problems. We can restrict our gifts to things like ropes, bags, knives, and nets. The Ilmatarans have all those things already; only the materials would differ, and since they have no way to make things of metal or polymers, the objects would not affect their society. In a few years, when the ropes and nets wear out and the knives corrode, no trace of us will remain."

"I suppose so. Very well—I approve."

"I do have one other thing to request. Could you arrange for some of the Guardians to give a demonstration of their weapons for the Ilmatarans?"

"Why?"

"I want these Ilmatarans to understand that we can harm them. I do not trust them. They appear to be a small, heavily armed band, traveling far from civilization and in no hurry to get anywhere. I suspect some community may have exiled them for some crime."

"Some kind of breakaway group?"

"Or social predators. Possibly both—they may follow a consensus based on using force against nonmembers."

"Ah, yes. A common feature of primitive societies," said Irona.

"Indeed," said Tizhos without a hint of sarcasm. "So a demonstration of our weapons would make it much easier to prevent conflict."

"I approve. Now go and get some food and rest, Tizhos. You look exhausted."

* * *

STRONGPINCER and Shellcrusher approach the town cautiously. Strongpincer doesn't remember ever robbing anyone around here, but news does travel and townies are always suspicious. This is the third town he remembers visiting on this journey. The two of them are working their way along the edge of the shallows, cutting across the rifts. Strongpincer figures news would travel easily along the rift trade routes.

A youngster on patrol at the edge of town stops them. "What is your business in Bubbling Vent?"

"Trade," says Strongpincer. "We have goods from Deep Fissure and the waters beyond the Shallow Basin."

The youngster pings them, loud enough to hear what they've been eating. "All right. You may pass into the town. Private lands are marked with stones. Town law applies in common areas. Only town militia may carry spears longer than their bodies. Interfering with drag nets means you must replace the lost catch and repair any damage."

"We promise to follow your laws."

The town is small, but it sits on a trade route so is likely to get lots of news. Strongpincer leads Shellcrusher to the market, an open space downcurrent of the main vent. There are only a few other vendors: another traveling trader with a string of immature towfins, one of the locals selling stingers, and a schoolmaster with some apprentices for sale. Strongpincer finds a clear spot near the stinger-seller and lays out his wares.

The odd flavor of his items diffusing through the water draws some business. First some idle apprentices and tenant workers come to feel what he's got. Then the landowners drift over.

"You're selling string?" asks one, feeling a reel of the strangers' cable with his feeding tendrils.

"It's as thin as string, but stronger than any rope."

"Nonsense," says the landowner.

"Break it, then," says Strongpincer. "You can have as much as you can break off the reel."

The landowner's a burly fellow with heavy pincers worn blunt by digging. He wraps a couple of loops of the cord around each pincer and pulls. He pulls harder. He pulls until his joints grind and the thick shell of his pincers begins to creak under the strain.

"That is tough!"

"It's flexible, too. You can knit it into nets which can hold anything."

"How much?" the burly fellow asks.

"Ten beads for a pincer's length." It's a ridiculous price. Normally cord is priced by the cable-length, not the pincer-length. But nobody objects. Burly asks for five lengths.

"How do you cut it?" asks an apprentice.

Strongpincer is glad the youth asked. "With this!" he whips out another alien tool—a kind of artificial pincer made of something harder than stone but as light as shell. He grips the handles in his pincers and snips off a length of cord.

They do great business, selling cord, some of the cutting tools, and some incredibly strong awls. Shellcrusher begins to complain of hunger, so Strongpincer sends her with some beads to buy food. She comes back with cakes of roe and a couple of bunches of worms. Strongpincer lets her eat first, then leaves her in charge of the stall while he crawls aside to enjoy his own food.

A local approaches. From her grooved pincers Strongpincer guesses she's the town rope-twister. She sits beside Strongpincer and listens to him eating for a while.

"That's amazing cord you've got," she says.

"Stronger than anything."

"I remember examining it after buying a reel. It feels like a

single fiber, not a twisted cord. And it doesn't taste like anything I recognize. Where does it come from?"

"Very far away," says Strongpincer.

"That's right—don't tell anyone. You've got a nice thing going and don't want to spoil it. I understand completely."

Strongpincer decides it's time. "It's difficult, selling my stuff
town to town. I don't know what's in demand and there are
bandits in the cold water. I don't know when I'm getting
cheated or when I'm asking too much. I worry about townsfolk
robbing me."

"A merchant's life is full of uncertainty," she agrees.

"I remember hearing about strange creatures," he says.
"Things nobody remembers anything about. Do you recall hearing anything like that?"

"Strange creatures? Are you interested in things of that sort?
Because Spinylegs is the fellow you should talk with, then."

"Why?"

"He likes to learn about things. I believe he knows about
every kind of creature in the sea. And anything he can't recall
touching himself is in one of his reels of writing. I expect he's
got more cord than I do, but all tied in knots."

Strongpincer is puzzled. "Why? Is he a schoolmaster?"

"No, he just likes to know things. And he's a landowner so
he can afford to waste beads on it."

A fool, Strongpincer decides. But possibly a useful one. If this
landowner likes to waste his wealth learning things, maybe he
knows what Strongpincer is trying to discover. "Where does he
live?"

"He has the Great Stone property—but he's not there now.
Nobody but apprentices running the place."

"Well where is he, then?"

"He's on a journey. A friend of his called Longpincer has a
big property downcurrent from here about a thousand cables.

Spinylegs visits him to talk about animals and plants and old things."

"Downcurrent along the rift?"

"Yes. If you plan to go there, be sure to mention I'm sending you."

"I intend to." Perfect! Strongpincer imagines that he and Shellcrusher are capable of bullying a couple of foolish land-owners into telling what he needs to know. And if they have some valuable items lying around, so much the better.

BROADTAIL is helping some of Longpincer's ten-ants put guy lines on a standing net when an apprentice pings him. "Excuse me, Broadtail, sir, but the boss wants you."

"Very well. Here—hold on to this post, and when it's just leaning into the current tell them to tie off the line."

He swims back to the house, where a clutch of adults are gathered. There's a strange towfin with a large cargo bundle beneath it, and an adult giving some kind of commercial pitch.

"Cable absolutely unbreakable by any pull! Netting so fine even the tiniest swimmers can't pass through!"

Longpincer swims up to intercept Broadtail and takes him aside. "You hear them?"

"I do. A pair of traveling merchants. What of it?"

"Listen to the talk some more."

The merchant booms, "I challenge any adult—any pair of adults—to sever this cord. You can use any tool you wish, but you cannot cut it! Anyone care to try?"

"Absurd," says Broadtail to Longpincer. "Borrow one of Builder 1's tools and snip it in half!"

"I have felt and tasted this merchant's wares, Broadtail. They are very like some of the Builder tools and gear."

"But how?"

"I am not sure. Possibly another group of Builders, selling

their gear to a merchant in exchange for help? Possibly some cache of theirs, now in the grip of scavengers? Or—possibly Builder 1 is not telling us everything."

"Builder 1 speaks of strangers unlike him, occupying his home and driving him into the wilderness."

"Could these things be theirs?" Longpincer asks.

"That captures a netful of other questions," says Broadtail. "Is this merchant a thief selling stolen goods of those other strangers, or are they his by trade, or is he their servant?"

"Let us speak with him."

The two scientists approach the merchant. He is selling a length of un-cuttable cord to one of Longpincer's tenants, and the landowner waits courteously until the trade is done.

"Come aside with me," says Longpincer. "I have matters of importance to discuss."

The merchant scuttles over, and as he approaches, Broadtail catches a familiar tang in the water. He knows this adult. Who is he? The memory of Onepincer's school comes to mind. The bandit! He risks seeming rude and pings the fellow to make sure—a little larger and not quite so smooth-shelled, but it's unmistakably the same adult. Strongpincer is his name. Broadtail says nothing, not wishing to open his pincer yet.

"Sir, your wares are extraordinary," says Longpincer. "Can you tell me where they are made?"

"Far away. Very far indeed."

"How far? I own craftwork from beyond the shallows and even from the deep basins. None of it resembles this at all. Let me put you at ease—I am only curious because I am a scholar. I have no wish to trespass on your trade."

"Oh, surely not," says Strongpincer. "But others may, and a secret makes many echoes when it's spoken."

"Yet I suspect I know the origin of these things," says Longpincer casually. "I offer you one of my beads if you will answer a single question: are the makers adults like ourselves?"

There is a long silence before Strongpincer speaks. "No."

"Two beads for a second answer. How many limbs do the makers have?"

"I cannot answer," Strongpincer replies promptly.

Broadtail taps quietly on Longpincer's tail. "Leave him. Must talk privately."

"I must beg your pardon," says Longpincer. "I must determine how much of your goods I need—and what I can afford to trade. Please excuse me."

Strongpincer turns back to the throng of tenants while Longpincer and Broadtail hurry off to the entryway of the house.

"He is a bandit. I remember him robbing a schoolmaster, and I suspect him of attacking my exploring party. He calls himself Strongpincer."

"His refusal to answer my second question is significant," says Longpincer. "He knows there are two kinds of strangers with differing numbers of limbs. And I suspect he knows they are in conflict."

Once again Broadtail is startled by Longpincer's thinking. "True!"

"But we do not know where his loyalty stands."

"That I can answer," says Broadtail. "He is a bandit and his loyalty is to himself."

"We can also deduce that he is not allied with the stranger you call Builder 1."

"I believe his goods are stolen," says Broadtail. "It makes perfect sense: this bandit comes across the other strangers— the ones I call Squatters. Perhaps he overcomes one in an ambush, or perhaps he simply takes a cache of goods left unguarded.

He wishes to conceal this, so he answers you evasively when you ask about the origin of the items."

Longpincer considers this. "But how does he know of Builder 1's people, then?"

"I cannot explain that," Broadtail admits. "It is extremely unlikely for one bandit to come across two sets of strangers by chance."

"Then there are three possible sources of his knowledge: the Builders, the Squatters, and—ourselves," says Longpincer.

"I recall Builder 1 being entirely ignorant of how to tap out words at our first meeting. That rules out his people."

"And this bandit is a stranger here, which rules out any of us. A good thing, too—I should hate to think any of the Company were trying to gain knowledge secretly, hoarding it like scarce roe instead of passing it around generously."

"Which leaves the Squatters," says Broadtail. "This bandit is their hired worker. But doing what? If the Squatters hold Builder 1's home, why send someone to search for him? Surely no creature could be so evil as to harry poor Builder 1 from shelter to shelter."

"Spying," says Longpincer. "They fear Builder 1, and wish to know if he plans revenge against them. Anyone would, in such a situation. So they hire this bandit to seek him out and report on what he is doing."

"I suggest that I wait with some of the Company just outside your boundaries and kill this spy as he leaves. I promise you a share of his goods," says Broadtail.

"I wish to know more before planning action," says Longpincer. "I propose serving this merchant, or bandit, a very large meal and giving him as many stings as he wants. The food makes him content, the stings make him irresponsible—I imagine him telling us much he might otherwise keep secret."

"But what do you intend when the dinner is done?"

"I think it best to let him go."

"I imagine him telling the Squatters! Isn't it better for him to simply disappear into your trash midden?"

"I do not have the reputation of a landowner who kills and robs passing merchants, Broadtail. Bitterwater is remote and I worry about traders avoiding my place if they fear being robbed. Besides, we have no way to know if he suspects the Builders are here."

"He isn't deaf, and neither are your tenants and servants. Can you keep all of them silent about such amazing news?"

"I don't know. But I do know I don't want you attacking this adult."

Broadtail is unhappy, but agrees. He sets himself the task of remaining with the bandit, keeping him away from the shelter inhabited by the Builders. He sits and listens as the "merchant" sells a great deal of strong cord, some unbreakable tools, and a quantity of superfine netting. Longpincer's tenants and staff buy all he is willing to sell.

The merchant takes payment in Longpincer's beads, then sends off his helper to spend them. That means Broadtail can't keep both of them in hearing at once.

He hears Holdhard nearby and gets her to help. "Stay here and listen to the merchant. Ask him many questions, keep him here. Do not speak of the Builders."

"I understand," she says.

"Good." He crawls after the merchant's helper. He recognizes her flavor in the water: she's the big one who can crack an adult's shell with her pincers.

He stays back, just close enough to hear her scuttling along. She probably knows he's behind her. Broadtail remembers the attack on his expedition and grows more angry. He hopes she doesn't like him following her. He hopes she tries to fight him. A fight makes everything simple: even Longpincer's strong notions of hospitality don't extend to strangers brawling with guests.

But if she does notice him, she gives no sign and shows no anger. She visits Longpincer's storehouses and the homes of his more prosperous tenants. She trades Longpincer's beads for small, valuable goods: fertile eggs, hot-water crops, diamonds. All very sensible.

Broadtail feels momentary doubt. Maybe they are just merchants. He might be mistaken about them being bandits. They might have an innocent explanation of where the goods come from.

Then her course bends toward the shelter holding the Builders. Innocent or not, he can't let her ping them. Broadtail leaves the ground and swims, beating his flukes noisily and dodging past nets and rigging.

The big female turns. He must sound hostile, swimming toward her like some hunter, for she raises her open pincers and braces herself. Broadtail forces himself to slow and drop to the bottom a couple of arm-lengths away from her.

"I come to warn you," he says. "You are walking toward danger."

"Danger?" she says. Her speech is slow and overly precise. A real cold-water barbarian, this one.

"Poison things grow over there," he says, gesturing. "They make adults sick. Stay away."

"What poison things?" She folds her pincers slowly.

Broadtail is a scholar and remembers being a landowner. He begins to reel off the most alarming poison growths he can think of. "There's a nasty colony of gill-blight down there, and since nobody wants to go clear them out some stinging tendril-worms are nesting as well. So please, stay away."

"Very well," she says, though he suspects she doesn't believe him. Too bad. She's just a visitor here anyway. If Longpincer—or Broadtail acting on his behalf—wants to keep something secret, he has every right to do so. If she doesn't like it she can leave, and Broadtail rather likes that idea.

She alters course and trundles toward some of the smaller tenant homes. Broadtail considers his mental map of the estate. From those homes she can cut back toward where the Builders are staying by following the sandy slope. He decides to wait there for a while and intercept her.

He finds a comfortable spot where the sand isn't too unstable and sits quietly. While he waits his thoughts wander, but he is well-fed and does not sleep.

Broadtail thinks about his own place in the world. For now he is Longpincer's guest, but he hopes to change that. He remembers meeting others like that—adults with some accomplishment but no property, living off some admiring landowner. It can be a good life, but it does not survive the death of the admirer. When an apprentice inherits, the permanent guests are the first to go. If they are lucky, and still fit, they may stay on as tenants or servants.

Broadtail is not a greedy adult, but he does have his pride. That is not what he imagines for himself. But what does he imagine? What does he want? In the quiet he tries to hear his own thoughts.

He does not imagine owning land again. Every property has too many apprentices waiting to inherit. He remembers cases of landowners naming a favored friend as heir and they always end badly. Legal challenges, labor troubles, sometimes ambush and murder in open water. And Longpincer is devoted to the Bitterwater property.

Not a guest, not a landowner. A crafter, perhaps? Living as a tenant but earning his own way? He is nearly as good at netmaking as any professional, and of course he is an excellent writer. Can one get paid for that? Not very well.

Fishing is tiring and leaves little opportunity for scholarship. He is not a good trader. He has no taste for mercenary soldiering. He knows a lot about plumbing and flow, but every landowner is a self-proclaimed expert about that.

What he wants to do is to study the Builders and learn about the worlds beyond the ice. Is there a way to get paid for that? Broadtail doesn't know of one.

A sound draws his attention. Someone is approaching along the slope from the direction of the tenant homes. It sounds like the big bandit female. She passes a few arm-lengths below him without noticing him, heading for the Builders' shelter.

His position is perfect. He can spring down on her and get a pincer behind her head-shield before she hears him. It is the logical thing to do—she is a bandit, a murderer herself. The secret of the Builders must be protected.

Broadtail sits quietly and lets her pass. It is far easier to plan and talk about killing someone by surprise than to do it. The bandits are capable of it, but Broadtail realizes that he is not. "You!" he calls out.

She hears him and turns, pincers raised unambiguously to fight.

"I remind you that place is not safe. The landowner forbids anyone to go there."

"I do not remember him telling me. You are not the owner. I go where I choose."

"I don't wish to fight you," says Broadtail.

"Then let me pass. I am not afraid to fight you."

Broadtail feels the frustration of all vent-dwellers speaking with barbarians. For a civilized adult, being peaceable and willing to negotiate is an admirable thing, worthy of praise. But

among the barbarians those who do not fight are quickly bullied to death. And this barbarian is bigger than Broadtail.

"As you choose," he says. "But I go now to tell Longpincer.
You are not behaving as a proper visitor and I imagine you and
your companion being expelled for this foolishness."

"I am not afraid of you," she says again.

STRONGPINCER and Shellcrusher leave the
settlement, tired and hungry. He is rather annoyed at being
forced to go without eating any of the wonderful-tasting meal he
remembers. The packed travel food seems dull and unsatisfying.

But they have important news for their patrons, and perhaps
it is best not to wait. Shellcrusher is certain that the creatures
they seek are concealed at Bitterwater.

He caches the trade goods, stripping down to just enough food
for a fast swim back. Strongpincer has the faint echo of an idea:
he suspects his patrons plan to attack Bitterwater and recapture
the creatures there. Strongpincer imagines the landowner and
many of his apprentices dying in that fight. Which leaves the
vent in need of a new master. Why not . . . Strongpincer? With
Shellcrusher and his alien patrons supporting him, he does
not imagine any tenant daring to oppose him.

As they swim he half-dozes, letting his thoughts wander
even as he keeps up a steady beat of his tail. A warm house of
his own. Servants to make meals whenever he wants. Thick
layers of weeds and crawlers on his shell. Nothing to do but
molt and grow.

"I RECALL her getting close enough to the Builders'
shelter to ping it," says Broadtail.

"Do you recall the reason for not stopping her?" asks Sharpfrill.

"She is a very large barbarian bandit. I am not. And it is not my property to fight on."

Those who know his history tap quiet explanations to the others.

"I remember specifically asking Broadtail to avoid violence," says Longpincer. "It is never proper to attack a visitor who commits no harm or theft."

"But now they go to tell the Squatters what they remember hearing," Broadtail points out. "I suggest we plan our course."

"Your Builder friends are my guests," says Longpincer. "They are under my protection."

"Then how do we protect them?" asks Broadtail. "Builder 1 says he fears the Squatters coming here and attempting to recapture them."

"I am sending out scouts now to alert us of their coming," says Longpincer. "Beyond that, we simply wait. My apprentices and tenants all know what to do in case of attack."

"NOW that they know, maybe we should give up," said Rob.

"You are afraid?" asked Alicia.

"Of course I'm afraid! In particular I'm afraid you'll get hurt. Last time it was just the two of us and they could afford to be careful. This time—it's going to be ugly. There's going to be microtorps flying all over, and it sounds like the Sholen have some Ilmataran thugs working for them, and God knows what else."

"We will think of ways to trick them. You have been very clever."

"That's bullshit and you know it. Maybe we can fool a drone, but what about a Sholen microtorp? They blew up Dickie when he tried to fight."

She was quiet for a while. "I cannot simply give up, Robert. And we have no place we can run away to."

"Will you promise me one thing, at least? That you'll surrender? No glorious last stand?"

"I promise—if you will do the same."

"Okay, then. I'll try to be very clever one last time."

TIZHOS and Irona stood on the sea bottom near the moon pool entrance to Hitode Station. Their Ilmataran allies floated a few meters away while one laboriously tapped out a message.

"He says they have found the Terrans," said Tizhos.

"Excellent!" said Irona. "Tell them we leave in—oh, six hours. That should be enough time for everyone to rest and prepare. He must show us where they are."

"He does mention what sounds like a problem. The humans have taken refuge in an Ilmataran community."

"As we suspected. That does sound bad. Ask him how large a community. We need to know how many Ilmatarans know about them."

"If the community includes a large number of individuals I fear we cannot preserve the secret."

"Never mind that," said Irona. "Get specific directions to this community and try to locate it on the maps we have of the sea bottom. I must begin preparing the Guardians."

As Irona paddled up into the station, Tizhos consulted her lexicon and tapped out a message to the waiting Ilmatarans. "Immobility here. Food. Multiple swimming. Fighting."

They seemed to understand, and Tizhos handed out the supplies of small creatures from the drift nets. She tried to engage the pair who understood the number-code language in conversation.

"Adults grasp fighting?" she asked.

"Grasp fighting quickly," the Ilmataran replied, and Tizhos found that highly depressing. The more she understood about the Ilmatarans, the more she found herself disliking these allies Irona had recruited. They seemed little more than thieves, preying upon the labor of the vent settlements.

She knew how they must appear to Irona—small groups with a tight consensus, living in wild regions, attacking those who sought to manipulate the environment instead of accommodating to it. Noble primitives. But to Tizhos they seemed like entropy itself, constantly warring with the little outposts of knowledge and order.

Two of the larger Ilmatarans snatched the food away from one of the others and threatened him with their big pincers when he tried to take some back. Tizhos tossed a few extra dead swimmers his way. He got one or two, but the bigger ones grabbed the rest.

When they finished eating, she called up the map display and began trying to figure out where the Terrans had hidden. The Ilmatarans used prevailing currents rather than the inertial grid of her own navigation system, which made the task much more difficult. Fortunately they had a reasonably standardized and accurate system for measuring distance.

After more than twenty minutes she believed she had an accurate fix. All their route descriptions seemed to lead back to one isolated vent community—the one where the human Henri Kerlerec had died.

Scientists. The Ilmatarans at the vent had dissected Henri Kerlerec because they wanted to learn. Now Irona wanted to attack them and prevent them from learning. Tizhos felt ill.

ROB surfaced in the hatchway of the repurposed elevator capsule and opened his helmet. "They're coming! Broadtail says one of Longpincer's scouts just reported in."

"How long do we have?" Alicia called down from her hammock.

"No way to tell. Quantified linear time is still a crazy theory around here. I figure a minimum of one hour. Probably more than that—if they're smart they'll let their 'tarans rest up before the fighting starts. Broadtail and Longpincer are having a war council down at the main house. Wake up Josef and come on when you're ready."

FOURTEEN

THE scout gives her report to the assembled company. "I remember swimming as far as these stones on my patrol. I remember resting there and hearing this sound." She imitates it: a steady chaotic churning noise superimposed on a heavy rhythmic swish-swish.

"I hear swimming adults and a towfin, but what is that other noise?" asks Longpincer.

"The Squatters," says Broadtail. "They make paddling noises like the Builders, but with a tail beat."

"Can we study how your Builders swim?" asks Raggedclaw.

"Certainly," says Broadtail. "After the battle."

"What battle?"

"The Squatters come here to fight," Longpincer explains gently.

"What? Why?" Raggedclaw sounds highly irritated at the news.

"They wish to steal Broadtail's Builders."

"That is impossible! I still wish to learn how they can stand erect without a shell," says Raggedclaw.

"Which is why we fight the Squatters," says Longpincer.

"How many do you remember hearing?" Broadtail asks the scout, desperate to get the conversation back on course.

"Twenty-two adults and one large towfin, and maybe twelve of the alien swimmers."

"The adults are bandits and wild children," says Broadtail. "They carry spears and their own strong pincers, but little else."

"My people all remember many fights with bandits," says Longpincer. "Raiders are only brave if they are winning. Stand firm against them and they flee."

There is a loud commotion of scrapes and thumps, and three of the Builders come into the room. Builder 2 raises a forelimb. "Greeting. Adults build fight reel."

"Yes," says Broadtail. "We know how to fight the bandits, but not the Squatters. Can you tell us what to expect?"

Builder confers with the other two before replying.

"Squatters carry"—a long pause and much Builder chatter—"spear tools stab adult one cable."

"How is this possible?" asks Longpincer. "No creature, not even an alien, can carry a spear a cable long."

"It is possible we are not understanding something," says Broadtail. He asks Builder, "How can a spear be a cable?"

"Not spear. Push swim spear stab adult. Or swim spear loud sound."

The remaining Bitterwater Company scholars listen in puzzlement. "Sounds like babble to me," says Raggedclaw.

Broadtail asks Builder 2 to show them what it means. There follows a remarkable demonstration as the alien takes several items and uses its upper limbs to propel them through the water away from it. No adult has limbs that can do that, and all the company present think it is quite impressive.

"I think it means bolt-launchers!" says Broadtail. Longpincer orders several bolt-launchers brought and demonstrated for the Builders. They chatter excitedly, and Builder 2 says "Yes" several times.

"Well, if that's all we have to worry about there is little danger," says Longpincer. "Bolt-launchers may be a threat to soft-skinned beings like Builders or Squatters, but I know my shell is thick enough to stop one unless it is very close."

But something is nagging at Broadtail's thoughts. "I remember capturing the hanging shelter. The Squatter makes Crestback fly apart. I think that may be what the Builders mean."

"Builder 2 may exaggerate."

"Or not." Broadtail clicks a question to Builder 2: "Launch bolt cable?"

"Cable, two cable," it laboriously replies. "Bolt swim."

"I think I understand," says Broadtail to the Company. "The Squatter weapons have bolts which swim through the water— like the Builder moving shelter, only smaller. And then they burst apart like a thin-walled pipe. They may be very dangerous indeed."

"I imagine having such a weapon," says Longpincer. "In battle I stay far from my enemies and slay them with bolts, but they cannot stab me because they cannot reach me."

They all think about that for a while. The Company members who are craftworkers are intrigued, imagining a town protecting itself against raiders with a handful of armed militia. Those who own remote properties like Longpincer imagine bandits capable of standing off and slaughtering defenders.

"We must fight them as though stalking swift prey," says Holdhard. "Stay silent until they are close enough to grasp."

Broadtail keeps up a running translation of the important remarks for the benefit of the aliens.

"Builder head silent," Builder 1 points out. "Squatter head silent."

Broadtail reminds the others. "The Squatters have the same silent sense as the Builders. They can find us without pinging. We must do more than remain still and quiet to surprise them."

ROB and Broadtail were placed well forward, watching and listening for signs of the Sholen force. If the attackers were trying to be silent, they'd need lights to keep together and see where they were going. If they were staying dark, they'd need the occasional active sonar ping. Either way, one of the two scouts would notice.

It occurred to Rob that just a few days ago it would have been impossible for him to sit on the sea bottom in silence and total darkness this long without completely freaking. Now it almost felt restful. He had deliberately chosen an uncomfortable spot so that the hard stones pressing into his chest and thighs would help him keep awake.

He felt around for his spear. It was a two-meter piece of "wood" (more like biological fiberglass, really) from an Ilmataran "plant." The tip was a leaf-shaped piece of carved obsidian, wickedly sharp. If everything went according to plan, at some point in the near future Rob was going to try to push that obsidian spearpoint into the vital organs of a Sholen or enemy Ilmataran.

Back before the ultimatum, or even during the first "camping trip" period in the Coquille, such a thought would have been completely absurd, like imagining himself biting off his own left thumb. Except for one or two inconclusive grade-school spats and an embarrassing drunken shoving match in college, Rob had never intentionally harmed another person.

Now he felt no reluctance at all. He'd been angry with the Sholen pretty much constantly since Gishora and Tizhos had first stepped out of the elevator. Now at least he could let it out.

He was afraid for himself, of course, and for Alicia. Just about any injury here would be fatal, and she would certainly be in the thick of it, carrying the same kind of spear.

He held the spear loosely, just resting his hand on the shaft, ready to pick it up.

Something caught his attention. Out in the blackness he could see a faint spark. No, two sparks. Were they tiny and close up, or far away? He moved his head around, trying to get some parallax. The sparks stayed put. They looked like two stars now, faintly green.

He reached over to Broadtail and tapped from memory, "Adults come."

The Ilmataran clicked softly in acknowledgment, and the two of them turned and began moving back to the defensive positions around the Bitterwater vent. Rob didn't dare show a light, so he held onto a trailing line attached to Broadtail's harness and did his best to keep up.

They followed a wide zigzag course, pausing occasionally for Broadtail to quietly ping out a warning to the fighters lying hidden on the seafloor. Nearly a quarter of Longpincer's retainers were currently dispersed on the silty bottom about a hundred meters in front of the vent mound, buried under a thin layer of mud and old netting. The Ilmatarans were very good at masking their sonar signatures, but the humans had been hard-pressed to make sure they couldn't be seen by Sholen eyes. How do you teach a blind being how not to be seen? Ultimately, the answer was just to cover them up and hope for the best.

The plan was for the camouflaged fighters to wait until the invaders were among them, then suddenly attack at close range. According to Broadtail, this was a well-known tactic mentioned in many of the Ilmataran classic books on warfare. They were gambling that neither the alien Sholen nor their semiliterate Ilmataran bandit allies had heard of the ploy.

Up ahead Rob could hear the faint constant rumble of the Bitterwater vent. There were tall nets rigged all around the heart of Longpincer's holding. Again, standard tactics against barbarian raiders. They had to either try to get through the nets, in which case the defenders could move in with spears, or swim up over the barrier, exposing their thin-shelled undersides to bolts from below.

Broadtail clicked out a password and one of Longpincer's apprentices untied a section of net to let them in. Rob left Broadtail and followed a guideline to where his drones were waiting. There were two of them still operational, and Rob had spent an afternoon converting them into weapons. There was nothing subtle about the armed drones: since he couldn't come up with a decent explosive warhead, Rob had just attached the largest of Alicia's dissecting knives to the front of each drone, just above its camera eye. Once the fighters outside the netting engaged the enemy, Rob was to pilot the two drones and attack as many of the Sholen as he could. A few ripped suits and damaged hoses would certainly hamper them.

He covered himself with camouflage netting—no sense in letting the Sholen see him—and warmed up the link to the drones. His poor robot fish were weeks overdue for maintenance, but they were performing superbly. In a little while they'd be scrap metal corroding in the silt of Ilmatar.

Josef and the sub were gone. It had taken a long argument but at last they'd convinced him that their most important remaining asset shouldn't be anywhere near the battlefield. If the Sholen captured the last camp, it would be up to Josef to decide whether he should give up or fight on. Rob knew that Josef would never let the *Mishka* fall into enemy hands. He hoped Josef would find a way to scuttle the sub and then surrender, rather than going out like Captain Nemo.

Rob reached down and found his spear. It might still come

to that. He sent Alicia a quick message over their local network.

"Here they come. I love you."

BROADTAIL and Longpincer confer just inside the net barrier.

"You are certain?"

"Builder 1's silent sense detects them. They approach."

"All is ready here. I need only sound the signal." Longpincer pats the signaling device. It resembles an ordinary snapper, but the stick in it is nearly as thick as one of Broadtail's minor limbs. When it snaps, he imagines the sound carrying as far as Continuous Abundance.

"I suggest waiting until they reach the nets," says Broadtail, and then immediately regrets it.

"I remember doing this many times before," Longpincer points out. "Please do not lecture me like an apprentice on my own land."

"I mean no offense."

"Of course not. All of us are poised with pincers ready. Are you hungry? There is a pile of food back by the house flow channel. All must be full and strong to fight."

"I am full."

"Then let us listen."

They wait in silence. Broadtail can hear the nets waving in the current, the rumble of the vent, and a persistent hiss from a leaking flow conduit nearby. As he relaxes he picks up more distant sounds: one of Longpincer's apprentices fidgeting as he waits near the net, the irritating high-pitched buzz Builders sometimes make, the faint clicking of scavengers crawling over Longpincer's house, and, far away but all-pervasive, the creak of the ice above the world.

And now he hears the invaders. They are about three cables

distant. The bandit adults ping one another carelessly. The devices of the Squatters make a steady hum. The Squatters themselves swim noisily. He remembers a truism: *the weak are silent when the strong make noise.* Well, that is true enough now. But there is another old saying; he remembers tying it into a reel when first learning to write: *a noisy swimmer is soon silenced.*

Though he knows the Bitterwater vent is Longpincer's, Broadtail cannot rid himself of the feeling that he is the one defending his own property. The Builders are *his* discovery, and these Squatters and their bandit servants wish to take them away from him. He will not allow it. Broadtail takes up his spear and waits for something to stab with it.

TIZHOS was miserable. The journey seemed to last forever: a two-day push through endless black water, sealed up in her suit with the smell of her own anger and fear, struggling to keep up with the Ilmatarans and Irona's Guardians. Her suit's foodmaker could never create enough broth to satisfy her, and the flavorings seemed particularly artificial today.

From time to time, Irona switched on the laser link to make leader-like noises. "The humans endanger this entire planet," he said. "We must drive them away and leave it once again pure and undefiled! All our efforts lead to this moment. We cannot fail!"

Tizhos noted wryly that not even the Guardians cheered Irona's harangues anymore. But neither did any of them question the consensus. Since Irona had selected all of them personally, they shared his devotion to the ideal of Tracelessness.

The war party moved past a jumble of ancient stones, rounded by the water but obviously carved by Ilmataran tools. It felt oddly comforting, Tizhos thought, to live in a world where somebody *made* everything, even the rocks. Back on Shalina so much effort went into erasing traces of the past, coaxing the planet into a carefully maintained imitation of wildness.

She looked back at the two great native animals being guided by their Ilmataran allies. They were beautiful creatures, shaped almost like aircraft, with rippling delta wings and a gaping mouth like a jet intake. One was towing a net filled with food for the Ilmataran troops, but the second had a mysterious payload that Irona refused to let Tizhos get close to.

According to the navigation display, they were only seven or eight hundred meters from the Ilmataran settlement where the humans were hiding. Irona called a halt as they reached a low ridge that gave some visual cover.

"Tizhos," he said over the private link. "Tell the Ilmataran troops to get ready. When I give the order, have them move forward to attack the complex."

"What about me? Where do you want me to go?"

"Stay close to me. I need you to translate for the Ilmatarans."

"Irona, I believe we should give them one last chance to surrender. Perhaps when they see how many we have brought they will give up."

"I consider the situation too far gone for that. The humans did not take the opportunity to surrender before. I do not believe they will do so now. It seems foolish to alert them to our presence."

"So you actually intend to just plunge in and begin attacking?"

"Of course. All moral beings find fighting a terrible thing, yet we must do it to preserve this world. Now I want you to remain quiet, Tizhos."

Tizhos could smell her suit flooding with aggression pheromones, and kept herself rigidly quiet and still until the air cleaners could scrub them away. Isolated from each other in their suits, both she and Irona were limited to sound communication only, forcing them to be as emotionless and hierarchical as humans.

Two of the Ilmataran teamsters guided the second towfin to a position on the other side of Irona and began untying their mysterious payload. Tizhos sidled over to get a look while Irona and the other Sholen Guardians were getting ready. The objects the creature had hauled all the way from Hitode were a pair of big streamlined cylinders with propellers and guidance fins at the back. Irona had kept them secret ever since they had come down from the surface with a supply drop.

Were they giant impellers? But they had no controls or handles. Camera drones? Perhaps the first camera drones in Shalina's oceans had been that large; not even the humans used anything so bulky. Maybe they were some kind of long-range drone with lots of batteries on board. But why have them towed, then?

Then Tizhos realized what the things were. She called up the reference on her helmet computer to be sure. During the age of warfare, ships and submarines in Shalina's oceans had used self-propelled explosive carriers that looked very much like these objects. They were torpedoes.

She searched frantically through her computer files, looking for anything about the effects of such weapons. She finally located something in, ironically enough, a description of human military technology. Tizhos did a little calculating, let out a noise of terror, and did the math again just to be sure. Her suit reeked of fear.

"Irona!" Tizhos scrambled across the sea bottom to where the other Sholen were gathered in a last-minute tactical conference. "Irona, I must make an objection! Those explosive devices— you must not use them!"

Irona activated the private link and Tizhos could hear irritation in his voice. "Do not broadcast every detail of our tactical plan. The humans have drones and, thanks to your careless-ness, may have heard you."

"Tell me the explosive power of these devices."

"First explain why I should tell you anything. I lead this ex-pedition."

"Irona, I fear you do not understand the power of these weapons! The shock from an underwater explosion may kill or injure individuals up to a hundred meters away."

"I understand that perfectly, Tizhos. I had them made and brought them for just that reason. Now please stop interfer-ing." Irona switched off the link and resumed his conversation with the others.

Tizhos was shaken. Was Irona willing to use torpedoes ca-pable of sinking an oceangoing ship just to kill three humans? It seemed impossible. Didn't he realize how many Ilmatarans would be killed?

And then Tizhos understood. *Of course* Irona knew how many of the natives would die. He had planned on it. They were in contact with the humans. Tainted and corrupted, in Irona's mind. Infected with the knowledge of the universe be-yond the ice. Irona wished to kill them all and return Ilmatar to its pristine innocence.

She had to stop this, right away. Tizhos turned and began hurrying back to the torpedoes. Perhaps she could disable them somehow. She covered perhaps ten meters before two of the Guardians grabbed her, pinning her limbs and bearing her down to the sea bottom. They pulled her arms and midlimbs behind her back and bound them with lengths of cord. She struggled and thrashed, but they were younger and stronger.

Irona turned Tizhos over and jammed the tip of a tool into her helmet speaker. Tizhos heard plastic snap. "I don't want you distracting the natives or alerting the humans," he told her. "You may wait here for the end of the battle. If I feel particularly generous afterward, perhaps I will bring you back to the station."

Tizhos switched to laser link. "Who will communicate with the Ilmatarans if I stay here a prisoner?"

"I have all your notes. I can certainly tell them 'forward' when the time comes."

Tizhos went to general broadcast. "Listen, all of you! Irona plans to use explosives against the native settlement. Dozens may die. You cannot allow—"

"Please do not humiliate yourself, Tizhos," said Irona. "They all know and understand the operational plan. We have a consensus. All agree that we prefer the sacrifice of a few Ilmatarans to seeing this world ravaged by human exploiters or Ilmatarans copying human methods."

"*I* do not agree! You do not have a consensus!" Tizhos struggled against her bonds, but the Guardians were trained in subduing and securing violent offenders. "You cannot just ignore my objections!"

"Tell me why I cannot," said Irona.

"Irona, your plan seems—" Tizhos stopped and groped for the right word, finally choosing something archaic and absolute, the kind of moral judgment that had sent millions of Sholen to war in barbaric times. "It *is* wrong!"

For a moment, nobody said anything. The others were all startled at what Tizhos had said. Finally Irona spoke. "You have humiliated yourself enough, Tizhos. Stop talking. We must go now." They switched to a secure link and swam off.

Tizhos struggled. She thrashed about. She tried to crawl toward the torpedoes. She screamed inside her helmet until her ears hurt. She tried to get someone—anyone—to answer her laser messages. Finally she lay helpless in the cold muck, her joints aching and the cable cutting into her limbs. Maybe her suit would tear and let her die.

DR. VIKRAM Sen waited until the Sholen expedition were all on their way. That still left a pair of the Sholen soldiers in Hitode.

He went to the kitchen and made himself a cup of tea, drank it, then took the largest carving knife from the rack and went to the little Operations office that adjoined the common room. His hands were perfectly steady, he noticed.

One of the two Sholen was in Operations, watching the sonar imager for signs of the returning war party. Dr. Sen had read a text on Sholen anatomy, so he drove the knife into her neck just to the right of the spinal bone, sliding it between the bone and the neck muscle into the right nerve trunk.

She cried out, a sound like a crow's call, and swung her left midlimb at him. The blow caught him in the side, and he could hear a rib break even before he felt it.

The Sholen tried to get up but fell. Her whole right side wasn't working. Sen grabbed the chair and smashed it down on her, over and over, not caring what he hit. She tried to ward off the blows with her left arm and midlimb. The spindly aluminum tubing of the chair began to bend after he hit her a couple of times, but he didn't care.

In desperation she used her one working leg to sweep Sen's feet out from underneath him. They wrestled for the chair but eventually she got a grip on it with her left midlimb and yanked it away from him. He kicked her in the face, but she bit his foot, her carnivore teeth punching through his slippers and crunching on bone.

Sen kicked her in the eye with his other foot and scrambled free. There were more chairs in the common room. More knives in the kitchen.

The other Sholen soldier came through the entrance from

Hab Two and saw what was happening. He drew his weapon from its chest holster and fired as Dr. Sen reached the knife rack. The bullet hit him in the shoulder, and Sen wondered idly if any major arteries were severed. He never felt the second shot, which drilled neatly into the back of his head.

BROADTAIL hears the bandits approach. There are about a dozen, all big and swimming strongly. They come straight on, advancing in a line with no attempt to hide, swimming about a body-length above the bottom.

Half a cable now; surely they must be among the hidden skirmishers by now. Can Longpincer hear them? Why doesn't he sound the alarm? Broadtail shifts his spear in his grip.

The crack from Longpincer's signal snapper startles him. The noise is so loud that it almost sounds as though his own shell is splitting. The echo lets him sense the entire battlefield very distinctly. There are fourteen of the bandits, advancing in a line with the ends slightly forward of the center. He doesn't know if this is accident or good tactics on their part, but it is a classic formation. The defenders must either split up to fight the two pincers and thus risk being split down the middle by the center, or clump together and thus risk being outflanked.

Now the bottom behind and among the attackers erupts in a swirl of silt and pincers as the hidden fighters reveal themselves. The line dissolves into a series of small battles.

Broadtail recalls Longpincer telling the hidden fighters, "Strike quickly, then flee. Do not stay and become surrounded. If they disperse to pursue you, so much the better."

Three of the five hidden fighters remember that advice. Broadtail hears spears crunching into shells as they stab up into unshielded bellies or between back plates from behind. There are sounds of distress and anger and the three swim up and then sprint for the netting with angry bandits behind them.

But two don't get away in time. Roughtail is surrounded in open water by four of the bandits. They stab at him from all sides, pinging and clicking angrily. He fights one off, turns to face another, but the pincers keep jabbing in. His movements become random and weary. One of them grapples him from behind, bending back a pincer until there is an ugly crack and Roughtail cries out. Then all four are upon him, gripping, piercing, and cracking until he sinks to the bottom.

Shortfeeler is a little more fortunate. She hears a bandit above her and realizes she can't swim free of them, so she drops back to the sea bottom and holds her spear up in challenge. With her underside protected and her legs solidly braced she is a hard target: the bandits must risk getting past the spearpoint to poke ineffectually at her shell.

Two of them stay with her, trying to get in under the spear and flip her over, but she gives ground, backing away and keeping the weapon between them and her. Finally one drops to the bottom and rushes in with pincers folded. She catches him dead-center in the headshield with her spear, and the force of the impact drives the point through his shell. The bandit gives a last cry as his resonator chamber is breached, leaving him deaf and mute.

But the spearpoint is caught, and while Shortfeeler tries to free it the second one drops on her back and gets a pincer into one of her shoulder joints. She breaks away and tries to swim for it, but the bandit is faster and catches her before she can reach the netting. With one pincer useless, Shortfeeler must drop her spear. They grapple, there is the crack of a shell splitting, and Shortfeeler stops moving. Horribly, she isn't quite dead, and Broadtail hears her faint clicks and pings until the bandits reach the netting.

* * *

ROB couldn't show any lights for fear of giving away his position to the Sholen, but he kept the passive sonar on and could at least get a vague impression of the battle. The crack of Longpincer's signal device nearly burst his eardrums even with the automatic volume cutoff, and then he watched the image on his faceplate as blurry shapes emerged from the sea bottom and started mixing it up with the invaders.

After a bit Rob noticed something interesting: all the sonar images on the battlefield beyond the netting were very much alike. They all had the echo pattern of rigid, segmented objects—Ilmatarans with their armored shells. Where were the Sholen?

Time for one Robert J. Freeman to earn his pay. He activated Drone One and sent it swimming back toward the main thermal vent at the center of the settlement. He hoped the column of rising water could mask the sound of its little motor.

The drone stayed in the rising water column until it was two hundred meters above the sea bottom. Rob ordered it to circle wide around the battlefield to where the Ilmataran attackers had first come into view. Were the Sholen back there?

Yes. The drone's camera picked up a constellation of pale yellow-green stars on the bottom, just past a low ridge. There were eight Sholen in suits, with safety lights glowing softly.

"Gotcha!" Rob muttered.

Four of the Sholen were spread out in a line along the ridge, apparently hunkered down on the sea bottom. In the dim light Rob could see them holding weapons—the same microtorp guns they'd been carrying at the Coquille raid. It seemed weird to Rob that they were just hanging back and not doing anything, but then the drone's hydrophone picked up the faint whoosh of the weapons. He checked his local sonar image: the Ilmataran attackers were about to reach the netting. He just had time to shout a warning before the explosions.

* * *

BROADTAIL is braced and ready to start jabbing his spear through the netting at the attackers when the world fills with noise. It is far louder than even Longpincer's signal device. He can feel the sound with his entire body, and his head feels like it is shattering. After the painful pulse of sound there is silence. Is he deaf? He taps the front of his head and hears it very faintly, but that is all.

Something is holding his spear. He tugs on it and jerks it free. Probing with it reveals something soft in front of him. The netting has collapsed!

The attackers must be almost as deaf as he is, and Broadtail is getting used to fighting things he cannot hear. He turns his spear sideways and holds it forward, hoping one of them will brush against it. Slowly the world comes back into existence around him, although every sound is accompanied by a throb of pain.

A large adult is two body-lengths away, ahead and to Broadtail's right. She is moving slowly with her pincers extended, feeling around. Evidently she hears him at almost the same moment, for suddenly she rushes forward.

Broadtail swings his spear, jabbing the butt end into the front of her head and stopping her charge long enough for him to reverse his weapon and brace himself.

She tries to shove the spearpoint out of the way with her pincers and rush in, but Broadtail scuttles sideways, keeping the point between them. He prods at her head, hoping to force her back, but she holds her ground and the spear grates along her shell. She bursts forward before Broadtail can get his spear back into place, and now she's almost in pincer-reach.

The bandit raises her pincers and lunges at Broadtail, stabbing down onto his back, trying to find a weak spot in his shell. He folds his own pincers and pushes forward, getting his head underneath hers and then shoving. He feels a jolt of pain from near his tail flukes as one pincer strikes home, but it angers him more than it harms him. He slams against the bandit's underside with all his strength and she loses her grip on the sea bottom.

The two of them are now curled around each other in a ball, rolling about the bottom. Broadtail feels the bandit's powerful pincers getting a grip on his tail. Is she trying to crack him? She is, and he can feel the stress in his shell.

In desperation he probes her underside with his pincer tip, but her flailing legs keep him from finding a gap. The pressure on his back is almost unbearable. Then the bandit gives a twitch and lets go. He feels her body settle to the bottom next to him. He tastes blood in the water.

A small adult drops down in front of him and pulls a spear out of the bandit's back. He recognizes Holdhard by flavor. "Thank you," he says.

ROB waited for his ears to stop ringing and risked a visual look around with his lamp. There were four big gaps in the netting where the volley of microtorps had hit the support poles. The 'tarans on both sides were staggering around looking disoriented. Hearing bangs that loud must have hit them like a flashbulb in the eyes. One of them was down and not moving; Rob couldn't tell if it was one of Longpincer's people or an attacker.

Time to put a stop to that! He launched Drone Two, once again using the water column above the vent for concealment. While it was on its way he switched his link back to Drone One, keeping station above the Sholen position.

Rob picked his target almost at random: one of the faint green glows among the line of Sholen soldiers. The third one from the left. He designated it, then sent the drone into a power-dive toward its target. The signal lag meant he was just an observer, watching a series of still images as the Sholen grew larger and more distinct. His intended victim must have heard the drone approach, because the final clear frame showed him turning, his face indistinct within his helmet, mouth open.

Then there was a hash of visual static with fragments of blurry images. Then the link went dead. Had the drone even hit its target? Maybe Drone Two could tell him. Rob switched links and steered his last weapon on a long curving course around to the north. Since he'd dropped One on them from above, he kept Two hugging the sea bottom. As the drone got closer to the Sholen position, Rob adopted a scoot-and-freeze pattern of movement, staying undercover and out of sight as much as possible.

Soon he was within a few tens of meters of the Sholen position. The drone camera could pick up several of their safety lights, and the passive sonar detected eight Sholen. The firing line of Sholen soldiers with microtorp guns were on the move, grouping into pairs with one facing toward Longpincer's house and one guarding the firer's back. Good; he'd accomplished something. He didn't know if getting them moving was good or bad.

Time for a different kind of mischief. Maybe he could mess with their supplies or something? Or find whoever was in charge of the whole attack?

He moved the drone to a point about twenty meters behind the firing line. Sonar detected a pair of the big grazers Broadtail called "towfins" tethered by some rocks, with a single Ilmataran minding them. He didn't dare bring the drone too close to any Ilmataran—they'd hear it coming long before even a computer-enhanced Sholen hydrophone would notice.

The camera detected a faint light just ahead of the two animals. Slowly and quietly, Rob guided the drone toward it. A long-exposure still image resolved a pair of big cylinders sitting on the sea bottom. The light was coming from an indicator panel on the side of one. Some kind of self-propelled cargo pods, Rob guessed. Which meant the Sholen had enough supplies to fight all day if they wanted to. There was no way he could damage something like that with a knife blade mounted on a camera drone. He moved on, looking for something he could hurt.

ANOTHER series of deafening blasts makes Broadtail want to curl into a ball. He clutches the rock he stands on, hoping his sense returns before a barbarian plunges a pincer into him.

Someone taps numbers on his tail. "Move back to the house." It is Holdhard. She leads him by one feeler. Broadtail tastes the water and starts working his way up the gradient of warmth and minerals toward the main vent until he runs into one of the guidelines, then follows that.

He stumbles over a body that has a familiar flavor. It is Strongpincer, the bandit. Broadtail cannot imagine the bandit charging this far, so he suspects the blast of tossing the body past the front line.

Out of curiosity, he feels the dead bandit's harness and finds the stone box. He tucks it into his own carrying pouch. "I remember refusing to pay you, and now it is free. You are a very bad trader," he tells the corpse.

His hearing is starting to return and he listens. The netting is gone, and half a dozen bandits are swimming over the tangled wreckage. Time to get into a house. With solid stone at their back even a small group of scholars and apprentices can hold off any number of bandits. Broadtail wonders how they can withstand the exploding swimmer weapons.

* * *

ROB'S ears were still ringing from the second volley of microtorps when an Ilmataran tapped him on the helmet. Since it wasn't trying to gut him with its pincers, he figured it must be one of the good guys. His lexicon translated the message as "Builder swim structure," which sounded like an order to retreat. He banged an okay on his chestplate.

Inside the house he wouldn't be able to maintain the link. Time for Drone Two to go out in glory.

He checked the drone's sonar and noticed a big noise source nearby. It sounded like something splashing, or trying to swim very clumsily. On the camera he could make out a very streaky image of a Sholen thrashing about on the sea bottom. Huh? Rob moved the drone closer.

It was a Sholen, all right. Lying on the bottom, with its limbs held in a very weird position. The front two limb pairs were held against its back, and the rear pair were parallel to the tail. The Sholen was hog-tied. It was a prisoner.

Why the hell were the Sholen tying one another up in the middle of a battle? Was this part of their constant sex thing?

It would be really easy for the drone to stab this Sholen in the throat, just below the helmet ring, and let it drown on blood and seawater. Rob thought about that, then maneuvered the drone to a position behind the Sholen. If whoever was in command of this attack felt it necessary to tie someone up, it seemed obvious to Rob that cutting the cables binding him would be a good thing.

TIZHOS felt something prodding at her hands. Some kind of native organism? She stopped wriggling. Maybe it would crawl around to where she could get a look at it. She felt the cable binding her upper arms snap. The creature had freed her? She reached for her multipurpose tool and cut the cables on her midlimbs and legs, then turned to look at her rescuer.

It was a drone. Human-built, with a crude blade affixed to its nose. Why had it freed her?

No time. Her speaker was broken, so she shouted as loudly as she could, hoping the sound would carry through her hood and the water, "Get everyone away from the house! Irona wishes to kill you all! He has torpedoes! Very large! Get away!"

Tizhos didn't wait for an answer, even if the human controlling the drone had understood her at all. She scrambled across the sea bottom toward the two torpedoes. Her arm and midlimb joints were stiff and painful, and her suit's medical system was completely out of painkillers. She called for a big dose of stimulants and some confidence-building pheromones to help her tough it out.

The torpedoes hadn't moved. She tried to establish a link, but Irona had prudently locked her out of the command web. Well, if high-tech methods wouldn't work, perhaps primitive methods would. Tizhos made her tool narrow and sharp, and began jabbing at the control panel of the torpedo. She smashed sensors, indicators—anything that looked vulnerable. The tough plastic resisted her blows, but she got the blade into a seam and pried with all her strength until she heard a satisfying snap. Behind the panel was a block of circuitry sealed in plastic. Tizhos began stabbing it, holding the tool in both midlimb hands and using her whole body to drive it. Her suit reeked of aggression, and she found it oddly pleasant.

She ripped out the fragments of circuitry and groped inside for anything else she could ruin. She slashed what seemed like a hydraulic line and saw a cloud of fluid leak into the ocean like blood.

Enough damage. Time to move on. She clambered over to

the second torpedo and made ready to stab its controls. Suddenly it began making a loud hum, and rose up off the bottom.

Tizhos got on top of it, trying to weigh it down, but it surged forward, then rolled, slamming her into the silt. When she looked up again it was ten meters away, rising and accelerating. She struggled after it, but the machine moved smoothly away.

Half a minute later there was a flash and a concussion that tumbled Tizhos head over tail along the sea bottom for a dozen meters.

She steadied herself, waited for her suit's sonar and inertial navigation systems to recover, and wondered what to do next. Irona had won the battle; that much seemed obvious. Even if any of the humans and their native allies had survived, the Guardians would be able to round them up without any difficulty.

Tizhos realized, rather vaguely, that she herself might not survive very long. Would Irona even bother to take her back to Shalina for treatment of her behavior? Or would they just stuff her body into the plasma furnace along with the dead humans and let her ashes discolor Ilmatar's surface for a few centuries?

When a Guardian found her, Tizhos followed her to the shattered settlement where Irona and the others were searching through the rubble. The water was still full of sediment, so it was like walking in heavy fog.

The elevator capsule lay on its side, caved in and flooded. The front of the native house had collapsed. Tizhos saw at least four Ilmataran bodies left scattered by the blast. She couldn't tell if they were some of Irona's native allies or the ones helping the humans.

"You failed," said Irona when he noticed Tizhos. "We need only gather up the human artifacts and any native records here, then we return to the base and finish dismantling it."

"I intend to bear witness to this crime," said Tizhos. "I shall inform the Consensus what you have done here. Tell me if you will order your Guardians to murder me also; I desire to know."

"I see no more need for violence here," said Irona, and even without smelling him Tizhos could tell he was afraid. "This world seems safe now. After we take you back home for treatment, I plan to lead expeditions against all the other human bases and colonies. I hope we do not need to kill any others."

Tizhos made no reply. She sat amid the rubble as the others continued their search. After a long swim from the base and a battle, the Guardians looked exhausted. Finally even Irona noticed and called a rest. "Two hours for rest and food, then we resume work."

The Guardians gathered at the torpedo impact point, where the force of the blast had cleared away rubbish and left a nice open area. They dropped to the sea bottom and lay as limp as sleeping humans.

Irona came over to Tizhos and sat. "I want you to promise me you do not intend to run away. Otherwise I must tie your limbs again."

"I have no place to run to," she said. "I suggest you return to the base and allow the Guardians to rest and recover. You can bring a work party to clear away all the human artifacts later."

"Scavengers may come before we can remove everything. I believe it best to get everything now."

"Tell me what you plan to do with it all."

"The incinerator on the surface can dispose of everything. After it reduces everything to ash, we will dismantle it and take away the pieces. No trace of any alien presence will remain on this world."

"You could save the native records. They have little mass, and would improve our knowledge of this civilization."

"No," said Irona. "They would only tempt you and others who think the same way. You would wish to learn more. Only probes at first, but then would come crewed missions. Where the explorers go, conquerors and exploiters always follow. We can only avoid moral fault by remaining at home, on our own world in our own communities."

Tizhos couldn't answer that; she could smell her own sadness and depression. The idea of returning to Shalina and living in a Consensus that thought the way Irona did made her want to die.

Perhaps she could accompany the human prisoners back to Earth. Assuming, of course, that Irona really intended to send them home.

"Tell me what will happen to the prisoners," said Tizhos.

Irona didn't reply. Tizhos looked at him and saw that Irona was staring at a swirl of dark material in the water. After a moment Tizhos realized that the dark stuff was coming from a hole in Irona's suit, just below the helmet. There was some kind of pointed object studded with little barbs sticking out of the hole. As Tizhos watched, the tapered object slid back into the hole and then Irona fell over sideways in a cloud of blood and bubbles.

An Ilmataran was standing behind Irona, cleaning blood off one pincer with its feeding tendrils. Then it advanced on Tizhos.

"I surrender! I will not fight!" She bowed her head and held her front arms straight out from her body in the traditional pose of surrender, then realized that looked an awful lot like the Ilmataran threat posture. So she tucked in her arms and tried to curl into a ball.

The Ilmataran placed one sharp pincer-tip at the back of Tizhos's neck and rattled off a loud series of clicks and pops. A moment later Tizhos heard someone banging tools together, and then a human was rolling her onto her back and peering into her helmet.

"Tizhos!" said Robert Freeman. "Are you okay?"

Tizhos indicated her broken speaker, then shouted inside her helmet. "I feel no injury!"

"Good. I was afraid Longpincer might have stabbed you. He's pretty pissed off about his house."

"Tell me if the Ilmatarans escaped."

"Most of them—about a dozen. Some of Longpincer's apprentices and a couple of the scientists were still up on the battle line when the torpedo hit. The rest of us were swimming like hell in the other direction."

"I apologize for not disabling both weapons."

"What?"

"I apologize!"

"There's no need. You saved our lives."

"I could not permit Irona to kill you all."

An Ilmataran came over to Robert Freeman carrying two microtorp guns. Robert Freeman took them, then tapped a reply on the Ilmataran's shell. He examined the guns, clipped one to his utility harness, and held the other one ready to shoot. "Cool guns," he said.

Tizhos looked over at the Guardians. Most of them were standing with arms extended while Ilmatarans and another human with a microtorp gun watched over them. Two of the Guardians lay on the sea bottom, with blood clouding the water around them.

"Tell me what you plan to do now," said Tizhos.

"Now? Now we're all going back to Hitode Station. I'm going to eat something that isn't an emergency bar, and take a fucking *shower.* Broadtail's coming with us. Longpincer and his people have to rebuild here."

"I must join the other Sholen," said Tizhos, getting up off the sea bottom.

"It's okay. You've always been a pretty decent person; I trust

you. Heck, you saved our lives when the rest of them were trying to kill us all."

"That does not alter the fact that I belong with them. I dis-
agreed with Irona and he treated me wrongly, but I will not
join with you."

"I guess I understand. Can you tell them we won't hurt anyone as long as they cooperate? It's a long way back to Hitode
and if we start fighting nobody's going to make it alive."

"I will tell them. I do not desire any more killing."

TWENTY days later, Commander Jorge Hernandez
floated in the command pod of the expedition support vehicle
Marco Polo, looking over the shoulder of the sensor specialist at
a display of the gas giant Ukko and its moons. "Anything?"

"Not that I can see. Optical's clear, radio's quiet, and there's
nothing on infrared. If there were Sholen here, I think they
must be gone."

Commander Hernandez didn't want to admit it, but he was
tremendously relieved. The *Polo* had deployed a whole constellation of sensor platforms, missiles, and laser mirrors, but everyone aboard knew that in an actual fight none of them would
accomplish much more than using up some of the enemy's
munitions. It was precisely because the *Marco Polo* was not a
military vehicle that UNIDA had agreed to send it to Ilmatar.
All of Earth's real combat-effective, purpose-built warcraft
were scattered around Earth and Mars, waiting to meet a
Sholen attack. The peacetime UNICA had changed hats and
become the UN Interstellar Defense Agency, and explorers like
Hernandez suddenly found themselves military officers.

Hernandez didn't exactly relish being expendable, so the
absence of any Sholen spacecraft was the best news he'd had in
a while. If it was true, of course. They might be hiding somewhere, possibly behind Ilmatar or one of the other moons.

They could even have some supertech way of fooling his sensors.

Still, better to find out now, before the braking burn, when he still had enough fuel to run for home. "Send a tightbeam to the surface station on Ilmatar. Tell them we're here and ask for a sitrep."

Moss sent the message for five minutes, then shook his head. "I'm not getting any response. Chances are the Sholen took everyone prisoner."

"Or bombed the place flat. Keep trying until T minus ten minutes on the burn clock."

"Wait a sec! I'm getting something. It sounds like Morse code. They must've lost their radio mast." Moss called up a Morse code cheat sheet. "Here it comes: 'Sho left two weeks ago, took sixteen, four dead, fixing damage.'"

"Ask them what happened! How did they drive off the Sholen? Do they need anything?"

"It says, 'Sho captured base, Ilmatarans made them go, OK for now.' Wait, there's more: 'Send all string cord etcetera on lander, Ilmats want to learn.'"

"Okay," said Hernandez, utterly baffled. "Flight: go ahead with the braking burn as planned." In a quieter voice he added, "I'm going down in the first lander. I want to hear the full story."

"ADULT swims grasping human on stone," said Broadtail. He and Rob were floating in the nice warm outflow from the station reactor, watching a mixed team of humans and Ilmatarans load the sub's power plant onto the cargo rack on top of the elevator. The elevator capsule was all pumped out and reattached to the cable, ready for a trip up to the surface.

"We can't stay any longer," said Rob. "It's not safe here. The Sholen might come back, maybe with more spacecraft and troops."

"Many adults stab Squatters."

"Yeah, you guys kicked ass." Rob wondered idly how his computer was going to translate that phrase. "But it's not right to expose you to more risk because of us. We're buttoning up the base, and when the trouble with the Sholen is over, we'll send back an ambassador."

"Human swims downward to house?"

"Sure. Later. We, uh, swim toward coming back."

"Builder 1 swims downward?"

"No, not me. I can't come back. I've spent enough time under high pressure already. Even with the drugs I'm at risk for nerve damage. The docs will veto that for sure."

"Adult swims upward."

"What?"

"Adult swims upward to house with many humans. Adult swims through ice. Adult swims past large spheres."

"Broadtail, I don't know if you can ever leave Ilmatar. There's the whole pressure thing, and—"

"Adult grasps many reels. Adult grasps numbers. Adult holds tools. Adult swims past large spheres."

"Well, I'm sure you'll get into space someday. Maybe we could build you some kind of pressure tank to travel in. Lifting all that water's going to be a bitch and a half, but we'll figure something out."

Broadtail reached into one of his belt pouches and handed something to Rob. It was a box made of stone, about as big as a baseball. He could feel a seam where the lid fit on it.

"Is this for me? You want me to keep it or just look at it?"

"Adult places stone inside human house."

"Aw, thank you, Broadtail. This is really nice. Did you make this?" Rob carefully lifted the lid off and looked inside. He was quiet for a long time, and when he spoke again he was trembling despite the warm water. "Where did you get this, Broadtail?"

⌒ month later, the last lander rose from Ilmatar carrying two passengers, four tons of specimens and artifacts—and ten human and Sholen corpses, packed together in a single cargo pod.

Alicia still felt a little odd in the thin air on board. Even after an extra-slow ascent in the restored elevator capsule, she was still saturated with argon and trace gases. She could almost feel them oozing out of her body. Her sinuses were completely blocked and her face felt bloated.

The interior of the lander was wonderfully warm and dry. Alicia ran her hand sensuously over the clean fabric seat cover. She had already vowed to spend her first month back on Earth in Tunis, or maybe Las Vegas, baking herself in the desert sunlight all day and sleeping on clean sheets every night.

In the seat next to her, Robert sat silently, occasionally looking at the little carved stone box in his hands. He had been nearly comatose since they'd left Hitode. During the elevator ride she had been so tired and hungry herself that she hadn't minded, especially with six people jammed into the elevator and no privacy. But it would be a very long trip home if Robert was going to be morose the whole way.

From the flight deck she could hear radio chatter and the occasional terse remark by the pilots. Through the window she could see the white surface of Ilmatar rolling past, marked with lines and faint blotches. A screen above her seat showed the expedition ship, surrounded by a halo of drones and shuttles.

At last Alicia could stand the silence no longer. "What's the matter?" she asked. "You have been a living corpse ever since we left Hitode. Is something wrong? Traumatic stress?"

"Broadtail gave me this," said Rob. "He got it from one of the bandits; where the bandit got it from is anyone's guess but the surface erosion suggests it's pretty damn old."

"Why does that make you sad?"

"I'm not sad. I'm just—here. See for yourself." He handed Alicia the little stone box. She opened it and looked at the object inside, nestled snugly in the little niche that had protected it—how long?

"Go ahead," he said. "Look through it."

She picked it up carefully by the edges and held it up to the light. It was scratched and chipped, but not yet opaque.

It was a lens.